The Dreamer

The Dreamer

by Mary Newton Stanard

Copyright © 5/13/2015
Jefferson Publication

ISBN-13: 978-1512197501

Printed in the United States of America

All rights reserved. No part of this book may be reprinted or reproduced or utilized in any form or by any electronic, mechanical, or other means, now known or hereafter invented, including photocopying and recording, or in any form of storage or retrieval system, without prior permission in writing from the publisher.'

The Dreamer

Contents

TO THE READER 4
THE DREAMER 4
CHAPTER I. 4
CHAPTER II. 7
CHAPTER III. 10
CHAPTER IV. 14
CHAPTER V. 17
CHAPTER VI. 24
CHAPTER VII. 28
CHAPTER VIII. 32
CHAPTER IX. 36
CHAPTER X. 42
CHAPTER XI. 45
CHAPTER XII. 49
CHAPTER XIII. 52
CHAPTER XIV. 54
CHAPTER XV. 57
CHAPTER XVI. 62
CHAPTER XVII. 65
CHAPTER XVIII. 69
CHAPTER XIX. 73
CHAPTER XX. 78
CHAPTER XXI. 84
CHAPTER XXII. 88
CHAPTER XXIII. 92
CHAPTER XXIV. 95
CHAPTER XXV. 102
CHAPTER XXVI. 107
CHAPTER XXVII. 113
CHAPTER XXVIII. 120
CHAPTER XXIX. 124
CHAPTER XXX. 129
CHAPTER XXXI. 133
CHAPTER XXXII. 138
CHAPTER XXXIII. 147

The Dreamer

TO THE READER

This study of Edgar Allan Poe, poet and man, is simply an attempt to make something like a finished picture of the shadowy sketch the biographers, hampered by the limitations of proved fact, must, at best, give us.

To this end I have used the story-teller's license to present the facts in picturesque form. Yet I believe I have told a true story—true to the spirit if not to the letter—for I think I have made Poe and the other persons of the drama do nothing they may not have done, say nothing they may not have said, feel nothing they may not have felt. In many instances the opinions, and even the words I have placed in Poe's mouth are his own—found in his published works or his letters.

I owe much, of course, to the writers of Poe books before and up to my time. Among these, I would make especial and grateful acknowledgment to Mr. J.H. Ingram, Professor George E. Woodberry, Professor James A. Harrison and Mrs. Susan Archer Weiss.

But more than to any one of his biographers, I am indebted to Poe himself for the revelations of his personality which appear in his own stories and poems, the most part of which are clearly autobiographic.

M.N.S.

THE DREAMER

CHAPTER I.

The last roses of the year 1811 were in bloom in the Richmond gardens and their petals would soon be scattered broadcast by the winds which had already stripped the trees and left them standing naked against the cold sky.

Cold indeed, it looked, through the small, smoky window, to the eyes of the young and beautiful woman who lay dying of hectic fever in a dark, musty room back of the shop of Mrs. Fipps, the milliner, in lower Main Street—cold and friendless and drear.

She was still beautiful, though the sparkle in the great eyes fixed upon the bleak sky had given place to deep melancholy and her face was pinched and wan.

She knew that she was dying. Meanwhile, her appearance as leading lady of Mr. Placide's company of high class players was flauntingly announced by newspaper and bill-board.

The advertisement had put society in a flutter; for Elizabeth Arnold Poe was a favorite with the public not only for her graces of person and personality, her charming acting, singing and dancing, but she had that incalculable advantage for an actress—an appealing life-story. It was known that she had lately lost a dearly loved and loving husband whom she had tenderly nursed through a distressing illness. It was also known that the husband had been a descendant of a proud old family and that the same high spirit which had led his grandfather, General Poe, passionately denouncing British tyranny, to join the Revolutionary Army, had, taking a different turn with the grandson, made him for the sake of the gifted daughter of old England who had captured his heart—actress though she was—sever home ties, abandon the career chosen for him by his parents, and devote himself to the profession of which she was a chief ornament. A brief five years of idylic happiness the pair had spent together—happiness in spite of much work and some

The Dreamer

tears;—then David Poe had succumbed to consumption, leaving a penniless widow with three children to support. The eldest, a boy, was adopted by his father's relatives in Baltimore. The other two—a boy of three years in whom were blended the spirit, the beauty, the talent and the ardent nature of both parents, and a soft-eyed, cooing baby girl—were clinging about their mother whenever she was seen off the stage, making a picture that was the admiration of all beholders.

The last roses of the year would soon be gone from the gardens, but Mrs. Fipps' windows blossomed gallantly with garlands and sprays more wonderful than any that ever grew on tree or shrub. Not for many a long day had the shop enjoyed such a thriving trade, for no sooner had the news that Mr. Placide's company would open a season at the theatre been noised abroad than the town beaux addressed themselves to the task of penning elegant little notes inviting the town belles to accompany them to the play, while the belles themselves, scenting an opportunity to complete the wreck of masculine hearts that was their chief business, addressed themselves as promptly to the quest of the most ravishing theatre bonnets which the latest Paris fashions as interpreted by Mrs. Fipps could produce. As that lady bustled back and forth among her customers, her mouth full of pins and hands full of ribbons, feathers, flowers and what not, her face wore, in spite of her prosperity, an expression of unusual gravity.

She could not get the lodger in the back room off her mind.

Mr. Placide, who had been to see the sick woman, was confident that her disorder was "nothing serious," and that she would be able to meet her engagements, and charged the thrifty dealer in fashionable head-gear and furnished rooms by no means to let the fact that the star was ill "get out." But the fever-flush that tinged the patient's pale cheeks and the cough that racked her wasted frame seemed very like danger signals to good Mrs. Fipps, and though she did not realize the hopelessness of the case, her spirits were oppressed by a heaviness that would not be shaken off.

Ill as Mrs. Poe, or Miss Arnold, as she was still sometimes called, was, she had managed by a mighty effort of will and the aid of stimulants to appear once or twice before the footlights. But her acting had been spiritless and her voice weak and it finally became necessary for the manager to explain that she was suffering from "chills and fevers," from which he hoped rest and skillful treatment would relieve her and make it possible for her to take her usual place. But she did not appear. Gradually her true condition became generally known and in the hearts of a kindly public disappointment gave place to sympathy. Some of the most charitably disposed among the citizens visited her, bringing comforts and delicacies for her and presents for the pretty, innocent babes who all unconscious of the cloud that hung over them, played happily upon the floor of the dark and bare room in which their mother's life was burning out. Nurse Betty, an ample, motherly soul, with cheeks like winter apples and eyes like blue china, and a huge ruffled cap hiding her straggly grey locks from view—versatile Betty, who was not only nurse for the children and lady's maid for the star, but upon occasion appeared in small parts herself, hovered about the bed and ministered to her dying mistress.

As the hours and days dragged by the patient grew steadily weaker and weaker. She seldom spoke, but lay quite silent and still save when shaken by the torturing cough. On a Sunday morning early in December she lay thus motionless, but wide-eyed, listening to the sounds of the church-bells that broke the quiet air. As the voice of the last bell died away she stirred and requested, in faint accents, that a packet from the bottom of her trunk be brought to her. When this was done she asked for the children, and when Nurse Betty brought them to the bedside she gave into the hands of the wondering boy a miniature of herself, upon the back of which was written: "For my dear little son Edgar, from his mother," and a small bundle of letters tied with blue ribbon. She clasped the baby fingers of the girl about an enameled jewel-case, of artistic workmanship, but

The Dreamer

empty, for its contents had, alas, gone to pay for food. She then motioned that the little ones be raised up and allowed to kiss her, after which, a frail, white hand fluttered to the sunny head of each, as she murmured a few words of blessing, then with a gentle sigh, closed her eyes in her last, long sleep.

The baby girl began to whimper with fright at the suddenness with which she was snatched up and borne from the room, and the boy looked with awe into the face of the weeping nurse who, holding his sister in one arm dragged him away from the bedside and out of the door, by the hand. There was much hurried tramping to and fro, opening and closing of doors and drawing to of window-blinds. These unusual sounds filled the boy with a vague fear.

That night the children were put to bed upon a pallet in Mrs. Fipps' own room and Mrs. Fipps herself rocked the baby Rosalie to sleep and gave the little Edgar tea-cakes, in addition to his bread and milk, and told him stories of Heaven and beautiful angels playing upon golden harps. The next day the children were taken back to their mother's room. The shutter to the window which let in the one patch of dim light was now closed and the room was quite dark, save for two candles that stood upon stands, one at the foot, the other at the head of the bed. The air was heavy—sickening almost—with the odor of flowers. Upon the bed, all dressed in white, and with a wreath of white roses on her dark ringlets, lay their mother, with eyelids fast shut and a lovely smile on her lips. She was very white and very beautiful, but when her little boy kissed her the pale lips were cold on his rosy ones, as if the smile had frozen there. It was very beautiful but the boy was a little frightened.

"Mother—" he said softly, pleadingly, "Wake up! I want you to wake up."

The weeping nurse placed her arm around him and knelt beside the bed.

"She will never wake up again here on earth, Eddie darling. Never—nevermore. She has gone to live with the angels where you will be with her some day, but never—nevermore on earth."

With that she fell to weeping bitterly, hiding her face on his little shoulder.

The child, marvelling, softly repeated, "Nevermore—nevermore." The solemn, musical word, with the picture in the dim light, of the sleeping figure—asleep to wake nevermore—and so white, so white, all save the dusky curls, sank deep into his young mind and memory. His great grey eyes were wistful with the beauty, and the sadness, and the mystery of it all.

The next day the boy rode in a carriage with Mrs. Fipps and Nurse Betty who had left off the big white cap and was enveloped from head to foot in black, up a long hill, to a white church in a churchyard where the grass was still green between the tombstones. The bell in the white steeple was tolling slowly, solemnly. Soft grey clouds hung over the steeple and snow-flakes as big as rose-leaves began to fill the air. Presently the bell ceased tolling and he and Nurse Betty moved up the aisle behind a train of figures in black, with black streamers floating from their sleeves. The figures bent beneath a heavy burden. It was long and black and grim, but the flowers that covered it were snow-white and filled the church with a sweet smell. A white-robed figure led the way up the aisle, repeating, as he walked, some words so solemn and full of melody that they sounded almost like music. The church was dim, and quiet, and nearly empty. The organ began to play—oh, so softly! It was very beautiful, but still the boy shuddered, for he dimly realized that the grim box held the sleeping form that seemed to be his mother, but was not his real mother. *Her* kisses were not frozen, and *she* was in Heaven with the angels.

The choir sang sweet music and the white-robed priest said more solemn words that were like spoken music; then the procession moved slowly down the aisle again and out of the door. The bell in the steeple was silent now, and the organ was silent. Silently the procession moved—silently the snow came down. Silently and softly, like white flowers. The green graves were white with it now, like the flowers on the coffin lid; but the open grave in the churchyard corner, near the wall—it was dark, and deep and terrible! The boy's heart almost stood still as, clinging to Nurse Betty's hand, he stared into its yawning mouth. He felt that he would choke—would suffocate. They were lowering the box into that deep, dark pit! What if the sleeping figure should awake, after all—awake to the darkness and narrowness of that narrow bed!

With a piercing shriek the child broke from his nurse's hand and thrust himself upon the arm of one of the black figures who held the ropes, in a wild effort to stay him; then, still shrieking, was borne from the spot.

CHAPTER II.

"Since it seems you have set your heart upon this thing, I do not forbid it; but remember, you are acting in direct opposition to my judgment and advice, and if you ever live to regret it (as I believe you shall) you will have no one but yourself to blame."

John Allan's voice was harsher, more positive, than usual; his shoulders seemed to square themselves and a frowning brow hardened an always austere face. His whole manner was that of a man consenting against his will. His young wife hung over his chair vainly endeavoring to smooth, with little pats of her fair hands, the stubborn locks that *would* stand on end, like the bristles of a brush, whatever she did. Her soft and vivacious beauty was in striking contrast to the strength and severity of his rugged and at the same time distinguished countenance. His narrow, steel-blue eyes, deep sunk under bushy brows and a high, but narrow, forehead, were shrewd and piercing; his nose was large and like a hawk's beak. His face too, was narrow, with cheek-bones high as an Indian's. His mouth was large, but firmly closed, and the chin below it was long and prominent and was carried stiffly above the high stock and immaculate, starched shirt-ruffles. Her figure, as she leaned against the chair's high back, was slender and girlish,—childish, almost, in its low-necked, short-waisted, slim-skirted, "Empire" dress, of some filmy stuff, the pale yellow of a Marshal Niel rose. Her face was a pure oval with delicate, regular features. Her reddish-brown hair, parted in the middle, was piled on top of her small head, and airy little curls hung down on her brow on either side of the part. Her eyes—the color of her hair—were gentle and sweet and her mouth was tenderly curved and rosy. With her imploring attitude, the sweetness of her eyes and mouth and the warmth of her plea, her fresh beauty glowed like a flower, newly opened. All unmoved, John Allan repeated,

"You will have no one but yourself to blame."

Her ardor undimmed by the chariness of the consent she had gained, she showered the lowering brow with cool, delicate little kisses until it grew smooth in spite of itself.

"Oh, I know I never shall regret it, John," she cooed. "He is such a beautiful boy—so sweet and affectionate, so merry and clever! Just what I should like our own little boy to be, John, if God had blessed us with one."

"I grant you he seems a bonny little lad enough, Frances. But I realize, as it seems you do not, the risk of undertaking to rear as your own the child of any but the most unquestionable parentage. I confess the thought of introducing into my family the son of professional players is extremely distasteful to me."

"But John, dear, you know these Poes were not ordinary players. The father was one of the Maryland Poes and I understand the mother came of good English stock. She certainly seemed to be a lady and a good, sweet woman, poor thing! The Mackenzies

The Dreamer

have decided to adopt the baby Rosalie, though they have children, as you know; and with this charming little Edgar for my very own I shall be the happiest woman alive."

"Well, well, keep your pretty little pet, but if he turns out to be other than a credit to you, don't forget that you were warned."

And so the little Edgar Poe—the players' child—became Edgar Allan, with a fond and admiring young mother who became at once and forever his slave and whose chief object in life henceforth was to stand between him and the discipline of a not intentionally harsh or unkind, but strict and uncompromising father; who though he too was fond of the boy, in a way, and proud of his beauty and little accomplishments, was constantly on the lookout for the cloven foot which his fixed prejudice against the child's parentage made him certain would appear.

In her delight over her acquisition, Frances Allan was like a child with a new toy. She almost smothered him with kisses when, accepting her bribe of a spaniel pup and his pockets full of sugar-kisses, he agreed to call her "Mother." With her own fingers she made him the quaintest little baggy trousers, of silk pongee, and a velvet jacket, and a tucker of the finest linen. His cheap cotton stockings were discarded for scarlet silk ones, and for his head, "sunny over with curls" of bright nut-brown, she bought from Mrs. Fipps, the prettiest peaked cap of purple velvet, with a handsome gold tassel that fell gracefully over on one shoulder. Thus arrayed, she took him about town with her to show him to her friends who were ecstatic in their admiration of his pensive, clear-cut features, his big, grey eyes and his nut-brown ringlets; of his charming smile and the frank, pretty manner in which he gave his small hand in greeting.

"Oh, but you should hear him recite and sing," the proud foster-mother would say. "And he can dance, too."

She gave a large dinner-party just to exhibit the accomplishments of her treasure—actually standing him upon the table when it had been cleared, to sing and recite for the guests. Even her husband unbent so far as to applaud vigorously the modest, yet self-possessed grace with which the mite drank the healths of the assembled company—making a neat little speech that his new mother had taught him.

The boy's young heart responded to the affection of the foster-mother to a certain degree; but, mere baby though he was, his real heart lay deep in the grave on the hill-top, where the earthly part of that other mother was lying so still, so white, with the roses on her hair and the frozen smile on her lips.

The churchyard on the hill was but a short distance away from his new home, and as spring opened, became a favorite resort of nurses and children. The negro "mammy" who had replaced Nurse Betty used often to take him there, and often, as she chatted with other mammies, her charge would wander from her side to the grave against the wall, where he would stretch his small body full length upon the turf and whisper the thoughts of his infant mind to the dear one below; for who knew but that, even down under ground she might be glad to hear, through her white sleep, her little boy's words of love and remembrance—though never, nevermore she could see him on earth. He would even imagine her replies to him, until the conversations with her became so real that he half believed they were true.

At night, when bed-time came, he said his prayers at the knee of his pretty new mother, who told him jolly stories and sang him jolly songs, and patted him and soothed him with caresses which he found very agreeable, and accepted graciously. But he always took the miniature which had been his dying mother's parting gift to bed with him and he was glad when the new mother kissed him goodnight and put out the light and softly closed the door behind her; for it was then, with the picture close against his breast, that the visions

The Dreamer

came to him—the visions of angels making sweet music upon golden harps and among them his lost mother, with her sweet face saddened but made sweeter still by that thought of nevermore.

Oh, that wondrous word nevermore! Its music charmed him, its hopelessness filled and thrilled him with a strange, a holy sorrow, in which there was no pain.

With the lovely vision still about him, the picture still clasped to his breast, he would sink into healthful sleep to wake on the morrow a bright, joyous boy, alive to all the pleasures of the new day—delighting in the beauties of blue sky and sunshine, of whispering tree and opening flower, ready for sport with his play-fellows and his pets, and full of all manner of merry pranks and jokes. For in the frame of this small boy there dwelt two distinct personalities—twin brothers—yet as utterly unlike as strangers and foreigners, thinking different thoughts, speaking different languages, and dominating him—spirit and body—by turns. One of these we will call Edgar Goodfellow—Edgar the gay, the laughter-loving, the daring, the real, live, wholesome, normal boy; keen for the society of other boys and liking to dance, to run, to jump, to climb, even to fight. The other, Edgar the Dreamer, fond of solitude and silence and darkness, for they aided him to wander far away from the everyday world to one of make believe created by himself and filled with beings to whom real people were but as empty shadows; but a world that the death and burial of his beautiful and adored young mother and the impression made upon him by those scenes, had tinged with an eternal sadness which hung over it as a veil.

The life of Edgar the Dreamer was filled with the subtle charm of mystery. It was a secret life. The world in which he moved was a secret world—an invisible world, to whose invisible door he alone held the key. Edgar the Dreamer was himself an invisible person, for the only outward difference between him and his twin brother, Edgar Goodfellow, lay in a certain quiet, listless air and the solemn look in his big, dark grey eyes which his playmates—bored and intolerant—took as indications that "Edgar was in one of his moods," and his foster-father—eyeing him keenly and with marked displeasure—as an equally unmistakable indication that he was "hatching mischief."

There were times when in the midst of the liveliest company this so-called "mood" would possess the child. He would fall silent; his mouth would become pensive, his dark grey eyes would seem to be impenetrably veiled; his chin would drop upon his hand; he would seem utterly forgetful of his surroundings. The familiar Edgar—Edgar Goodfellow—would have given place to Edgar the Dreamer, who though apparently of the company, would really have slipped through that invisible portal and wandered far afield with the playmates of his fancy.

At such times Mrs. Allan would say, "Eddie, what are you thinking about?" And brought back to her world with a jolt, the boy would answer quickly (somewhat guiltily it seemed to Mr. Allan—noting the startled expression),

"Nothing." It was his first lie, and a very little one, but one that was often repeated; for he that would guard a secret must be used to practice deception.

Mr. Allan would say, "Wake up, wake up, child! Only the idle sit and stare at nothing and think of nothing. You'll be growing up an idle, trifling boy if you give way to such a habit."

Between the Allans and Edgar the Dreamer a great gulf lay—for how should a dreamer of day-dreams reveal himself to any not of his own tribe and kind? Upon Edgar Goodfellow Mrs. Allan doted. All of her friends agreed with her that so remarkable a child—one so precocious and still so attractive—had never been seen, and Mr. Allan was secretly, as proud of his wrestling, running, riding and other out-door triumphs as his wife was of his pretty parlor accomplishments. Their friends agreed too, that she made him the best of mothers, barring the fact (for which weakness she was excusable—he was such a love!) that she spoiled him, and perhaps permitted him to rule her too absolutely. Was he grateful? Oh, well, that would come in time. Appreciation was not a quality to be expected in children, and what more natural than that the boy should accept as a matter of course the good things which she made plain it was her chief pleasure in life to shower upon him? She was indeed, as good a mother as it was possible for a mother without a highly developed imagination to be.

A most lovely woman was Frances Allan, justly admired and liked by all who knew her. She was pretty and gracious and sunny-tempered and sweet-natured; charitable—both to society and the poor—and faithful to her religious duties. Withal, a notable house-keeper, given to hospitality, fond of "company" and gifted in the art of making her friends feel at home under her roof. If she was not gifted with a lively imagination she did not know it, and so had not missed it. As Mr. Allan's wife she had not needed it. And so she lavished upon Edgar Goodfellow everything that heart could wish. She delighted to provide him with pets and toys and good things to eat, and to fill his little pockets with money for him to spend upon himself or upon treating his friends. Fortunately, the other Edgar—Edgar the Dreamer—was not dependent upon her for his pleasures, for the beauties of sky and river and garden and wood which nourished his soul were within his own reach.

If Mrs. Allan had known Edgar the Dreamer, she would have been puzzled and alarmed. If Mr. Allan had known him he would have been angry. A man of action was John Allan. A canny Scotchman he, who owed his success as a tobacco merchant to energy and strict attention to business. If there were dreams in the bowl of the pipe, there was no room for them in the counting-house of a thrifty dealer in the weed. Meditation had no part in his life—was left out of his composition. He believed in *doing*. Day-dreaming was in his opinion but another name for idling, and idling was sin.

The son of their adoption vaguely realized the lack of kinship—the impossibility of contact between his nature and theirs, and as time went on drew more and more within himself. The life of Edgar the Dreamer became more and more secret. So often however, did the warning against his idle habit fall upon his ears that the plastic conscience of childhood made note of it—confusing the will of a blind human guardian with that of God. The Eden of his dreams, guarded by the flaming sword of his foster-father's wrath, began to assume the aspect (because by parental command denied him) of an evil place—though none the less sweet to his soul—and it was with a consciousness of guilt that he would steal in and wander there.

Thus the habit that nurtured God-given genius, branded as sin, and forbidden, might have been broken up, altogether or in part, had not the special providence that looks after the development of this rare exotic transplanted it to a more fertile soil—a more congenial clime.

CHAPTER III.

Upon a mellow September afternoon three years after the newspapers had announced the death, in Richmond, Virginia, of Elizabeth Arnold, the popular English actress, generally known in the United States as Mrs. Poe, the ancient town of Stoke-Newington, in the suburbs of London, dozing in the shadows of its immemorial elms, was aroused to a mild degree of activity by the appearance upon its green-arched streets of three strangers—evidently Americans. It was not so much their nationality as a certain distinguished air that drew attention upon the dignified and proper gentleman in

The Dreamer

broadcloth and immaculate linen, the pretty, gracious-seeming and fashionably dressed lady and especially the little boy of six or seven summers with the large, wistful eyes and pale complexion, and chestnut ringlets framing a prominent, white brow and tumbling over a broad, snowy tucker. He wore pongee knickerbockers and red silk stockings and on his curls jauntily rested a peaked velvet cap from which a heavy gold tassel fell over upon his shoulder.

The denizens of old Stoke-Newington gazed upon this prosperous trio with frank curiosity; the reader has already recognized John Allan and his wife, Frances, and little Edgar Poe—their adopted child.

The sun was still hot, and the refreshing chill in the dusky street, under its arch of interlacing boughs, was grateful to the tired little traveller. As he moved along, clinging to Mrs. Allan's hand, his big eyes gazing as far as they might up the long, cool aisle the trees made, the hazy green distance invited his mystery-loving fancy. The odors of a thousand flowering shrubberies were on the air and he felt that it was good to be in this dreaming old town—as old, it seemed to him, as the world; and there was born in him at that moment, though he could not have defined it, a sense of the picturesquesness, the charm, the fragrance, of old things—old streets, old houses, old trees, old turf and shrubberies, even—with their haunting suggestions of bygone days and scenes.

They passed the ancient Gothic church, standing solemn and serene among its mossy tombs. In the misty blue atmosphere above the elms the fretted steeple seemed to the boy to lie imbedded and asleep, but even as he gazed upon it the churchbell, sounding the hour, broke the stillness with a deep, hollow roar which thrilled him with mingled awe and delight.

Ah, here indeed, was a place made for dreaming!

In the midst of the town lay the Manor House School where the scholarly Dr. Bransby, who preached in the Gothic church on Sundays, upon week-days instructed boys in various branches of polite learning—and also frequently flogged them. This school was the destination of the three strangers from America, for here the foundations of young Edgar's education were to be laid during the several years residence of his foster-parents in London, in which city the boy himself would pass his holidays and sometimes be permitted to spend week-ends.

The ample grounds of the school were enclosed from the rest of the town by a high and thick brick wall, dingy with years, which seemed to frown like a prison wall upon the grassy and pleasantly shaded freedom without. At one corner of this ponderous wall was set a more ponderous gate, riveted and studded with iron bolts, and surmounted with jagged iron spikes. As the boy passed through it he trembled with delicious awe which was deepened by the ominous creak of the mighty hinges. He fancied himself entering upon a domain of mystery and adventure where all manner of grim and unearthly monsters might cross his pathway to be wrestled with and destroyed. The path to the house lay through a small parterre planted with box and other shrubs, and beyond stretched the playgrounds.

As for the house itself, that appeared to the eyes of the boy as a veritable palace of enchantment. It was a large, grey, rambling structure of the Elizabethan age. Within, it was like a labyrinth. Edgar wondered if there were any end to its windings and incomprehensible divisions and sub-divisions—to its narrow, dusky passages and its steps down and up—up and down; to its odd and unexpected nooks and corners. Scarce two rooms seemed to him to be upon the same level and between continually going down or up three or four steps in a journey through the mansion upon which Dr. Bransby guided him and his foster-parents, the dazed little boy found it almost impossible to determine upon which of the two main floors he happened to be. It was afterward to

The Dreamer

become a source of secret satisfaction to him that he never finally decided upon which floor was the dim sleeping apartment to which he was introduced soon after supper, and which he shared with eighteen or twenty other boys.

The business of formally entering the pupil about whom the Allans and Dr. Bransby had already corresponded, in the school, was soon dispatched, and once more the iron gate swung open upon its weirdly complaining hinges, then went to again with a bang and a clang, and the little boy from far Virginia, with the wistful grey eyes and the sunny curls was alone in a throng of curious school-fellows, and in the dimness, the strangeness, the vastness of a hoary, mysterious mansion full of echoes, and of quaint crannies and closets where shadows lurked by day as well as by candle-light. Alone, yet not unhappy—for Edgar the Dreamer was holding full sway. With the departure of his foster-father, all check was removed from his fancy which could, and did, run riot in this creepy and fascinating old place, and at night he had to comfort him the miniature of his mother from which he had never been parted for an hour, and which he still carried to bed with him with unfailing regularity.

He had always known that his mother was English-born, and somehow, in his mind, there seemed to be some mystic connection between this ancient town and manor house and the green graveyard in Richmond, with its mouldy tombstones and encompassing wall.

Not until the next morning was the new pupil ushered into the school-room—the largest room in the world it seemed to the small, lonely stranger. It was long, narrow and low-pitched. Its ceiling was of oak, black with age, and the daylight struggled fitfully in through pointed, Gothic windows. Built into a remote and terror-inspiring corner was a box-like enclosure, eight or ten feet high, of heavy oak, like the ceiling, with a massy door of the same sombre wood. This, the newcomer soon learned was the "sanctum" of the head-master—the Rev. Dr. Bransby—whose sour visage, snuffy habiliments and upraised ferule seemed so terrible to young Edgar that on the following Sunday when he went to service in the Gothic church, it was with a spirit of deep wonder and perplexity that he regarded from the school gallery the reverend man with countenance so demurely benign, with robes so glossy and so clerically flowing, with wig so minutely powdered, so rigid and so vast, who, with solemn step and slow, ascended the high pulpit.

Interspersed about the school-room, crossing and recrossing in endless irregularity, were benches and desks, black, ancient and time-worn, piled desperately with much bethumbed books, and so beseamed with initial letters, names at full length, grotesque figures and other multiplied efforts of the knife, as to have lost what little of original form might have been their portion in days long departed. A huge bucket with water stood at one extremity of the room and a clock, whose dimensions appeared to the boy to be stupendous, at the other.

But it was not only Edgar the Dreamer who came to Manor House School, who passed out of the great iron gate and through the elm avenues to the Gothic church on Sundays, and who regularly, on two afternoons in the week, made a decorous escape from the confinement of the frowning walls, and in company with the whole school, in orderly procession, and duly escorted by an usher, tramped past the church and into the pleasant green fields that lay beyond the quaint houses of the village. Edgar Goodfellow was there too—Edgar the gay, the frolicsome, the lover of sports and hoaxes and trials of strength.

Upon the evening of the young American's arrival, his schoolmates kept their distance, regarding him with shy curiosity, but by the recess hour next day this timidity had worn off, and they crowded about him with the pointed questions and out-spoken criticisms which constitute the breaking in of a new scholar. The boy received their sallies with

The Dreamer

such politeness and good humor and with such an air of modest dignity, that the wags soon ceased their gibes for very shame and the ring-leaders began to show in their manner and speech, an air of approval in place of the suspicion with which they had at first regarded him.

When the questions, "What's your name?"—"How old are you?"—"Where do you live?" "Were you sick at sea?"—"What made you come to this school?" "How high can you jump?"—"Can you box?" "Can you fight?"—and the like, had been promptly and amiably answered, there was a lull. The silence was broken by young Edgar himself. Drawing himself up to the full height of his graceful little figure and thumping his chest with his closed fist, he said, "Any boy who wants to may hit me here, as hard as he can."

The boys looked at each other inquiringly for a moment—they were uncertain, whether this was a specimen of American humor or to be taken literally. Presently the largest and strongest among them stepped forward. He was a stalwart fellow for his years, but his excessively blond coloring, together with the effeminate style in which his mother insisted upon dressing him, caused the boys to give him the name of "Beauty," which was soon shortened into "Beaut," and had finally become "the Beau."

"Will you let *me* hit you?" he asked.

"Yes," replied Edgar. "Count three and hit. You can't hurt me."

As "the Beau" counted, "One—two—three"—Edgar gently inflated his lungs, expanding his chest to its fullest extent, and then, at the moment of receiving the blow, exhaled the air. He did not stagger or flinch, though his antagonist struck straight from the shoulder, with a brawny, small fist.

The rest of the boys, in turn, struck him—each time counting three—with the same result. Finally "the Beau" said,

"*You* hit *me*."

Edgar counted, "One—two—three"—and struck out with clenched fist, but "the Beau" not knowing the trick, was promptly bowled over on the grass—the shock making quick tears start in his forget-me-not blue eyes.

The boys were, one and all, open and clamorous in their admiration.

"Pshaw," said young Edgar, indifferently. "It's nothing. All the boys in Virginia can do that."

"Can you play leap-frog?" asked "Freckles"—a wiry looking little fellow, with carotty locks and a freckled nose, whose leaping had hitherto been unrivalled.

"I'll show you," was the reply.

Instantly, a dozen backs were bent in readiness for the game, and over them, one by one, vaulted Edgar, with the lightness of a bird, his brown curls blowing out behind him, as his baggy yellow thighs and thin red legs flew through the air.

"Freckles" magnanimously owned himself beaten at his own game.

"Let's race," said "Goggles"—a lean, long-legged, swathy boy, with a hooked nose and bulging, black eyes.

Like a flash, the whole lot of them were off down the gravel walk, under the elms. Edgar and "Goggles"—abreast—led for a few moments, then Edgar gradually gained and came out some twenty feet ahead of "Goggles," and double that ahead of the foremost of the others.

It was not only these accomplishments in themselves that made the American boy at once take the place of hero and leader of his form in this school of old England, but the quiet and unassuming mien with which he bore his superiority—not seeming in the least to despise the weakest or most backward of his competitors, and good-humoredly initiating them all into the little secrets of his success in performing apparently difficult feats.

It was the same way with his lessons. Without apparent effort he distanced all of his class-mates and instead of pluming himself upon it, was always ready to help them with their Latin or their sums, whose answers he seemed to find by magic, almost.

CHAPTER IV.

During the winter before Edgar went to Stoke-Newington, he had attended an "infant school," in Richmond, taught by a somewhat gaunt, but mild-mannered spinster, with big spectacles over her amiable blue eyes, a starchy cap and a little bunch of frosty corkscrew curls on each side of her face. As a child, she had played with Mr. Allan's father on their native heath, in Ayrshire, and to her, little Edgar was always her "ain wee laddie." She had spoiled him inordinately and unblushingly. Also, as she contentedly drew at the pipe filled with the offerings of choice smoking-tobacco which he frequently turned out of his pockets into her lap, she had taught him to read in her own broad Scottish accent, and to cypher.

She had furthermore drilled him in making "pothooks and hangers," with which he covered his slate in neat rows, daily. But it was at the Manor House, in Stoke-Newington, that he was initiated into the mysteries of writing. His hands were as shapely as a girl's, with deft, taper fingers that seemed made to hold a pen or brush, and he soon developed a neat, small, but beautifully clear and graceful hand-writing.

This new accomplishment became at once a delight to him, and as time went on opened a new world to Edgar the Dreamer, who now began, when he could snatch an opportunity to do so unobserved, to put down upon paper the visions of his awakening soul. Sometimes these scribblings took the form of little stories—crudely conceived and incoherently expressed, but rich in the picturesque thought and language of an exceptionally imaginative and precocious child. Sometimes they were in verse. For subjects these infant effusions had generally to do with the lonely grave in the churchyard in Richmond and the sad joy of the heart that mourns evermore; with the beauty of flowers—the more beautiful because doomed to a brief life; with the Gothic steeple, asleep in the still, blue air, and the bell in whose deep iron throat dwelt a note that was hollow and ghostly; with the great wall around the Manor House grounds and with the mighty gate that swung upon hinges in which the voice of a soul in torment seemed to be imprisoned, and with other things which filled him with a terror that

"was not fright, But a tremulous delight."

His learning to write bore still another fruit.

When Mrs. Allan had first adopted him and set apart a room in her home for him, she had placed in a little cabinet therein the packet of letters his dying mother had given him. She had not opened the packet, for she felt that the letters were for the actress's child's eye alone. He, when he looked at it, did so with a feeling of mixed reverence and fascination which was deepened by his inability to decipher the secrets bound together by the bit of blue ribbon tied around it. How the sight of the packet recalled to him that sad, that solemn hour in which it had been given into his hands! When getting him ready for boarding-school, Mrs. Allan had packed the letters with his other belongings, for she was a woman of sentiment, and she felt the child should not be parted from this gift of his dying mother. But at length, when a knowledge of writing made it possible for him to read the letters, he was possessed with a feeling of shrinking from doing so, as one might shrink from opening a message from the grave.

The Dreamer

What grim, what terrible secrets, might not the little bundle of letters reveal!

It was not until his fifth and last year at Stoke-Newington that Edgar decided one day to look into the packet. He was confined to his bed by slight indisposition and so had the dormitory to himself and could risk opening the letters without fear of interruption. He untied the blue ribbon and the thin, yellowed papers, with fragments of their broken seals still sticking to them, fell apart. He picked up the one bearing the earliest date and began to read. It was from his father to his mother immediately after their betrothal. His interest was at once intensely aroused and in the order in which the letters came, he read, and read, and read, with the absorption with which he might have read his first novel. They were a revelation to him—a revelation of a world he had not known existed, though it seemed, it lay roundabout him—these love-letters of his parents, literally throbbing with the exalted passion of two young, ardent, poetic spirits. The boy had not dreamed that anything so beautiful could be as this undying love of which they wrote and the language in which they made their sweet vows to each other. His own heart throbbed in answer to what he read. His imagination was violently wrought upon and exquisite feelings such as he had never known before awakened in his breast.

Under the spell of the letters the child-poet fell in love—not with any creature of flesh and blood, for his entire acquaintance and association was with boys—but with the ideal of his inner vision. From that time, his poetic outbursts came to be filled with—more than aught else—the surpassing beauty, the worshipful goodness, the divine love of woman. He was a naturally reverent boy, but for these more than mortal beings, as they appeared to his fancy, was reserved the supreme worship of his romantic soul. Indeed, the adoration of his ideal woman—perfect in body, in mind and in soul, became, and was to be always, a religion to him.

To imagine himself rescuing from a dark prison tower, hid in a deep wood, or from a watery grave in a black and rock-bound lake, at midnight, some lovely maiden whose every thought and heart-beat would thenceforth be for him alone—this became the entrancing inward vision of Edgar the Dreamer—the poet—the lover, at whom Edgar Goodfellow with whisper as insistent as the voice of Conscience, scoffed and sneered, seeking to make him ashamed; but all in vain.

Of course it was to follow, as the night the day, that the boy would find someone in whom to dress his ideal. Upon a Sunday soon after his falling in love, he saw the very maiden of his dreams in the flesh. It was in the Gothic church. From the remote pew in the gallery where he sat with his school-mates, he looked down upon a wonderful vision of white and gold in one of the principal pews of the main aisle. Clad all in white and with a shower of golden tresses falling over her shoulders, she was like a glorious lily or a holy angel. Her eyes, uplifted in the rapture of worship, he divined, rather than saw, were of the hue of heaven itself. He loved her at once, with all his soul's might. Her name? Her home? These were mysteries—sacred mysteries—whose unfathomableness but added to her charm.

After that, service in the Gothic church was a much more important event to The Dreamer than before—an event looked forward to with trembling from Sunday to Sunday. After that too, upon his periodical week-day walks with the school, he would look up at the quaint old homesteads they passed, with their hedged gardens, ivied walls and sweet-scented shrubberies, and try to guess which was the house-wonderful in which she dwelt. Then suddenly, one sweet May afternoon, he discovered it.

It was, as was fitting, the most antique, the most distinguished mansion of them all. He saw her through the bars of the stately entrance gate as she sat beside her mother, on a garden-seat, tying into nosegays the flowers that filled her lap. Stupified by the shock of the discovery, he stood rooted to the ground, letting his school-mates go on ahead of him. She was much nearer him than she had been in the dusky church, and upon closer view,

The Dreamer

she seemed even more lovely, more flower-like, more angelic than ever before. He stared upon her face with a gaze so compelling that she looked up and smiled at him; then, with sudden impulse, gathered her flowers in her apron, and running forward, handed him through the gate, a fragrant, creamy bud that she happened at the moment to have in her hand.

As in a dream, he stretched his fingers for it. He tried to frame an expression of thanks, but his lips were dry and though they moved, no sound came. She had returned at once to her seat beside her mother, and the voice of the usher (who had just missed him) sharply calling to him to "Come on!" was in his ears. He hurried forward, trembling in all his limbs. Twice he stumbled and nearly fell. The bud, he had quickly hidden within his jacket—it was too holy a thing for the profane eyes of his school-fellows to look upon.

When strength and reason came back to him he was like a new being. Happiness gave wings to his feet and he walked on air. A divine song seemed to be singing in his ears. Mechanically, he went through the regular routine of school, with no difference that others could see. To himself, heart and soul—detached and divorced from his body—seemed soaring in a new and beautiful world in which lessons and teachers had no place, no part. Whenever it was possible for him to do so unobserved, he would snatch the rose from his bosom and kiss and caress it. He only lived to see Sunday come round.

But on the next Sunday and the next she was absent from her accustomed place. Such a thing had not happened before since he had first seen her. He was filled with the first real anxiety he had ever known. Here was a mystery in which there was no charm!

The Wednesday after the second Sunday upon which he had missed her was a day dropped out of heaven. The mild, early summer air that floated through the open windows into the gloomy, oak-ceiled schoolroom, was ambrosial with the breathings of flowers. Young Edgar could not fix his thoughts upon the page before him. The out-of-door world was calling to him. He found himself listening to the birds in the trees outside and gazing through the narrow, pointed windows at the waving branches.

Suddenly his heart stopped. The deep, sweet, hollow, ghostlike voice of the bell in the steeple, tolling for a funeral, was borne to his ears. In a moment his fevered imagination associated the tolling with the absence of his divinity from her pew, and in spite of passionately assuring himself that it could not be, and recalling how lovely and full of health she had been when he saw her through the gate, he was possessed by deep melancholy.

The days and hours until Sunday seemed an age to him—an age of foreboding and dread—but they at last passed by. In a fever of anxiety, he walked with the rest of the boys to church, and mounted the steps to the school gallery.

It was early; few of the worshippers had arrived, but in a little while there was a stir near the door. A group of figures shrouded in the black habiliments of woe were moving up the aisle—were entering *her* pew, from which alas, *she* was again absent!

Then he knew—knew that she would enter that sacred place *nevermore!*

After the service there were inquiries as to the cause of a commotion in the gallery occupied by the Manor House School, and it was said in reply that the weather being excessively hot for the season, one of the boys had fainted.

The Dreamer

CHAPTER V.

The June following young Edgar's eleventh birthday found him in Richmond once more. The village-like little capital was all greenery and roses and sunshine and bird-song and light-hearted laughter, and he felt, with a glow, that it was good to be back.

In the five years of his absence he had grown quite tall for his age, with a certain dignity and self-possession of bearing acquired from becoming accustomed to depend upon himself. All that was left of the nut-brown curls that used to flow over his shoulders were the clustering ringlets that covered his head and framed his large brow. His absence had also wrought in him other and more subtle changes which did not appear to the friends who remarked upon what a great boy he had grown—a maturity from having lived in another world—from having had his thoughts expanded by new scenes and quickened by the suggestions of historic association and surroundings.

But with his return, England and Stoke-Newington sank into the shadowy past—their spell weakened, for the time being, by the thought-absorbing, heart-filling scenes of which he had now become a part. The years at the Manor House School were as a dream—*this* was the real thing—*this* was Home. *Home*—ah, the charm of that word and all it implied! His heart swelled, his eyes grew misty as he said it over and over to himself. The clatter of drays "down town" was like music in his ears, the dusty streets of the residential section were fair to his eyes for old time's sake. How he loved the very pavement under his feet, rough and uneven as it was; how dearly he loved the trees that he had climbed (and would climb again) which stretched their friendly boughs over his head!

In a state of happy excitement he rushed about town, visiting his old haunts to see if they were still there, and "the same."

"Comrade," his brown spaniel—his favorite of all his pets—had grown old and sober and had quite forgotten him, but his love was soon reawakened. The boys he had played with, too, had almost forgotten him, but his return called him to mind again and put them all in a flutter. A boy who had lived five years on the other side of the ocean and had been to an English boarding school, was not seen in Richmond every day. Mrs. Allan gave him a party to which all of the children in their circle were invited. In anticipation of this, he had purchased in London, out of the abundance of pocket-money with which his doting foster-mother always saw to it he was provided, a number of little gifts to be distributed among the boys at home. These, with the distinction his travels gave him, made him the man of the hour among Richmond children. And how much he had to tell! At Stoke-Newington it was always the boys at home that were the heroes of the stories he spun by the yard for the entertainment of his school-fellows—the literal among whom had come to believe that there was no feat a Virginia boy could not perform. Now that he was in Richmond, the Stoke-Newington boys themselves loomed up as the wonder-workers, and his playmates listened with admiration and with such expression as, "Caesar's ghost!"—"Jiminy!"—"Cracky!" and the like, as he narrated his tales of "Freckles," "Goggles," "the Beau," and the rest.

One of his first visits after reaching home was to his old black "Mammy," in the tiny cottage, with its prolific garden-spot, on the outskirts of the town, in which Mr. Allan had installed her and her husband, "Uncle Billy," before leaving Virginia.

"Mammy" was expecting him. With one half of her attention upon the white cotton socks she was knitting for her spouse and the other half on the gate of her small garden through which her "chile" would come, she sat in her doorway awaiting him. She was splendidly arrayed in her new purple calico and a big white apron, just from under the iron. Her gayest bandanna "hankercher" covered her tightly "wropped" locks from view and the snowiest of "neckerchers" was crossed over her ample bosom. Her kind, black countenance was soft with thoughts of love.

"Uncle Billy," too, was spruced for the occasion. Indeed, he was quite magnificent in a "biled shut," with ruffles, and an old dresscoat of "Marster's." His top-boots were elaborately blacked, and a somewhat battered stove-pipe hat crowned his bushy grey wool. Each of the old folks comfortably smoked a corn-cob pipe.

"Mammy" saw her boy coming first. She could hardly believe it was he—he was so tall—but she was up and away, down the path, in a flash. Half-way to the gate that opened on the little back street, she met him and enveloped him at once in her loving arms.

"Bless de Lord, O my soul!" she repeated over and over again in a sort of chant, as she held him against her bosom and rocked back and forth on her broad feet, tears of joy rolling down her face.

"De probable am returned," announced Uncle Billy, solemnly.

"G'long, Billy," she said, contemptuously. "He ain' no *probable*. He jes' Mammy's own li'l' chile, if he *is* growed so tall!"

"I'se only 'peatin' what de Good Book say," replied Uncle Billy, with dignity.

Edgar was crying too, and laughing at the same time.

"Howdy, Uncle Billy," said he, stretching a hand to the old man as soon as he could extricate himself from Mammy's embrace. "My, my, you do look scrumptious! How's the rheumatiz?"

"Now jes' heah dat! Rememberin' uv de ole man's rheumatiz arter all dis time!" exclaimed the delighted Uncle Billy. "'Twus mighty po'ly, thankee, li'l Marster, but de sight o' you done make it better a'ready. I 'clar 'fo' Gracious, if de sight of you wouldn' be good for so' eyes! Socifyin' wid dem wile furren nations ain' hu't you a bit—'deed it ain't!"

"How did you expect them to hurt me, Uncle Billy?" asked Edgar, laughing.

"I was 'feard dey mought make a *Injun*, or sum'in' out'n you."

"G'long, Billy," put in his wife, with increased contempt, "Marse Eddie ain' been socifyin' wid no Injuns—he been socifyin' wid kings an' queens' settin' on dey thrones, wid crowns on dey haids an' spectres in dey han's! Come 'long in de house, Honey, an' set awhile wid Mammy."

As they crossed the threshold of the humble abode, Edgar looked around upon its familiar, homely snugness with satisfaction—at the huge, four-post bed, covered with a cheerful "log cabin" quilt made of scraps of calico of every known hue and pattern; at the white-washed walls adorned with pictures cut from old books and magazines; at the "shelf," as Mammy called the mantel-piece, with its lambrequin of scalloped strips of newspaper, and its china vases filled with hundred-leaf roses and pinks; at the spotless bare floor and homemade split-bottomed chairs; at the small, but bright, windows, with their rows of geraniums and verbenas, brilliantly blooming in boxes, tin-cans and broken-nosed tea-pots.

Almost all that Mammy could say was,

"Lordy, Lordy, Honey, how you has growed!" Or, "Jes' to think of Mammy's baby sech a big boy!"

Presently a shadow crossed her face. "Honey," she said, "You gittin' to be sech a man now, you won't have no mo' use fur po' ole Mammy. Dar won't be a thing fur her to do fur sech a big man-chile."

The Dreamer

"Don't you believe that, for a minute, Mammy," was the quick reply. "I was just wondering if you had forgotten how to make those good ash-cakes."

"Now, jes' listen to de chile, makin' game o' his ole Mammy!" she exclaimed. "Livin' so high wid all dem hifalutin' kings an' queens an' sech, an' den comin' back here an' makin' ten' he wouldn' 'spise Mammy's ash-cakes!"

"I'm in dead earnest, Mammy. Indeed, indeed and double deed, I am. Kings and queens don't have anything on their tables half as good as one of your ash-cakes, with a glass of cool butter-milk."

"Dat so, Honey?" she queried, with wonder. "Den you sho'ly shall have some, right away. Mammy churn dis ve'y mornin', and dars a pitcher of buttermilk coolin' in de spring dis minute. You des' make you'se'f at home an' I'll step in de kitchen an' cook you a ash-cake in a jiffy. Billy, you pick me some nice, big cabbage leaves to bake it in whilst I'm mixin' de dough, an' den go an' git de butter-milk an' a pat o' dat butter I made dis mornin' out'n de spring."

Edgar and Uncle Billy followed her into the kitchen where she deftly mixed the cornmeal dough, shaped it in her hands into a thick round cake, which she wrapped in fresh cabbage leaves and put down in the hot ashes on the hearth to bake. Meantime the following conversation between Edgar and the old "Uncle:"

"Uncle Billy do you ever see ghosts now-adays?"

"To be sho', li'l' Marster, to be sho'. Sees 'em mos' any time. Saw one las' Sunday night."

"What was it like, Uncle Billy?"

"Like, Honey?—Like ole Mose, dat's what t'wus like. Does you 'member Mose whar useter drive de hotel hack?"

"Yes, he's dead isn't he?"

"Yes, suh, daid as a do' nail. Dat's de cur'us part on it. He's daid an' was buried las' Sunday ebenin'—buried deep. I know, 'ca'se I wus dar m'se'f. But dat night when I had gone to bed an' wus gittin' off to meh fus' nap, I was woke up on a sudden by de noise uv a gre't stompin' an' trompin' an snortin' in de road. I jump up an' look out de winder, an' I 'clar' 'fo' Gracious if dar warn't Mose, natchel as life, horses an' hack an' all, tearin' by at a break-neck speed. I'se seed many a ghos' an' a ha'nt in meh time, uv *humans*, but dat wus de fus' time I uver heard tell uv a horse or a hack risin' f'um de daid. 'Twus skeery, sho'!"

Before Edgar had time for comment upon this remarkable apparition, Mammy set before him the "snack" she had prepared of smoking ash-cake and fresh butter, on her best china plate—the one with the gilt band—and placed at his right hand a goblet and a stone pitcher of cool butter-milk. A luncheon, indeed, fit to be set before royalty, though it is not likely that any of them ever had such an one offered them—poor things!

Edgar did full justice to the feast and was warm in his praises of it. Then, before taking his leave, he placed in Mammy's hands a parcel containing gifts from the other side of the water for her and Uncle Billy. There is nothing so dear to the heart of an old-time negro as a present, and as the aged couple opened the package and drew out its treasures, their black faces fairly shone with delight. Mammy could not forbear giving her "chile" a hug of gratitude and freshly springing love, while Uncle Billy heartily declared,

"De Lord will sho'ly bless you, li'l' Marster, fur de Good Book do p'intedly say dat He do love one chufful giver."

To young Edgar's home-keeping playmates, he seemed to be the luckiest boy in the world, and indeed, his brief existence had been up to this time, as fortunate as it appeared

The Dreamer

to them. Even the beautiful sorrow of his mother's death had filled his life with poetry and brought him sympathy and affection in abundant measure.

But bitterness was soon enough to enter his soul. His thoughts from the moment of his return to Richmond, had frequently turned to the white church and churchyard on the hill—and to the grave beside the wall. Thither he was determined to go as soon as he possibly could, but it was too sacred a pilgrimage to be mentioned to anyone—it must be as secret as he could make it; and so he must await an opportunity to slip off when he would be least apt to be missed. He chose a sultry afternoon when Mr. and Mrs. Allan were taking a long drive into the country. He waited until sunset—thinking there would be less probability of meeting anyone in the churchyard after that hour than earlier—and set out, taking with him a cluster of white roses from the summer-house in the garden.

It was nearly dusk when he reached the church and climbed the steps that led to the walled graveyard, elevated above the street-level. Never had the spot looked so fair to him. The white spire, piercing the blue sky, seemed almost to touch the slender new moon, with the evening star glimmering by her side. The air was sweet with the breath of roses and honeysuckle, and the graves were deeply, intensely green. Long he lay upon the one by the wall, near the head of which he had placed his white roses—looking up at the silver spire and the silver star and the moon's silver bow—so long that he forgot the passage of time, and when he reached home and went in out of the night to the bright dining-room, blinking his great grey eyes to accustom them to the lamp-light, supper was over.

The keen eyes of John Allan looked sternly upon him from under their fierce brows. The boy saw at once that his foster-father was very angry.

"Where have you been?" he demanded, harshly.

"Nowhere," replied the boy.

"What have you been doing all this time?"

"Nothing," was the answer.

"Nowhere? Nothing? Don't nowhere and nothing me, Sir. Those are the replies—the lying replies—of a boy who has been in mischief. If you had not been where you shouldn't have been, and doing as you shouldn't have done, you would not be ashamed to tell. Now, Sir, tell me at once, where you have been and what you have been doing?"

The boy grew pale, but made no reply, and in the eyes fixed on Mr. Allan's face was a provokingly stubborn look. The man's wrath waxed warmer. His voice rose. In a tone of utter exasperation he cried, "Tell me at once, I say, or you shall have the severest flogging you ever had in your life!"

The boy grew paler still, and his eyes more stubborn. A scowl settled upon his brow and a look of dogged determination about his mouth, but still he spoke not a word.

Mrs. Allan looked from one to the other of these two beings—husband and son—who made her heart's world. The evening was warm and she wore a simple white dress with low neck and short sleeves. Anxiety clouded her lovely face, yet never had she looked more girlishly sweet—more appealing; but the silent plea in her beautiful, troubled eyes was lost on John Allan, much as he loved her.

"Tell him, Eddie dear," she implored. "Don't be afraid. Speak up like a man!"

Still silence.

She walked over to the table where the boy sat before the untouched supper that had been saved for him, and dropped upon one knee beside him. She placed her arm around him and drew him against her gentle bosom—he suffering her, though not returning the caress.

"Tell *me*, Eddie, darling—tell Mother," she coaxed.

The Dreamer

The grey eyes softened, the brow lifted. "There's nothing to tell, Mother," he gently replied.

Mr. Allan rose from his chair. "I'll give you five minutes in which to find something to tell," he exclaimed, shaking a trembling finger at the culprit; then stalked out of the room.

In his absence his wife fell upon the neck of the pale, frowning child, covering his face and his curly head with kisses, and beseeching him with honeyed endearments, to be a good boy and obey his father. But the little figure seemed to have turned to stone in her arms. In less than the five minutes Mr. Allan was back in the room, trimming a long switch cut from one of the trees in the garden as he came.

"Are you ready to tell me the truth?" he demanded.

No answer.

Still trimming the switch, he approached the boy. Frances Allan trembled. Rising from the child's side, she clasped her husband's arm in both her hands.

"Don't, John! Don't, please, John dear. I can't stand it," she breathed. He put her aside, firmly.

"Don't be silly, Frances. You are interfering with my duty. Can't you see that I must teach the boy to make you a better return for your kindness than lying to hide his mischief?"

"But suppose that he is telling the truth, John, and that he has been doing nothing worse than wandering about the streets? You know the way he has always had of roaming about by himself, at times."

"And do you think roaming about the streets at this time of night proper employment for a boy of eleven? Would you have him grow up into a vagabond? A boy dependent upon the bounty of strangers can ill afford to cultivate such idle habits!"

The boy's already large and dark pupils dilated and darkened until his eyes looked like black, storm-swept pools. His already white face grew livid. He drew back as if he had been struck and fixed upon his foster-father a gaze in which every spark of affection was, for the moment, dead. He had been humiliated by the threat of a flogging, but the prospect of the hardest stroke his body might receive was as nothing to him now. His sensitive soul had been smitten a blow the smart of which he would carry with him to his last day. "Dependent upon the bounty of strangers,"—*of strangers!*

Up to this time he had been the darling little son of an over-fond mother, and though his foster-father had been at times, stern and unsympathetic with him, no hint had ever before dropped from him to indicate that the child was not as much his own as the sons of other fathers were their own—that he was not as much entitled to the good things of life which were heaped upon him without the asking as an own son would have been. His comforts—his pleasures had been so easily, so plentifully bestowed that the little dreamer had never before awaked to a realization of a difference between his relation with his parents and the relation of other children with theirs. Brought face to face with this hard, cold fact for the first time, and so suddenly, he was for the moment stunned by it. He felt that a flood of deep waters in which he was floundering helplessly was overwhelming him.

A deep silence had followed the last words of Mr. Allan, who continued to trim the switch, while his wife, sinking into a chair, bowed her face in her arms, folded upon the table, and began to cry softly. The gentle sounds of her weeping seemed but further to infuriate her husband.

"Come with me," he commanded, placing his hand on the shoulder of the child, who unresistingly suffered himself to be pushed along toward his foster-father's room. Frances Allan broke into wild sobbing and placed her fingers against her ears that she might not

The Dreamer

hear the screams of her pet. But there were no screams. Silently, and with an air of dignity it was marvellous so small a figure could command, the beautiful boy received the blows. When one's soul has been hurt, what matters mere physical pain? When both the strength and the passion of Mr. Allan had been somewhat spent, he ceased laying on blows and asked in a calmed voice,

"Are you ready to tell me the truth now?"

In one moment of time the child lived over again the beautiful hour at his mother's grave. He saw again the silver spire and the silver half-moon and the silver star—smelled the blended odors of honeysuckle and rose, made sweeter, by the gathering dews, and felt the coolness and freshness of the long green grass that covered the grave. Who knew but that deep down under the sweet grass she had been conscious he was there—had felt his heart beat and heard his loving whispers as of old, and loved him still, and understood, though she would see him nevermore? Share the secret of that holy hour with anyone—of all people, with this wrathful, blind, unsympathizing man who had just confessed himself a stranger to him? Never!

A faint smile, full of peace, settled upon his poet's face, but he answered never a word.

There was a stir at the door. John Allan looked toward it. His wife stood there drying her eyes. He turned to the boy again.

"Go with your mother and get your supper," he commanded.

"I don't want it," was the reply.

"Well, go to bed then, and tomorrow afternoon you are to spend in your own room, where I hope meditation upon your idle ways may bring you to something like repentance."

The boy paused half-way to the door. "Tomorrow is the day I'm going swimming with the boys. You promised that I might go."

"Well, I take back the promise, that's all."

"Don't you think you've punished him enough for this time, John?" timidly asked his wife.

"No boy is ever punished enough until he is conquered," was the reply. "And Edgar is far from that!"

Mrs. Allan, with her arm about the little culprit's shoulder went with him to his room. How she wished that he would let her cuddle him in her lap and sing to him and tell him stories and then hear him his prayers at her knee and tuck him in bed as in the old days before he went to boarding-school! Her heart ached for him, though she had no notion of the bitterness, the rebellion, that were rankling in his. As she kissed him goodnight she whispered,

"You shall have your swim, in the river, tomorrow, Eddie darling; I'll see that you do."

"Don't you ask *him* to let me do anything," he protested, passionately. "I'm going without asking him. He disowned me for a son, I'll disown him for a father!"

He loved her but he was glad when the door closed behind her so that he could think it all out for himself in the dark—the dear dark that he had always loved so well and that was now as balm to his bruised spirit. The worst of it was that he could not disown John Allan as a father. He had to confess to himself with renewed bitterness that he was indeed, and by no fault of his own—a helpless dependent upon the charity of this man who had, in taunting him with the fact, wounded him so grievously. His impulse was to run away—but where could he go? Though his small purse held at that moment a generous amount of spending money for a boy "going on twelve," it would be a mere nothing toward taking him anywhere. It would not afford him shelter and food for a day, and he knew it—it would not take him to the only place where he knew he had kindred—

The Dreamer

Baltimore. And what if he could get as far as Baltimore, would he care to go there? To assert his independence of the charity of John Allan only to throw himself upon the charity of relatives who had never noticed him—whom he hated because they had never forgiven his father for marrying the angel mother around whose memory his fondest dreams clung?

No, he could not disown Mr. Allan—not yet; but the good things of life received from his hands had henceforth lost their flavor and would be like Dead Sea fruit upon his lips. Hitherto, though he knew, of course, that he was not the Allans' own child, he had never once been made to feel that he was any the less entitled to their bounty. They had adopted him of their own free will to fill the empty arms of a woman with a mother's heart who had never been a mother, and that woman had lavished upon him almost more than a mother's love—certainly more than a prudent mother's indulgence. He had been the most spoiled and petted child of his circle, and the bounty had been heaped upon him in a manner that made him feel—child though he was—the joy that the giving brought the giver, and therefore no burden of obligation upon himself in receiving. If Mr. Allan had been strict to a point of harshness with him, at times, Mr. Allan was a born disciplinarian—it seemed natural for him to be stern and unsympathetic and those who knew him best took his stiffness and hardness with many grains of allowance, remembering his upright life and his open-handed charities. He had administered punishment upon the little lad when he was naughty in the years before he went away to school, and the little lad had taken his medicine philosophically like other naughty boys—had cried lustily, then dried his eyes and forgotten all about it in the pleasure which the goodies and petting he always had from his pretty, tender-hearted foster-mother at such times gave him. But *this* was different. He was a big lad now—very big and old, he felt, far too big to be flogged; quite big enough to visit his mother's grave, if he chose, without having to talk about it. And he had not only been flogged because he would not reveal his sacred, sweet secret, but had had his dependence upon charity thrown up at him!

Henceforth, he felt, his life would be a lonely one, for he now knew that he was different from other boys, all of whom (in his acquaintance) had fathers to whose bounty they had a right—the right of sonship. Yes, he was a very big boy (he told himself) and he had not cried when he was flogged, but under the cover of the kindly dark, hot tears of indignation, hurt pride and pity for his own loneliness—his singularity—made all his pillow wet.

Comfort came to him from an unexpected source. The door of his room had been closed, but not latched. It was now pushed open by "Comrade," his old spaniel, who made straight for his side, first pushing his nose against his face and then leaping upon the bed and nestling down close to him, with a sigh of satisfaction. The desolate boy welcomed this dumb, affectionate companionship. The feel of the warm, soft body, and the thought of the velvety brown eyes which he could not see in the dark, but knew were fixed upon him with their intense, loving gaze, were soothing to his overwrought nerves. Here was something whose love could be counted upon—something as dependent upon him as he was upon Mr. Allan; yet what a joy he found in the very dependence of this devoted, soft-eyed creature! Never would he taunt Comrade with his dependence upon charity.

"No;" he said, his hands deep in the silky coat, "I would not insult a dog as he has insulted me! Never mind, Comrade, old fellow, we'll have our swim in the river tomorrow, and he may flog me again if he likes."

But he was not flogged the next day. An important business engagement occupied Mr. Allan the whole afternoon, and when he came in late, tired and pre-occupied, he found Edgar fresh and glowing from his exercise in the river, the curls still damp upon his forehead, quietly eating his supper with his mother. *She* knew, but tender creature that she was, she was prepared to do anything short of fibbing to shield her pet from another out-burst. But John Allan, still absorbed in business cares, hardly looked toward the boy, and asked not a question.

CHAPTER VI.

The home of the Allans was never quite the same to Edgar Poe after that night. A wall had been raised between him and his foster-father that would never be scaled. He was still indulged in a generous amount of pocket money which he invariably proceeded to get rid of as fast as he could—lavishing it upon the enjoyment of his friends as freely as it had been lavished upon him. He had plenty of pets and toys, went to dancing school, in which his natural love of dancing made him delight, and was given stiff but merry little parties, at which old Cy, the black fiddler played and called the figures, and the little host and his friends conformed to the strict, ceremonious etiquette observed by the children as well as the grown people of the day.

For these indulgences Frances Allan was chiefly responsible. The one weak spot in the armor of austerity in which John Allan clothed himself was his love for his wife, and it was often against what he felt to be his better judgment that he acquiesced in her system of child-spoiling. He felt a solemn responsibility toward the boy, and he did his duty by him, as he saw it, faithfully. It was not in the least his fault that he did *not* see that under the broad white brow and sunny ringlets was a brain in which, like the sky in a dew-drop, a whole world was reflected, with ever changing pageantry, and that the abstracted expression in the boy's eyes that he thought could only mean that he was "hatching mischief," really indicated that the creative faculty in budding genius was awake and at work.

For a child Edgar's age to be making trials at writing poetry Mr. Allan regarded as sheer idleness, to be promptly suppressed. Indeed, when he discovered that the boy had been guilty of such foolishness, he emphatically ordered him not to repeat it. To counteract the effects of his wife's spoiling of her adopted son, he felt it his duty to place all manner of restrictions upon his liberty, which the freedom-loving boy, with the connivance of his mother and the negro servants who adored him, disregarded whenever it was possible. Though bathing in the river was (except upon rare occasions) prohibited, Edgar became before summer was over, the most expert swimmer and diver of his years in town, and many an afternoon when Mr. Allan supposed that he was in his room, to which he had been ordered for the purpose of disciplining his will and character, or for punishment, he was far beyond the city's limits roaming the woods, the fields, or the river-banks— joyously, and without a prick of conscience (for all his disobedience) feeding his growing soul upon the beauties of tree, and sky, and cliff, and water-fall.

And so, in spite of the melancholy moods in which he was occasionally plunged by the bitterness which had found lodgment in his breast, the summer was upon the whole a happy one to the boy. He was so young and the world was so beautiful! He could not remember always to be unhappy. Edgar Goodfellow, as well as Edgar the Dreamer, revelled in the world of Out-of-Door. To the one all manner of muscular sport and exercise was as the breath of his nostrils; to the other, whose favorite stories were ancient myths and fairy-tales, all natural phenomena possessed vivid personality. He loved to

The Dreamer

trace pictures in the clouds. In the rustling of corn or the stirring of leaves in the trees, or in the sound of running waters he heard voices which spoke to him of delightsome things, bringing to his full, grey eyes, as he hearkened, a soft, romantic look, and touching his lips and his cheeks with a radiant spirituality.

The cottage, on Clay Street, to which the Allans had removed soon after their return from England, was in a quiet part of the town. The window of Edgar's own, quaint little room in the dormer roof, with its shelving walls, gave him a fair view of the sky, and brought him sweet airs wafted across the garden of old-fashioned flowers below. Here, such hours as he spent from choice or by command were not lonely, for, sitting by the little window, many a story or poem was thought out; or buried in some favorite book his thoughts would be borne away as if on wings to a world where imagination was king.

In the fall he was entered at Mr. Clarke's school. The school-room, with its white-washed walls and the sun pouring in, unrestricted, through the commonplace, big, bare windows, was very different from the great, gloomy Gothic room at old Stoke-Newington—so full of mystery and suggestion—but Edgar found it a pleasant place in which to be upon that cool fresh morning in late September, when he made its acquaintance. He felt full of mental activity and ready to go to work with a will upon his Latin, his French and his mathematics. Since his return from England, in June, he had become acquainted with most of the boys who were to be his school-fellows, and he took at once to the school-master, Professor Clarke, of Trinity College, Dublin—a middle-aged bachelor of Irish birth, an accomplished gentleman and a very human creature, with a big heart, a high ideal of what boys might be and abundant tolerance of what they generally were. If he had a quick temper, he had also a quick wit, and a quick appreciation of talent and sympathy with timorous aspirations.

It had been Master Clarke's suggestion that his new pupil, who was known as Edgar Allan, should put his own name upon the school register. Edgar, looking questioningly up into Mr. Allan's face, was glad to read approval there, and with a thrill of pride he wrote upon the book, in the small, clear hand that had become characteristic of him:

"Edgar Allan Poe."

He was proud of his name and proud of his father, of whom he remembered nothing, but in whose veins, he knew, had run patriot blood, and who had had the independence to risk all for love of the beautiful mother of worshipped memory. It was with straightened shoulders and a high head that he took the seat assigned him at the clumsy desk, in the bare, ugly room of the school in which he was to be known for the first time as *Edgar Poe*. He felt that in coming into his own name he had come into a proud heritage.

Mr. Clarke's Irish heart warmed toward him. He divined in the big-browed, big-eyed boy a unique and gifted personality and proceeded with the uttermost tact to do his best toward the cultivation of his talents. The result was that Edgar not only acquitted himself brilliantly in his studies, but progressed well in his verse-making, which though, since Mr. Allan's prohibition, it had been kept secret in his home, was freely acknowledged to teacher and school-fellows.

By his class-mates he was deemed a wonder. He was so easily first among them in everything—in the simple athletics with which they were familiar, as well as in studies—and his talent for rhyming and drawing seemed to set him upon a sort of pedestal.

In the first blush of triumph these little successes gave him, young Edgar's head was in a fair way to be turned. He saw himself (in fancy) the leader, the popular favorite of the whole school. Indeed, he flattered himself he had leaped at a single bound to this position at the moment, almost, of his entrance. But he soon began to see that he was mistaken. While he was conscious of the unconcealed admiration of most, and the ill-concealed envy of a few of the boys, of his mental and physical abilities, he began, as time went on, to suspect—then to be sure—that for some reason that baffled all his ingenuity to fathom, he was not accorded the position in the school that was the natural reward for superiority of endowment and performance. This place was filled instead by Nat Howard, a boy who, he told himself, he was without the slightest vanity bound to see was distinctly second to him in every way.

He noticed that whatever Nat proposed was invariably done, so that he was forced either to follow where he should have led, or be left out of everything. Often when he joined the boys listening with interest to Nat's heavy jokes and talk, a silence would fall upon the company, which in a short while would break up—the boys going off in twos and threes, leaving him to his own society or that of a small minority composed of two or three boys for the most part younger than himself, who in spite of the popular taste for Nat, preferred him and were captivated by his clever accomplishments.

That there was some reason why he was thus shut out from personal intimacy by school-mates who acknowledged and admired his powers he felt sure, and he was determined to ferret it out. In the meantime his heart, always peculiarly responsive to affection, answered with warmth to the devotion of the small coterie who were independent enough to swear fealty to him. He helped them with their lessons, initiated them into the mysteries of boxing and other manly exercises, went swimming and gunning with them, and occasionally delighted them by showing them his poems and the little sketches with which he sometimes illustrated his manuscript, in the making.

It must be confessed that there was little in these compositions to set the world afire. They would only be counted remarkable as the work of a school-boy in his early teens, and were practice work—nothing more. They served their purpose, then sank into the oblivion which was their meet destiny. But to Jack Preston, Dick Ambler, Rob Stanard and Rob Sully, and one or two others, they were master-pieces.

These boys, as well as Edgar, were giving serious attention to their linen, the care of their hands, and the precise parting of their hair, just then; and a close observer might often have detected them in the act of furtively feeling their upper lips with anxious forefinger in the vain hope of discovering the appearance—if ever so slight—of a downy growth thereupon. For they, as well as he, were making sheep's eyes at those wonderful visions in golden locks and jetty locks, with brown eyes and blue eyes, with fluttering ribbons and snowy pinafores, known as "Miss Jane Mackenzie's girls," who were the inspiration of most of their poet-chum's invocations of the muse. The little hymns in praise of the charms of these girls were generally adorned with pen or pencil sketches of the fair charmers themselves.

Poor Miss Jane had a sad time of it. As the accomplished principal of a choice Young Ladies Boarding and Day School, she enjoyed an enviable position in the politest society in town. Parents of young ladies under her care congratulated themselves alike upon her strict rule and her learning, her refinement of manners and conversation and her distinguished appearance. She was tall and stately and in her decorous garb of black silk that could have "stood alone," and an elegant cap of "real" lace with lavender ribbons softening the precise waves of her iron-grey hair, she made a most impressive figure—one that would have inspired with profound respect any male creature living saving that incorrigible non-respecter of persons and personages, especially of lady principals—the Boy. For the "forming" of young ladies, Miss Jane had a positive forte, but the genus boy was an unknown quantity to her, and worse—he was a positive terror. For one of them to invade the sacred precincts of her school, or its grounds, seemed to her maiden soul rank sacrilege; to scale her garden wall after dark for the purpose of attaching a letter to a string let down from a window to receive it, was nothing short of criminal. For one of her

The Dreamer

girls to receive offerings of candy and original poetry—*love poetry*—from one of these terrible creatures; such an offence was unspeakably shocking.

Yet discovery of such offences happened often enough to give her repeated shocks, and to confirm her in her belief in the total depravity, the hopeless wickedness of all boys—especially of John Allan's adopted son.

In spite of her vigilance, Edgar Poe found the means to outwit her, and to transmit his effusions, without difficulty, to her fair charges, who with tresses primly parted and braided and meek eyes bent in evident absorption upon their books, were the very pictures of docile obedience, and bore in their outward looks no hint of the guilty consciences that should, by rights, have been destroying their peace.

Miss Jane was the sister of Mr. Mackenzie who had adopted little Rosalie Poe. Rosalie was, at Miss Jane's invitation, a pupil in the school, but (ungrateful girl that she was) she became, at the suggestion of her handsome and charming brother Edgar, whom she adored, the willing messenger of Dan Cupid, and furthered much secret and sentimental correspondence between the innocent-seeming girls and the young scamps who admired them.

In these fascinating flights into the realms of flirtation, as in other things, Edgar's friends acknowledged his superiority—his romantic personal beauty and his gift for rhyming giving him a decided advantage over them all; but they acknowledged it without jealousy, for there was much of hero worship in their attitude toward him, and they were not only perfectly contented for him to be first in every way but it would have disappointed them for him not to be. The captivating charm of his presence, in his gay moods, made it unalloyed happiness for them to be with him. They were always ready to follow him as far as he led in daring adventure—ready to fetch and carry for him and glowing with pride at the least notice from him.

Some boys would have taken advantage of this state of things, but not so Edgar Goodfellow. He, for his part, was always ready to contribute to their pleasure, and fairly sunned himself in the unstinting love and praise of these boys who admired, while but half divining his gifts. Their games had twice the zest when Eddie played with them—he threw himself into the sport with such heartfelt zeal that they were inspired to do their best. Many a ramble in the woods and fields around Richmond he took with them, telling them the most wonderful stories as he went along; but sometimes, quite suddenly, during these outings, Edgar Goodfellow would give place to Edgar the Dreamer and they would wonderingly realize that his thoughts were off to a world where none of them could follow—none of them unless it were Rob Sully, who was himself something of a dreamer, and could draw as well as Edgar.

The transformation would be respected. His companions would look at him with something akin to awe in their eyes and tell each other in low tones not to disturb Eddie, he was "making poetry," and confine their chatter to themselves, holding rather aloof from the young poet, who wandered on with the abstracted gaze of one walking in sleep—with them, but not of them.

There were other, less frequent, times when his mood was as much respected, when added to the awe there was somewhat of distress in their attitude toward him. At these times he was not only abstracted, but a deep gloom would seem to have settled upon his spirit. Without apparent reason, melancholy claimed him, and though he was still gentle and courteous, they had a nameless sort of fear of him—he was so unlike other boys and it seemed such a strange thing to be unhappy about nothing. It was positively uncanny.

At these times they did not even try to be with him. They knew that he could wrestle with what he called his "blue devils" more successfully alone. A restlessness generally accompanied the mood, and he would wander off by himself to the churchyard, the river,

The Dreamer

or the woods; or spend whole long, golden afternoons shut up in his room, poring over some quaint old tale, or writing furiously upon a composition of his own. When he looked at the boys, he did not seem to see them, but would gaze beyond them—the pupils of his full, soft, grey eyes darkening and dilating as if they were held by some weird vision invisible to all eyes save his own; and indeed the belief was general among his friends that he was endowed with the power of seeing visions. This impression had been made even upon his old "Mammy," when he was a mite of a lad. Many a time, when he turned that abstracted gaze upon her, she had said to him,

"What dat you lookin' at now, Honey? You is bawn to see evil sho'!"

And now a glimpse of Edgar Goodfellow—the normal Edgar, whom his chums saw oftenest and loved best, because they knew him best and understood him best.

It was a late Autumn Saturday—one of the Saturdays sent from Heaven for the delight of school-children—bracing, but not cold; and brilliant. Little Robert Sully looked pensively out of the window thinking what a fine day it would be for a country tramp, if only he were like other boys and could take them. But Rob was of frail build and constitution and could never stand much exertion. In his eyes was the expression of settled wistfulness that frequent disappointment will bring to the eyes of a delicate child; in the droop of his mouth there was a touch of bitterness, for he was thinking that not only did his weak body make it impossible for him to keep up with the boys, but that it was no doubt, a relief to the boys to leave him behind—that when he could be with them he was perhaps a drag on their pleasure. No doubt they would make a long day of it, this bright, bracing Saturday, for the persimmons and the fox-grapes were ripe and the chinquapin and chestnut burrs were opening. Tears of self-pity sprang to his eyes, but they were quickly dashed away as he heard his name called and saw his beloved Eddie, flushed and glowing with anticipated pleasure, at the gate.

"Come along, Rob," he was calling. "We are going to the Hermitage woods for chinquapins, and you must come too. Uncle Billy is going for a load of pine-tags, and we can ride in his wagon, so it won't tire you."

The other boys were waiting at the corner, all at the highest pitch of mirth, for they saw that their idol, Eddie, was in one of his happiest moods, which would mean a morning of unbounded fun to them. And the ride with old Uncle Billy who, with black and shiny face, beaming upon them in an excess of kindliness, hair like a full-blown cotton-boll, and quaint talk, was an unfailing source of delight to them!

The Saturday freedom was in their blood. Off and away they went in the jolly, rumbling wagon, past houses and gardens, and fields and into the enchanting, autumn-colored woods, where "Bob Whites" were calling to each other and nuts were dropping in the rustling leaves or waiting to be shaken from their open burrs.

As they jolted along, the steady stream of conversation between Edgar and Uncle Billy was as good as a play to the rest of the boys—Edgar, with grave, courteous manner, discoursing of "cunjurs" and "ha'nts" with as real an air of belief as that of the old man himself.

CHAPTER VII.

The allegiance of his little band of boon companions was all the sweeter to the young poet because he realized more and more fully as the years of his school-days passed that for some reason unknown to himself he was systematically, and plainly with intention,

The Dreamer

denied intimacy with Nat Howard and his followers—*snubbed*. As has been said, they did not hesitate to acknowledge his success in all sorts of mental and physical trials of skill, but in a formal, impersonal way. There was never the least familiarity in their intercourse with him. This, naturally, produced in him a reserve in his manner toward them that they unreasonably attributed to "airs." Their coldness wounded and chilled the sensitive boy as much as the love of his devoted adherents warmed him.

It was not until near the end of his third session in the school that the riddle was, quite suddenly, solved. Edgar Poe was now in his fifteenth year. One perfect May day, when the song of birds, the odors of flowers, the whisper of soft breezes and the languor of mellow sunshine outside of the open school windows were wooing all poetic souls to come out and live, and let musty, dry books go to the deuce, little Rob Sully found it impossible to fix his mind upon his Latin. As for Edgar's mind, it was plain from his expression that it was far afield; but then Edgar had the power of knowing his lessons intuitively, almost. Rob only "got" his by faithful plodding. When their respective classes were called, Edgar recited brilliantly, while Rob seemed like one befuddled and, making a dismal failure, was bidden to stay in and study at recess. A look of utter woe settled upon his thin, pallid face, which lifted as, impelled to look toward Edgar's desk, he caught his friend's eyes fixed upon him with their charming smile. He knew well what the eyes were saying:

"Don't worry, Rob, I'll stay in and help you."

And stay in the owner of the eyes did, patiently going over and over the lesson with the confused boy until the hard parts were made easy. Finally, when he saw that Rob had mastered it, Edgar walked out into the yard for the few minutes left of recess. The boys were all drawn up in a group a little way from the house and were being harangued by his rival, Nat Howard. His chums, Rob Stanard, Dick Ambler and Jack Preston, were standing together a few feet apart from the rest. Their faces were very red and the haranguing seemed to be addressed directly to them. Edgar stopped where he was, wondering what it was all about, but shy of joining a crowd over which Nat was presiding.

The speaker's voice rose to a higher key.

"I'll tell you, boys," he was saying, "if you persist in intimacy with this fellow, you needn't expect to be in with me and my crowd."

"We don't want you and your crowd," was the response. "He's worth all of you rolled into one."

Edgar's heart stood still. "Was Nat Howard talking about *him*?"

The voice went on: "I grant you the fellow's smart enough and game enough, but he's not in our class, and I, for one, won't associate with him intimately."

"His family's one of the oldest and most honorable in the country," said Robert Stanard. "I've heard my father say so."

"Yes, but his father must have been a black sheep to run away with a common actress—"

The harangue was brought to an abrupt end. The enraged Edgar had sprung forward and, with a blow in the face, struck Nat Howard down. Nat's friends were lifting him up and wiping the blood from his face and dusting his clothing, while Edgar's own friends gathered around him as if to restrain him from repeating the attack. He shook them off, gazing with contempt upon his limp and half-stunned adversary.

"I'll not hit him again until he repeats his offence," he assured the boys, "but I want him and all other cowardly dogs to know what's waiting for them when they insult the memory of my father and mother. Yes! my mother was an actress! God gave her the gifts

The Dreamer

to make her one and she had the pluck to use them to earn bread for herself and for her children. Yes! she was an actress! She had the lovely face and form, the high intelligence and the poetic soul for the making of a perfect woman or for the interpreter of genius—for the personification of a Juliet, a Rosalind or a Cordelia. Yes! she was an actress! And I'm proud of it as surely as I'm proud she's an angel in Heaven! And I'm proud that my father—the son of a proud family—had the spirit, for her sweet sake, to fly in the face of convention, to count family, fortune and all well lost to become her husband, and to adopt her profession; to learn of her, in order that he might be always at her side to protect her and to live in the light of her presence. If I had choice of all the surnames and of all the lineage in the world, I would still choose the name of Poe, and to be the son of David and Elizabeth Poe, players!"

The boys were silent. The school bell was ringing and Edgar Poe, still pale and trembling with passion, turned on his heel and strode, with head up, in the direction of the door. Rob Stanard and Rob Sully walked one on each side of him, while Dick Ambler and Jack Preston and several others among his adherents, followed close. A little way behind the group came the other boys, their still half-dazed leader in their midst. Good Mr. Burke (who had succeeded Mr. Clarke as school-master) guessed as they came in and took their seats that there had been an altercation of some kind, and that his two brag scholars had been prominent in it; but he was wise in his generation and allowed the boys to settle their own differences without asking any questions unless he were appealed to, when his sympathy and interest were found to be theirs to count upon.

The afternoon session was unsatisfactory, but the master was in an indulgent mood and apparently did not notice what each boy felt—a confusion and abstraction. There was a palpable sense of relief when the closing hour came.

At dinner that day Edgar was silent and evidently under a cloud, and scarcely touched his food. Frances Allan looked toward him anxiously and her husband suspiciously. When his lack of appetite was remarked upon, he, truthfully enough, pleaded headache. Mrs. Allan was all sympathy at once.

"You study too hard, dear," she said. "You may have a holiday tomorrow if you like, and go and spend the day in the country with Rosalie and the Mackenzies."

"No, no," replied the boy. "I'll just stay quiet, in my room, this evening. I'll be all right by tomorrow."

"What have you been eating?" demanded John Allan, gruffly.

"Nothing, since breakfast, Sir," was the reply.

"Headaches are for nervous women. When a healthy boy complains of one, and declines dinner, it generally means that he has been robbing somebody's strawberry patch or up a cherry-tree, stuffing half-ripe fruit," he said in the acid, suspicious tone that the boy knew. It was beyond John Allan's powers to imagine any but physical causes for a boy's ailments.

Not until the door of his own little bed-room was closed behind him did Edgar Poe even try to collect his thoughts. Then he sat down at his window and looked out over the fragrant garden to the quiet sky, contemplation of which had so often soothed his spirit, and tried to readjust the inner world he lived in, in accordance with the discovery he had just made. A first such readjustment his world had experienced three years before, when Mr. Allan had taunted him with his dependence upon charity. Before that time the world, as he knew it, had held only love and beauty—sorrow, as he had seen it, being but a solemn and poetic form of beauty. The change in such a world made by the discovery

The Dreamer

that his being an adopted son set him apart in a class different from other boys—a class unlovely and loveless—had been great, had stolen much of the joy from living; but he was very young then, and the joy of mere living and breathing was strong in his blood, and he had gradually become accustomed—hardened, if you will—to the idea of his dependence upon charity.

But here was a change far more terrible, and coming at a time when he was old enough to feel it far more keenly. He was indeed, in a class by himself—he was held in contempt because of what his angel mother had been! His holy of holies had been profaned, the sacred fire that warmed his inner life had been spat upon. It seemed he had been from the beginning despised, though he had not dreamed it, for that which he held most dear—of which he was most proud. The little, aristocratic, puffed-up world he lived in would doubtless always despise him; but that was because of its narrowness and ignorance for which he, in turn, would despise it. With the whimsical, half-belief he had always had that the dead remain conscious through their long sleep, he wondered if his beautiful young mother, with the roses on her hair, down under the green earth, was not aware of the love and loyalty of her boy and if her spirit soaring the highest heavens, would not aid him in carrying out the resolution which in the bitterness of his soul, he then and there made—the resolution to bring this mean little, puffed up world to do honor to his name—to her name, of which he was prouder in this hour when others would trample it in the dust than he had ever been before.

Young boy though he was, he was conscious of his God-given endowments. He felt that the divine fire of poetic feeling in his breast was an immortal thing. Up to this time, his singing had been as the singing of a wood-bird—an impulse, a necessity to express the thoughts and feelings of his heart. He had never looked far enough ahead to consider whether he should or should not publish his work; but now ambition awoke—full-grown at its birth—and set him afire. From those parents whose memory had been insulted he had received (God willing it) the precious heritage of brilliant intellect. He would put the work of this intellect—his stories and his poems—into books. He would give them to the wide world. He would win recognition for the name of Poe.

He drew from within his coat the miniature of his mother—her dying gift. He gazed upon it long and tenderly, and with it still exposed to view brought from his desk the little packet of yellowed letters in their faded blue ribbon. He knew them by heart, but he read them—each one—over again, as carefully as if it had been the first time. They were not many and those not long; but ah, they were sweet!—those tender, quaint love-letters that had passed between his parents in their brief courtship and married life. His father's so manly so strong—like the letters of a soldier. His mother's so modest, so tender. They did not stir his pulses so wildly now as they did upon his first reading of them, when a little lad at old Stoke-Newington—but they were no less beautiful to him now than then. The sentences made him think of the dainty, sweet aroma of pressed roses.

He tied the packet up again and kissed letters and picture, as if to seal the promise he was making them, then restored them to their hiding-places. With the bitter knowledge that had come to him, he felt that years had passed over him—that he would never be young again—this boy of fourteen!

He raised his deep, pensive eyes once more to the quiet sky and his spirit cried to Heaven to grant him power to accomplish this task he had set himself: to lift the loved name of his parents from the dust where it lay, and to set it high in the temple of fame, wreathed with immortal myrtle.

His resolution gave to his poetic face and his slender figure an air of mastery, as though some new, high quality had been born within him.

The Dreamer

CHAPTER VIII.

In the days that followed, Edgar's friends found him unusually silent, yet not morose. Serenity sat on his broad, thoughtful brow and in his great, soft eyes. Nat Howard and his chums gave him the cold shoulder and wore, in his presence, the air of offended dignity which the small-minded are apt to assume when conscious of being in the wrong or of having committed an injury which the victim has received with credit and the offender has not forgiven. It is so much easier to grant pardon for an injury received than for one given!

Edgar's own friends were more emphatic in their devotion to him than ever—racking their young brains for ways in which to show their loyalty and frequently looking into his face with the expression of soft adoration and trust one sees in the eyes of a faithful dog. Edgar was touched and gratified, and his sweet, spontaneous smile often rewarded their efforts; but his face would soon become grave again and the boys were aware that the mind of their gifted friend was busy with thoughts in which they had no part. This gave them an impression of distance between them and him. He all of a sudden, seemed to have become remote, as though a chasm, by what power they knew not, had opened between them—making their love for him as "the desire of the moth for the star." They knew that he was more often than ever before working upon his poetical and other compositions, but these were seldom shown, or even mentioned, to them.

Each boy in his own way sought to bridge the gulf that separated them from their idol. Robert Sully missed his Latin lesson on purpose in the hope that Eddie would stay in and help him. And Eddie did, but wore that same detached air in which there was no intimacy or comfort. When the lesson was learned Edgar took a slate from the desk before them, rubbed off the problem that was upon it, and quickly wrote down a little poem of several stanzas. He held it out, with a smile, to Rob, telling him that while teaching him his lesson he had been practicing "dividing his mind," and that while one part of his brain had been putting English into Latin the other part had composed the verses on the slate.

The dumfounded Rob read the verses aloud, but before he could express his amazement Edgar had taken the slate from him and, with one swipe of the damp spunge, obliterated the rhymes.

"Write them on paper for me, please," plead Robert.

The brilliant smile of the boy-poet flashed upon him. "Oh, they were not worth keeping," said he, indifferently. "They were merely an exercise." And picking up his books and hat, he walked out of the door, whistling in clear, high, plaintive notes one of the melodies of his favorite Tom Moore.

The boy left behind looked after him with a troubled heart and misty eyes. This wonderful friend of his was as kind as ever, yet he seemed changed. It was clear that he had "something on his mind."

"Will you go swimming with me this evening, Eddie?" said Dick Ambler one day when school was out.

"With all the pleasure in life," was the hearty response.

Dick went home to his dinner with a singing heart. If anything could bring Edgar down from the clouds to his own level, surely it would be bathing together. He certainly could not make poetry while diving and swimming, naked, in the racing and tumbling falls of James River. A merry battle with those energetic waters kept a fellow's wits as well as his muscles fully occupied.

But even this attempt was a failure. If Edgar made any poetry while in the water he did not mention it; but he was absent-minded and unsociable all the way to the river and

The Dreamer

back—sky-gazing for curious cloud-forms, listening for bird-notes and hunting wild-flowers, and talking almost none at all.

In the water he seemed to wake up, and never dived with more grace, or daring; but no sooner had they started on the way home than he was off with his dreams again.

Rob Stanard was more successful in his attempts to interest his friend. In spite of their intimacy at school and on the playground Edgar had up to this time never visited the Stanard home. Rob had enlisted his mother's sympathy in the orphan boy and she had suggested that he should invite Edgar home with him some day. It now occurred to Rob that this would be a good time to do so, and knowing his friend's fondness for dumb animals, he offered his pets as an attraction—asking him to come and see his pigeons and rabbits. His invitation was accepted with alacrity.

Edgar had seen Rob's mother, but only at a distance. He knew her reputation as one of the town beauties, but lovely women were not rare in Richmond, and, beauty-worshipper though he was, he had never had any especial curiosity in regard to Mrs. Stanard. He was altogether unprepared for the vision that broke upon him.

Instead of going through the house, Rob had piloted him by way of a side gate, directly into the walled garden, sweet and gay with roses, lilies and other flowers of early June.

Mrs. Stanard, who took almost as much pleasure in her children's pets as they did, was standing near a clump of arbor-vitae, holding in her hands a "willow-ware" plate from which the pigeons were feeding. She was at this time, though the mother of Edgar's twelve-year-old chum, not thirty years of age, and her pensive beauty was in its fullest flower. Against the sombre background the arbor-vitae made, her slight figure, clad in soft, clinging white, seemed airy and sylphlike. Her dark, curling hair, girlishly bound with a ribbon snood, and her large brown eyes, were in striking contrast to her complexion, which was pale, with the radiant and warm palor of a tea-rose or a pearl. Her features were daintily modelled, and like slender lilies were the hands holding the deep blue plate from which the pigeons—white, grey and bronze, fed—fluttering about her with soft cooings.

The picture was so much more like a poet's dream than a reality, that the boy-poet stepped back, with an exclamation of surprise.

"It is only my mother," explained Rob. "She'll be glad to see you."

The next moment she had perceived the boys, and with quick impulse, set the plate upon the ground and came forward, and before a word of introduction could be spoken, had taken the visitor's hand between both her own fair palms, holding it thus, with gentle, gracious pressure, in a pretty, cordial way she had, while she greeted him.

The soft eyes that rested on his face filled with kindness and welcome.

"So this is my Rob's friend," she was saying, in a low, musical voice. "Rob's mother is delighted to see you for his sake and for your own too, Edgar, for I greatly admired *your* gifted mother. I saw her once only, when I was a young girl, but I can never forget her lovely face and sweet, plaintive voice. It was one of the last times she ever acted, and she was ill and pale, but she was exquisitely beautiful and made the most charming Juliet. She interested me more than any actress I have ever seen."

Edgar Poe longed to fall down and kiss her feet—to worship her. Her beauty, her gentleness and her gracious words so stirred his soul that he grew faint. Power of speech almost left him, and, vastly to his humiliation, he could with difficulty control his voice to utter a few stumbling words of thanks—he who was usually so ready of speech!

If she noticed his confusion she did not appear to do so. Her heart had been touched by all she had heard from her son of the lonely boy, and she had also been interested in accounts of his gifts that had come to her from various sources. The beauty, the poetry,

The Dreamer

the pensiveness of his face moved her deeply—knowing his history and divining the lack of sympathy one of his bent would probably find in the Allan home, for all its indulgences.

She sat on a garden-bench and talked to him for a time, in her gentle, understanding way, and then, not wishing to be a restraint upon the boys, (after placing her husband's fine library at Edgar's disposal, and urging him to come often to see Rob) withdrew into the house.

The motherless boy looked after her until she had disappeared, and stared at the door that had closed upon her until he was recalled from his reverie by the voice of his friend, suggesting that they now see the rabbits. Edgar looked at the gentle creatures with unseeing eyes, though he appeared to be listening to the prattle of his companion concerning them. Suddenly, in a voice filled with enthusiasm and with a touch of awe in it, he said:

"Rob, your mother is divinely beautiful—and *good*."

"Bully," was the nonchalant reply. "The best thing about her is the way she takes up for a fellow when he brings in a bad report or gets into a scrape. Fathers always think it's their sons' fault, you know."

Edgar flushed. "*Bully*—" he said to himself, with a shudder. The adjective applied to her seemed blasphemy.

Aloud, he said, "She's an angel! She's the one I've always dreamed about."

"You dreamed about mother when you had never seen her?" questioned the astonished Rob. "What did you dream?"

"Nothing, in the way you mean. I meant she is like my idea of a perfect woman. The kind of woman a man could always be good for, or would gladly die to serve."

"Well, I'm not smart enough to think out things like that, Eddie, but Mother certainly is all right. What you say about her sounds nice, and she'd understand it, too. I just bet that you and mother'll be the best sort of cronies when you know each other better. She likes all those queer old books you think so fine, and she knows whole pages of poetry by heart. When you and she get together it will be like two books talking out loud to each other. I won't be able to join in much, but it will be as good as a play to listen."

The young poet bent his steps homeward with but one thought, one hope in his heart, and that a consuming one: to look again upon the lovely face, to hear again the voice that had enthralled him, had taken his heart by storm and filled it with a veritable *grande passion*—the rapturous devotion of the virgin heart of an ardent and romantic youth. First love—yet so much more than ordinary love—a pure passion of the soul, in which there was much of worship and nothing of desire. Surely the most pure and holy passion the world has ever known, for in it there was absolutely nothing of self. Like Dante after his first meeting with Beatrice, this Virginia boy-poet had entered upon a *Vita Nuova*—a new life—made all of beauty.

What difference did the taunts of schoolmates, the hardness of a foster-father make now? The wounds they made had been gratefully healed by the balm of her beauteous words about his mother. Those old wounds were as nothing—neither they nor anything else had power to harm him now. In the new life that had opened so suddenly before him he would bear a charmed existence.

He went to his room before the usual hour that night, for he wanted to be alone with his dreams—with his newest, most beautiful dream. To his room, but not to bed. Life was too beautiful to be wasted in sleep. He lighted his lamp and holding his mother's picture within its circle of light, gazed long and devotedly upon it. Did she know of the great light that had shone out of what seemed a sunless sky upon her boy? Had she, looking out

The Dreamer

from high Heaven, seen the gracious greeting of the beautiful being who was Madonna and Psyche in one? Had she heard her own cause so sweetly championed, her own name so sweetly cleared of opprobrium?

He threw himself upon his lounge and lay with his hands clasped under his curly head, still dreaming—dreaming—dreaming—until day-dreams were merged into real dreams, for he was fast asleep.

In his sleep he saw the lady of his dreams in a situation of peril, from which he joyfully rescued her. He awoke with a start. His lamp had burned itself out but a late moon flooded the room with the white light that he loved. A breeze laden with odors caught from the many rose-gardens and the heavier-scented magnolias, now in full bloom, it had come across, stirred the curtain. His nostrils, always sensitive to the odors of flowers, drank it in rapturously. So honey-sweet it was, his senses swam.

He arose and looked out upon the incense-breathing blossoms, like phantoms, under the moon. A clock in a distant part of the house was striking twelve. How much more beautiful was the world now—at night's high noon—than at the same hour of the day.

All the house, save himself, was asleep. How easy it would be to escape into this lovely night—to walk through this ambrosial air to the house-worshipful in which *she* doubtless lay, like a closed lily-flower, clasped in sleep.

A mocking-bird—the Southland's nightingale—in, some tree or bush not far away, burst into passion-shaken melody that seemed to voice, as no words could, his own emotion.

Down the stair he slipped, and out of the door, into the well-nigh intoxicating beauty of the southern summer's night. Indeed, the odors of the dew-drenched flowers—the moonlight—the bird-music, together with his remembrance of his lady's greeting, went to his head like wine.

As he strolled along some lines of Shelley's which had long been favorites of his, sang in his brain:

"I arise from dreams of thee In the first sweet sleep of night, When the winds are breathing low And the stars are shining bright. I arise from dreams of thee, And the spirit in my feet Has led me—who knows how?— To thy chamber-window, sweet!

"The wandering airs they faint On the dark, the silent stream; The champak odors fail Like sweet thoughts in a dream; The nightingale's complaint, It dies upon her heart, As I must die on thine, Oh, beloved, as thou art!

"Oh, lift me from the grass! I die, I faint, I fail! Let thy love in kisses rain On my lips and eyelids pale. My cheek is cold and white, alas! My heart beats loud and fast. Oh, press it close to thine again, Where it will break at last."

The words of the latter half of this serenade were meaningless as applied to his case. To have quoted them—even mentally—in any literal sense, would have seemed to him profanation; yet the whole poem in some way not to be analysed or defined, expressed his mood—and who so brutal as to seek to reduce to common-sense the emotions of a poet-lover, in the springtime of life?

At length he was before the closed and shuttered house, standing silent and asleep. Opposite were the grassy slopes of Capitol Square—with the pillared, white Capitol, in its midst, looking, in the moonlight, like a dream of old Greece. *Her* house! He looked upon its moonlit, ivied walls with adoration. A light still shone from one upper room. Was it *her* chamber? Was she, too, awake and alive to the beauty of this magic night?

His heart beat tumultuously at the thought. Then—Oh, wonder! His knees trembled under him—he grew dizzy and was ready, indeed, to cry, "I die, I faint, I fail!" She crossed the square of light the window made. In her uplifted hand she carried the lamp from which the light shone, and for a moment her slight figure, clad all in white as he had seen her in the garden a few hours before, and softly illuminated, was framed in the ivy-wreathed casement. But for a moment—then disappeared, but the trembling boy-lover and poet seemed to see it still, and gazed and gazed until the light was out and all the house dark.

He stumbled back through the moonlight to his home, he crept up the creaking stair again, to his little, dormer-windowed room; but sleep was now, more than ever, impossible.

Though the lamp had gone out, a candle stood upon a stand at the head of his bed. He lighted it, and by its ray, wrote, under the spell of the hour, the first utterance in which he, Edgar Poe, ascended from the plane of a maker of "promising" verse, to the realm of the true poet—a poem to the lady of his heart's dream destined (though he little guessed it) to make her name immortal and to send the fame of his youthful passion down the ages as one of the world's historic love-affairs.

What was her name? he wondered. He had never heard it, but he would call her Helen—*Helen*, the ancient synonym of womanly beauty, but the loveliest Helen, he believed, that ever set poet-lover piping her praise.

And so, "To Helen," were the words he wrote at the top of his page, and underneath the name these lines:

"Helen, thy beauty is to me Like those Nicean barks of yore, That gently o'er a perfumed sea, The weary, wayworn wanderer bore To his own native shore.

"On desperate seas long wont to roam, Thy hyacinth hair, thy classic face, Thy Naiad airs have brought me home To the glory that was Greece And the grandeur that was Rome.

"Lo! in yon brilliant window-niche How statue-like I see thee stand! The agate lamp within thy hand, Ah! Psyche, from the regions which Are Holy Land!"

CHAPTER IX.

With his meeting with "Helen," a new life, indeed, seemed to have opened for Edgar the Dreamer. Not only had her own interest and sympathy been aroused, but her husband, a learned and accomplished judge of the Supreme Court of Virginia, also received him cordially and became deeply interested in him, and he found in their home what his own had lacked for him, a thoroughly congenial atmosphere.

"Helen" Stanard listened kindly to his boyish rhapsodies about his favorite poets, and encouraged him to bring her his own portefolio of verses, which he did, all but the ones addressed to herself—these he kept secret. She read all he brought her carefully, and intelligently criticised them in a way that was a real help to him.

As has been said, when Mr. Allan had discovered that his adopted son was a rhymster, he had rebuked him severely for such idle waste of time, and in a vain attempt to clip the wings of Pegasus, threatened him with punishment if he should hear of such folly again. Mrs. Allan, on the contrary, though she was not a bookish woman, had protested against her husband's command—urging that Edgar be encouraged to cultivate his talent. The ability to compose verse seemed to her, in a boy of Edgar's age, little short of miraculous, and, proud of her pet's accomplishment, she heaped indiscriminate praise upon every line that she saw of his writing.

The boy, hardly knowing which way to escape, between these two fires that bade fair to work the ruin of his gift, turned eagerly to his new friend. "Helen" gently told him that

The Dreamer

she believed his talent to be a sacred trust, and that he would be committing sin to bury it—even though by so doing he should be fulfilling the wishes of his foster-father to whom he owed so much. He must, however, not forget his duty to Mr. Allan in regard to this matter, as in other things, but treat his views with all the consideration possible. Above all things, he was never to depart from the truth in talking to him, but to tell him in a straightforward and respectful way that he believed it his duty when poetical thoughts presented themselves to his mind, to set them down, and even to encourage and invite such thoughts.

At the same time, she earnestly warned him against being overmuch impressed by the flattering estimates of his work of his friends, especially of his mother, who was far too partial to him, personally, to be a safe judge of his writings.

A happier summer than is often given mortals to know, Edgar the Dreamer passed at the feet of the lovely young matron who had become a sort of mother-confessor to him. Happiness which, with a touch of the superstition that was characteristic of him he often told himself was too perfect to last. What was it that made him feel sometimes in looking upon her under the serene sky of that ideal summer that a cloud no bigger than a man's hand threw its shadow upon her? Was it that faint hint of sadness in her dark eyes or the ethereal radiance of her pale complexion that while thrilling him with delight in the exquisite quality of her beauty, filled him with foreboding?

Ere the frosts of autumn had robbed her garden of its glory, blighting sorrow had fallen upon her tender mother-heart in the death of a darling baby girl. Beneath this blow the health of sweet "Helen," always frail, succumbed, and her home became thenceforth as a living tomb, in which the few who ever saw her again trod softly and spoke in hushed voices.

When the earliest roses were in bloom in her garden two years after Edgar Poe first saw her there, she lay in her coffin, and for him, the world seemed to have come to an end.

She was laid to rest in the new cemetery on Shockoe Hill, not far from the Allan home. The bier was followed by its black procession of mourners, and no one knew that the heart of a youth who followed too, but at a distance, was breaking. Though husband and children and brother and sister were bowed with grief, he told himself that there was among them no sorrow like unto his sorrow who had not even the right of kinship to mourn for her. Of what business of his (he fancied, out of the bitterness of his soul, the world saying) of what business of his was her death? What business had he to mourn?

Again his feet kept time to the old refrain of never, nevermore, that hammered in his brain—a refrain that to the unrealizing ear of the child of three had been sad with a beautiful, rhythmic sadness that was rather pleasurable than otherwise; that to the youth of sixteen was still musical and beautiful, though filled with despair.

As at many another time his poetical gift gave him a merciful vent for his pent up feeling, so now it came to his aid, and upon the night of the day when she was laid to rest he poured out his sorrow in "The Paean"—which he was afterwards to revise and rename, "Lenore"—

"An anthem for the queenliest dead that ever died so young— A dirge for her, the doubly dead in that she died so young."

As during his childhood, and afterwards, he had found a mournful pleasure in visiting the grave of his mother, in the churchyard on the hill; so now he found a blessed solace, in his terrible loneliness, in pilgrimages to the shrine (for as such he held the grave of his saint) in the new cemetery. These pilgrimages he usually made at night—his grief was too sacred a thing to be flaunted in broad daylight. Many a night during the spring and

The Dreamer

summer found him slipping down the stair, when the house was asleep, and taking his way through the silent city of Slumber to that even more silent city of Death.

Oh, that those that lay there not much more still than they who lay asleep in their beds in that other city, might arise like them with the morrow's sun!

Often, as he walked along, drinking in the perfumed night air that he loved—the night breeze gratefully lifting the ringlets from his fevered brow—often he thought of that first summer's night when with the sweet words of Shelley's serenade: "I arise from dreams of thee," singing themselves in his heart, he had gone with light feet to worship beneath her window.

Ah, the world was young then, for sweet hope was alive!

The iron gates of the cemetery were locked, but the wall was not very high. To scale it but added zest to his adventure. He would be a knight unfit for his vigil if he were to let himself be so easily balked.

Within the wall the odors of flowers were even heavier, more oppressively sweet than without, and the silence surpassed the silence of the outer city even as the stillness of the sleepers here surpassed the stillness of those yonder.

He listened and listened to the silence. Surely if she should speak, even from down under the ground he could hear her across this silence which was as a void—a black and terrible void.

His first pilgrimages were by moonlight, but when the moonless nights came he continued his vigils. He would have known the way by that time with his eyes shut.

Sometimes he was afraid—horribly afraid. He seemed, in the shadows, to descry weird phantom-shapes, moving stealthily; in the silence to hear ghostly whispers; sometimes he fancied he heard *the silence itself*! But in the very fear that clutched his throat there was a fascination—a lure—that made it impossible to turn back.

His sorrow was exquisite; his terror was exquisite; his loneliness was oh, how exquisite! Yet in courting them all, here in the dead of night, prone on her grave, he found the only balm he knew—the only sympathy; for to his fancy the dark and the quiet had always seemed sentient things and he felt that they gave him a sympathy he did not—could not ask of people.

A breathless night in July found him at the familiar tryst at an earlier hour than was his wont. He lay upon the grass at her feet with his hands clasped under his head and his face turned up to the stars. There was moonlight as well as starlight, and in its silvery radiance his features, always pale, had the frigid whiteness of marble. The wide-open eyes that stared upward to the stars, were larger, darker than in daylight, and more full of brooding; the white brow, with its crown of dark ringlets was whiter and more expansive.

In a dormer-windowed cottage overlooking a rose garden, on Clay Street, an erect gentleman in an uncompromising stock and immaculate ruffles, with narrow blue eyes under a beetling brow, and a somewhat hawk-like nose, sharply questioned a fair and graceful lady, with an anxious expression on her flower-face, as to why "that boy" did not come home to his supper. But they were used by now, to the boy's strange, wayward whims, and so did not marvel much. Only—they had not seen him since the feat that had set the town ringing with his name and it seemed to them that it would have been natural for him to come home in the flush of his triumph and tell them about it.

Edgar Poe had that day created the sensation of the hour by swimming from the Richmond wharves to Warwick—a distance of six miles—in the midsummer sun.

Richmond was a fair and pleasant little city in those days, in spite of the fact that our boy-poet found in it so much to make him melancholy. "The merriest place in America,"

The Dreamer

Thackeray called it some years later, and would probably have said the same of it then had he been there. The blight of Civil War had not touched the cheerful temper of its people; the tenement row had not crowded out grass and flowers. It was more a large village than a town, with gracious homes—not elbowing each other for foundation room, but standing comfortably apart, amid their green lawns, and with wide verandahs overhanging their many-flowered gardens.

"After tea," on warm nights, the houses overflowed into these verandahs, and there was much visiting from one to another—much light-hearted talk and happy laughter; the popular theme being whatever happened to be "the news."

It was the day of contentment, for wants were moderate and plentifully supplied; the day of satisfaction in wholesome domestic joys; the day of hospitality without grudging; the day when sweetness extracted from little pleasures did not need spicing, for palates were not jaded; the day of the ideal simple life.

Upon this night, as on other nights, young girls who were not yet "gone to the springs" floated along the fashionable promenades, in airy muslins, with their cavaliers beside them. Groups of gentlemen and ladies sat on the porches and children played hide-and-seek, chased fire-flies, or sat on the steps and listened to the talk of their elders. And everywhere, in all of the groups, the chief topic was the boy, Edgar Poe, and his wonderful swim.

And the boy who had in an afternoon become, for the time being at least, the foremost figure in town, knew it, but did not care.

To lie alone on the grass by the grave of his dead divinity and gaze at the far stars, and brood upon his young sorrows—this gave him more satisfaction than to be the central figure of any one of the groups singing his praise; filled him with a romantic despair that to his high-strung soul had a more delicately sweet flavor than positive pleasure.

As to the erect gentleman in the high stock and the pretty lady with the tender, anxious face—they had, for the present, no part in his thoughts. It was wrong and ungrateful of him that they should not have, and if he had remembered them he would have known that it was wrong and ungrateful; but he would not have cared. And as for his food—he had supped royally, and without compunction, upon the fruit of an inviting orchard to which he had helped himself, unblushingly, upon his way into town.

A reckless mood, born of the restlessness that was in his blood, was upon him.

The truth was, that poignant as was his pleasure in dwelling upon his poetical sorrow for the adored "Helen"—his "lost Lenore"—it did not fully satisfy him. His youthful heart was hungry for response to his out-poured sentiment, for the more robust diet of mutual love. In plain English, Edgar Poe wanted, and wanted badly, a sweetheart, though he did not suspect it.

When, finally, he scaled the cemetery wall and took his way homeward he did not go directly to the dormer-windowed cottage where the erect gentleman and the pretty lady awaited him. Just as he was approaching it he heard Elmira Royster's guitar in the porch opposite, and he crossed the street and entered the Royster's gate.

The Roysters and Allans had been neighbors for years and he and Elmira had been "brought up together." At the sound of approaching footsteps the guitar grew suddenly silent and a slight, rather colorless girl in a white dress, with a white flower in her fluffy blonde hair, came from out the shadow of the microphilla rose that embowered the porch and stood in the full light of the moon, giving him greeting.

The Dreamer

"Oh, I'm so glad to see you, Eddie," she said. "All of the family but me have gone to a party, and I'm so lonesome! Besides, I, like everybody else in town, want a chance to congratulate you."

"Congratulate?" he replied, with a shrug, as he took a seat beside her, under the roses, "Congratulate? In their hearts they all despise me." Then with a smile,

"You see the blue devils have the upper hand of me tonight, Myra."

"Well, they are fibbing devils if they tell you you are despised. Dick Ambler was over at your house looking for you a little while ago, and he stopped by and told me about your swim. He said he and the other boys that followed you in the boat had never seen anything so exciting in their lives. They were expecting you to give out any minute and so much afraid that if you did you would go under before they could get hold of you. When you won the wager they were so proud and happy that they were almost beside themselves."

"Oh, I know Dick and the rest are the best and truest friends a fellow ever had—bless their hearts—but they are the exceptions."

"Nonsense! There's not a boy in town tonight who would not give his head to be in your shoes, and" (shyly) "the girls are all wild about you."

The hero smiled indulgently. No woman was ever thrown with Edgar Poe, from his birth up, but in some fashion or degree, loved him, and to him all women were angels. He never, as boy or man, entertained a thought or wrote a line of one of them that was not reverent. He admired, in varying degree, all types of feminine loveliness, but Myra, though he liked her, was not the style that he most cared for. He had always thought her too "washed out." The soul that shone through her rather prominent, light-blue eyes was too transparent, too easily read. He found more interesting the richer-hued brunette type, and the complex nature that goes with it; the flashes of starlight, the softness and the warmth, of brown eyes; the mysteries that lie in the shadow of dusky lashes; the variety of rich, warm tones in chestnut and auburn tresses.

But Myra was a revelation to him tonight. He had never dreamed that she could look so pretty—*so very pretty*—as she did now in her white dress, with the moonlight filtering through the foliage upon her fair hair and her face (turned full of liking and undisguised admiration upon him) and her lovely arms, bared to the elbow. She had an ethereal, fairy-like appearance that was bewitching, and in his despondent mood, her frank praise was more than sweet. Still his answer was as bitter as ever,

"Oh, well, what does it all amount to? They would say the same of any acrobat in a circus whose joints were a bit more limber than those of the rest of his tribe. That does not remove their contempt for me, personally."

"I don't feel contempt for you, Eddie," she gently replied—just breathing it.

(Myra was really wonderful tonight. He had not known her voice could have so much color in it; and the white flower in her hair—a cape-jessamine, its excessively sweet fragrance told him—gave her pale beauty the touch of romance it had always lacked). The poetic eyes that looked into hers mellowed, the cynical voice softened:

"Don't you Myra? Well, you'd better cultivate it. Its the fashion, and it's the only feeling I'm worth."

"Eddie," she said earnestly—tenderly, "I want you to promise me that you won't talk that way any more—at least not to *me*—it hurts me."

Her hand, on his sleeve, was as fair as a petal from the jessamine flower in her hair. He took it gently in his.

"Dear little Myra, little playmate—" he said. "You are my friend, I know, and have been since we were mere babies, in spite of knowing, as you do, what a naughty, idle,

The Dreamer

disobedient boy I've been, deserving every flogging and scolding I've gotten and utterly unworthy all the good things that have come my way—including your dear friendship."

"You are breaking your promise already," she said. "You *shall not* run yourself down to me. I think you are the nicest boy in town!"

There was nothing complex about Myra. Her mind was an open book, and he suddenly found he liked it so—liked it tremendously. Her unveiled avowal of preference for him was most soothing to his restless, dissatisfied mood.

"Thank you, Myra," he said tenderly, kissing the flower-petal hand before he laid it down. He had a strong impulse to kiss *her*, but resisted it, with an effort, and abruptly changed the subject.

"Did you know that we are going to move?" he asked. "And that I'm going to the University next winter?"

"*To move?*" she questioned, aghast. "Where?"

"To the Gallego mansion, at Fifth and Main Streets. Mr. Allan has bought it. The dear little mother, who, I'd say, if you'd let me, is so much better to me than I deserve, is full of plans for furnishing it and is going to fit up a beautiful room in it for me. It will be a delightful home for us, and quite grand after our modest cottage, but do you know I'm goose enough to be homesick at the thought of giving up my little den under the roof? Myself and I have had such jolly times together in it!"

She had scarcely heard him, except the first words and the stunning facts they contained. There was a minute's silence, then she spoke in a changed, quivering voice.

"Then that will be the end of our friendship, I suspect! When you get out of the neighborhood, and are off most of the time at the University, we will doubtless see little more of you."

Her clear blue eyes were shining up at him through tears. Her mouth was tremulous as a distressed child's. The appeal met an instant response from the tender-hearted poet. *Both* the flower-like hands were captured this time, and held fast, in spite of their fluttering. The excessively sweet fragrance of the blossom in her hair was in his nostrils. Her quick, short breaths told him of the tempest in her tender young bosom.

"Myra, little Myra, do you care like that?" he cried. "Then let the friendship go, and be my dear little sweetheart, won't you? I'm dying of loneliness and the want of somebody to love and to love me—somebody who understands me—and you do, don't you, Myra, darling?"

She was too happy to answer, but she suffered him to put his arms around her and kiss her soft pale hair—and her brow—and her tremulous mouth—the first kisses of love to him as well as to her. And ah, how sweet!

He laughed happily, lifted out of his gloom by this new, this deliriously sweet dream.

"Do you know, little sweetheart," he said, in a voice that was bubbling with joy, "I feel that you have cast those devils out of me forever. It was you that I wanted all the time, and did not know it. Some of these days, when I've been through college and settled down, we will be married, and wherever our home is, we must always have a porch like this, with a rose on it, and" (kissing her brow) "you must always wear a jessamine in your hair."

And so the boy-poet and his girl play-mate, very much to their own surprise, parted affianced lovers, and a long vista of sunlit days seemed to beckon The Dreamer.

The Dreamer

CHAPTER X.

The session at the University did not begin until the middle of February, so love's young dream was not to be interrupted too soon. Meantime, its sweetness was only enhanced by thought of the coming separation. The affair had too, the interest of secrecy, for the youthful lovers well knew the storm of opposition that would be raised, in both their homes, if it should be discovered. This need of secrecy made frequent meetings and exchange of vows impossible, but it gave to such as occurred the flavor of stolen sweets and kept the young sinners in a tantalized state which was excruciating and at the same time delightful, and which still further fed the flames and convinced them of the realness and intensity of their passion.

When they did meet, their awed, joyous confessions of mutual love charmed the lonely, romantic boy by their very novelty. In them his fairest dreams were fulfilled. How sweet it was in these rare, stolen moments, to crush the pure young creature, who would be his own some day, against his wildly beating heart—how passing sweet to hear against his ear her whispered, hesitating vows of deep, everlasting love!

In his pretty new room overlooking the terraced garden of the stately mansion which had become his home, Edgar Poe plunged headlong into Byron, and in the mood thus induced, penned many a verse, no worse and not much better than the rhymes of lovelorn youths the world over and time out of mind, to be copied into Myra's album.

Between the love-making and preparation for college, time took wings. In what seemed an incredibly short space summer and fall were gone, Christmas, with its festivities, was over and the new year—the year 1826—had opened.

It was upon St. Valentine's Day that, with a feeling of solemnity worthy of the act, the seventeen year old lover and student wrote the name Edgar Allan Poe, and the date of his birth, upon the matriculation book of the University of Virginia—open for its second session. Upon the day before the beauty and the poetry—*the inspiration*—of the place had burst upon him, and this first impression still held his soul in thrall.

Here, in this fair Virginia vale, ringed about with the heaven-kissing hills of the Blue Ridge, the scholastic village conjured by Jefferson's fertile imagination lay before him in the clear, winter sunshine. Its lawns and its gardens were just now white with an unbroken blanket of new-fallen snow; the young trees which had been planted in avenues along the lawns, but which were as yet hardly more than shrubs, glittered with icicles, and above them rose the classic columns of the colonnaded dormitories and professors' houses; while at one end of the oblong square the majestic dome and columns of the Rotunda stood out against the sky. As the entranced Dreamer gazed and gazed, trying to imagine what it must be like by moonlight—what it would be in spring—what (a few years later, when the trees should have grown large enough to arch the walks) in summer—he told himself that surely in this garden-spot of the Old Dominion, bricks and mortar had sprung into immortal bloom, and he found himself quoting a line of his own:

"The glory that was Greece and the grandeur that was Rome."

Upon his earliest opportunity he sat down and wrote Myra a rhapsody upon it all. Her presence, he felt, and he wrote her, was all needed to make the place a paradise.

Under his name upon the matriculation book he had written, with confidence:

"Schools of Ancient and Modern Languages." In the school of Ancient Languages were taught (according to the announcement for the year) "Hebrew, rhetoric, belles-lettres ancient history and geography;" in the school of Modern Languages, "French, Spanish, Italian, German, and the English language in its Anglo Saxon form; also modern history and modern geography." A list, one would think, to daunt the courage of a seventeen year old student and make him feel that he had the world on his shoulders.

The Dreamer

It was quite the contrary with The Dreamer. He felt instead that he had suddenly developed wings. Learning came easy to him. He was already a good French and Latin scholar, and the rest did not frighten him. Not only was he not in the least burdened by thought of the work he was cutting out for himself, but he was elated by a sense of freedom such as he had never known before. Always before, both at home and at school, he had been under surveillance. But now he was to be a partaker of the benefits of Mr. Jefferson's theories of the treatment of students as men and gentlemen—letting their conduct be a matter of *noblesse oblige*.

In the youth of seventeen this sudden withdrawal of oversight and regulation produced an exhilaration that was indeed pleasurable. Among the unfrequented hills known as the "Ragged Mountains," not far away, was a wild and romantic region that invited him to fascinating exploration—perhaps adventure. Instead of having to beg permission or to steal off upon the solitary rambles which he loved, to this enchanting country, he could, and did, go when he chose, openly, and with no questions asked or rebukes given.

He held up his head with a new confidence at the thought, and took his dreams of ambition and love, whenever he could allow himself time to do so, to the enticing new region (as unlike anything around Richmond as if it were in a different world) adjacent to which, for the time, his lot lay.

He did not neglect his classes, however. They were regularly attended and his standing was excellent; so the professors had no cause for making inquiry into the pursuits of his private hours. The library, too, in the beautiful Rotunda, was a new, if different, field for his exploration and one that gave him great delight, for he found there many volumes of quaint and curious lore whose acquaintance he had never before made.

His imaginary wings were soon enough to be clipped—his exhilaration to drop from him as suddenly as it had come.

He did not hear from Myra!

He watched eagerly for the mails, and as day after day passed without bringing him a letter, deep dejection claimed him. Finally he wrote to her again—and then again—and again—frantically appealing to her to write to him and assure him of her constancy if she would save his life.

Still, no word from her.

The truth was that Myra, at home in Richmond, was awaiting each mail-time as feverishly as he. The faint suggestion of rose her cheeks usually wore, had entirely disappeared and deep circles caused by lack of sleep and lost appetite made her light blue eyes appear more prominent than ever before. The ethereal look that had been her chief claim to beauty had become exaggerated into a ghastliness that was not in the least bewitching. She, like Edgar, had pocketed her pride and followed her first letter with others more and more expressive of her tender maiden passion; but her father, who had begun to suspect an affair between her and the players' son a short time before Edgar left for the University, had kept diligent watch for the passage of letters, and had successfully intercepted them.

And so the unhappy pair pined and sighed and gloomed, each reckoning the other faithless and believing that life was forever robbed of joy.

Edgar Poe had never really loved the girl. He had merely loved the dream to which her tender words and timid caresses gave an adorable reality; but now in his disappointment at not hearing from her he felt that her love and loyalty to him were the only things in the world worth having and persuaded himself that without her there as no incentive to live

The Dreamer

or to strive. His misery was increased by an over-whelming homesickness, to escape from which, he wandered restlessly about, vainly seeking excitement and forgetfulness.

In this mood, he eagerly accepted an invitation to spend the evening from a class-mate whose room in "Rowdy Row" had a reputation for conviviality. His own room, shared by a quiet and steady Richmond boy with whom he had a slight acquaintance at home, was in one of the cloister-like dormitories opening upon the main lawn.

While Edgar Poe had been a somewhat wayward and at times a disobedient boy, at home, he had never been a *bad* boy except when judged by John Allan's standards, and had never been in the least wild. Wines were used upon the table of his foster-father, as upon the tables of other gentlemen whose homes he had visited, and he had always been permitted to drink a small quantity at a time, at dinner, or to sip a little mint-julep from the goblet passed around before breakfast and supposed to be conducive to appetite and healthful digestion; but he had never thought of exceeding this allowance. As to cards, he knew nothing of them save as an innocent, social pastime in which he found pleasure, as in all other games and sports—especially such as required exercise of ingenuity or mental skill.

The evening in "Rowdy Row" was therefore a revelation, as well as a diversion to him. As he approached the end of this arcaded row in which his new friend's room was situated his interest received a spur from the sounds of hilarity that greeted him, and his spirits began to rise. In a few moments more he found himself in the midst of a group of exceedingly jolly youths evidently prepared to make a night of it. Several of them were gathered about a huge bowl in which they were mixing a variety of punch which they called "peach-honey." Others were seated around a card table while one of their number entertained the rest with what seemed to be almost magical tricks. These Edgar joined. His interest was immediately aroused and he fixed his eyes with intentness upon the juggler. The tricks were new to him, but he soon amazed the crowd by showing the solution of them all.

Finally, the punch was declared to be ready; other packs of cards were produced and the real sport of the evening began. It was Edgar's first experience in drinking with boys and his conscience, not yet hardened to it, kept him in check without worrying him enough to destroy his pleasure. Somewhat of his old exhilaration returned to him at the bare thought, for he felt himself a man, following his own will and yet not disobeying any direct command.

In spite of much urging, he only drank one glass of the peach-honey, but thanks to a jovial ancestor of whom he had never heard, but of some of whose sins (in accordance with the ancient law) he bore the marks in his temperament, he was peculiarly susceptible to the influences of strong drink, and as he drained the glass at a gulp, a new freedom seemed to enter his soul. The dejection which had oppressed him dropped from him instantly, and with his great eyes glowing like lamps with new zest in life, he sat down at a card table to be initiated into the mysteries of the fascinating game of *loo*, which had lately become the fashion, and at the same time into his first experience in playing for money.

He had beginner's luck—held good hands and won straight through the game. His success, with the effects of the punch, developed his wittiest vein and Edgar Goodfellow assumed complete ascendancy.

His new acquaintances were charmed, and encouraged his mood by loud applause and congratulated themselves upon having added to their number such good company.

From that night Edgar Poe's new friends, who constituted what was known as the "fast set" at the University, became his boon companions. It was in the card-table, much more than the punch-bowl that the charm for him lay, for the gambling fever had entered his blood with his first winnings, but in the combination of the two he found, for the present, a sure cure for his "blue devils."

Alas, Helen! Where was your sweet spirit that it did not hover, as guardian angel, about the head of this wayward child of genius in his hour of sore need, when temptations gathered thick around his pathway and there was no one to steer him into safer waters; no one to restrain his feet from their first blind steps toward that Disaster to which ruinous companionship invited him, with syren voice?

True, his staid room-mate, Miles George, raised his voice in warning against the dangerous intimacies he was forming but Miles' view seemed extreme to him. Besides, he found at the University the same caste feeling that had cut him off from familiar intercourse with the leaders among his Richmond schoolmates. It was but natural, therefore, that he should have turned gratefully, to the society where his welcome was sure.

Finally words passed between him and Miles, ending in a formal meeting, with seconds on both sides. Their only weapons were their fists, and they shook hands afterward; but the idea of continuing to share the same bed-room was out of the question. Of the vacant rooms to be had, Edgar promptly decided upon Number 13, Rowdy Row, and the second step in a wrong direction quickly followed the first.

He was hailed by the rest of the "Row" with delight, and he promptly decided to return their many hospitalities in his new room, which he proceeded to elaborately prepare for their reception.

The result was an early and noisy house-warming. The guests were filled with admiration to find the walls of Number 13 decorated in honor of the occasion with charcoal sketches representing scenes from Byron's works done by the clever hand of the new occupant himself. They also found Edgar Goodfellow in the character of host, presiding over his own card-table and his own bowl—a generous one—of peach-honey, in the highest feather and his most captivating mood.

CHAPTER XI.

Erelong Number 13 was the liveliest and most popular room in the Row, but of the orgies held there the faculty rested in blissful unconsciousness. At class-time young Poe was invariably in his place and invariably the pale, thoughtful, student-like and faultlessly neat and gentle-mannered youth whose intelligent attention and admirable recitations were the joy of his masters. They heard rumors that he was something of a poet and were not surprised, the suggestions of ideality in the formation of his brow and the expression of his eyes hinted at such talent, and so long as he did not let the Muse come between him and his regular work, he should not be discouraged or restrained.

Indeed, in spite of the sway of Edgar Goodfellow at this time, Edgar the Dreamer was often present too, and during solitary tramps into the wild fastenesses of the Ragged Mountains, he not only conceived many fancies to be worked into poems, but made mentally, the first draft of a story to win fame.

The love of no real woman came to supplant the seemingly faithless Elmira, and though he still carried his mother's miniature with him and gazed often and fondly upon it, the sense of nearness between her spirit and his and the soul satisfaction he had found in this nearness in the past, were gone. The gambling fever that had fired his veins and the nightly potations of peach-honey created an excitement and restlessness that blurred the images his memory held of the angel mother who had dominated his childhood and of the madonna-like mistress who had filled the dreams of his early youth. These holy dreams

The Dreamer

became for the time being, a reproach to him, for they aroused his conscience to an unpleasant activity which required more frequent recourse to peach-honey to quiet.

Love was, nevertheless, as necessary to this poet's soul as meat and drink were to his body, and in the No Man's Land, "out of space, out of time," which his fancy created and where it loved to stray, he fashioned for himself the weirdest, strangest lady ever loved by mortal. The name he gave her was "Ligeia." She laid upon him no exactions, chastened him with no rebukes, demanded of him no service save that he should dream—and dream—and dream; for was not she herself formed from "such stuff as dreams are made of?"

The music of nature had long possessed a sort of personality for Edgar Poe, and now the voices, the motions, the numberless colors of the world about him took definite shape in his fancy of a wonderous fairy-woman whom he worshipped with an unearthly, poetic passion that was compared to the passion of the normal man to flesh and blood woman as moonlight to sunshine—a passion which was luminous without heat.

Dim and elusive as is the very conception of "Ligeia" to the ordinary mind, she was perfectly real to her creator. In the summer-night breeze he heard the music of her voice and felt the delicious coolness of her caress. Tall, swaying trees spoke to him of her height, her majesty and her grace. He perceived the softness and lightness of her footfalls in the passage of evening shadows across a lake or meadow, the perfection of her features in the form and finish of flower petals and the delicate tints of her beauty in the coloring of flowers; the raven hue and sweeping length of of her tresses in the drowning shades of midnight and the entrancing veil of her lashes in deep mysterious woods; and when, in fancy, he looked beneath that veil into her eyes, as unfathomable as the ocean itself, he was struck dumb with reverence and wonder, for they held in keeping all the secrets of the moon and the stars, of dawn and sunset, of green things growing and flowers in bloom, of the butterfly in the crysalis and on the wing, of still waters and of running brooks.

To the inner vision of this most unusual youth, "Ligeia"—this myth called into being by the enchantment of his own fancy—not only became as real as if she had been flesh and blood; his pagan soul bowed down before her and she blotted from his mind, for the time, all thought or consciousness of more robust womanhood. She became, in imagination, the sharer of his studies, the wife of his bosom, and he sat at her feet and gladly learned from her the beautiful, strange secrets of this fearfully and wonderfully made world.

He was sometimes haunted by another, and a far less agreeable vision. In spite of the absence of restraint under which he lived and the fact that between his dreams, his books and his dissipations there seemed little opportunity left for the still, small voice to make itself heard, there were times when his better self shook off slumber and rose before him like a ghost that, for all his efforts, would not be laid—a ghost like him in all regards save for the sternness of its look and of the voice which accused him in whispers to which all others ears were deaf, but his own intensely, horribly sensitive.

It was generally at the very height of excitement in play, when he had just been dealt a hand which he told himself, with exultation, would win him all the money in the pool, or, perhaps at the moment when he raised the glass to his lips, anticipating the delicious exhilaration of the seductive peach-honey, that the unwelcome spectre would, with startling suddenness, appear before his eyes. His face would blanch, his own voice become almost as hoarse as the warning whisper that was in his ear, and with trembling hand he would put down the cards or the cup and refuse to have anything more to do with the evening's sport.

The Dreamer

His companions at first thought these attacks the result of some physical weakness but finally became accustomed to them and attributed them to his "queerness."

Thus the youthful poet passed his year at college—dividing his time between his dreams, his classes and his carousals. The session closed in December. The final examinations occupied the early part of the month and when the faculty met upon the 14th., it was found that Edgar Poe had not only stood well in all of his studies, but in two of them—Latin and French—he had taken the highest honors.

In spite of this, and of the fact that at no time during the session had he come under the censure of the faculty, a startling revelation was made. Edgar Poe, model student as he seemed to be, whose only fault—if it could be called a fault—as the faculty knew him, had been a tendency toward a romantic dreaminess that had led him upon lonely rambles among the hills rather eccentric in a boy of seventeen; Edgar Poe, the quiet, the gentlemanly, the immaculately neat, the scholarly, the poetic, had been a spendthrift and a reckless gambler. His debts, for a boy of his age, were astounding. No one was more amazed at the sum of them than Edgar himself. He had always had the lordly indifference to money, and the contempt for keeping account of it, that was the natural result of being used to have what seemed to him to be an unlimited supply to draw upon, with the earning of which he had nothing to do. As to hoarding it, he would as soon have thought of hoarding the air he breathed which came to him with no less effort. He was, unfortunately, as heedless of what he owed as what he spent—lavishing it upon his companions as long as it lasted and when his supply of cash was exhausted running up accounts with little thought of a day of reckoning—though of course he fully intended to pay.

His mind was, indeed, too much engrossed with the charming creations of his brain to leave him time for brooding upon such sordid matters as the keeping of accounts, or the making of two ends meet. The amount of his indebtedness was now, however, sufficient to give him a shock which thoroughly aroused him, and he was genuinely distressed; for he had no wish to ruthlessly pain his foster-father. The haunting better self not only arose and confronted him, but remained with him, keeping close step with him and upbraiding him and condemning him in the whisper audible to his quick imagination and so terrifying.

Still, the thought that Mr. Allan had plenty of money, and that no severe sacrifice would be needful for the payment of his debts relieved his penitence of much of its poignancy. That Mr. Allan would settle these "debts of honor," as he called them, as the fathers and guardians of boys as reckless as himself had done, he had not the slightest doubt. But, as will be seen, he reckoned without Mr. Allan.

He wrote Mrs. Allan a dutiful letter, confessing all and expressing his sorrow, and begging to be permitted to repay Mr. Allan for settling his affairs at the University with work as a clerk in the counting house.

The letter filled the tender heart of the foster-mother with yearning. The sum frightened her, though she, like the boy, comforted herself with the thought that her husband could pay it without embarrassment. Still, she trembled to think of his wrath. Her chief feeling was one of sympathy for her erring, penitent boy. How natural it was for one of his age to be led away by evil associates! All boys—she supposed—must sow some wild oats, though few, she was confident, showed such a beautifully penitent spirit, and it would be a small matter in future years when he should have become the great and good man she knew he was going to be.

How noble it was of him to offer to give up or postpone the completion of the education so dear to his heart and tie himself to a desk in that tiresome counting-house in

The Dreamer

order to pay his debts—he that was born to shine as a poet. She exulted that he had offered to make such a sacrifice, but he should never make it, never while *she* had breath in her body to protest!

How her heart bled for him in his sorrow over his wrong-doing! How she longed to fold his dear curly head against her breast and tell him that he was quite, quite forgiven! She would reward him for the splendid stand in his classes and at the same time make him forget his troubles on account of the debts by giving him the loveliest imaginable Christmas. Uncle Billy must search the woods for the brightest greens, the prettiest holly; for the house must look its merriest for the home-coming of its young master, covered with honors! There must be mistletoe, too she told herself, her mouth dimpling and a suspicion of a twinkle flashing out from under her dewy lashes. The fatted calf should be killed, her boy should make merry with his friends.

The dear letter was kissed and cried over until it took much smoothing on her knee to make it presentable to hand over to her husband for perusal. Her fingers were still busy stroking out the crumples, though her tears were dried, and her thoughts were happily engaged with plans for a Christmas party worthy to celebrate the home-coming of her darling, when Mr. Allan came in to supper. She was brought back to recollection of the confession in the letter and her apprehensions as to how it would be received, with a start, and before timidly handing her husband the open letter, she began preparing him for its contents and excusing the writer.

"A letter from Eddie, John, dear. He has stood splendidly in his classes, but asks your forgiveness for having done wrong in his spare time. He is so manly and noble in his confession, John, and in his offer to make reparation!"

John Allan's face clouded and hardened instantly.

"What is this? Confession? Reparation?—Give me the letter!"

But she held it away from him.

"It seems he has gotten into a card-playing set who have led him away further than he realized. Oh, don't look like that, John! He is so young, and you know how evil association can influence the best of boys!"

But the storm gathered fast and faster on John Allan's face.

"Card-playing? Do you mean the boy has been gambling? Give me the letter."

She could withhold it no longer, but as he sat down to read it she threw herself upon an ottoman at his feet and clasping his knees hid her face against them, crying,

"Oh, John, have pity, have pity!"

But even as she sobbed out the words, she felt their futility. She knew that there was no pity to be expected from the owner of that face of stone, that eye of steel.

As he read, his rage became too great for the relief of an outburst. A still, but icy calm settled upon him. For some minutes he spoke no word and seemed unconscious of the tender creature so appealing in her loveliness and in the humility of her attitude, beseeching at his knee. The truth was, that much as he loved her, his contempt for what he called her "weakness" for the son of her adoption, but added to his harshness in judging the boy.

Presently he arose, impatiently pushing her away from him as he did so, saying;

"Pack my bag and order an early breakfast. I'm going to take the morning stage for the University."

It was a difficult evening for the little foster-mother. In the stately, octagon-shaped dining-room soft lamplight was cheerily reflected by gleaming mahogany and bright silver and china, upon which was served the most toothsome of suppers; but the meal was almost untouched and the mere pretense of eating was carried through in silence and gloom. In the drawing-room, afterward, the firelight leaped saucily against shining andirons and fender, bringing forgetfulness of the frosty night outside, while the carved wood-work and the great mirrors and soft-hued paintings, in their gilded frames, on the walls, and the deep carpets on the floors spoke of comfort. But the beautiful room was a mockery, for the promised comfort, was not there—only futile luxury. Upon that bright hearth was warmth for the body, but none for the spirit, for before it sat the master and mistress—the presiding geniuses of the house—upon whose oneness the structure of the *home* must stand, or without it fall into ruin; there they sat, wrapped in moods so out of sympathy and tune that speech was as impossible between them as if they had been of different tongues, and each unknown to the other.

Meantime, Edgar Poe was spending his last hours at the University in the dust and ashes of self-condemnation and regretful retrospection No farewell orgie celebrated his leave-taking. Only one of his friends was invited to his room that night and he no denizen of "Rowdy Row," but the quiet, irreproachable librarian. To this gentle guest The Dreamer confided his past sins and his penitence, while he laid upon the glowing coals the year's accumulation of exercise books, and the like, which had served their purpose and were finished and done with, and watched the devouring flames leap from the little funeral pyre they made into the chimney.

More than anything he had ever done in his life, he told his companion, he regretted the making of the gambling debts for which Mr. Allan would have to advance the money to pay. But, as has been said, he reckoned without Mr. Allan, who settled all other obligations, but utterly ignored the so-called "debts of honor."

"Debts of honor?" he queried with contempt. "Debts of *dishonor*, I consider them."

And that was his last word upon the subject.

CHAPTER XII.

The late January night was bitterly cold, and clear as crystal. There was a metallic glitter about the round moon, shining down from a cloudless, blue sky—too bright to show a star—upon the black and bare trees and shrubbery in the terraced garden of the Allan homestead.

Edgar Poe looked from his casement upon the splendor of the beautiful, but frigid and unsympathetic night. Bitterness was in his heart contending with a fierce joy. At last it had come—the breach with Mr. Allan—and he was going away! He knew not where, but he was going, going into the wide world to seek fame and fortune.

He had much to regret. He loved Richmond—loved it for the joy and pain he had felt in it; for the dreams he had dreamed in it. He loved it exceedingly for the two dear graves, one in the churchyard on the hill and one in the new cemetery, that held his beloved dead.

Yes, he was sorry to leave this *home*-city, if not of his birth, at least of his childhood and early youth, and his soul was still shaken by the scene with his foster-parents through which he had just passed. But in spite of all, his heart—rejoicing in the nearness of the freedom for which he had so fiercely longed, sang, and stilled his sorrow.

But a few weeks had passed since his return from the University. A few weeks? They seemed to him years, and each one had left a feeling of increased age upon his spirit.

The home-coming had not been altogether unhappy—humiliating as it was. In spite of the black looks of his foster-father, the little mother (bless her!) had welcomed him with out-stretched arms and eyes beaming with undimmed love. Never had she been more tenderly sweet and dear. She had given the most beautiful Christmas party, with all his

The Dreamer

best friends invited, and everything just as she knew he would like it. Her husband had frowningly consented to this, but her tears and entreaties were all of no avail to win his consent for the boy's return to college. Vainly had she plead his talents which she believed should be cultivated, and the injustice (since they had voluntarily assumed the responsibility of rearing him) of cutting short his education at such an early age. John Allan was adamant.

And so, after the holidays, he had taken his place in the counting-house of "Ellis and Allan."

Distasteful as the new work was to the young poet, he was determined to stick to it, and would probably have done so, but the strict surveillance he soon realized he was under (as if he could not be trusted!) and the manner of Mr. Allan who rarely spoke to him except when it was absolutely necessary, and seemed to regard him as a hopeless criminal, would have been unbearable to a far less proud and sensitive nature than Edgar Poe's. Both at the office and at home, Mr. Allan's narrow, steel-colored eyes seemed to keep constant watch, under their beetling brows, for faults or blunders; and it seemed to the driven boy that no matter what he did or said, he should have done or said just the reverse. He felt constantly that a storm was brewing which must sooner or later, certainly break, and that night it had burst forth with all the fury of the tempest which has been a long time gathering.

He hardly knew what had brought it on, or how it had begun. Its violence was so great as to almost stun him until at length, without being more than half conscious of the significance of his own words he had asked if it would not be better for him to go away and earn his own living; and then came his foster-father's startlingly ready consent, with the warning that if he did go he must look for no further aid from him.

His heart ached for the pretty, tender little mother. How soft the arms that had clung about his neck, the lips that had pressed his hot brow! How piteous her dear tears! They had almost robbed him of his resolution, but he had succeeded in steeling himself against this weakness. He had folded her close in his arms and kissed her, and vowed that, come what might, he could never forget her or cease to love her, and that he should always think of her as his mother and himself as her child. Then he had put her gently from him for, for all his vows, she was inseparably bound up in the old life from which he was breaking away—his life as John Allan's adopted son—she could have no real place in his future.

Yet the tie that bound him to her was the strongest in his life and could not be severed without keen pain. In the world into which he was going to fight the battle of life (he told himself) memory of her would be one of his inspirations.

But where was that battle to be fought, and with what weapons? He had been brought up as a rich man's son, and with the expectation of being a rich man's heir. He had been trained to no money-making work, physical or mental; and now he was to fare forth into the great world where there was not a familiar face, even, to earn his bread! What could he do that would bring him the price of a loaf?—

Did the question appal him? Not in the least. He had youth, he had health, he had hope, he had his beloved talent and the secret training he had given himself toward its cultivation. His "heart-strings were a lute"—he felt it, and with an optimism rare for him he also felt that he had but to strike upon that lute and the world must needs stop and listen.

What he did not have was experience and knowledge of the world. Little did he dream how small a part of the busy hive would turn aside to hear his music or how little poetry had to do with the earning of daily bread.

The Dreamer

His trunk was standing open, half packed, though his destination was still undecided; and among the first things that had gone into it was a box containing a number of small rolls of neat manuscript. As he thought of them his heart warmed and his eyes grew soft.

"The world's mine oyster, and with my good pen I'll open it," he joyously paraphrased. But toward what part of the world should he turn his face—to what market take his precious wares? That was the all-important question! How much his fortune might depend upon his decision!

As he stood at the window, he stared into the brilliancy and the shadows of the icy, unresponsive night—seeking a sign. But the cold splendor of the cloudless sky and glittering moon and the inscrutible shadows in the garden below where the leafless trees and bushes cast monster shapes upon the frozen ground, alike mocked him.

Presently there was the first hint of softness in the night. It came like a sigh of tender pity across the stillness and he bent his head to listen. It was the voice of the faintest of breezes blowing up from the south and passing his window. He threw wide his arms to empty space as if to embrace some invisible form.

"Ligeia, Ligeia, my beautiful one," he breathed, invoking his dream-lady, "Be my counsellor and guide! Let thy sweet voice whisper whither I must go!"

But the voice was silent and all the night was still again.

He turned from the window and threw himself into his arm-chair, letting his eyes rove about the room as though he would seek a sign from its walls. Suddenly he sat erect, his dilated pupils fixed upon a point above the chimney-piece—upon a small picture. It was a little water-color sketch done by the hand of his versatile mother, and found among her belongings after her death. Like her miniature and her letters, the picture had followed him through his life and had always adorned the walls of his room. Often and over he had studied it until he knew by heart every stroke of the brush that entered into its composition. Yet he stared at it now as if he had never seen it before. Finally he took it down from its place on the chimney and held it in his hands, gazing upon it in deep abstraction.

Underneath the picture was written its title: "Boston Harbor—Morning," and upon its back,

"For my little boy, Edgar, who must love Boston, the place of his birth, and where his mother found her best and most sympathetic friends."

The picture gave him the sign! With rising excitement he decided that it must be accepted. To Boston, of course, he would go. Boston, the place of his birth and where his angel mother had found her "best, most sympathetic friends."

He would get away as early the next morning as possible, he told himself. He would waste no time in goodbyes, for, he remembered with some bitterness, there were few to say goodbye to. The boys were all off at college again, now that the holidays were over, and as for Myra, she had quickly consoled herself and was already a wife! He had addressed some reproachful verses to her as a bride; then dismissed her from his thoughts.

He arose and placed the picture carefully in the trunk with the rest of his treasures and then went to bed to fall into the easy slumber of one whose mind is well made up.

A few days later Edgar Poe had looked with delight and ineffable emotion upon the real Boston Harbor, with its rocky little islets and its varied shipping and its busy wharves, and—for him—its suggestions of one in Heaven.

The Dreamer

CHAPTER XIII.

Upon his arrival in Boston, our errant knight, before setting out upon his quest for the Fame and Fortune to whose service he was sworn, spent some hours in wandering about the old town, with mind open to the quickening influences of historic association and eye to the irregular, picturesque beauty about him.

It was one of those rare days that come sometimes in the month of February when, though according to the callendar it should be cold, there is a warmth in the sunshine that seems borrowed from Spring. Tired out by his tramp, young Edgar at length sat down upon a bench in the Common, under an elm, great of girth and wide-spreading. The sunshine fell pleasantly upon him, through the bare branches. Roundabout were other splendid, but now bare elms and he sat gazing upward into their sturdy brown branches and dreamily picturing to himself the beauty of these goodly trees clothed in the green vesture of summer. Suddenly, by a whimsical sequence of suggestion, the pleasure he felt in the sunshine of February as it reached him under the tree in Boston Common, vividly called to mind the refreshing coolness of the shade of the elms, in full leaf, as he, a little lad of six, had walked the streets of old Stoke-Newington for the first time.

There was little relation between that first and this present parting with the Allans, yet in his mind they became inseparably connected. He recalled his happiness in his first essays at composition, made at the Manor School, and told himself that, though he did not know it at the time, that was the first step toward his life work. He was now, here in Boston, the city of his birth, about to take the second; for the hour had arrived when his work would be given to the world!

Across his knees he held the box containing his precious manuscripts. He arose from the bench and turning toward the lower end of the Common, walked, with brisk, hopeful step down town, in the direction of a well-known publishing house whose location he had already ascertained.

Edgar Poe had known sorrow, real and imaginary; he was now to have his first meeting with Disappointment, bitter and grim.

Of all the persons who had ever seen his work, every one had been warm in its praise— everyone saving John Allan only. Some had been positively glowing. True, they had not been publishers, yet among them there had been gentlemen and ladies of taste and culture. But here was a different matter. Here was a personage with whom he had not reckoned, but who was the door, as it were, through which his work must pass into the world. He was unmistakably a personage. His bearing, though modest, spoke of power. His dress, though unobtrusive, was in the perfect taste which only the prosperous can achieve and maintain. His features were cast in the mold of the well-bred. He was past middle age and his naturally fine countenance was beautiful with the ennobling lines which time leaves upon the face of the seeker after truth. He was courteous—most Bostonians and many publishers are. He was sympathetic. He was undoubtedly intellectual, but the eyes that regarded through big, gold-rimmed spectacles, the romantic beauty, the prominent brow and the distinguished air of the sweet-voiced youth before him, wore a not only thoughtful, but something more—a distinctly shrewd and practical expression. In them was no awe of the bare mention of "original poetry."

He took the little rolls of manuscript into his strong, and at the same time smooth and well-shapen hands, and drew them out to their full length with the manner of one who handled as good every day. He cast his eyes rapidly down the sheets—*too* rapidly, it seemed to the poet—with a not unkind, yet critical air, while the sensitive youth before him turned red and white, hot and cold, by turns, and learned something of the horrors of the Inquisition.

The Dreamer

It was really but a very short space, but to the boy who seemed suspended between a life and a death sentence, it was an age.

Finally, he experienced something like a drowning sensation while he heard a voice that barely penetrated the flood of deep waters that was rolling over his head, saying words that were intended to be kind about the work showing promise, in spite of an absence of marketable value.

"Marketable value?" Heavens! Was he back in John Allan's counting house? What could the man mean? It was as literature, not as merchandize that he wanted his poetry to be judged!

In his dismay, he stammered something of the sort, only to be told that when his poetry was made into a book it would become merchandize and it mattered not how good, as poetry—it might be, the publisher could do nothing with it unless as merchandize it would probably be valuable too.

Then—he had been politely bowed out, with his package still under his arm!

During the few minutes he had spent in the publisher's office the sky had become overcast and a biting east wind had blown up from the river; but the change in the outside world was as nothing to that within him. He had not known how large a part of himself was his dream of becoming a poet. It now seemed to him that it was all of him—had from the beginning of his life been all of him. Since those old days at Stoke-Newington, he had been building—building—building—this castle in the air; now, at one fell blow, the whole fabric was laid in ruin!

Weakness seized his limbs and deep dejection his spirits. His life might as well come to an end for there was nothing left for him to live for. How indeed, was he to live when the only work he knew how to do had "no marketable value?" The money with which Mrs. Allan supplied him, before he left home—"to give him a start"—would soon be exhausted. What if he should not be able to make more?

Though he was in the city of his birth, he found himself an absolute stranger. If any of those who had been sympathetic friends to his mother were left, he had no idea who or where they were.

He went back to the lodgings he had engaged to a night of bitter, sleepless tossing.

But with the new day, youth and hope asserted themselves. He decided that he would not accept as final the verdict of any one publisher, though that one stood at the head of the list. With others, however, it was just the same; and another night of even greater wretchedness followed.

Upon his third day in Boston (he felt that he had been there a year!) he wandered aimlessly about, spirit broken, ambition gone. Finally, in Washington Street, he discovered, upon a small door, a modest sign bearing the legend:

"Calvin F.S. Thomas. Printer."

With freshly springing hope, he entered the little shop and was received by a pale, soft-eyed, sunken-chested and somewhat threadbare youth of about his own age, who in reply to his inquiry, announced himself as "Mr. Thomas."

Between these two boys, as they stood looking frankly into each other's eyes, that mysterious thing which we call sympathy, which like the wind "bloweth where it listeth and no man knoweth whence it cometh or whither it goeth," sprang instantly into being. The one found himself without his usual diffidence declaring himself a poet in search of a publisher, and the other was at once alert with interest.

Calvin Thomas had but just—timorously, for he was poor as well as young—set up his little shop, hoping to build up a trade as a printer. To be a publisher had not entered into his wildest imaginings—much less a publisher for a poet! But he was, like his visitor, a dreamer, and like him ambitious. Why should he not be a publisher as well as a printer? The poet had not his manuscripts with him, but offered to recite some extracts, which he did, with glowing voice and gesture—explaining figures of speech and allusions as he went along.

Edgar Poe sat easily upon a high stool in the little shop. His dress was handsome and, as always, exquisite in its neatness and taste. His whole appearance and bearing were marked by an "air" which deeply impressed the young printer who had promptly fallen under the spell of his personal charm. He had laid his hat upon the desk, baring the glossy brown ringlets that clustered about his large, pale brow. His clear-cut features were mobile and eager; his dark grey eyes full of life. His voice had a wonderful musical quality, becoming passionate when, as at present, his feeling was deeply aroused.

His poetry, recited thus, gained much of distinction. Its crudities would have been lost, to a great extent, even upon a critic. But Thomas was no critic. He was simply a dreamy, half-educated youth with a mind open to the beautiful and the romantic. The flights of the poet's fancy did not seem to him obscure or too fantastic. They admitted him to a magic world in which he sat spell-bound until silence brought him back to his tiny bare shop which seemed suddenly to have been glorified.

"It is wonderful—*wonderful!*" he breathed.

He began to picture himself as not only sharing the wealth, but the fame which the publication of these gems was bound to bring. But he had to explain that he was poor, and that he could not bring out the poems without financial aid. The money which had been given Edgar to set out in the world with, was already dwindling, but he managed to subscribe a sum which Thomas declared would be sufficient, with the little he himself could add, for the printing of a modest edition, in a very modest garb.

CHAPTER XIV.

In the Allan mansion, in Richmond, there was a stillness that was oppressive. No young foot-falls sounded upon the stair; no boyish laughter rang out in rooms or hall. There were handsome and formal dinners occasionally, when some elderly, distinguished stranger was entertained, but there were no more merry dancing parties, with old Cy playing the fiddle and calling the figures.

Frances Allan, fair and graceful still, though looking somewhat out of health and "broken," as her friends remarked to one another, trod softly about the stately rooms with no song on her lip, no gladness in her step. Her husband was grown suddenly prematurely old and his speech was less frequent and harsher than before. He was more immersed in business than ever and was prospering mightily, but the fact seemed to bring him no satisfaction. Even the old servants had lost much of their mirth. Their black faces were grown solemn and their tread heavy. They looked with awe upon their mistress when, as frequently happened, they saw her quietly enter "Marse Eddie's" room and close the door behind her.

In that room and there alone, the fair, gentle, woful creature gave free reign to the grief of her stricken mother-heart. The room was kept just as her boy had left it, for she constantly hoped against hope that he would return. Hers was the aching, pent-up grief of a mother whose child is dead, yet she is denied the solace of mourning.

Here was the bed which had pillowed his dear, sunny ringlets. Here were his favorite chair—his desk—his books. In a little trunk against the wall were his toys with some of the pretty clothes made with her own fingers, in which it had been her pride to dress him when he was a wee laddie. How she loved to finger and fondle them!

The Dreamer

Fifteen years she had been his mother—now this was all she had! Somewhere in the same world with her he was living, was walking about, talking, eating, sleeping; yet he was dead to her! Oh, if she could only know that he was happy, that he was well, that he lacked nothing in the way of creature comfort; if she could know where he was, picture him at work or in his leisure hours, it would not be so hard to bear.

But she knew nothing—nothing—save that he had gone to Boston.

One letter she had had from him there—such a dear one!—she knew it by heart. In it he had called her "Mother" and assured her of his constant love and thought of her. He had arrived safely, he said, and would soon be busy making his living. Boston was a fine city and full of interest to him. When his ship came in he was going to have her come on and pay him a visit there. He would write again when he had anything worth telling.

Days had passed—weeks—and no word had come. Had he failed to obtain employment? Had he gone further—to New York, perhaps, or Philadelphia? She did not know. Oh, if she could but *know*!

Was he ill? Fear clutched her heart and made her faint. The suspense was terrible, and she had no one to go to for sympathy—no one. She dared not mention her anxiety to her husband; it made him furious. He could not stand the sound of Eddie's name, even—her darling, beautiful Eddie! Her arms felt so empty they ached.

Winter was passing. The garden that Eddie loved so dearly was coming to life. The crocuses for which he always watched with so much interest were come and gone. The jonquils were in bloom and the first sweet hyacinths, blue as turquoises, she had gathered and put in his room. It cheered her to see them there. Somehow, they made the room look more "ready" than usual—as if he might come home that day.

He did not come, but something else did. A letter with the Boston post-mark she had so longed to see, and a small, flat package addressed to her in his dear hand. She broke the seal of the letter first—she was so hungry for the sight of the familiar, "Mother dear," and to know how he fared.

It was a short letter, but, ah, the blessed relief of knowing he was well and happy! And *prospering*—prospering famously—for he told her he was sending her the first copy off the press of his book of poems! It was a *very little* book, he said, but it was a beginning. He felt within him that he would have much bigger and better things to show her erelong. For the present, he was hard at work making ready for a revised and enlarged edition of his book, if one should be called for.

There was a jubilant note in the letter that delighted her and communicated itself to her own spirits. She eagerly tore the wrappings from the package, and pressed the contents against her lips and her heart. It was but a slender volume, cheaply printed and bound, but it was her boy's first published work and a wonderful thing in her eyes. She already saw him rich and famous—saw him come home to her crowned with honor and success—*vindicated.*

She turned the pages of the book. He had written upon the fly-leaf some precious words of presentation to her. She kissed them rapturously and passed on to the title-page:

"Tamerlane and Other Poems. By a Bostonian. Boston: Calvin F.S. Thomas, Printer."

She was still gloating over her treasure when the brass knocker on the front door was sounded, and a minute later Myra Royster—now Mrs. Shelton—was announced. Taking the book with her, she tripped downstairs, singing as she went, and burst in upon Myra as she sat in state in the drawing-room, in all her bridal finery.

Myra noticed as she kissed her, her glowing cheeks and shining eyes.

"How well you are looking today, Mrs. Allan," she exclaimed.

The Dreamer

"It is happiness, dear. I've just had such a delightful letter from Eddie, and this darling little book. It is his poems, Myra!"

Myra was all interest. "To think of knowing a real live author!" she exclaimed. "I was sure Eddie would be famous some day, but had no idea it would come so soon."

"Don't you wish you had waited for him?" teased Mrs. Allan, laughing happily.

They chatted over the wonderful news until nearly dinner-time, and after they had parted Mrs. Allan sat at the window watching for her husband to come home that she might impart it to him at the earliest moment possible. But when at last he appeared she put off the great moment until after dinner, and then when he was comfortably smoking a fragrant cigar she approached him timidly and placed the letter and the book in his lap without a word.

"What's all this?" he questioned sharply.

She made no reply, but hovered about his chair, too excited to trust herself to speak.

He picked up the letter and read it with a deepening frown, then opened the book and ran his eyes hurriedly down one or two of its pages. At length he spoke:

"So this is the way he's wasting his time and, I dare say, his money too. Will the boy ever amount to anything, I wonder?"

The happiness in Frances Allan's face gave place to quick distress.

"Oh, John," she cried, "Don't you think it amounts to anything for a boy of eighteen to have written and published a book of poetry?"

"Poetry? This stuff is bosh—utter bosh!"

For the first time in her life, there was defiance in her gentle face. Her clinging air was discarded. She raised her head and with flashing eyes and rising color, faced him.

"You think that, because you cannot understand or appreciate it," she retorted, with spirit. "Neither do I understand it, but I can see that it is wonderful poetry. If he can do this at eighteen I have no doubt he will make himself and us famous before many years are past!"

Her husband's only reply was an astonished and piercing stare which she met without flinching, then turned and swept from the room, leaving him with a feeling of surprise to see that she was so tall.

Her self assertion was but momentary. As she ascended the stair and entered Eddie's room, all the elasticity was gone from her step, all the brightness from her cheeks and eyes and, still clasping her boy's letter and book to her heart, she threw herself upon his bed and burst into a passion of tears.

Meantime, the elms on Boston Common were clothed with tender April green and under foot sweet, soft grass was springing. In this inspiring cathedral walked Edgar Poe, his pale face and deep eyes, passionate with the worship of beauty that filled his soul, lifted to the greening arches above him, his sensitive ears entranced with the bird-music that fluted through the cool aisles. His mind was teeming with new poems in the making and with visions of what he should do if his book should sell.

But it did not sell. The leading magazines acknowledged its receipt in their review columns, but with the merest mention, which was exceedingly disconcerting. It was discussed (but with disappointment) for a week by his friends at home and at the University, to whom he sent copies. Then was forgotten.

And now its author was, for the first time within his recollection, beginning to feel the pinch of poverty. His money was almost gone and he saw no immediate hope of getting more. He moved to the cheapest boarding house he could find but he did not mind that so

The Dreamer

much as the prospect that faced him of soon beginning to present a shabby appearance in public. His shoes were already showing wear, and he found that to keep his linen as immaculate as he had always been accustomed to have it cost money and he actually had to economize in the quantity of clothing he had laundered. This to his proud and fastidious nature was humiliating in the extreme.

He and Calvin Thomas held frequent colloquies as to ways and means of giving his book wider circulation. He visited the offices of the several newspapers of the town in the hope of getting work in the line of journalism—reporting, reviewing, story-writing, anything in the way of the only business or profession for which he felt that he had any aptitude or preparation; but without success.

At length the sign of "Calvin F.S. Thomas, Printer" had suddenly disappeared from the little shop in Washington Street, and a dismal "To Let," was in its place.

At about the same time Mrs. Blanks lost the handsome, quiet young gentleman, who had evidently seen better days, from her unpretentious lodging house, and the walks under the elms in Boston Common were no longer trodden by The Dreamer from Virginia.

CHAPTER XV.

Where was Edgar Poe?—

Twice since he shook the dust of Richmond joyfully from his feet, fair Springtide had visited the terraced garden of the Allan home. Twice the green had come forth, first like a misty veil, then like a mantle enveloping its trees and its shrubs, its arbors and trellises; twice the procession of flowers, led by the crocuses in their petticoats of purple and yellow, had tripped from underground; twice the homing birds had built in the myrtles and among the snowy pear and cherry blossoms and filled all the place with music. Twice, too, in this garden, the pageant of spring and summer and sunset-hued autumn had passed, the birds had flown away again and winter snows had covered all with their whiteness and their silence.

And still the garden's true-lover, the poet, The Dreamer, was a wanderer, where?—

Oh, beautiful "Ligeia," was it not your voice that now and again whispered in the tree-tops and among the flowers? Could you not—did you not, bring news of the wanderer?

If she did, there was no human being to whom her language was intelligible, and the trees and the flowers keep their secrets well.

Within the homestead there was little change save a deepening of the quietness that had fallen upon it. In the master of the house there was no visible difference. There are some men who seen from year to year seem as unchanging as the sphinx. It is only after a long period that any difference in them can be detected and then they suddenly appear broken and aged. The fair lady of the manor was as fair as ever, but with the pale, tremulous fairness of a late star in the grey dawn of a new day in which it will have no part. Her bloom, her roundness, her gaiety—all these were gone. She spent more time than ever in the room which, waiting for its roving tenant, became more and more like a death chamber. The silence there was not now broken by her sobs even, for it was with dry-eyed grief that she watched and waited for her boy, these days—watched and waited and prayed. Ah, how she prayed for him, body and soul! Prayed that wherever he might be, he might be kept from harm and strengthened to resist temptation.

Was it her agonized petitions that kept him to the straight and narrow path of duty during those two years amid uncongenial surroundings and hard conditions?

The Dreamer

Who knows?

Yet the chair and the desk and the books and the vases of fresh flowers on the mantel, and the fire-wood resting on the shining andirons ready for a match, and the reading lamp with trimmed wick and bright chimney on the table, and the canopied white bed still waited, in vain, his coming.

Many months had passed since the name of Eddie had been spoken between husband and wife, but though she held her peace, like Mary of old, like Mary too, she pondered many things in her heart. He, loving her well, but having no aptitude for divining woman's ways, indulged in secret satisfaction, for he took her silence to mean that she was coming to her senses, and regarding the boy as he did. That she no longer importuned him to enquire into Edgar's whereabouts with the intention of inviting him home was a source of especial relief to him.

Then, upon a day two years after she had triumphantly placed Eddie's book and letter in his hands, it was his turn to bring her a letter.

"You see the bad penny has turned up again," he remarked, dryly.

She looked questioningly at the folded sheet. Its post-mark was Fortress Monroe and the hand-writing was not familiar to her.

"What is it?" she asked.

"A letter from Dr. Archer. He's surgeon at the fort, you know. Read it. It is about Edgar."

With shaking hands and a blanched face she spread open the sheet. A nameless dread possessed her. A letter about Eddie—not from him—and from a surgeon! For a moment darkness seemed to descend upon her and she could not make out the characters before her. She pressed her hand upon her heart. In sudden alarm, her husband rushed to a celaret nearby and brought out a decanter of wine. Pouring a glass he pressed it to her lips.

"Eddie," she gasped, as soon as she could speak. "Is he well?"

In spite of John Allan's anxiety, he was irritated, and showed it.

"Pshaw, Frances!" he exclaimed. "I hoped you had forgotten the boy. Yes, he's well, and, I'm glad to say, in a place where he is made to behave."

She calmed herself with an effort and began to read the letter. The story it told had a smack of romance.

Dr. Archer had (he wrote) been called to the hospital in the fort to see a private soldier by the name of Edgar A. Perry, who was down with fever. The patient spoke but little but the Doctor was struck with his marked refinement of look and manner, and there was something familiar to him about the prominent brow and full grey eyes, though the name was strange to him. His attention was aroused and he could not rid himself of the impression that he had seen the young man before. He mentioned the fact to some of the officers and found at once that his patient was a subject of deep interest to them. They felt sure (they told him) that he had a story. His polished manners and bright and cultivated conversation seemed to them incongruous with the duties of a private soldier, and they laughingly said that they suspected they were entertaining an angel unawares. Yet his duties were performed with the utmost faithfulness and efficiency. He had never been heard to speak of himself or his past in a way which would throw any light upon his history, and his reserve was of the kind which was bound to be respected. Dr. Archer had grown (he wrote) more and more interested in his patient as he became better acquainted with him, and being convinced that the young man had for some reason, gotten out of his proper sphere, he determined to try and help him back to it.

The Dreamer

By the time the young soldier was convalescent the Doctor had won his confidence and obtained from him the confession that the name of Perry was an assumed one, and that he was none other than Mr. Allan's adopted son, Edgar Poe, whom Dr. Archer had not seen since he was a small boy.

The discovery of his identity had greatly increased the good Doctor's interest and he and the officers of the fort were of the opinion that as young Poe had made a model soldier (having been promoted to the rank of sergeant-major, for good conduct) the best thing that could be done for him was to secure his discharge and get him an appointment to West Point. This, Mr. Allan could bring about, he thought, through men of influence whose friendship the Doctor knew he enjoyed. Edgar had enlisted for five years. He had confessed that at the time he had been almost upon the point of starvation and had turned to the army when every effort to find other means of livelihood had failed.

The Doctor and other officers thought that it would be a great sacrifice to leave a young gentleman of Edgar's abilities to three more years of such uncongenial life.

He was quite recovered and in accordance with a promise made the Doctor, was writing to Mr. Allan at that moment.

"Did Eddie's letter come too?" Mrs. Allan asked, as she finished the one in her hand.

Without a word, her husband handed it over to her. In it Edgar expressed much contrition for the trouble which his larger experience in life told him he had cost his foster-father, and asked his forgiveness. He also asked that Mr. Allan would follow the suggestion of Dr. Archer, and apply for a discharge from the army for him, and an appointment to West Point.

He had not written his "Mother" in the past because he had unfortunately nothing to tell which he believed could give her any pleasure, but he sent her his undying love.

Frances Allan looked through wet lashes into her husband's face, but her eyes were shining through the tears.

"Oh, John," she said breathlessly, "You will have him to come and make us a little visit before he goes to West Point, won't you?"

"I'll have nothing to do with him!" was the emphatic reply. "He seems to be getting along very well where he is. Let him stick it out!"

Feeling how vain her pleadings would be, yet not willing to give up hope, she wept, she prayed, she hung upon John Allan's neck. She brought every argument that starved motherhood could conceive to bear upon him.

To think that Eddie was in Virginia—just down at Old Point! The cup of joy was too near her lips to let it pass without a mighty effort. But finally she gave up and shrank within herself, drooping like the palest of lilies.

Then came a day when a stillness such as it had never known before hung over the Allan home. The garden was at its fairest. The halls and the drawing-rooms, with their rich furnishings and works of art were as beautiful as ever; but there was not even a bereaved mother, with an expression on her face like that of Mary at the foot of the cross, to tread the lonely floors. The luxurious rooms were quite, quite empty—all save one— an upper chamber, where upon a stately carved and canopied bed lay all that was mortal of Frances Allan, like a lily indeed, when pitiless storm has laid it low!

The learned doctors who had attended her had given long Latin names to her malady. In their books there was mention of no such ailment as heartbreak, and so happily, the desolate man left to preside in lonely state, over the goodly roof-tree which her presence had filled and made sweet and satisfying, was spared a suspicion even, of the real cause of her untimely end.

The Dreamer

His one consuming desire for the present was that all things should be done just as she would wish, and so—all minor bitternesses drowned in the one overwhelming bitterness of his loss—he scribbled a few hurried lines to Edgar Poe acquainting him with the sad news and telling him to apply for a leave and come "home" at once.

But the mails and travel were slow in those days, and when the young soldier reached Richmond the last, sad rites were over, and for the third time in his brief career the grave had closed over a beautiful woman who had loved him and upon whose personality had been based in part, that ideal of woman as goddess or angel before which his spirit throughout his life, with all its vicissitudes, bowed down. As the lumbering old stage crawled along the road toward Richmond, he lived over again the years spent in the sunshine of her presence. Her death was a profound shock to him. How strange that one so fair, so merry, so bubbling with *life* should cease to be! Would it always be his fate, he wondered, to love where untimely death was lying in wait?

Upon the night when he reached "home" and every night till, his furlough over, he returned to his post of duty at Fortress Monroe, he lay in his old room with his old household gods—his books in their shelves, his pictures on the walls, his desk and deep arm-chair, and other objects made dear by daily use in their accustomed places, and "the lamplight gloating o'er," around him. He was touched at the sweet, familiar look of it all and at the thoughtfulness of himself of which he saw signs everywhere. Could it be that he had been two years an exile from these homelike comforts or had it been only one of his dreams? In spite of the void her absence made, it was good to be back—good after his wanderings to come into his own again.

In the hush and loneliness of those few days under the same roof, the grief-stricken man and youth, their pride broken by their common sorrow, came nearer together than they ever had been before. It seemed that the gentle spirit of her whom each had loved hovered about them, binding them to each other by invisible, but sacred, cords. John Allan spoke to the players' son in tones that were almost fatherly and with quick response, the tender-hearted youth became again the Edgar of the days before reminders of his dependence upon charity had opened his eyes to the difference between a real and an adopted father.

Under this reconciling influence, the youth poured out expressions of penitence for the past and made resolutions for the future and Mr. Allan promised to apply for the desired appointment to West Point, but added that thereafter, he should consider himself relieved of all responsibility concerning Edgar.

This blunt and ungracious assurance strained the bond between the adopted father and son; the promised letter of application to the Secretary of War, ruthlessly shattered it. That his indulgencies during his year at the University of Virginia, so freely and earnestly repented, should have been exposed in the letter seemed to the boy unnecessary and cruel, but the man who had been fifteen years his father, the husband of her over whom the grave had but just closed and who had always loved him—Edgar—as an own and only son, had seen fit to add to the declaration,

"He left me in consequence of some gambling debts at the University," a disclaimer of even a sentimental interest in him!

"Frankly, Sir," the letter said, "I do declare that Edgar Poe is no relation to me whatever; that I have many in whom I have taken an active interest in order to promote theirs, with no other feeling than that every man is my care, if he be in distress."

Edgar Poe duly presented the letter, but the bitterness which during his brief visit home had been put to sleep, raised its head and robbed him of all pleasure in his anticipated change and of much of the incentive to put forth his best effort in it. He felt that the result of this ungracious letter must be to blot the new leaf which he had so ardently desired to turn with shadows of his past which no effort of his own could entirely obliterate.

For the soreness of finding himself disowned as Mr. Allan's son—this time publicly, in a manner—he found somewhat of balm in the letter of cordial praise addressed to the Honorable Secretary of War in his behalf, by the father of his old friend, Jack Preston. Mr. Preston described him as a young gentleman of genius who had already gained reputation for talents and attainments at the University of Virginia, and added,

"I would not write this recommendation if I did not believe he would remunerate the Government at some future day by his services and talents, for whatever may be done for him."

Happily for the, at times, morbidly, sensitive youth, he had soon forgotten the sting caused by the letter in a return to the dreams which he regarded as not only the chief joy but the chief business of his life; for though he was preparing himself for the profession of a soldier, he had never for a moment, forsworn the Muse of Poetry. For a whole year before being transferred to Fortress Monroe he had been stationed at Fort Moultrie, in Charleston harbor. There his wonderful dream-lady, "Ligeia," had seemed especially near to him, and often, when the day's work was done and he recognized her voice in the music of the waves or felt her kiss in the soft, southern air, blown across spicey islets, he would up and away with her across the world, on the moon's silver track; or on nights when no moon came up out of the sea, would wander with her through the star-sown sky.

There was one fair star that invited his fancy with peculiar insistence. It seemed to beckon to him with the flashes of its beams. He questioned "Ligeia" of it and she told him that it was none other than Al Aaraaf, the great star discovered by Tycho Brahe, which after suddenly appearing and shining for a few nights with a brilliancy surpassing that of Jupiter, disappeared never to be seen again; never except by him—The Dreamer—to whom it was given not only to gaze upon it from the far earth, but, with her as his guide, to visit it and to explore its fairy landscape where the spirits of lost sculptures enjoyed immortality.

The result of this flight of fancy to a magical world was the poem, "Al Aaraaf."

He spent the interim between his honorable discharge from the army and his entrance at West Point in a happy visit to Baltimore, where he made the acquaintance of his father's kindred and succeeded in publishing the new poem, with a revised edition of the old ones.

For the first time, his work appeared under his own signature:

"Al Aaraaf, Tamerlane and Minor Poems. By Edgar A. Poe."

The new poem was unintelligible to the critics—but what of that? he asked himself. One of his optimistic moods was upon him. He despised the critics for their lack of perception and as he held the slim volume in his hands and gazed upon that, to him, wondrous title-page, his countenance shone as though it had caught the reflection of the magic star itself. What mattered all the wounds, all the woes of his past life? He had entered into a land where dreams came true!

For the first time, too, his work received recognition as poetry, in the literary world. It was but a nod, yet it was a beginning; and it pleased him to think that this first nod of greeting as a poet came to him from Boston, where his mother had found "her best, most sympathetic friends." Before publishing his new book he had sent some extracts from it to Mr. John Neal, Editor of the *Yankee and Boston Literary Gazette*, who promptly gave them a place in his paper, with some kind words commending them to lovers of "genuine poetry."

"He is entirely a stranger to me," wrote the Boston editor, of the twenty-year-old poet, "but with all his faults, if the remainder of Al Aaraaf and Tamerlane are as good as the

The Dreamer

body of the extracts here given, he will deserve to stand high—very high—in the estimation of the shining brotherhood."

In a burst of gratitude the happy poet wrote to Mr. Neal his thanks for these "very first words of encouragement," he had received.

"I am young," he confided to this earliest friend in the charmed world of letters, "I am young—not yet twenty—*am* a poet if deep worship of all beauty can make me one—and wish to be so in the common meaning of the word."

CHAPTER XVI.

Upon a dark and drizzling November night of the year 1830, four cadets of West Point Academy sat around a cosy open fire in Room 28, South Barracks, spinning yarns for each other's amusement.

One of them—the one with the always handsome and scholarly, at times soft and romantic, but tonight, dare-devil face, was easily recognizable as Edgar the Goodfellow, frequently appearing in the quite opposite character of Edgar the Dreamer, and commonly known as Edgar Poe. His fellow cadets had dubbed him, "the Bard." Two of this young man's companions were his room-mates in Number 28, "Old P," and "Gibs," and the third was a visitor from North Barracks.

Taps had sounded sometime since, and the Barracks were supposed to be wrapt in slumber, but for these young men the evening had just begun. Several hours had elapsed since supper and it is a well-known fact that there is never a time or a season when a college boy is not ready to eat. Someone suggested that politeness demanded they should entertain their guest with a fowl and a bottle of brandy from Benny Haven's shop, and proposed that they should draw straws to determine which of the three hosts should fetch the necessary supplies. They had no money, but the accommodating "Bard" agreed to sacrifice his blanket in the cause of hospitality; and armed with that and several pounds of tallow candles, "Gibs," upon whom the lot had fallen, set forth to run the blockade to Benny's. This was a risky business, for the vigilance of Lieutenant Joseph Locke, one of the instructors in tactics who was also a sort of supervisor of the morals and conduct of cadets, was hard to elude. As one of the Bard's own effusions ran,

"John Locke was a very great name; Joe Locke was a greater, in short, The former was well known to Fame, The latter well known to Report."

The best that Benny would give, in addition to the bottle, for the blanket and candles, was an old gander, whose stentorian and tell-tale voice he obligingly hushed by chopping off its head. Under cover of the darkness and the storm, "Gibs" succeeded in safely returning to the Barracks but not until his hands and his shirt were reeking with the gander's gore. "The Bard," who was anxiously awaiting the result of the foraging expedition ventured outside to meet him. When he beheld the prize, he exclaimed, in a whisper,

"Good for you! But you look like a murderer caught red-handed."

His own words, almost before they left his lips, suggested to him an idea for a mammoth hoax—the best they had tried yet, he told himself. He hastily, and in whispers, unfolded it to "Gibs," whom he found all sympathy, then returned alone, to his friends in Number 28, reporting that he had seen nothing of their messenger, and expressing fear that he had met with an accident.

All began to watch the door with anxiety. After some minutes it burst open and "Gibs," who had carefully laid the gander down outside, staggered into the room, appearing to be

The Dreamer

very drunk and brandishing a knife, which he had rubbed against the fowl's bleeding neck. "Old P." and the visitor from North Barracks, too frightened for words, sat as though rooted to their chairs, while "the Bard" sprang to his feet and in a horror-stricken voice, exclaimed,

"Heavens, Gibs! What has happened?"

"Joe Locke—Joe Locke—" gasped "Gibs."

"Well, what of Joe Locke? Speak man!"

"He won't report me any more. I've killed him!"

"Pshaw!" exclaimed "the Bard," in disgust. "This is another of your practical jokes, and you know it."

"I thought you would say that, so I cut off his head and brought it along. Here it is!"

With that he quickly opened the door and picked up the gander and, whirling it around his head, dashed it violently at the one candle which was thus knocked over and extinguished, leaving the room in darkness but for a few smouldering embers on the hearth, and with the gruesome addition to the company of what two of those present believed to be the severed head of Lieutenant Locke.

The visitor with one bound was out of the room through the window, and made good his escape to his own quarters in North Barracks, where he spread the astounding news that "Gibs" had murdered Joe Locke; it was certainly so, for his head was then in Number 28, South Barracks.

"Old P." nearly frozen with fright, did not move from his place, and it was with some difficulty that "the Bard" and "Gibs" brought him back to a normal condition and induced him to assist in preparing the fowl which had played the part of Joe Locke's head, in the little comedy, for the belated feast—which was merrily partaken of, but without the guest of honor.

Edgar Poe had entered West Point in July, but hardly had its doors closed behind him when his optimism gave place to wretchedness and he began to feel that his appointment was a mistake. He had taken a fine stand in his classes, but he recognized at once a state of things most unpleasant for him for which he had not been prepared. As in his schooldays in Richmond and at the University, a number of the boys had withheld their intimacy from him on account of caste feeling, so now at West Point he found history repeating itself, but with a difference. In Richmond and at the University it had been as the child of the stage and as a dependent upon charity, that the line was drawn against him. With the aristocratic cadets, it was because of his promotion from the ranks. Yet the very experience which brought their contempt upon him gave him a sense of superiority that made their manner toward him the harder to bear, and drilling with green boys after having been two years a soldier, he found most irksome.

While the snubbing to which he was subjected was general enough to make his situation extremely unpleasant, however, it was by no means unanimous. "Gibs" and "Old P." his convivial room-mates in Number 28, took him to their hearts at once, and he really liked them when he was in the mood for companions of their type, but they wore cruelly upon his nerves when the divine fire within him was burning. So indeed would any room-mates, for at home always, and most of the time at the University, one of his chief comforts had been his own room where he could shut out all the world and be alone with his dreams.

There was, at West Point, nothing like a repetition of his course at the University. The trouble which his attack of gambling fever had gotten him into had proved a severe but wholesome lesson, and he had let cards alone at once and forever. In his ignorance of his own family history, he did not know that for one of his blood, the only safety lay in total abstinence from the cup that cheers, but the intense and instantaneous excitement he found a single glass of wine produced in his brain—an excitement amounting almost to madness—was in itself a warning to him, and kept him strictly within the bounds of moderation.

There were times, however, when with a chicken and a bottle of brandy, purchased secretly from old Benny, and smuggled, at great hazard, into the room, Edgar Goodfellow could, with zest join his rolicking room-mates in making merry, and in spite of his strict adherence to the single glass, generally out-do them at their own games.

But there was no place in that room for Edgar the Dreamer; and between the spirit-dulling routine and discipline of classes and drills with youths for the most part younger than himself and inferior in mentality and cultivation, but who bore themselves as his superiors, and the impossibility of an hour of solitude, the lovely "Ligeia" became unreal and remote. He could no longer catch the sounds of her voice, or feel her presence near. His muse, too, had become shy and difficult and when she deigned to visit him at all, it was generally in the quite new character of jester in cap and bells, under whose influence he dashed off humorous and satirical squibs at the expense of the professors and students, of which the lines on Lieutenant Locke are a specimen. These he recited for the benefit of the little parties that gathered in Number 28, by whom they were regarded as master-pieces of wit and were circulated through the school.

But he took no real pleasure in this perversion of his poetical gift, and feeling his soul cramped and cabined by the uncongeniality of his surroundings, he soon became convinced that West Point was not the place for him, and that he should leave it as soon as possible. He wrote Mr. Allan of his dissatisfaction—begging his assistance in securing a discharge. At no time would this request have been granted but it came at the most inopportune moment imaginable.

Some time before, certain ladies in Richmond who professed "to know the signs," had given out the interesting news that Mr. Allan was "taking notice." True it was that though such a thing had seemed impossible, his stocks were higher and more precisely folded than ever, his broadcloth was of a finer texture, his knee-buckles shone with a brighter lustre, but the most marked change in him was a certain springiness of gait altogether new to his silk-stockinged calves, and almost youthful, and a pleased expression of the hitherto stern eyes and mouth which made his usually solemn vizage look as if it might break out into smiles at any moment.

The signs, the ladies said, dated from the arrival of at "Powhatan," the country seat of the Mayo family, just below Richmond, of a fair guest—Miss Louisa Patterson, of Philadelphia. This lady was no longer young, according to the severe standards of that time of early marriages and correspondingly early "old-maidenhood," but so much the better, as she was therefore of suitable age for the elderly though spruce and prosperous widower. She was, withal, a decidedly personable woman with the elegant manners and conversation of the inner circles of the exclusive, stately society in which she had been nurtured—just the woman, the fair prophetesses said, to rule over John Allan (for everybody knew that a man who ruled his first wife was invariably ruled by his second) and to preside with distinction and taste over his drawing-room and his board. She was as suitable, in fact for the wife of ripe age as the flower-like Frances had been for the wife of youth. So Richmond gave its unqualified approval.

Nothing could have been more out of harmony with the sound of the "mellow wedding bells" pealing for this happy pair, than a reminder of the first wife of the bridegroom in the shape of a letter from Edgar Poe.

The Dreamer

When Poe had entered West Point his foster-father had drawn a long breath of relief. He believed that the idle youth with whom his dead wife had been so strangely infatuated was off his hands for good and all. When the letter came to jar upon his new dream of love he was irritated, and in his brief mention of the matter to his bride it was very apparent, and left upon her mind the impression that Frances Allan must have been a weak and silly creature indeed, to have fancied an idle, ungrateful boy who spent his time drinking, gambling and scribbling ridiculous poetry. *And the son of an actress!* It would have been impossible for such a low character and herself to have remained under the same roof for a day, she was sure, and she told her husband so—imparting to her tone somewhat of the pity she felt to think of his having been yoked for years to such a morally frail specimen of womanhood as she conceived the first Mrs. Allan to have been.

So Mr. Allan's letter of refusal to help Edgar escape the life that was growing more and more irksome to him was as decided as it was brief. But Edgar was unshaken in his resolve to get away as soon as possible. In the meantime, finding no outlet for his restless creative faculty that would not remain inactive though there was no opportunity for its satisfaction, he gave himself over by turns, to deepest dejection and wildest hilarity.

Finally, as no other relief was at hand, he decided to force his discharge by deliberate and systematic neglect of the rules. The plan succeeded so well that before the session was out he was expelled from the Academy for disobedience of orders and failure to attend roll-calls, classes and guard-duty.

CHAPTER XVII.

Happily, the restraints of the Academy and his environment there, instead of crushing out young Edgar's impulse to dream and to put his dreams into writing (as a longer period of the same restraints and conditions might have done) had but quickened and strengthened these very impulses, and he had now but one wish, one aspiration in regard to his newly acquired freedom, and that was to dedicate it to the art of literature which had become more and more his passion and his mistress, and which since he had given up all idea of the army, he was resolved to make his sole profession.

His first step toward this end was to arrange, before leaving New York, for a new edition of his already published work, adding some hitherto unpublished poems which even in the unsympathetic atmosphere of Number 28 South Barracks had been undergoing a refining process in the seething crucible of his brain.

The money for this venture dropped into his lap, as it were, for when the new friends in whom he had confided passed the word around that "the Bard" was going to get out a book of poetry, the cadets (in anticipation of a collection of ditties cleverly hitting off the peculiarities and characteristics of the professors) to a man, subscribed in advance—at seventy-five cents per copy. In appreciation of their recognition of his genius, and little guessing what manner of book they expected it to be, "the Bard" gratefully dedicated the new volume "To the United States Corps of Cadets."

Happy it was for him that he was not present to hear those he had thus honored set up their throats in unanimous expressions of disgust when—the dedication leaf turned—they were confronted by a reprint of "Tamerlane" and "Al Aaraaf," with the shorter poems, "To Helen," "A Pæan," "Israfel," "Fairy-Land," and other "rubbish," as they promptly pronounced the entire contents of the book.

"Listen, fellows!" said one of the disgusted lot, with the open volume in his hand.

The Dreamer

"'In Heaven a spirit doth dwell Whose heartstrings are a lute. None sing so wildly well As the angel, Israfel, And the giddy stars (so legends tell) Ceasing their hymns, attend the spell Of his voice, all mute.'"

As he finished this opening stanza of what posterity has ranked as one of the most exquisite lyrics in the English tongue, but which was received by the audience of cadets with guffaws of derision, the reader closed the book with a snap, and dashed it across the room and into the open fire.

"Did you ever hear crazier rubbish?" he asked, with contempt. "Highway robbery, I call it, to send us such stuff for our good, hard cash!"

"The joke's on us this time, and no doubt about it," said the also chagrinned, but more philosophically inclined "Gibs." "The Bard means well, though, and no doubt he thinks the stuff is poetry."

"Old P." solemnly tapped his forehead with his forefinger.

"Something wrong here," he remarked, ominously, "I suspected it all along."

The business of getting his book published dispatched, the poet's thoughts turned lovingly toward Richmond which he still called "home," and carpet-bag in hand and a package of copies of his book which he intended as presents to his old chums under his arm, he set out upon the journey thither.

The streets of New York had been cold and bleak but he told himself as he journeyed, that April days at home were quite different. The grass would be already green upon the hillsides, many of the trees in leaf, and the dear spring flowers in bloom. He pictured the ample comforts of the Allan homestead, and of his own room in it, with its familiar furnishings. Of course he had no idea of looking to Mr. Allan for support—his pen must give him that now—but during the visit which he was going to make "at home" it would be pleasant to sleep once more in that room with all of its associations, though many of these were with the blunders of a blinded youth.

As he thought of Mr. Allan and his last meeting with him, his heart softened. He would try and keep their intercourse upon the friendly basis upon which his last sad visit home had placed it; would as far as possible, put himself in his foster-father's place and see things as he saw them.

How desolate the widowed man had seemed in the big, empty house during those chill, sorrow-stricken, February days! No wonder he had sought escape from his desolation in another marriage—his loneliness without the lovely little mother must have been unbearable. What was the new wife like, he wondered? Was she like the lady of the manor he remembered? Could there be another such gentle, tender, flower-like woman on earth?

In his unworldly, unpractical dreamer's soul it did not occur to him for one moment that her existence might make him any less Mr. Allan's adopted son, or even that, with all the rooms in the big house at her disposal, she might have taken a fancy to rearrange the one which, from the time the house became Mr. Allan's property, had been "Eddie's room," and which had so long stood ready for his occupancy—dedicated as it was to his own belongings.

At last he was on the sacred soil!

How fair and comfortable the old homestead looked in its setting of greening lawn and flowering garden, with the pleasant sunshine of the April afternoon over all! How cheerful—how ample—how homelike!

The Dreamer

He ran up the steps of the commodious front porch and was on the point of opening the door when some impulse he could not define made him pause and, instead of turning the knob, announce himself with a rap upon the shining brass knocker.

One of the old family servants whom he had known and loved from his infancy, and with whom he had always been a pet, opened the door, and with beaming face and eager voice greeted him with the enthusiastic hospitality of his kind—lifting up his voice and his hands in praise to God that he was once more in this world permitted to look upon the face of "Marse Eddie."

The whilom young master of the house was equally, if less picturesquely, warm in his expressions of pleasure at seeing the old man again, and gave him his carpet-bag with instructions to take it to his room and to tell Mrs. Allan that he was there.

The venerable darkey's face fell. The "new Mistis" had "changed the house around some," he explained, apologetically, and "Marse's Eddie's" things had been moved to one of the servants' rooms, but "Marse Eddie's" old room was a guest chamber, and he "reckoned" that would be the place to take the bag.

The visitor's whole manner changed at once—*froze*. The flush of pleasure died out of his face and left it pale, cold and stern. A fierce and unreasonable rage possessed him. *She had dismantled the room that his little mother had arranged for him and sent his things to a servant's room!* Was this insult intentional, he wondered?

To his mind, his "little Mother" was so entirely the presiding genius of the place—he could not realize the right of anyone, not even a "new mistis," to come in and "change the house around."

Cut to the quick, he directed the old butler to leave the bag where it was and to let Mrs. Allan know that he was in the drawing-room.

No announcement could have given that lady greater surprise. She regarded Edgar's leaving West Point after her husband's letter, as direct disobedience, and his presenting himself at her door as the height of impertinence. Something of this was in the frigid dignity with which she received him—standing, and drawn up to the full height of her imposing figure.

She had never been within speaking distance of anyone drunk to the point of intoxication, but, somehow, she had received an impression that this was pretty generally the case with the young man now before her, and when he began somewhat incoherently (in his foolish rage) to ask her confirmation of the old servant's statement that his room had been dismantled, she was convinced that it was his condition at the moment. Turning, with the grand air for which she was noted, to the hoary butler who stood in the doorway between drawing-room and hall, respectfully awaiting orders as to "Marse Eddie's" bag, she said,

"Put this drunken man out of the house!"

The aged slave stood aghast. Between the stately new mistress whom it was his duty to serve, and the beloved young master whose home-coming had warmed his old heart, what should he do?

He stood in silence, his lined black face filled with sadness, his chin in his hand, his eyes bent in sorrow and shame upon the floor. What should he do?—

Fortunately, the new mistress did not see his indecision as she swept from the room, and "Marse Eddie" quickly relieved him of the embarrassing dilemma by picking up the carpet-bag and passing out of the door, closing it behind him.

It was all a mistake—a miserable mistake; but one of those mistakes in understanding between blind, prejudiced human beings by which hearts are broken, souls lost.

The Dreamer

At the foot of the steps Edgar Poe paused and looked back at the massive closed door. *Never—nevermore*, it seem to say to him.—*Never—nevermore!*

While he had been inside the house one of those sudden changes in the face of nature of which his superstitious soul always made note, had taken place. A shower from a passing cloud had filled the depressions in the uneven pavement, where before only sunshine lay, with little pools of water, and had left the trees "weeping," as he fancifully described them to himself.

He walked along the wet streets for a few steps, by the side of the wall that enclosed house and grounds. Then he paused again and looked over into the dripping garden while he held consultation with himself as to what he should do next. As he looked the breath of drenched violets greeted his nostrels. He noticed that the lilacs were coming into blossom. The fruit trees already stood like brides veiled in their fresh bloom. The tulip and hyacinth and daffodil beds were gay with color. How their newly washed faces shone in the sunshine, just then bursting through the clouds!

Near him, just inside the wall, was a bed of lily-of-the-valley. He was seized with an almost irresistible desire to go down upon his knees by it and search among the glistening green leaves to see if the lilies were in bloom.

But the garden-gate, like the house door, was closed upon him and seemed to repeat the fateful word—Nevermore.

Whither should he turn his steps? To Mr. Allan's office?—Never!

His intention had been to submit himself to Mr. Allan as far as his self-respect would let him. To consult him in regard to the literary career he felt himself committed to now that (as he recalled with satisfaction) the bridges between him and any other profession were burnt behind him. His own plan, upon which he was resolved to ask Mr. Allan's opinion, would be to seek a position in the line of journalism which would give him a living while he was waiting for his more ambitious work to find buyers.

But since the interview with Mrs. Allan he realized the folly of this dream.

Then, whither should he go?—To the chums of his boyhood?—Rob Stanard, Dick Ambler, Rob Sully, Jack Preston, where were they?—Good, dear friends they had been, but it seemed so long since they had played together! What should they find to say to each other now? They were busy with their various avocations and interests—what room in their hearts and homes could there be for a wanderer like himself?

At the age of one and twenty, at the springtime of his life, as of the year—he felt himself to be as friendless, as much a stranger in the city which he called home, as Rip Van Winkle after his long sleep had felt in his. The only spots toward which he could turn with any confidence for sympathy were those two quiet cities within this city where lay his loved and lovely dead—"The doubly dead in that they died so young."

"How different my life would be if they had lived!" he murmured to the flowers.

Yet how fair was this world in which he had no place—even to a mere looker-on. How fair was this mansion, in its setting of April green and bloom, which had once owned him as its young—its future master. Above it Hope stretched her shining wings, but the hope was not for him. For him the closed door and the closed gate said only, "no more—nevermore."

But whither should he go?—whither?

As he turned from the garden and walked slowly, aimlessly, down the street, his great grey eyes fixed ponderingly upon the breaking clouds, a rainbow—bright symbol of promise—spanned the heavens. His eyes widened, his lips parted at the wonder and the beauty and the suddenness of it.

Whither should he go? Behold an answer meet for a poet!

The Dreamer

Whither?—Whither?—The dark eyes in the pale cameo face turned skyward—the eyes of him who had declared himself to be a deep worshipper of all beauty grew more dreamy. Whither, indeed, but to the end of the rainbow!

By what "path obscure and lonely," the quest would lead him he knew not, but he would follow it to the bitter end, for there, perchance, he would find if not the traditional pot of gold, at least a wreath of laurel.

As he wandered down the street, his eyes still upon the bow, his dream was suddenly interrupted by the hearty voice of one of his boyhood's friends, and his sister Rosalie's adopted brother, Jack Mackenzie.

"Hello, Edgar!" he cried. "Did you drop from the clouds? Evidently, for I see your head is still in them."

He returned the greeting with joy. How good it was to feel the hand-clasp of friendship and welcome! He had always liked Jack—for the moment he loved him.

"And where are you bound—you and your bag?" asked Jack. "Not to Mr. Allan's, for you are going in the wrong direction."

"No," replied The Dreamer, with a whimsical smile. "I was going there, but I found the door shut, so I changed my mind, and had just decided to make the end of the rainbow my destination."

Jack's spontaneous laugh rang out. "The same old Edgar!" he said. "Well I won't interfere with your journey except to defer it a bit. You are going home with me, to 'Duncan Lodge,' now—at least to supper and spend the night; and to stay as much longer as pleases you. Rose and the rest will be delighted to see you."

CHAPTER XVIII.

Where was Edgar Poe? Again the question was being asked. In many quarters and with varying degrees of interest it was repeated. But it still remained unanswered.

In Richmond it was asked by the chums of his youth as they sat under their comfortable vines and fig-trees, or stopped each other on a corner for a few moments' social chat, or—catching some one of the rumors that were afloat concerning the gifted companion of their golden days—looked up from their desks in office or counting-house to ask each other the question. Their faces were keen with interest for their admiration and affection for The Dreamer had been sincere; yet it was not strong enough after the lapse of years to make any one of them lay down work and go forth to seek a solution of the mystery. Such an errand not one of them felt to be his business. A quixotic errand it would indeed have been considered and one which, if half the rumors were true, might have necessitated a journey to the ends of the earth, to prove but a fool's errand after all.

The oft-repeated question was one with which John Allan little concerned himself. A robust son and heir had come in his late middle age to fill all his thoughts with new interest and plans for the present and the future. The patter of little feet of his own child on the stairs and halls of his home, drowned the ghostly memories of other and less welcome footfalls that had once echoed there.

He too, had heard rumors of the adventures and the misadventures of Edgar Poe, but he did not consider it his business, as it was certainly not his pleasure, to investigate them.

In Baltimore too, the question was asked by the kinsfolk whose acquaintance Edgar had made during his visit there. But they had never held themselves in the least responsible for this eccentric son of their brother David, the actor—the black sheep of the family.

The Dreamer

Surely it was none of *their* business to follow him upon any chase his foolish fancy might lead him.

But still, when the rumors that were rife reached their ears, it was with no small degree of curiosity that they asked each other the question: Where was Edgar Poe?—What had become of him?—Had he, as some believed, met death upon the high seas or in a foreign land?—Was he the real hero of stories of adventure which floated across the ocean from Russia—from France—from Greece?

He had certainly contemplated going abroad—the Superintendent of West Point Academy had had a letter from him sometime after he left there, declaring his intention of seeking an appointment in the Polish army. Had he gone, or was he, as some would have it, going in and out among them, there in Baltimore, but unknown and unrecognized—his identity hidden under assumed name and ingenious disguise?

Who could tell?

The wonder of it was not in the existence of the unanswered question—of the mystery—but that the question could remain unanswered—the mystery remain unsolved—and no attempt be made to lift the veil. That a young man, a gentleman, of prominent connections, of handsome features and distinguished bearing and address, of rare mental gifts and cultivation, and of magnetic personality, could disappear from the face of the earth—could, almost before the very eyes of his fellows, step from the glare of the world in which he moved into the abyss of absolute obscurity or impenetrable mystery, and create no stir—that no one should deem it his or her business to seek or to find an answer to the question, a reading of the riddle.

Not until two years after Edgar Poe had turned his back upon the closed door of the Allan mansion, in Richmond, and stepped, as it seemed from the edge of a world in which he was not wanted into the unknown, did such an one arise. And that one was, as an especially good friend of Edgar Poe's was most likely to be—a woman.

Between this woman:—Mrs. Maria Poe Clemm—a widow of middle age, and The Dreamer, there existed the close blood-tie of aunt and nephew, for she was the own sister of his father, David Poe.

More than that—there existed, though they had never seen each other, a soul kinship rare between persons of the same blood, and which (for all they had never seen each other) she, with the woman's unerring instinct that sometimes seems akin to inspiration, divined. She too was something of a dreamer, with an ear for the voices of Nature and a mind open to the influences of its beauty, but with a goodly ballast of strong common sense.

She was but a young girl when her handsome and idolized brother David scandalized the family by marrying an actress and himself taking to the stage. But she had seen the bewitching "Miss Arnold" at the theatre in Baltimore—had, with fascinated eyes, followed her twinkling feet through the mazy dance, had listened with charmed ears to her exquisite voice, had sat spell-bound under her acting. To her childish mind, the stage had become a fairy-land and Miss Arnold its presiding genius. That brother David should love and marry her seemed like something out of a fairy book. *She* did not blame brother David; she secretly entirely approved of him.

In her later years the death of the husband of her own youth who had been romantically, passionately loved, had left her penniless but not disillusioned; with her own living to get and a little daughter with a face like a Luca Della Robbia chorister, and a voice that went with the face, but who had the requirements of other flesh and blood children, to be provided for. This child was the sunshine of the lonely widow's life, yet she only in part filled the great mother's heart of her. Nature had made her to be the mother of a son as well as a daughter, then mockingly, it would seem, denied her.

The Dreamer

But in her dreams she worshipped the son she had never borne, and deep in her heart was stored, like unshed tears, the love she would have lavished upon him had her whole mission in life been fulfilled.

She had heard little of her brother David's son Edgar, but that little had always interested her. She was living away from Baltimore during his visit there just before he entered West Point, and so she did not meet him; but upon the death of her husband, soon afterward, she had returned to the home of her girlhood, and established herself in modest, but respectable quarters, to earn a livelihood for the little Virginia and herself by the use of her skillful needle.

It was soon afterward that with a concern which no one but herself had felt, she learned of the mystery surrounding the whereabouts of her nephew.

She yearned over the wanderer and longed to mother him, as, somehow, she knew he needed to be mothered. She kept near her a copy of his last little book of poems which she had read again and again. In the earlier ones she saw a loose handful of jewels in the rough, yet she recognized the sparkle which distinguishes the genuine from the false. In the later ones she perceived gems "of purest ray serene," polished and strung and ready to be passed on from generation to generation—priceless heir-looms.

She was a tall woman, and deep-bosomed, with large but clear-cut and strong features, and handsome, deepset gray eyes which habitually wore the expression of one who has loved much and sorrowed much. She had been called stately before her proud spirit had bowed itself in submission to the chastenings of grief—since when she had borne the seal of meekness. But there was a distinction about her that neither grief nor poverty could destroy. She was so unmistakably the gentle-woman. In the simple, but dainty white cap, with its floating strings, which modestly covered her dark waving hair, the plain black dress and prim collar fastened with its mourning pin, she made a reposeful picture of the old-fashioned conception of "a widow indeed."

Her hands were not her least striking feature. They were large, but perfectly modelled, and they were deft, capable, full of character and feeling. In their touch there was a wonderfully soothing quality. In winter they always possessed just the pleasantest degree of warmth; in summer just the most grateful degree of coolness. No one ever received a greeting from them without being impressed with the friendliness, the sympathy of their clasp.

As she bent her fine, deeply-lined face over them, and the work they held, while the little Virginia sat nursing a doll at her feet, she often stitched into the garments that they fashioned yearnings, thoughts, questionings of the youth—her brother's child—whose picture, as she had conceived him from descriptions she had heard, she carried in her heart. She knew too well the weakness that was his inheritance and she knew too, what perils were in waiting to ensnare the feet of untried youth—poor, homeless and without the restraining influences of friends and kindred—whatever their inheritance might be.

Sometimes she felt that the yearning was almost more than she could bear, and that she must arise and go forth and seek this straying sheep of the fold of Poe. But alas, she was but a woman, without money and without a clue upon which to begin to work save such as wild, improbable and contradictory rumors afforded. That was, after all, what she most needed—a clue. If she could only find a clue, poor as she was, she would follow it to the ends of the earth!

Upon a summer's day two years after Edgar's disappearance, and when she had almost given up hope, the clue came. It was placed in her hand by her cousin, and Edgar's, Neilson Poe, who had no faith in its value but passed it on to her as it had come to him— "for what it was worth," as he expressed it.

The Dreamer

It was a strange story that Mrs. Clemm's cousin Neilson told her, and which had been told him, he said, by an acquaintance of his from Richmond who had known Edgar Poe in his boyhood.

It seems that this Richmond man had during a visit to Baltimore gone to a brickyard to arrange for the shipment home of bricks for a new house he was building. As he sat in the office talking to the manager of the yard, a line of men bearing freshly molded bricks to the kiln passed the open window. There was something about the appearance of one of the laborers that struck the Richmond man as familiar and he turned quickly to the manager and asked the name of the man, pointing him out. The name given him was a strange one to him and he dismissed the matter from his thoughts and returned to his business talk.

Upon his way to his hotel, however, the appearance of the brick-carrier, and the impression that somewhere, he had seen him before, returned to his mind and it came upon him in a flash, first that the likeness was to Edgar Poe, and then the conviction that the man was none other than Poe himself, though emaciated and aged to a degree that, with his shabby dress and unshaven chin, made him scarcely recognizable. Though he had been but a casual acquaintance of Edgar's, he was deeply touched at seeing him so evidently in distress, and returned to the brickyard early the next morning for the purpose of speaking to him and of helping him back into the sphere in which he belonged and from which he had so long disappeared. But the man he sought was not there and no one knew where his lodgings were. He was a recent employe of the yard, they said, and so gloomy and unsociable that he had made no friends. He was capable of a great amount of work, which he performed faithfully, but kept to himself and had little to say to anybody.

Upon the day before he had looked ill and had stopped work before the day was over. He was evidently suffering from exhaustion, but had declared that he needed nothing, and after sitting down to rest upon a pile of bricks for a while, had gone off to his home—wherever that might be—as usual, alone.

This story Neilson Poe set down as highly sensational. He did not believe, he said with a laugh, that his cousin, when found, would be doing anything half so energetic or useful as carrying bricks—he would have more hope of him if he could believe it. The laborer's real, or fancied, likeness to Edgar was but a case of chance resemblance, that was all.

But that was not enough for Maria Clemm. She folded her sewing and laid it away with an air of finality which plainly said that she had found other and more pressing work to do. The sewing must wait a more convenient season.

Then she went out into the streets sweltering in the summer heat, and turned her face toward that obscure quarter of the town where human beings who could not afford to rest or to dine might at least secure a corner in which to "lodge" and the right, if not the appetite, to "eat," for an infinitesimal sum; for it was in this quarter that strange as it might, seem, her instinct told her her search must be made—in this quarter that Edgar Poe, the rich merchant's pampered foster-child, Edgar Poe, the poet, the scholar, the exquisite in dress, in taste and in manners, would be found.

When she did find him the mystery that had surrounded him was stripped of the last shred of its romance. In a room compared to which the little chamber back of the shop of Mrs. Fipps, the milliner, in which his mother had drawn her last breath, and in which Frances Allan had found and fallen in love with him, was luxurious, he lay upon a bed of straw thrown into a dark corner, tossing with fever and in his delirium, literally "babbling of green fields."

The kind-hearted, but ignorant and uncleanly slattern who sought with "lodgings to let" to keep the souls of herself and family in their bodies, gave him as much attention as the demands of a numerous brood of little slatterns and a drunken husband would permit, and sighed with real sorrow as she admitted that the "poor gentleman" was in a very bad way. It was her opinion he had seen better days she confided to the three other lodgers who were just then renting the three straw beds in the three other corners of the same dark, squalid and evil-smelling room. He was "so soft-spoken and elegant-like, if he *was* poor as a church mouse. Pity he had no folks nor nobody to keer nothin' about 'im."

It was not at once that Mrs. Clemm found him. She had sought him diligently in what would to-day be known as the slum districts of the city, descending the scale of respectability lower and lower until she thought she had reached the bottom, but without success.

Then, upon the fourth or fifth day of her search, late in the afternoon, when the little Virginia was watching anxiously from the sitting-room window for "Muddie's" return, a wagon stopped before her door and out of it and into the house was borne a stretcher upon which lay an apparently dying man—ghastly, unshaven, and muttering broken unintelligible sentences.

Keeping pace with the wagon as it crept along the street, might have been seen the stately, sad-eyed Widow Clemm. When the wagon stopped, she stopped, and directed the careful lifting of the stretcher from it. Then she turned and opened the door of her small house and led the way to her neat bed-chamber where, upon her own immaculate bed, the sick man was gently laid—henceforth, as long as need be, a cot in the sitting-room would be good enough for her.

The little Virginia, her soft eyes filled with wonder, had followed her mother upon tip-toe.

"Who is it, Muddie?" she questioned in an awed whisper.

The anxiety in the widow's face gave place to a look of exaltation which fairly transfigured her. Her deep eyes shone with the hoarded love for the son so long denied her. She gathered her little daughter to her breast and kissed her tenderly.

"It is your brother, darling," she gently said. "God has given me a son!"

Well she knew that he was not yet entirely her own—that she would have to wrestle fiercely with Death for his possession. But she had made up her mind that she would win the battle.

"Death *shall* not have him," she passionately told herself.

But the next moment, overwhelmed with a realization of human helplessness, she was upon her knees at his bedside, crying:

"Oh, God, do not let him die! I have but just found him! Spare him to me now, if but a little while!"

CHAPTER XIX.

For many days the sick man lay with eyes closed in uneasy sleep or open, but unseeing, and with body writhing and tongue loosed but incoherent, showing that these half-waking hours, as well as the sleeping ones, were "horror haunted."

Finally the most terrible of dreams visited him. The circumstances of his life had caused him from his infancy to dwell much upon the subject of death. He had oftentimes taken a gruesome pleasure in trying to imagine all the sensations of the grim passage into the "Valley of the Shadow"—even to the closing of the coffin-lid and the descent into the grave. Now, in his fever-dream, the dreadful details and sensations imagined in health came to him, but with tenfold vividness. At the point when in the blackness and

The Dreamer

suffocation of conscious burial horror had reached its extremest limit and the sufferer was upon the verge of real death from sheer terror, relief came. He seemed to feel himself freed from the closeness, the maddening fight for breath, of the coffin, and gently, surely, borne upward out of the abyss ... upward ... upward ... into air—light—life!

For a long while he lay quite still, too exhausted to move hand or foot—to raise his eyelids even; but content—more—happy, perfectly happy, in the glorious consciousness of being able just to lie still and breathe the sweet air of day.

Presently, as he began to feel rested, the great grey eyes opened. For the first time since the conqueror, Fever, had overthrown him and bound him to the uneasy bed of straw, they were clear as the sky after a storm—swept clean of every cob-web cloud; but their lucid depths were filled with surprise, for they opened upon a cool, light, homelike chamber. The walls around him were white, but were relieved here and there by restful prints in narrow black frames. The four-post bed upon which he lay was canopied and the large, bright windows were curtained with snowiest dimity, but the draperies of both were drawn and he could look out at the trees and the sky now roseate with the hues of evening. In a set of shelves that nearly reached the ceiling stood row on row of friendly looking books. Upon a high mahogany chest of drawers, with its polished brass trimmings and little swinging looking-glass, stood a white and gold porcelain vase filled with asters—purple, white and pink—while before it, in a deep arm-chair, a little girl of ten or eleven years, with a face like a Luca della Robbia chorister, or like one of the children of sunny Italy that served for old Luca's model, was curled up, stroking a large white cat which lay purring in her lap.

Upon the child the wondering eyes of the sick man lingered longest and to her they returned when their survey of the rest of the room was done. Suddenly, impelled by the steadiness of his gaze, she lifted her own dark, soft eyes and let them rest for a moment upon his. She started—then was up and across the floor in a flash, carrying the cat upon her shoulder.

"Muddie, Muddie," she cried from the door, "The new Buddie is awake!"

Then, still carrying her pet, she walked, to his bedside and gazed earnestly and unabashed into the "new Buddie's" face. Her eyes had the velvety softness of pansy petals and as they looked into the eyes of the sick man recalled to his clearing mind the expression of mixed love and questioning in the eyes of his spaniel, "Comrade," the faithful friend of his boyhood.

At length he spoke.

"Who is 'Muddie'?"

"She's my mother, and you are my new brother that has come to live with us always."

A radiant smile illumined the pale and haggard face. "Thank Heaven for that!" he said. "And who brought me up out of the grave?"

The child was spared the necessity of puzzling over this startling question. *Surely it was no other than she*, he thought—she who at this moment appeared at the open door—the tall figure of a woman or angel who in the next moment was kneeling beside him with a heaven of protecting love in her face. *She it was, no other!* Through all of his dreams he had been dimly conscious of her—saving him from death and despair. Now for the first time, in the light of life, and in his new consciousness he saw her plainly.

Edgar Poe's convalescence was slow but it was steady, and even in his weakness he felt a peace and happiness such as he had rarely tasted. This frugal but restful home in which he found himself, with the ministrations of "Muddie" and "Sissy," as he playfully called

The Dreamer

his aunt and the little cousin who had adopted him as her "Buddie," were to him, after his struggle with hunger, fever and death, like a safe harbor to a storm-tossed sailor.

The little Virginia claimed him as her own from the beginning. As long as he was weak enough to need to be waited upon her small feet and hands never wearied in his service but as he grew better, it was he who served her. There never were such stories as he could tell, such games as he could play, and he took her cat to his heart with gratifying promptness. When they walked out together the world seemed turned into a fairyland as with her hand held fast in his he told her wonderful secrets about the clouds, the trees, the flowers, the birds and even about the stones under her feet. It was fascinating to her too, to lie and listen to him read and talk with "Muddie." She was not wise enough to understand much that they said, but at night, when she had been tucked into bed, he would sit under the lamp and read aloud from one of the books in the shelves, or from the long strips of paper upon which he wrote and wrote; and though she did not understand the words, she delighted to listen, for his voice made the sweetest lullaby music.

With the return of health and strength, energy and the impulse for life's battle began to return to Edgar Poe, and with them a new incentive. He began to awaken to the fact that "Muddie" and "Sissy" were poor and that his presence in their home was making them poorer—that the struggle to support this modest establishment was a severe one, and that he must arise and add what he could to the earnings of the deft needle. The three little editions of his poems had brought him no money—he had begun to despair of their ever bringing him any. He had sometime since turned his attention to prose but the manuscripts of such stories as he had offered the publishers had come back to him with unflattering promptness. He began now, however, with fresh heart to write and to arrange a number of those that seemed to him to be his best, for a book, to which he proposed to give the title, "Tales of the Folio Club."

But the new tide of hope was soon at a low ebb. The editors and publishers would have none of his work.

When the repeated return to him of the stories, poems and essays he sent out had begun to make him lose faith in their merit and to question his own right to live since the world had no use for the only commodity he was capable of producing, "Muddie" came in one evening with an unusually bright, eager look in her eyes and a copy of *The Saturday Visitor* (a weekly paper published in Baltimore) in her hand.

"Here's your chance, Eddie," she said.

In big capitals upon the first page of the paper was an announcement to the effect that the *Visitor* would give two prizes—one of one hundred dollars for the best short story, and one of fifty dollars for the best poem submitted to it anonymously. Three well-known gentlemen of the city would act as judges, and the names of the successful contestants would be published upon the twelfth of October.

With trembling hands the discouraged young applicant for place as an author made a neat parcel of six of his "Tales of the Folio Club" and a recently written poem, "The Coliseum," and left them, that very night, at the door of the office of *The Saturday Visitor*.

How eagerly he and "Muddie" and "Sissy" awaited the fateful twelfth! The hours and the days dragged by on leaden wings. But the twelfth came at last. It found Edgar Poe at the office of the *Visitor* an hour before time for the paper to be issued, but at length he held the scarcely dry sheet in his hand and there, with his name at the end, was the story that had taken the prize—"The MS. Found in a Bottle."

More!—In the following wonderful—most wonderful words, it seemed to him—the judges declared their decision:

The Dreamer

"Among the prose articles were many of various and distinguished merit, but the singular force and beauty of those sent by the author of 'Tales of the Folio Club' leave us no room for hesitation in that department. We have awarded the premium to a tale entitled, 'The MS. Found in a Bottle.' It would hardly be doing justice to the writer of this collection to say that the tale we have chosen is the best of the six offered by him. We cannot refrain from saying that the author owes it to his own reputation as well as to the gratification of the community to publish the entire volume. These tales are eminently distinguished by a wild, vigorous and poetical imagination, a rich style, a fertile invention and varied, curious learning.

(Signed) "John P. Kennedy, J.H.B. Latrobe, James H. Miller, *Committee.*"

Here was the fulfilment of hope long deferred! Here was a brimming cup of joy which the widowed aunt and little cousin who had taken him in and made him a son and brother could share with him! It seemed almost too good to be true, yet there it was in plain black and white with the signatures of the three gentlemen whose opinion everyone would respect, at the end. What wealth that hundred dollars—the first earnings of his pen—seemed. What comforts for the modest home it would buy! This was no mere nod of recognition from the literary world, but a cordial hand-clasp, drawing him safely within that magic, but hitherto frowning portal.

He felt as if he were walking on air as he hurried home to tell "Muddie" and "Sissy" of his and their good fortune. And how proud "Muddie" was of her boy! How lovingly little "Sissy" hung on his neck and gave him kisses of congratulation—though but little realizing the significance of his success. And how he, in turn, beamed upon them! The grey eyes had lost all of their melancholy and seemed suddenly to have become wells of sunshine. In imagination he pictured these loved ones raised forever from want, for he told himself that he would not only sell for a goodly price all the rest of the "Tales of the Folio Club," but under the happy influence of his success he would write many more and far better stories still, to be promptly exchanged for gold.

Bright and early Monday morning he made ready (with "Muddie's" aid) for a round of visits to the members of the committee, to thank them for their kind words. His clothes, hat, boots and gloves were all somewhat worse for wear and his old coat hung loosely upon his shoulders—wasted as they still were by the effects of his long illness; but he whistled while he brushed and "Muddie" darned and carefully inked the worn seams, and finally it was with a feeling that he was quite presentable that he kissed his hands to his two good angels and ran gaily down the steps. Hope gave him a debonair mien that belied his shabby-genteel apparel.

A quarter of an hour later Mr. John Kennedy, prominent lawyer and the author of that pleasant book "Swallow Barn," then newly published and the talk of the town, answered a knock upon his office door with a quick, "Come in!"

At the same time he raised his eyes and confronted those of the young author whom he had been instrumental in raising from the "verge of despair."

The face of the older man was one of combined strength and amiability. Evidences of talent were there, but combined with common sense. There was benevolence in the expansive brow and kindliness and humor as well as character, about the lines of the nose and the wide, full-lipped mouth, and the eyes diffused a light which was not only bright but genial, and which robbed them of keenness as they rested upon the pathetic and at the same time distinguished figure before him. What the kindly eyes took in a glance was that the pale and haggard young stranger with the big brow and eyes and the clear-cut features, the military carriage and the shabby, but neat, frock coat buttoned to the throat where it met the fashionable black stock, and with the modest and exquisite manners, was a gentleman and a scholar—but poor, probably even hungry. They kindled with added

The Dreamer

interest when the visitor introduced himself as Edgar Poe—the author of "Tales of the Folio Club."

The strong, pleasant face and the cordial hand that grasped his own, then placed a chair for him, invited the young author's confidence—a confidence that always responded promptly to kindness—and he had soon poured into the attentive ear of John Kennedy not only profuse thanks for the encouraging words in the *Visitor* but his whole history. Deeply touched by the young man's refined and intellectual beauty—partially obscured as it was by the unmistakable marks of illness and want—by his frank, confiding manners, by the evidences in thought and expression of gifts of a high order, and by the moving story he told, Mr. Kennedy's heart went out to him and he sent him on his way to pay his respects to the other members of the committee, rejoicing in offers of friendship and hospitality and promises of aid in securing publishers for his writings.

Edgar Poe had been loved of women, he had been adored by small boys, he had received many material benefits from his foster father, he had been kindly treated by his teachers, but he was now for the first time taken by the hand spiritually as well as physically, by a *man*, a man of mental and moral force and of position in the world; a man, moreover, who with rare divination appreciated, out of his own strength, the weaknesses and the needs as well as the gifts and graces of his new acquaintance, and who took his dreams and ambitions seriously. The sane, wholesome companionship which The Dreamer found in him and at his hospitable fireside acted like a tonic upon his spirits and improvement in his health both of mind and body were rapid.

Though warning him against being over much elated at his success, and an expectation of growing suddenly either rich or famous, Mr. Kennedy was as good as his word in regard to helping him find a market for his work. A proud moment it was when the young author received a note from his patron inviting him to dine with Mr. Wilmer, the editor of *The Saturday Visitor* which had given him the prize, and some other gentlemen of the profession of journalism. But his pleasure was followed by quick mortification. *What should he wear?* Still holding the open note in his hand, he looked down ruefully at his clothes—his only ones. For all their brushing and darning they were unmistakably shabby—utterly unfit to grace a dinner-party. Nearly all of the hundred dollars which had seemed such a fortune had already been spent to pay bills incurred during his illness and to buy provisions for the bare little home which had sheltered him in his need and which had become so dear to his heart. No, he could not go to the dinner, but what excuse could he make that would seem to Mr. Kennedy sufficient to warrant him in not only declining his hospitality but putting from him the chance of meeting the editor of the *Visitor* under such auspices?

At length he decided that in this case absolute frankness was his only course.

"My dear Mr. Kennedy," he wrote,

"Your invitation to dinner has wounded me to the quick. I cannot come for reasons of the most humiliating nature—my personal appearance. You may imagine my mortification in making this disclosure to you, but it is necessary."

As he was about, in bitterness of soul, to add his signature a sudden thought caused him to pause, pen poised in air. A thought?—A temptation would perhaps be a better word. It bade him consider carefully before throwing away his chance. Who knew, who could tell, it questioned, how much might depend upon this meeting? His fortune might be made by it! Almost certainly it would lead to the sale of some more of his stories to the *Visitor*. Mr. Kennedy believed that it would have this result—for this purpose he had arranged it. After taking so much pains for his benefit he would undoubtedly be disappointed— seriously disappointed—if his plan should fail. Mr. Kennedy had been so kind, so generous—doubtless he would gladly advance him a sum sufficient to make himself presentable for the dinner—to be paid by the first check received as a result of the meeting. A very modest sum would do. He might manage it, he thought, with twenty dollars.

Finally, he drew his unfinished note before him again and added to what he had written,

"If you will be my friend so far as to loan me twenty dollars, I will be with you tomorrow—otherwise it will be impossible, and I must submit to my fate. Sincerely yours,

"E.A. Poe."

CHAPTER XX.

The dinner went off charmingly. In addition to several journalists, Mr. Latrobe and Mr. Miller who, with Mr. Kennedy, had formed the committee that awarded the prize to Edgar Poe, were there and the meeting between the young guest of honor and his patrons engendered a spirit of *bon-homie* that was palpable to all. Under its spell The Dreamer's spirits rose. Yet he was quiet, listening with deep attention to the conversation of his elders, but having little to say, until the repast was half over, when he responded to the evident desire of his host to draw him out. The conversation had turned upon a favorite theme of his—the power of words. He threw himself into it with zest, and with brilliant play of expression animating his splendid eyes and pale features, and the graceful, unrestrained gestures of one thoroughly at ease and entirely unconscious of self, he held the table spell-bound with a flow of sparkling talk in which his own exquisite choice of words delighted his hearers no less than the originality and beauty of his thought.

In the young editor of *The Saturday Visitor* he promptly found a second friend among men of letters. Mr. Wilmer, already prejudiced in his favor by the success of the "MS. Found in a Bottle," and its cordial reception by the public, and by Mr. Kennedy's warm words of recommendation, yielded at once to the witchery of the poetic eyes, the courtly manners and the charmed tongue, and not only befriended him by inviting and accepting his writings for publication, but gave him, as time went on, what proved to be a stimulant to good work as well as one of his greatest pleasures—the intimate companionship of a man of congenial tastes and near his own age.

The winter that followed was one of the happiest of The Dreamer's life—a lull in a tempest, a dream of peace within a dream of storm and stress.

He was soon able to return the twenty dollars to Mr. Kennedy. The newspapers kept him busy and while the returns were—so far—small, he was hopeful. He felt that he had made a beginning, and that the future promised well. His work was praised and he became something of a lion—the doors of many a proud Baltimore home opening graciously to his touch.

He cared little for general society, however. His greatest pleasure he found in his evenings with the Kennedys (for Mrs. Kennedy had taken him in as promptly as her husband) or in a canter far into the country on the saddle horse which Mr. Kennedy, noting his pallor and thinking that out-door exercise would be of benefit to him, kindly placed at his disposal, or in walks in the fields and lanes beyond the city with his new chum Wilmer. Many a fine afternoon saw these two cronies, often accompanied by the sprite, Virginia, with her airy movements and vivid beauty, rambling in the suburbs, and beyond, with heads close in intimate communion of thought and fancy.

The Dreamer

What he enjoyed most of all was the time spent at his desk, in the shelter of the new-found haven of rest, with the happy "Muddie" and "Sissy" nearby.

This little family circle was unique. There was an unmistakably oak-like element in the nature of the widow which was apparent to some degree even in her outward appearance, in the stateliness and dignity of her figure and carriage—an element of sturdiness and self-reliance which made it her pleasure to be clung to, looked up to, leaned upon. The character of her new-found son was, on the contrary, vine-like. He was constantly reaching out tendrils of craving for love, for appreciation, for understanding. More—for advice, for guidance. Such tendrils seeking a foot-hold, make a strong appeal to every womanly woman. She sees in them a call to her nobility of soul, to the mother that is a part of her spiritual nature—a call that gives her pleasant good-angel sensations, that soften her heart and flatter her self-esteem. To the Widow Clemm, with her self-reliance and her highly developed maternal instinct, the appeal was irresistible and between her and The Dreamer the ivy and oak relation was promptly established, while in the little Virginia he found a heartsease blossom to be loved and sheltered by both—the loveliest of heartsease blossoms whose beauty, whose purity and innocence and the stored sweets of whose nature were all for him.

The three lived, indeed, for each other only, in a dream-valley apart from and invisible to, the rest of the world, for their dreams of which it was constructed made it theirs and theirs alone. Their dreams piled beautiful mountains around the valley through which peace flowed as a gentle river, while love and contentment and innocent pleasures were as flowers besprinkling the grass and speaking to their hearts of the love and the glory of God, and the fancies with which they beguiled the time were as tall, fantastic trees, moved by soft zephyrs. And because of the bright flowers ever springing in the green turf that carpeted the valley, they named it the *Valley of the Many-Colored Grass*. And to the three the dream-valley, with its peace and its beauty and its sweet seclusion, was the real world, while all the wilderness outside of it, where other men dwelt was the unreal.

One happy effect of these peaceful days upon The Dreamer was that there was in them no temptation to excess—no restless craving for excitement. The Bohemian—the Edgar Goodfellow—side of him found, it is true, an outlet, but a harmless one. He found it in the genial atmosphere of the Widow Meagher's modest eating-house where he and his new crony, Wilmer, passed many a jolly hour. The widow, an elderly, portly dame, with a kind Irish heart and keen Irish wit, had the power of diffusing a wonderful cheerfulness around her. Her shop was clean, if plain, her oysters were savory, if cheap. Like all women, she petted Edgar Poe, and hearing from Wilmer that he was a poet, she at once gave him the name by which the West Point boys had called him, and to all of the frequenters of her shop he was known as "the Bard."

Her shop had not only an oyster counter, but a bar and a room for cards and smoking but these had little attraction for Poe at this period of his career—much to the widow's dissatisfaction, for she wished "the Bard" to be merry, and did not like to see him neglect what she honestly and unblushingly believed to be the really good things of life. But though to her pressing invitations, "Bard take a hand," "Bard take a nip," he was generally deaf, he was more accomodating when, after getting off an unusually clever bit of pleasantry (putting her customers into an uproar of laughter) she would turn to him with, "Bard put it in poethry." And put it "in poethry" he did—to the increased hilarity of the crowd.

The month of February brought an interruption to the smooth and pleasant course of The Dreamer's life. A long time had passed since he had heard anything of his friends

The Dreamer

down in Virginia, and it was therefore with quick interest that he broke the seal of a letter bearing the Richmond post-mark and addressed to him in the unforgotten hand of his early admirer, Rob Sully. Dear old Rob, the sight of the familiar hand-writing alone warmed The Dreamer's heart and brought the soft, melting expression to his eyes!

The object of the letter was to tell him that Mr. Allan was extremely ill—dying, some thought, though the end might not be immediate. Rob was taking it upon himself to write because he felt that Eddie ought to know. Mr. Allan had lately been heard to speak kindly of Eddie, he had been told, and it had occurred to him that Eddie might like to come on and have a word of forgiveness from him before he died.

As "Eddie" read, the pleasure the first sight of the letter had given him turned to sudden, sharp pain. Mr. Allan and—*death*! He had never thought of associating the two. Under the influence of the shock his heart became all tenderness and regret.

He hurriedly packed his carpet-bag, kissed Mrs. Clemm and Virginia goodbye, and set out post-haste for Richmond and the homestead on Main and Fifth Streets.

He did not stop to lift the brass knocker this time. The forlorn details of his last visit, his lack of right to cross that threshold uninvited—what mattered such considerations now? They were, indeed, forgotten. Everything was forgotten—everything save that the man who had stood in the position of father to him was dying—dying without a word of pardon to him, the most wayward (he felt at that moment of severe contrition)—*the most wayward* of prodigal sons. Everything was forgotten save that he was having a race with death—a race for a father's blessing!

He flung wide the massive front door and hastened through the spacious hall, up the stair and into the room where the ill man sat in an arm-chair. On the threshold he paused for a moment. Mr. Allan saw and recognized him, and at once the misunderstanding of the actions of his adopted son for which he seemed to have a gift, asserted itself, construing the visit as an unpardonable liberty. The only motive Mr. Allan could imagine which could have prompted Edgar Poe to force himself, as it seemed to him, into his presence at this time was a mercenary one, and burning with indignation, his eyes gleaming with something like their old fire, he half raised himself from the chair.

"How dare you?" he screamed in the grating tones of angry old age. Then, grasping the cane at his side in trembling fingers and raising it with threatening gesture, he ordered his visitor to leave the room at once.

Edgar Poe stood aghast for a moment, then fled down the stair and out of the door and turning his back for the last time upon the house whose young master he had been, with the word "Nevermore" ringing like a knell in his ears, made his way again to the abode of love and peace in Baltimore, which held his whole heart and which had become his home.

A few weeks later Mr. Allan died, leaving the whole of his fortune to his second wife and her children.

It now became more important than ever for Edgar Poe to earn a living. In spite of the fact that Mr. Allan was known to have lost all regard for him, his friends had always believed that he would be remembered in the will. They believed that John Allan's rigid, sometimes even strained, idea of justice would cause him to provide for the boy for whom he had voluntarily, albeit against his own judgment, made himself responsible. The fact that the boy had turned out to be, in Mr. Allan's opinion, "trifling," that he refused to engage in any "useful" work and that at five and twenty years of age he had not established himself in any "paying business" would, those who knew Mr. Allan best believed, be with him but another reason for ensuring against want his first wife's spoiled

The Dreamer

darling who was evidently incapable of taking care of himself and therefore (so they believed he would argue) so much the more his care.

Possibly The Dreamer may have taken this view himself. However that may be, the opening of the will silenced all conjecture, and as has been said, made the need of his making his work produce money more pressing than ever. His friend Wilmer did his best for him—publishing his stories in *The Saturday Visitor* from time to time and paying him as well as he was able. But Wilmer and his paper were poor themselves. *The Visitor* was only a small weekly, with a modest subscription list. It had little to pay, however good the "copy" and that little and Mother Clemm's earnings put together barely kept the wolf from the door.

When the frequent and welcome summons to the bountiful board of the Kennedys came the young poet blushed for shame in the pleasure he could not help feeling in anticipation of the chance to satisfy his chastened appetite, and he often found himself fearing that the hunger with which he ate the good things which these kind friends placed upon his plate would betray the necessary frugality of the dear "Muddie's" house-keeping, which was one of the sacred secrets of the sweet home. Sometimes his pride would make him go so far as to decline delicious morsels in the hope of correcting such an impression, if it should exist.

He racked his brain to find a means of making his work bring him more money. Upon Mr. Kennedy's advice, he sent his "Tales of the Folio Club" to the Philadelphia publishing house of "Carey and Lea." After several weeks of anxious waiting he received a letter accepting the collection for publication but frankly admitting that his receiving any profit from the sale of the book was an exceedingly doubtful matter. They suggested, however, that they be permitted to sell some of the tales to publishers of the then popular "annuals," reserving the right to reprint them in the book. To this the author gladly consented and received with a joy that was pathetic the sum of fifteen dollars from "The Souvenir," which had purchased one of the tales at a dollar a printed page.

He and Wilmer put their heads together in dreams of literary work by which a man could live. One of these dreams took form in the prospectus of a purely literary journal of the highest class which was to be in its criticisms and editorial opinions "fearless, independent and sternly just."

But the scheme required capital and never got beyond the glowing prospectus.

In spite of the small sums that came to him as veritable God-sends from the sale of his stories and from odd jobs on the *Visitor* and other journals, Edgar Poe was poor—miserably poor. And just as he had begun to flatter himself that he did not mind, that he would bear it with the nonchalance of the true philosopher he believed he had become, it assumed the shape of horror unspeakable to him. Not for himself, if there were only himself to think of, he felt assured, he could laugh poverty—want even—to scorn; but that his little Virginia should feel the pinch was damnable!

Two years had made marked changes in Virginia. She was losing the formless plumpness of childhood and growing rapidly into a slight and graceful maiden—a "rare and radiant maiden," with the tender light of womanhood beginning to dawn in her velvet eyes and to sweeten the curves of her lips. A maiden lovelier by far than the child had been but with the same divine purity and innocence that had always been hers—that were his, for her beauty, her purity and innocence and the stored sweets of her nature were still for him alone and for him alone too, was her sweet companionship—her comradeship—of which he never wearied.

Under his guidance her mind had unfolded like a flower. She was beginning to speak fluently in French and in Italian. How he loved the musical southern accents on her tongue! And she was developing an exquisite singing voice. Her voice was her crowning

The Dreamer

grace—her voice was his delight of delights! As he gazed into the shadows that lay under her long black lashes and listened to her voice, with its hint of hidden springs of passion, his pulses stirred at the thought that this lovely flower of dawning womanhood was his little Virginia, and his own heart ached to think that any desire of hers should ever be denied.

In his desperation he thought of teaching and applied for a position in a school, but without success.

But relief was at hand.

While the Dreamer and his friend the editor of *The Saturday Visitor* had been building literary air-castles in Baltimore, a journal destined to take something approaching such a stand as their ideal was actually founded, in Richmond, under the title of *The Southern Literary Messenger*. Its owner and publisher, Mr. Thomas W. White, was no dreamer, but a practical printer and an enterprising man of business. Early in this year—the year 1835—Mr. White wrote to Mr. Kennedy, requesting a contribution from his pen for the new magazine, and, as was to be expected, Mr. Kennedy, with his wonted thoughtfulness of his literary protegé, wrote back commending to Mr. White's notice the work of "a remarkable young man by the name of Edgar Poe."

At Mr. Kennedy's suggestion Edgar bundled off some of the "Tales of the Folio Club" for Mr. White's inspection, with the result that in the March number of the *Messenger* the weird story "Berenice," appeared. It and its author became at once the talk of the hour, and when the history of "The Adventures of Hans Phaal" came out in the June number it found the reading public ready and waiting to fall upon and devour it.

Other stories and articles followed in quick succession and the pungent critiques and reviews of the new pen were looked for and read with as great interest as the tales.

In a glow over the prosperity which the popularity of the new writer was bringing his magazine, Mr. White wrote to him offering him the position of assistant editor, with a salary of five hundred and twenty dollars a year, to begin with. Of course the offer was to be accepted! The salary, small as it was, seemed to The Dreamer in comparison to the diminutive and irregular sums he had been accustomed to receive, almost like wealth. But its acceptance would mean, for the present, anyhow, separation—a break in the small home circle where had been, with all of its deprivations, so much of joy—a dissolving of the magical Valley of the Many-Colored Grass. Not for a moment, he vowed to Mother Clemm and Virginia, was this separation to be looked upon as permanent. Just so soon as he should be able to provide a home for them in Richmond he would have them with him again, and there they would reconstruct their dream-valley. But for the present—.

The present, in spite of the new prosperity, was unbearable!

In vain the Mother with the patience born of her superior years and experience, assured them that time had wings, and that the days of absence would be quickly past. To the youthful poet and the little maid who lived with no other thought than to love and be loved by him a month—a week—a day apart, seemed an eternity.

In the midst of their woe at the prospect a miracle happened—a miracle and a discovery.

It fell upon a serene summer's afternoon when the two children—they were both that at heart—wandered along a sweet, shady lane leading from the outskirts of town into the country. It was to be their last walk together for who knew, who could tell how long? The poet's great grey eyes wore their deepest melancholy and the little maid's soft brown ones too, were full of trouble, for had not their love turned to pain? They spoke little, for the love and the pain were alike too deep for words, but the heart of each was filled with broodings and musings upon the love it bore the other and upon the agony of parting.

The Dreamer

How could he leave her? the poet asked himself. His cherished comrade whose beauty, whose purity and innocence, the stored sweets of whose nature were for him alone? Into his life of loneliness, of lovelessness, of despair—a life from which everyone who had really cared for him had been snatched by untimely death and shut away from him forever in an early grave—a life where there had been not only sorrow, but bitterness—where there had been pain and want and homelessness and desolate wanderings and longings for the unattainable—where there had been misunderstanding and distrust and temptation and defeat—into such a life this wee bit of maidenhood—this true heartsease—had crept and blossomed, filling heart and life with beauty and hope and love—with blessed healing.

How could he leave her? To others she seemed wrapped in timid reserve. He only had the key to the fair realm of her unfolding mind. How could he bear to leave her for even a little while? How barren his life would be without her! How shorn of all beauty and grace!

And what would her life be without him, to whom had been offered up all her beauty and the stored sweets of her nature? Who would guard her from other eyes, that as her beauty and charm came to their full bloom might look covetously upon her?

For the first time (and the bare suggestion seemed profanation) it occured to him that a day might come when, as this slip of maidenhood walked forth in her surpassing beauty and her precious innocence and purity the eyes of a man might make note of her loveliness, her altogether desirableness—might rest upon her with hopes of possession—and he not there to kill him upon the spot. What if in his absence another's hand should be stretched to pluck his heartsease blossom—that left unguarded, unprotected by him, another should snatch it, in its beauty, its purity and innocence, to his bosom?

The thought was hell!

Faint and trembling, he gazed down upon her as they strolled along, compelling her soft eyes to meet his anguished ones. His face was white and strained with his misery. She was pale and trembling, too, and there was dew on the sweeping lashes, and as she lifted them and looked into his face she trembled more. He looked upon her, tenderly marvelling to see in her at once the loveliest of children and of women—a woman with her first grief!

There was heart-break in his voice, for himself and for her, as he murmured (brokenly) words of love and of comfort in her ear, and in her voice as she, brokenly, answered him.

The sun was setting—a pageant in which they both were wont to take exquisite delight—but they could not look at the glowing heavens for the heaven of love and of beautiful sorrow that each found in the eyes of the other.

Suddenly, they knew!

The knowledge burst upon them like an illumining flood. How or whence it came they could not tell, nor did they question—but they knew that the love they bore each other was no brother and sister love, but that what time they had been calling each other "Buddie," and "Sissy," there had been growing—growing in their hearts the red, red rose of romance—the love betwixt man and maid of which poets tell—knew that in that sweet, that sad, that wondrous eventide the rose had burst into glorious flower.

They trembled in the presence of this sweetest miracle. The beauty and solemnity of it well nigh deprived them of the power of speech. A divine silence fell upon them and they slowly, softly took their way homeward through the gathering dusk, hand in hand—but with few words—to tell the Mother.

To the widow their disclosure came as a shock. At first she thought the silly pair must be joking—then that they were mad. Finally she realized their earnestness and their happiness and saw that the situation was serious and must be dealt with with the utmost tact. Still, she could hardly believe what she saw and heard. Was it possible that the demure girl talking to her so seriously of love and marriage was her little Virginia—her baby? And that these two should have thought of such a thing! Cousins!—Brother and sister, almost!—And with such disparity in ages—thirteen and six-and-twenty!

She had lived long enough, however, to know that love is governed by no rules or regulations and besides, she had kept through all the changes and chances of her checkered life, a belief in true love as fresh as a girl's. This was too sacred a thing to be carelessly handled—only, it was not what she would have chosen.... Yet—was it not?

A new thought came to her—a revelation—inspiration—what you will, and sunk her in deep revery.

Why was this not what she would have chosen? Why not a union between her children—her all? Her own days were fast running out. She could not live and make a home for them always—then, what would become of them? She would die happy, when her time came, if she could see them in their own home, bound by the most sacred, the most indissoluble of ties—bound together until death should part them!

She fell asleep with a heart full of thankfulness to God for his mercies.

A quite different view of the matter was taken by other members of the Poe connection in Baltimore—particularly the men, who positively refused to regard the love affair as anything more than sentimental nonsense—"moonshine"—they called it, which would be as fleeting as it was foolish. Their cousin, Judge Neilson Poe, who had made a pet of Virginia, was especially active in his opposition and brought every argument he could think of to bear upon the young lovers and upon Mrs. Clemm in his endeavor to induce them to break the engagement; but he only succeeded in sending Virginia flying with frightened face to "Buddie's" arms, vowing (as, much to Cousin Neilson's disgust, she hung upon his neck) that she would never give him up, while "Buddie," holding her close, assured her, in the story-book language that they both loved, that "all the king's horses and all the king's men" would not be strong enough to take her from him.

CHAPTER XXI.

Midsummer found Edgar Poe in Richmond and regularly at work upon his new duties in the office of *The Southern Literary Messenger*. He felt that if he had not actually reached the end of the rainbow, it was at least in sight and it rested upon the place of all others most gratifying to him—the dear city of his boyhood whose esteem he so ardently desired. Most soothing to his pride, he found it, after his several ignominious retreats, to return in triumph, a successful author, called to a place of acknowledged distinction, for all its meagre income.

The playmates of his youth—now substantial citizens of the little capital—called promptly upon him at his boarding-house. They were glad to have him back and they showed it; glad of his success and glad and proud to find their early faith in his powers justified, their early astuteness proven.

All Richmond, indeed, received him with open arms and if there were some few persons who could not forget his wild-oats at the University and his seeming ingratitude to Mr. Allan, who they declared had been the kindest and most indulgent of fathers to him, and who did not invite him to their homes or accept invitations to parties given in his honor, they were the losers—he had friends and to spare.

Yet he was not happy. The ivy had been torn from the oak and there was no sweet heartsease blossom to make glad his road—to made daily—hourly—offerings to him and

The Dreamer

him alone of the beauty, physical and spiritual, that his soul worshipped—of beauty and of unquestioning love and sympathy and approbation. In other words, The Dreamer was sick, miserably sick, with the disease of longing; longing for the modest home and the invigorating presence of the Mother; longing that was exquisite pain for the sight, the sound, the touch, the daily companionship of the child who without losing one whit of the purity, the innocence, the charm of childhood, had so suddenly, so sweetly become a woman—a woman embodying all of his dreams—a woman who lived with no other thought than to love and be loved by him.

Life, no matter what else it might give, life without the soft glance of her eye, the sweet sound of her voice, the pure touch of her hand within his hand, her lips upon his lips, was become an empty, aching void.

After two years of the sheltered fireside in Baltimore whose seclusion had made the dream of the Valley of the Many-Colored Grass possible, the boarding-house with its hideous clatter, its gossip and its commonplaceness was the merest make-shift of a home. It was stifling. How was a dreamer to breathe in a boarding-house? He was even homesick for the purr and the comfortable airs of the old white cat!

Whenever he could he turned his back upon the boarding-house and tried to forget it, but the clatter and the gossip seemed to follow him, their din lingering in his ears as he paced the streets in a fever of disgust and longing. For the first time since Edgar Poe had opened his eyes upon the tasteful homelikeness of the widow Clemm's chamber and the tender, dark eyes of Virginia searching his face with soft wonder, the old restlessness and dissatisfaction with life and the whole scheme of things were upon him—the blue devils which he believed had been exorcised forever had him in their clutches. Whither should he fly from their harrassments? By what road should he escape?

At the answer—the only answer vouchsafed him—he stood aghast.

"No, no!" he cried within him, "Not that—not that!" Seeking to deafen his ears to a voice that at once charmed and terrified him, for it was the voice of a demon which possessed the allurements of an angel—a demon he reckoned he had long ago fast bound in chains from which it would never have the strength to arise. It was the voice that dwelt in the cup—the single cup—so innocent seeming, so really innocent for many, yet so ruinous for him; for, with all its promises of cheer and comfort it led—and he knew it—to disaster.

Bitterly he fought to drown the sounds of the voice, but the more he deafened his ears the more insistent, the clearer, the more alluring its tones became.

And it followed him everywhere. At every board where he was a guest the brimming cup stood beside his plate, at every turn of the street he was buttonholed by some friend old or new, with the invitation to join him in the "cup of kindness." At every evening party he found himself surrounded by bevies of charming young Hebes, who, as innocent as angels of any intention of doing him a wrong, implored him to propose them a toast.

How could he refuse them? Especially when acquiescence meant escape from this horrible, horrible soul-sickness, this weight that was bearing his spirits down—crushing them.

Therein lay the tempter's power. Not in appetite—he was no swine to swill for love of the draught. When he did yield he drained the cup scarce tasting its contents. But ah, the freedom from the sickness that tortured him, the weight that oppressed him! And ah, the exhilaration, physical and mental, the delightful exhilaration which put melancholy to flight, loosed his tongue and started the machinery of his brain—which robbed the past of regret and made the present and the future rosy!

It was in the promise of this exhilaration that the seductiveness of the dreaded tones lay.

The Dreamer

Even his kindly old physician, diagnosing the pallor of his cheeks and melancholy in his eyes as "a touch of malaria," added a note of insistence to the voice, as he prescribed that panacea of the day, "a mint julep before breakfast."

Yet he still sternly and stoutly turned a deaf ear to the voice of the charmer, while dejection drew him deeper and deeper into its depths until one day he found he could not write. His pen seemed suddenly to have lost its power. He sat at his desk in the office of the *Messenger* with paper before him, with pens and ink at hand, but his brain refused to produce an idea, and for such vague half-thoughts as came to him, he could find no words to give expression.

He was seized upon by terror.

Had his gift of the gods deserted him? Better death than life without his gift! Without it the very ground under his feet seemed uncertain and unsafe!

Then he fell. Driven to the wall, as it seemed to him, he took the only road he saw that led, or seemed to lead, to deliverance. He yielded his will to the voice of the tempter, he tasted the freedom, the exhilaration, the wild joy that his imagination had pictured—drank deep of it!

And then he paid the price he had known all along he would have to pay, though in the hour of his severest temptation the knowledge had not had power to make him strong. Neither, in that hour, had he been able to foresee how hard the price would be. That shadowy, yet very real other self, his avenging conscience, in whose approval he had so long happily rested, arose in its wrath and rebuked him as he had never been rebuked before. It scourged him. It held up before him his bright prospects, his lately acquired and enviable social position, assuring him as it held them up, of their insecurity. It pointed with warning finger to the end of the rainbow and the road leading to it seemed to have suddenly grown ten times longer and rougher than before.

Finally it held up the images of his two good angels, "Muddie," with her heart of oak, and her tender, sorrow-stricken face, and Virginia, whose soft eyes were a heaven of trustful love—whose beauty, whose purity and innocence, the stored sweets of whose nature were for him alone, and to whom he was as faultless, as supreme as the sun in heaven.

It was too much. The dejection into which his "blue devils" had cast him was as nothing to the remorse that overwhelmed him now. On his knees before Heaven he confessed that his last estate was worse than his first, and cried aloud for forgiveness for the past and strength for the future.

In this mood he sat down to write to Mr. Kennedy (who had been absent upon a summer vacation when he left Baltimore) a letter of acknowledgment for his benefactions—for whatever The Dreamer was, it is very certain that he was *not* ungrateful.

The date he placed at the top of his page was "September 11, 1835."

"I received a letter yesterday," he wrote, "which tells me you are back in town. I hasten therefore, to write you and express by letter what I have always found it impossible to express orally—my deep sense of gratitude for your frequent and effectual assistance and kindness.

"Through your influence Mr. White has been induced to employ me in assisting him with the editorial duties of his Magazine—at a salary of $520 per annum."

He had not intended to mention his troubles to Mr. Kennedy, but with each word he wrote the impulse to unburden himself which he always felt when talking to this kind, sympathetic man, grew stronger and he found his pen almost automatically taking an unexpected turn. It was out of the abundance of his anguished heart that he added:

The Dreamer

"The situation is agreeable to me for many reasons—but alas! it appears that nothing can now give me pleasure—or the slightest gratification. Excuse me, my Dear Sir, if in this letter you find much incoherency. My feelings at this moment are pitiable indeed. You will believe me when I say that I am still miserable in spite of the great improvement in my circumstances; for a man who is writing for effect does not write thus. My heart is open before you—if it be worth reading, read it. I am wretched and know not why. Console me—for you can. Convince me that it is worth one's while to live. Persuade me to do what is right. You will not fail to see that I am suffering from a depression of spirits which will ruin me if it be long continued. Write me then, and quickly. Urge me to do what is right. Your words will have more weight with me than the words of others—for you were my friend when no one else was."

Some men of more goodness than wisdom might have read this letter with impatience—perhaps disgust, and tossed it into the waste basket, not deeming it worth an answer, or pigeon-holed it to be answered in a more convenient season—which would probably never have arrived. It is easy to imagine the contempt with which John Allan would have perused it. Not so John Kennedy. Busy lawyer and successful man of letters and of the world though he was, he had gone out of his way to stretch a hand to the gifted starveling he had discovered struggling for a foothold on the bottommost rung of the ladder of literary fame, and had not only helped him up the ladder but had drawn him, in his weakness and his strength, into the circle of his friendship, and now he had no idea of letting him go. Mr. Kennedy was a great lawyer with a great tenderness for human nature, born of a great knowledge of it. He did not expect young men—even talented ones—to be faultless or to be fountains of sound sense, or even always to be strong of will. When he received Edgar Poe's wail he had just returned to his office after a long vacation and found himself over head and ears in work; but he responded at once. If it had seemed to him a foolish letter he did not say so. If it had shocked or disappointed him, he did not say so. He wrote in the kindly tolerant and understanding tone he always took with his protegé a letter wholesome and bracing as a breath from the salt sea.

"My dear Poe," he began, in his simple familiar way, "I am sorry to see you in such plight as your letter shows you in. It is strange that just at the time when everybody is praising you and when Fortune has begun to smile upon your hitherto wretched circumstances you should be invaded by these villainous blue devils. It belongs however, to your age and temper to be thus buffeted—but be assured it only wants a little resolution to master the adversary forever. Rise early, live generously, and make cheerful acquaintances and I have no doubt you will send these misgivings of the heart all to the Devil. You will doubtless do well henceforth in literature and add to your comforts as well as your reputation which it gives me great pleasure to tell you is everywhere rising in popular esteem."

This and more he wrote, in kind, encouraging vein, and closed his letter with a friendly invitation:

"Write to me frequently, and believe me very truly

"Yours,

"John P. Kennedy."

The same post that brought Mr. Kennedy's letter brought The Dreamer other mail from Baltimore—brought him letters from both Virginia and Mother Clemm.

They had an especial reason for writing, each said. They had news for him—news which was most disturbing to them and they feared it would be to him.

Disturbing indeed, was the news the letters brought. It drove him into a rage and aroused him into action which made him forget all of his late troubles.

The Dreamer

Their Cousin Neilson and his wife, they wrote him, had not ceased to bring every argument they could think of to bear upon Virginia to induce her to break her engagement and had finally proposed that they should take her into their home, treat her as an own daughter or young sister, providing for her all things needful and desirable for a young girl of her station, until her eighteenth birthday, after which if she and Edgar had not changed their minds, they could be married.

He dashed off and posted answers to the letters at once, making violent protest against a scheme that seemed to him positively iniquitous and pleading with "Muddie" to keep Virginia for him. But writing was not enough. He determined to answer in person.

A day or two later Virginia and her mother were in the act of discussing his letters, which had just come, when the sitting-room door quietly opened, and there stood the man who was all the world to them!

Virginia, with a scream of delight, was in his arms in a flash and began telling him, breathlessly, what a fright she had been in for fear "Cousin Neilson" would take her away and she would never see him again.

With a rising tide of tenderness for her and rage against their cousin, he kissed the trouble from her eyes.

"Don't be afraid, sweetheart," he murmured, "He shall never take you from me. I have come back to marry you!"

"To marry her?" exclaimed Mrs. Clemm. "At once, do you mean?"

"At once! Today or tomorrow—for I must be getting back to Richmond as soon as possible. Don't you see, Muddie, that this is just a plot of Neilson's to separate us? He never cared for me—he loves Virginia and is determined I shall not have her. But we'll outwit him! We'll be married at once. We'll have to keep it secret at first—until I am able to provide a home for my little wife and our dear mother in Richmond, but I will go away with peace of mind and leave her in peace of mind, for once she is mine only death can come between us. We will keep it secret dear," he added, with his lips on the dusky hair of the little maid who was still held fast in his arms. "We will keep it secret, but if Neilson Poe becomes troublesome you will only have to show him your marriage certificate."

Virginia joyfully agreed to this plan, while the widow, finding opposition useless, finally consented too—and the impetuous lover was off post-haste for a license.

It was a unique little wedding which took place next day in Christ Church, when a beautiful, dreamy looking youth, with intellectual brow and classic profile and a beautiful, dreamy-looking maid, half his age, plighted their troth. The only attendant was Mother Clemm in her habitual plain black dress and widow's cap, with floating cap-strings, sheer and snowy white. No music, no flowers, no witnesses even, save the widowed mother and the aged sexton who was bound over to strict secrecy.

But in the dim, still, empty church the beautiful words of the old, old rite seemed to this strange pair of lovers to take on new solemnity as they fell from the lips of the white robed priest and sank deep into their young hearts, filling and thrilling them with fresh hope and faith and love and high resolve.

CHAPTER XXII.

In the following spring Edgar Poe and Virginia Clemm were, strange as it may seem, principals in another wedding. The months intervening between the two ceremonies had been teeming with interest to them both—filled with work and with happiness just short

The Dreamer

of that perfect satisfaction—that completeness—that unattainable which it is part of being a mortal with an immortal mind and soul to be continually striving after, and missing, and will be until the half-light of this world is merged into the light ineffable of the one to come.

The Dreamer had returned from his brief visit to Baltimore a new man. The blue devils were gone. The heart and mind which they had made their dwelling-place were swept clean of every vestige of them and were filled to overflowing with a sweet and rare presence—the presence of her who lived with no other thought than to love and be loved by him; for he felt that her spirit was with him at every moment of the day, though her fair body was other whither. The consciousness of the secret he carried in his heart flooded his nature with sunshine. Because of it he carried his head more proudly—wore a new dignity which his friends attributed entirely to the success of his work upon the magazine. He was filled with peace and good will to all the world. He was happy and wanted everybody else to be happy—it was apparent in himself and in his work. In his dreamy moods his fancy spread a broader, a stronger wing, and soared with new daring to heights unexplored before. When Edgar Goodfellow was in the ascendency he threw himself with unwonted zest into the pleasures that were "like poppies spread" in the way of the successful author and editor—the literary lion of the town.

He had always been an enthusiastic and graceful dancer and now nothing else seemed to give him so natural a vent for the happiness that was beating in his veins. His feet seemed like his pen, to be inspired. He felt that he could dance till Doomsday and all the prettiest, most bewitching girls let him see how pleased they were to have him for a partner. In the brief, glowing rests between the dances he rewarded them with charming talk, and verses in praise of their loveliness which seemed to fall without the slightest effort from his tongue into their pretty, delighted ears or from his pencil into their albums.

There was at least one fair damsel—a slight, willowy creature with violet eyes and flaxen ringlets, who treasured the graceful lines he dedicated to her with a feeling warmer than friendship. She was pretty Eliza White, the daughter of his employer, the owner of the *Southern Literary Messenger*. She was herself a lover of poetry and romance, and a dreamer of dreams, all of which had erelong merged into one sweet dream so secret, so sacred that she scarce dared own it to her own inner self, and its central figure was her father's handsome assistant editor, who rested in blissful ignorance of the havoc he was making in her maiden heart, engrossed as he was in his own secret—his own romance.

New energy, new zest, new life seemed to have entered his blood. He had endless capacity for work as well as for pleasure and could write all day and dance half the night and then lie awake star-gazing the other half and rise ready and eager for the day's work in the morning. Such a tonic—such a stimulant did his love for his faraway bride and his consciousness of her love for him prove.

He was happy—very, very happy, but he desired to be happier still. The simple, beautiful words of the old, old rite uttered in the dim, empty church had woven an invisible bond between him and the maiden whom he loved to call in his heart his wife though the time when he could claim her before the world was not yet.

The miracle that this bond wrought in him was a revelation to him. Was the priest a wizard? Did the words of the ancient rite possess any intrinsic power of enchantment undreamed of by the uninitiated?

He had not believed it possible for mortal to love more wholly—more madly than he had loved the little Virginia before that sacred ceremony, but after it he knew there were heights of love of which he had not hitherto had a glimpse. Just the right to say to his heart "She is my own—my wife—" made her tenfold more precious than she had ever

The Dreamer

been before, but it also made the separation tenfold harder to bear—made it beyond his power to bear!

The Valley of the Many-Colored Grass had been dissolved—the spell that had brought it into being broken, by the separation, and he longed with a longing that was as hunger and thirst to reconstruct this magical world in which he and his Virginia dwelt apart with her who was mother to them both, in Richmond. And so, poor as he was, he arranged to bring Virginia and Mother Clemm to Richmond and establish them in a boarding house where he could see them often and wait with better grace the still happier day of making his marriage public.

The day came more speedily than they had let themselves hope. The popularity of the *Messenger* and the fame of its assistant editor had grown with leaps and bounds. The new year brought the welcome gift of promotion to full editorship, with an increase of salary. With the opening spring began plans for the divulging of the great secret—for public acknowledgment of the marriage. But how was it to be done?—That was the question! Edgar Poe knew too well the disapproval with which the world regarded secret marriages—with which he himself regarded them, ordinarily. His sense of refinement of fitness, of the sacredness of the marriage tie, revolted from the very idea.

In what fashion then, could he and his little bride proclaim their secret that would not do violence to their own taste or set a buzz of gossip going? That the horrid lips of gossip should so much as breathe the name of his Virginia—that Mrs. Grundy should dare shrug her decorous shoulders, if ever so slightly, at mention of that sacred name—. The bare suggestion was intolerable!

At last a solution offered itself to his mind. Not for an instant did he regret the sacred ceremony in Christ Church, Baltimore. Not for worlds would he have cut short for one moment of time the duration of the beautiful spiritual marriage when he had been able to say to himself: "She whose presence fills my heart and my life—whose spirit I can feel near me at my work, in my hours of recreation and in my dreams, is my wife." But of this exquisite, this inexpressibly dear union the world was in utter ignorance. It was known only to the Mother, the priest and the aged sexton. To these witnesses always, as to themselves, their marriage would date from the moment when the blessing was invoked above their bowed heads in Christ Church, but to the world—why not let it date from the day in which they would claim each other before the world, in Richmond?

The thing was most simple! A second ceremony in the presence of a few friends—a brief announcement in next day's paper—and their life would be begun with the dignity, the prestige, of public marriage.

The sixteenth of May was the day chosen for the event which was more like a wedding in Arcady than in latter-day society. As at the secret ceremony, the customary preparations for a wedding were conspicuously absent; yet was not the whole town gala with sunshine and verdure and May-bloom and bird-song?

Edgar Poe looked every inch a bridegroom as, with his girl-wife upon his arm, he stepped forth from Mrs. Yarrington's boarding-house, opposite the green slopes of Capitol Square. A bridegroom indeed!—plainly, but perfectly apparelled—handsome, proud, fearless—his great eyes luminous with solemn joy.

The simplest of white frocks became Virginia's innocence and beauty more than costly bridal array and the nosegay of white violets above her chaste bosom was her only ornament.

With this sweet pair came the happy mother and a little train of close friends. It was late afternoon. The sunshine was mellow and the air was filled with the delicious insense

The Dreamer

which in mid-May the majestic paulonia tree drops from its purple bells and which is the very breath of the warm-natured South.

No line of carriages stood at the door. No awning shut the picture they made from admiring eyes, but happily the little party chatted together as they strolled under overarching greenery to the corner of Main and Seventh Streets, where in the prim parlor of the Presbyterian minister, the words were pronounced which told the world that Edgar Poe and Virginia Clemm were one.

Upon the return of the party to Mrs. Yarrington's, a cake was cut, the health and happiness of the bride and groom were drunk in wine of "Muddie's" own make, and the modest festival was over.

How happy the young lovers and dreamers were in their home-making! Their housekeeping and furnishings were the simplest, but love made everything beautiful and sufficient. They had a garden in which they planted all their favorite flowers and to which came the birds—the birds with whom they had discovered a sudden kinship, for they too, were nesting—and filled it with music. And they sang and chatted as happily as the birds themselves as the pretty business progressed.

How delightful it was to receive their friends, together, in their own home and at their own board—Eddie's old friends, especially. Rob Stanard, now a prosperous lawyer, and Rob Sully whose reputation as an artist was growing, were the first to call and present their compliments to the bride and groom; and how cordial they were! How affectionate to Eddie—how warm in their expressions of friendship for the girl-wife!

Virginia found it the greatest fun imaginable to go to market with "Muddie," with a basket hanging from her pretty arm. The market men and women began to daily watch for the sweet face and tripping step of the exquisite child whom it seemed so comical to address as "*Mrs.* Poe," and who rewarded their open admiration with the loveliest smile, the prettiest words of greeting and interest, the merriest rippling laugh that rang through the market place and waked echoes in many a heart that had believed itself a stranger to joy.

And the Valley of the Many-Colored Grass was reconstructed in even more than its old beauty. The flowers of love and contentment and innocent pleasure that besprinkled its green carpet had never been so many or so gay, the dream-mountains that shut it in from the rest of the world were as fair as sunset clouds, and the peace that flowed through it as a river broke into singing as it flowed.

Meantime Edgar Poe worked—and worked—and worked.

Every number of the *Messenger* contained page after page of the brilliantly conceived and artistically worded product of his brain and pen. His heart—his imagination satisfied and at rest in the love and comradeship of a woman who fulfilled his ideal of beauty, of character, and of charm, whose mind he himself had taught and trained to appreciate and to love the things that meant most to him, whose sympathy responded to his every mood, whose voice soothed his tired nerves with the music that was one of the necessities of his temperament, a woman, withal, who lived with no other thought than to love and be loved by him—his harassing devils cast out by this true heartsease, Edgar Poe's industry and his power of mental production were almost past belief.

As he worked a dream that had long been half-formed in his brain took definite shape and became the moving influence of the intellectual side of his life. His literary conscience had always been strict—even exacting—with him, making him push the quest for the right word in which to express his idea—just the right word, no other—to its farthest limit. Urged by this conscience, he could rarely ever feel that his work was finished, but kept revising, polishing and republishing it in improved form, even after it had been once given to the world. He had in his youth contemplated serving his country as a soldier. He now began to dream of serving her as a captain of literature, as it were—as a defender of purity of style; for this dream which became the most serious purpose of his life was of raising the standard of American letters to the ideal perfection after which he strove in his own writings.

For his campaign a trusty weapon was at hand in the editorial department of the *Southern Literary Messenger*, which he turned into a sword of fearless, merciless criticism.

Literary criticism (so called) in America had been hitherto mere puffery—puffery for the most part of weak, prolix, commonplace scribblings of little would-be authors and poets. A reformation in criticism, therefore, Edgar Poe conceived to be the only remedy for the prevalent mediocrity in writing that was vitiating the taste of the day, the only hope of placing American literature upon a footing of equality with that of England—in a word, for bringing about anything approaching the perfection of which he dreamed.

The new kind of criticism to which he introduced his readers created a sensation by reason of its very novelty. His brilliant, but withering critiques were more eagerly looked for than the most thrilling of his stories, and though the little, namby-pamby authors whom the gleaming sword mowed down by tens were his and the *Messenger's* enemies for life, the interested readers that were gathered in by hundreds were loud in their praise of the progressiveness of the magazine and the genius of the man who was making it.

In the North as well as the South the name of Edgar Poe was now on many lips and serious attention began to be paid to the opinion of the *Southern Literary Messenger*.

CHAPTER XXIII.

Between his literary work, his home and his social life in Richmond, it would seem that every need of The Dreamer's being was now satisfied and the days of his life were moving in perfect harmony. But "the little rift within the lute" all too soon made its appearance. It was caused by the alarm of Mr. White, the owner and founder of the *Messenger*.

"Little Tom White" was a most admirable man—within his limitations. If he was not especially interesting, his daughter Eliza of the violet eyes was, and he was reliable—which was better. He had a kind little heart and a clear little business head and his advice upon all matters (within his experience) was safe. Though he saw from the handsome increase in the number of the *Messenger's* subscribers that his young editor was a valuable aid, he did not realize how valuable. Indeed, Edgar Poe and his style of writing were entirely outside of Mr. White's experience. They were so altogether unlike anything he had known before that in spite of the praise of the thousands of readers which they had brought to the magazine the dissatisfaction of the tens of little namby-pamby authors alarmed him. Edgar Poe found him one morning in a state of positive trepidation. He sat at his desk in the *Messenger* office with the morning's mail—an unusually large pile of it—before him. In it there were a number of new subscriptions, several letters from the little authors protesting against the manner in which their works were handled in the review columns of the magazine and one or two from well-known and highly respected country gentlemen expressing their disapproval of the *strangeness* in Edgar Poe's tales and poems.

The Dreamer

Mr. White appreciated the genius of his editor—within his limitations—but he was afraid of it and these letters made him more afraid of it. He saw that he must speak to Edgar—add his protest to the protests of the little authors and the country gentlemen and see if he could not persuade him to tone down the sharpness of his criticisms and the strangeness of his stories.

It was with a feeling of relief that he saw the trim, black-clad figure of the young editor and author at the door, for he would like to settle the business before him at once. His manner was grave—solemn—as he approached the subject upon which his employe must be spoken to.

"Edgar," he said, when good-mornings had been exchanged, "I want you to read these letters. They are in the same line as some others we have been receiving lately—but more so—decidedly more so."

"Ah?" said The Dreamer, as he seated himself at the desk and began to unfold and glance over the letters.

"Little Tom" watched his face with a feeling of wonder at the look of mixed scorn and amusement that appeared in the expressive eyes and mouth as he read. Finally the anxious little man laid his hand upon the arm of his unruly assistant, with an air of kindly patronage.

"You have talent, Edgar," he said, with a touch of condescension, "Good talent—especially for criticism—and will some day make your mark in that line if you will stick to it and let these weird stories alone. We must have fewer of the stories in future and more critiques, but milder ones. It is the critiques that the readers want; but in both stories and critiques you must put a restraint on that pen of yours, Edgar. In the stories less of the weird—the strange—in the critiques, less of the satirical. Let moderation be your watchword, my boy. Cultivate moderation in your writing, and with your endowment you will make a name for yourself as well as the magazine."

Edgar Poe was all attention—respectful attention that was most encouraging—while Mr. White was speaking, and when he had finished sat with a contemplative look in his eyes, as if weighing the words he had just heard. Presently he looked up and with the expression of face and voice of one who in all seriousness seeks information, asked,

"Is moderation really the word you are after, Mr. White, or is it mediocrity?"

The announcement at the very moment when the question was put, of a visitor—a welcome one, for he brought a new subscription—precluded a reply, and in the busy day that followed the broken thread of conversation was never taken up again. But the unanswered question left Mr. White with a confused sense which stayed with him during the whole day and at intervals all through it he was asking himself what Edgar Poe meant. Truly his talented employe was a puzzling fellow! Could it be possible that the question asked with that serious face, that quiet respectful air, was intended for a joke? That the impudent fellow could have been quizzing him? No wonder his stories gave people shivers—there was at times something about the fellow himself which was positively uncanny!

That he and "little Tom" would always see opposite sides of the picture became more and more apparent to The Dreamer as time went on and along with this difficulty another and a more serious one arose.

Though the amount of work—of successful work, for it brought the *Messenger* a steadily increasing stream of new subscribers—which he was now putting forth, should have surrounded the beloved wife and mother with luxuries and placed him beyond the reach of financial embarrassment, the returns he received from the entire fruitage of his brilliant talent—his untiring pen—at this the prime-time of his life—in the fullness of mental and physical vigour, was so small that he was constantly harrassed by debt and

The Dreamer

frequently reduced to the humiliating necessity of borrowing from his friends to make two ends meet.

The plain truth was gradually borne in upon him—the prizes of fame and wealth that for the sake of his sweet bride he coveted more earnestly than ever before, were not to be found, by him, in Richmond, or as an employe of Mr. White. But the hues of the bow of promise with which hope spanned the sky of his inward vision were still bright, and he believed that at its end the coveted prizes would surely still be found—provided he did not lose heart and give up the quest. Indications of the growth of his reputation at the North had been many. In the North the facilities for publishing were so much more abundant than in the South. The publishing houses and the periodicals of New York, of Boston, and of Philadelphia would create a demand for literary work—and from these large cities his message to the world would go out with greater authority than from a small town like Richmond.

It was not until the year 1838 that he finally resolved to make the break and sent in his resignation to the *Messenger*. In the three years since his first appearance in its columns the number of names upon its subscription list had increased from seven hundred to five thousand.

Though Edgar Poe's connection with the magazine as editor was at an end, Mr. White took pains to announce that he was to continue to be a regular contributor and the appearance of his serial story, "Arthur Gordon Pym," then running, was to be uninterrupted.

It was a far cry from the gardens and porches and open houses of Richmond to the streets of New York—from the easy going country town where society held but one circle, to a city, with its locked doors and its wheels within wheels. Indeed, the single circle in Richmond, bound together as it was by the elastic, but secure, tie of Virginia cousinship and neighborliness then regarded as almost the same thing as relationship, was practically one big family. Whoever was not your cousin or your neighbor was the next best thing—either your neighbor's cousin or your cousin's neighbor—so there you were.

Though Edgar and Virginia Poe and the Widow Clemm had no blood kin in Richmond they were, during those two years' residence there, taken into the very heart of this pleasant, kindly circle, and it was with keen homesickness that they realized that "in a whole cityful friends they had none."

But if this trio of dreamers felt strangely out of place in the streets of New York, they looked more so. As they sauntered along, in their leisurely southern fashion, their picturesque appearance arrested the gaze of many a hurrying passer-by. In contrast to the up-to-date, alert, keen-eyed crowd upon the busy streets, the air of distinction which marked them everywhere was more pronounced than ever. They gave the impression of a certain exquisite fineness of quality, combined with quaintness, that one is sensible of in looking upon rare china.

In and out—in and out—among the crowds of these streets where being a stranger he felt himself peculiarly alone, Edgar the Dreamer walked many days in his quest for work. Here, there and everywhere, his pale face and solemn eyes with less and less of hope in them were seen. He had been right in believing that his reputation was growing and had reached New York—yet no one wanted his work. The supply of literature exceeded the demand, he was told everywhere. It is true that he succeeded in placing an occasional article, for which he would be paid the merest pittance. Man should not expect to live by writing alone, he found to be the general opinion—he should have a business or profession and do his scribbling in the left-over hours.

The Dreamer

Still, his appearance at the door of a newspaper, magazine or book publisher's office, accompanied by the announcement of his name, brought him respect and a polite hearing—if that could afford any satisfaction to a man whose darling wife was growing wan from insufficient food.

One devoted friend he and his family made in Mr. Gowans, a Scotchman and a book-collector of means and cultivation, whose fancy for them went so far as to induce him to become a member of the unique little family in the dingy wooden shanty which they had succeeded in renting for a song. To this old gentleman, who had the reputation of being something of a crank, The Dreamer's conversation and Virginia's beauty and exquisite singing were never-failing wells of delight, while the generous sum that he paid for the privilege of sharing their home was an equal benefit to them and went a long way toward supplying the simple table. The little checks which "little Tom" White sent for the monthly instalments of "Arthur Gordon Pym," upon which his ex-editor industriously worked, were also most welcome. But with all they could scrape together the income was insufficient to keep three souls within three bodies, and three bodies decently covered.

Before the year in New York was out the rainbow was pale in the sky—its colors were faded and its end was invisible—obscured by lowering clouds. At the moment when it seemed faintest it came out clear again—this time setting toward Philadelphia, whose name the hope that rarely left him for long at a time whispered in The Dreamer's ear.

Why not Philadelphia? Philadelphia—then the acknowledged seat of the empire of Letters. Philadelphia—the city of Penn, the "City of Brotherly Love." There was for one of The Dreamer's superstitious turn of mind and his love of words and belief in their power, an attraction—a significance in the very names. He said them over and over again to himself—rolled them on his tongue, fascinated with their sound and with their suggestiveness.

He bade Virginia and "Muddie" keep up brave hearts, for they would turn their backs upon this cold, inhospitable New York and set up their household gods in the "City of Brotherly Love." The city of Penn, he added, was the place for one of his calling—laughing as he spoke, at the feeble pun—but there was new hope and life in the laugh. In Penn's city, even if disappointments should come they would be able to bear them, for how should human beings suffer in the "City of Brotherly Love?"

CHAPTER XXIV.

The year was waning—the year 1838—when Edgar Poe removed his family from New York. About the hour of noon, upon a pleasant day of the spring following, he might have been seen to turn from the paved streets of the "City of Brotherly Love," and to enter, and walk briskly along, a grassy thoroughfare of Spring Garden—a village-like suburb.

He was going home to Virginia and the Mother—to a new home in this village which they had been first tempted to explore by its delightful name and which they had found seeing was to love, for in its appearance the name was justified. The quiet streets were lined with trees just coming into leaf, in which birds were building, happy and unafraid, and spring flowers were blooming in little plots before many of the unpretentious homes.

The place also possessed a more practical attraction in the reasonableness of its house-rents. Delightfully low was the price asked for a small, Dutch-roofed cottage that was just to their minds. It was small, yet quite large enough to hold the three and their modest possessions, and about it hung a quaint charm that might have been wanting in a more ambitious abode. Though in excellent preservation it had a pleasantly time-worn air and there was moss, in velvety green patches, on its sloping roof. It was set somewhat back

The Dreamer

from the street, with a bit of garden spot in front of it, in whose rich soil violets and single hyacinths—blue and white—were blooming, and its square porch supported a climbing rose, heavy with buds, that only needed training to make it a bower of beauty.

After having tried several more or less unsatisfactory homes during their brief residence in Philadelphia, they felt that they had at last found one that filled their requirements, and had promptly moved in. There were no servants—maids would have been in the way they happily told each other—but Virginia and her mother had positive genius for neatness and order. At their touch things seemed to fly by magic into the places where they would look best and at the same time be most convenient, and it was astonishing how quickly the arrangement of their small belongings converted the cottage into a home.

It was with light heart and step that the master of the house took his way homeward to the mid-day meal. The periodicals of the "City of Brotherly Love" were keeping him busy, and there was at that moment money in his pocket—not much, but still it was money—that day received for his latest story.

As he drew near a corner just around which his new roof-tree stood, he stopped suddenly—in the attitude of one who listens. Peal after peal of rippling laughter was filling the air with music. In his vivid eyes, as he listened, shone the soft light of love and a smile of infinite tenderness played about his lips. Well he knew from what lovely, girlish throat came the merry sounds—sweet and clear as a chime of silver bells. A quickened step brought him instantly in view of her and the cause of her mirth.

She stood in the rose-hooded doorway leaning upon a broom. Her cheeks were pink with the exertion she had been making and her sleeves were rolled up, leaving her dimpled, white arms bare to the elbow. Her soft eyes were radiant and she was laughing for sheer delight in the picture the stately "Muddie" made white-washing the palings that enclosed the wee garden-spot from the street. When she saw her husband at the gate she dropped her broom and ran into his arms like a child.

"Oh, Buddie, Buddie," she cried, "are not our palings beautiful? Muddie did them for a surprise for you!"

"Buddie" was enthusiastic in admiration of the white palings and praised the gentle white-washer to the skies. Then the three happy workers went inside to their simple repast, which the sauce of content turned into a banquet.

The door had been left open to the sunshine and the result was an unexpected guest—a handsome tortoise-shell kitten which strayed in to ask a share of their meal. She paused, timidly, upon the threshold for a moment, then fixing her amber eyes upon The Dreamer, made straight for him and arching her back and waving her tail like a plume, in the air she rubbed her glossy sides against his ankle in a manner that was truly irresistible. All three gave her a warm welcome. Edgar regarded her appearance as a good omen; Virginia was delighted to have a pet, and "Catalina," as they named her, became from the moment a regular and favorite member of the family.

The cottage contained but five rooms—three downstairs (including the kitchen) and upstairs two, with low-pitched, shelving walls and narrow little slits of windows on a level with the floor. But as has been said, it was large enough—large enough to shelter love and happiness and genius—large enough to hold the dream of the Valley of the Many-Colored Grass, with its fair river and its enchanted trees and flowers, in which the three dreamers lived apart and for each other only.

It was large enough for the freest expansion the world had yet seen of the vivid-hued imagination of Edgar Poe.

The Dreamer

Night and day his brain was busy—"fancy unto fancy linking"—and the periodicals teemed with his work.

In *The American Museum*, of Baltimore appeared his fantastic prose-poem, "Ligeia," with his theory of the power of the human will for a text—his favorite of all of his "tales"—*his* favorite, in the weakness of whose own will lay the real tragedy of his life! In *The Gift*, of Philadelphia, appeared, a little later the dramatic "conscience-story," "William Wilson," with its clear-cut pictures of school-life at old Stoke-Newington. *The Baltimore Book* gave the thrilling fable, "Silence," to the world. The weirdly beautiful "Haunted Palace" and "The Fall of the House of Usher" followed in quick succession—in *The American Museum*.

"The Fall of the House of Usher," brought The Dreamer a pat-on-the back from "little Tom" White, who in writing of the tale in *The Southern Literary Messenger*, informed the world: "We always predicted that Mr. Poe would reach a high grade in American literature; only we wish Mr. Poe would stick to the department of criticism; there he is an able professor."

Wrote James Russell Lowell, of the same story,

"Had its author written nothing else it would have been enough to stamp him as a man of genius."

The cottage in Spring Garden was large enough too, for the sweet uses of hospitality. By the time the roses on the porch were open, friends and admirers began to find their way to it, and all who came through the white-washed gate and sat down in the green-hooded porch or passed through it into the bright and tasteful rooms felt the poetic charm which this son of genius and his exquisite bit of a wife and the stately mother with the "Mater Dolorosa" expression, threw over their simple surroundings.

Among those who found their way thither was "Billy" Burton, an Englishman, and an actor, who though a graduate of Cambridge was "better known as a commedian than as a literary man." He had written several books, however, and was the publisher of *The Gentleman's Magazine*, of Philadelphia. Here too, came intimately, Mr. Alexander, one of the founders of *The Saturday Evening Post*, to which The Dreamer was a frequent contributor, and Mr. Clarke, first editor of *The Post* and others of what Edgar Poe's friend, Wilmer, would have dubbed the "press gang" of Philadelphia.

To be intimate with The Dreamer meant to adore the little wife with the face of a Luca della Robbia chorister and the voice which should have belonged to one—with the merry, irresistible ways of a perfectly happy child,—and to revere the mother.

The cottage was also found to be large enough (as the fame of its master grew) to be the destination of letters from the literary stars of the day. Longfellow and Lowell and Washington Irving, on this side of the water, and Dickens, in England, were among Edgar Poe's numerous correspondents while a dweller in the rose-embowered cottage in Spring Garden.

In addition to the stories, poems, essays and critiques which the indefatigable Dreamer was putting out, he found time to publish a collection of his "Tales of the Grotesque and Arabesque," in book form. He was also (unfortunately for him) induced to prepare a work on sea-shells for the use of schools—"The Conchologist's First Book," it was called. This was unmistakably a mere "pot-boiler" and confessedly a compilation, but it set the little authors whose namby-pamby works the self-appointed Defender of the Purity of Style in American Letters had consigned to an early grave, like a nest of hornets buzzing about his ears.

"Plagarism!" was the burden of their hum.

The Dreamer

Even while the discordant chorus was being chanted, however, his wonderfully original tales continued to make their appearance at intervals—chiefly in *The Gentleman's Magazine*, whose editor, at "Billy" Burton's invitation, he had become.

In the midst of all this activity one of his old and most cherished dreams took more definite shape than ever before—the dream of becoming himself the founder of a magazine in which he could write as his genius and his fancy should dictate without having to be constantly making compromises with editors and proprietors—a periodical which would fulfil his ideal of magazine literature, which he predicted would be the leading literature of the future. With his prophetic eye he foresaw the high pressure under which the American of coming years would live, and he never lost an opportunity to express the opinion that the reader of the future would give preference to the essay, or story, or poem which could be read at a sitting—which would waste no time in preamble or conclusion, but in which every word would be chosen by the literary artist with the nicety with which the painter selects the exact tint he needs, and in which every word would tell. And such works he conceived it would be especially the province of the magazine to present.

He went so far as to prepare a prospectus and advertise for subscribers to *The Penn Monthly*, as he proposed naming this child of his hopes, and his proposition to enter the field of magazine publishing not only as an editor, but as a proprietor, bade fair to be the rock upon which he and his friend "Billy" Burton would split. They came to an understanding finally, however, for when Mr. Burton, a little later, decided to abandon *The Gentleman's Magazine* and devote himself exclusively to the theatre, he said to Mr. George R. Graham, the owner of *The Gasket*, to whom he sold out,

"By the way, Graham, there's one thing I want to ask, and that is that you will take care of my young editor."

Edgar Poe was at the moment lost in the happy dream of his own *Penn Monthly* which he conceived would not only take care of him and his family, but would give his genius free rein. He was resolved to put the best of himself into it, and the best of outside contributions he could succeed in procuring. Its criticisms should be "sternly just, guided only by the purest rules of Art, analyzing and urging these rules as it applied them; holding itself aloof from all personal bias, acknowledging no fear save that of outraging the right." It would "endeavor to support the general interests of the republic of letters—regarding the world at large as the true audience of the author," he determined, and he declared in his prospectus.

Dear to his heart as was this dream of dreams of his intellectual life, he was soon to realize that its fulfilment was not to be. At least—not yet, for he comforted his own heart and Virginia's and "Muddie's" with the assurance that it was but a case of hope deferred again.

As he was bracing himself for this fresh disappointment, Mr. Graham, the purchaser of *The Gentlemen's Magazine* which he proposed to combine with *The Casket* in the creation of *Graham's Magazine*, sat in his office with a paper before him which the initiated would have at once recognized as an Edgar Poe manuscript. It was a long, narrow strip, formed by pasting pages together endwise, and had been submitted in a tight roll which Mr. Graham unrolled as he read. The title at the top of the strip, in The Dreamer's neat, legible handwriting was, "The Man of the Crowd."

There was nothing gruesome about Mr. Graham. His candid brow, his kindling blue eye, his fresh-colored cheeks, the genial curve of his lip and his strong but amiable chin, spoke of a sunshiny nature, with neither taste nor turn for the weird. But, as he read, the strange "conscience-story" moved him—held him in a grip of intense interest—wove a

The Dreamer

spell around him. He was on the lookout for original material—undoubtedly he had it in this manuscript. He recalled "Billy" Burton's last words to him: "Take care of my young editor."

A smile lighted his pleasant face. He had his own mental endowments—generous ones—and without the least conceit he knew it; but he had no ambition to patronize genius.

"The writer of this story is quite able to take care of himself," he informed his inner consciousness, "And if I can only form a connection with him it will doubtless be a case of the young editor's taking care of me."

Upon the next afternoon Mr. Graham set out on a pilgrimage to Spring Garden. Though it was November the air was mild and the sunshine was mellow. Was the sky always so blue in Spring Garden, he wondered? He found the rose-embowered cottage without difficulty, for he had obtained minute directions. The roses were all gone but the foliage was still green and the little white-paled garden was bright with the sunset-hued flowers of autumn. Flowers and cottage stood bathed in the light of the golden afternoon—the picture of serenity. What marked this quaint, small homestead?—set back from the quiet village street—tucked away behind its garden-spot from the din of the world? What made it different from others of its neighborhood and character? Was it just a notion of his (Mr. Graham wondered) that made him feel that here was poetry pure and simple?—*visible* poetry?

With sensations of keen interest he lifted the knocker. Edgar Poe himself opened the door and his captivating smile, cordial hand-clasp and words of warm, as well as courtly, greeting raised the visitor instantly from the ranks of the caller to the place of a friend. Mr. Graham had met Edgar Poe before and had felt his charm, but he now told himself that to know him one must see him under his own roof, and in the character of host.

As the door was opened a flood of music floated out. A divinely sweet mezzo-soprano voice was singing to the accompaniment of a harp. As the master of the house flung wide the sitting-room door and announced the visitor, the sounds ceased, but the musician sat with her hands resting upon the gilded strings for a moment, her eyes turned in inquiry toward the door, then rose and with the simplicity of a child came forward to place her hand in that of Mr. Graham. Mother Clemm who sat near the window with a piece of sewing in her lap also arose, and with gentle dignity came forward to be introduced and to do her part in making the guest welcome.

As he took the seat proffered him and entered upon the exchange of commonplace phrases with which a visit of a comparative stranger is apt to begin, Mr. Graham's blue eyes gathered in the details of the reposeful picture of which he had become a part. The open fire, the sunshine lying on the bare but spotless floor, the vases filled with flowers, the few simple pieces of furniture so fitly disposed that they produced a sense of unusual completeness and satisfaction—the row of books, the harp, the cat dosing upon the hearth,—and finally, the people. The master of the house—distinguished, handsome, dominant, genial, his young wife, the embodiment of soft, poetic beauty, and the mother with her saint-like face and gentle, composed manner—her expressive hands busy with her needle work. Was it possible that such a home—such a household—was always there, keeping the even tenor of its way among the unpicturesque conventions of the modern world?

After the first formalities had been exchanged he had delicately intimated that he had come on business, but he soon began to see that whatever his business might be it was to be dispatched right there, in the bosom of the family. This was irregular and unusual, yet, somehow, it did not seem unnatural, and he found that the presence of the women of the poet's household was not the least restraint upon the freedom of their discussion.

The Dreamer

After some words of commendation of the story, "The Man of the Crowd," which he accepted for the next number of his magazine, he came to the real business of the afternoon.

"Mr. Poe," said he, "I believe you know that with the new year *The Gentleman's Magazine* and *The Casket* will be combined to form *Graham's Magazine* which it is my intention to make the best monthly, in contributed articles and editorial opinion, in this country. Mr. Poe I want an editor capable of making it this. *I want you.* What do you say to undertaking it?"

As he sat with his eyes fixed upon The Dreamer's eyes waiting for an answer he could not see the quick clasping of the widow's hands the uplifting of her expressive face which plainly said "Thank God," or the sudden illumination in the soft eyes of Virginia. But the transformation in the beautiful face of the man before him held him spell-bound. Edgar Poe's great eyes were glowing with sudden pleasure the curves of his mouth grew sweet, his whole countenance softened.

"This is very good of you, Mr. Graham," he said, his low, musical voice, warm with feeling. "Your offer places me upon firm ground once more. To be frank with you, the failure, through lack of capital, of my attempt to establish a magazine of my own (since the severing of my connection with Burton, which gave me my only regular income) has left me hanging by the eyelids, as it were, and I have been wondering how long I could hold on with only the small, irregular sums coming in from the sale of my stories to depend upon. Your offer at this time means more to me than I can express."

His girl-wife stole to his side and with pretty grace, unembarrassed by the presence of Mr. Graham, leaned over his chair and pressed her lips upon his brow.

"But you know, Buddie," she murmured in a voice that was like a dove's, "I always told you something would come along!"

Darkness fell and lamps were lighted, and still Mr. Graham sat on and on as though too fascinated by the charm of the little circle to move. To his own surprise he found himself accepting the invitation to remain to supper. The simple table was beautiful with the dainty touch of Mother Clemm and Virginia, and the very frugality of the meal seemed a virtue.

After supper his host, not the least of whose accomplishments was the rare one of reading aloud acceptably, was persuaded to read some of his own poems—Mr. Graham asking for certain special pieces. Among these were the lines "To Helen," which were recited with a fervor approaching solemnity.

"Tell him about Helen, Eddie," murmured Virginia, who sat by his side.

"Yes, do tell me!" urged Mr. Graham, quickly. And with his eyes brooding and dreamy, the poet went over, in touching and beautiful words, the story of what he always felt and declared to be "the first pure passion of his soul."

In the silence that followed he arose and took from the wall a small picture—a pencil-sketch of a lovely head.

"This is a drawing of her made by myself," he said. "It was done from memory, but is a good likeness. I needed no sitting to make her likeness."

When he had shown Mr. Graham the picture, he hung it back in its place and a gentle hush fell upon the little group. Speech seemed out of place after the moving recital and the four sat gazing into the embers, each sunk in his or her own dreams.

The poet was the first to speak.

"Some music Sissy," he said turning to Virginia. "I want Mr. Graham to hear you."

The Dreamer

She arose at once and seating herself at the harp, struck some soft, bell-like chords while she waited for "Buddie" to decide what she should sing.

"Let it be something sweet and low," he said, "and simple. Something of Tom Moore's, for instance. You know my theory, anything but the simplest music to be appreciated—to reach the soul—must be heard alone."

The harp accompaniment rippled forth, and in a moment more melted into the rich, sweet passionate tones of her voice as she told in musical numbers a heart-breaking story of love and parting.

Ballad after ballad followed while the little audience sat entranced. Finally when the singer returned to her seat by the side of her husband, the conversation turned upon music. Mr. Graham commented upon his host's theory that all music but the simplest should, for its best effect, be listened to in solitude.

"Yes," said The Dreamer, "It is (like the happiness felt in the contemplation of natural scenery) much enhanced by seclusion. The man who would behold aright the glory of God as expressed in dark valleys, gray rocks, waters that silently smile and forests that sigh in uneasy slumbers, and the proud, watchful mountains that look down upon all—the man that would not only look upon these with his natural eye but feed his soul upon them as a sacrament, must do so in solitude. And so too, I hold, should one listen to the deep harmonies of music of the highest class."

At length the hour came when Mr. Graham felt that he must tear himself away—bring this strange visit to an end. Before going he felt moved by an impulse to express something of the effect it had had upon him.

"Mr. Poe," he said, "I wish to thank you for one of the most delightful evenings of my life and for having taken me into the heart of your home. I can find no words in which to express my appreciation. Tonight, at your fireside, it seems to me that I have had for the first time in my life a clear understanding of the word happiness."

Edgar Poe smiled, dreamily.

"Why should we not be happy here?" he answered. "Concerning happiness, my dear Mr. Graham, I have a little creed of my own. If I could only persuade others to adopt it there would be more happy people—far more contented ones—in the world."

"And the articles of your creed?" queried Mr. Graham.

"Are only four. First, free exercise in the open air, and plenty of it. This brings health—which is a kind of happiness in itself—that attainable by any other means is scarcely worth the name. Second, love of woman. I need not tell you that my life fulfils that condition." (As he spoke, his eyes, with an expression of ineffable tenderness, wandered for a moment—and it seemed involuntarily—in the direction of his wife). "The third condition is contempt for ambition. Would that I could tell you that I have attained to that! When I do, there will be little in this world to be desired by me. The fourth and last is an object of unceasing pursuit. This is the most important of all, for I believe that the extent of one's happiness is in proportion to the spirituality of this object. In this I am especially fortunate, for no more elevating pursuit exists, I think, than that of systematically endeavoring to bring to its highest perfection the art of literature."

"I notice you do not mention money in your creed," remarked his guest.

"No, neither do I mention air. Both the one and the other are essential to life, and to the keeping together of body and soul. It goes without saying that the necessities of life are necessary to happiness. But money—meaning wealth—while it makes indulgence in pleasures possible, has nothing to do with happiness. Indeed the very pleasure it ensures often obscure highest happiness—the happiness of exaltation of the soul, of exercise of the intellect. What has money to do with happiness? It is a happiness to wonder—it is a

The Dreamer

happiness to dream. Your over-fed, jewel-decked, pleasure-drunk rich man or woman is too deeply embedded in flesh and sense to do either. No"—he mused, his eyes on the glowing coals in the grate, "No—I have no desire for wealth—for more than enough money to keep my wife and mother comfortable. They, like myself, have learned the lesson of being poor and happy. But I *must* keep them above want—I *will* keep them above want!" As he repeated the words the meditative mood dropped from him. He straightened himself in his chair with sudden energy, his voice trembled and sunk almost to a whisper, in place of the dreamy look his eyes flamed with passion.

"Mr. Graham," he exclaimed, "to see those you love better than your own soul in want, and, in spite of working like mad, to be powerless to raise them out of it, is hell!"

A second time the exquisite child-wife slipped quickly, noiselessly, to his side and with the same easy grace leaned over and touched his brow with her lips, but this time instead of moving away, remained hanging over the back of his chair, her fair hand gently toying with the ringlets on his brow. He was calm in an instant.

"I mean, of course, such a condition would be intolerable provided it should ever exist," he added.

As the visitor stepped from the cottage door into the chill of the bright November night, and made his way down the little path of flagstones—irregularly shaped and clumsily laid down, so that mossy turf which was still green, appeared between them—he felt that he was stepping back into a flat, stale and unprofitable world from one of the enchanted regions, "out of space, out of time," of Poe's own creation.

He had indeed, had a revelation of harmonious home-life such as he had not guessed existed in a work-a-day world—of the music, the poetry of living. He had had a glimpse into the Valley of the Many-Colored Grass.

CHAPTER XXV.

The next morning found Mr. Graham still under the spell of the evening with the Poes. He caught himself impatiently watching the clock, for the man under whose charm he had come was to call at a certain hour, to confer with him in regard to the magazine. He could hear him coming (stepping briskly and whistling a "Moore's Melody") before the rap upon the door announced him. He came in with the bright, alert air of a man ready for action for which he has appetite. His rarely heard laugh rang out, fresh and spontaneous, several times during the interview. His manners were at all times those of a prince, but Mr. Graham had never seen him so genial, so gay. The mantle of dreamer and poet had suddenly dropped from him, but the new mood had a charm all its own.

When business had been dispatched and they sat on to finish their cigars, Mr. Graham reiterated his expressions of pleasure in his visit of the evening before.

"You gave me food for thought, Mr. Poe," said he. "I've been pondering on that creed of yours for finding and keeping the secret of true happiness. It is about the most wholesome and sane doctrine I've met with for some time. I've determined to adopt it, and to, at least endeavor, to practice it."

His companion smiled.

"Good!" said he. "I only hope you'll have better success in living up to it than I have."

Mr. Graham's eyebrows went up. "I thought that was just what you did," was his answer.

The Dreamer

"So it is, at times; but when the blues or the imp of the perverse get hold of me all my philosophy goes to the devil, and I realize what an arch humbug I am."

"The imp of the perverse?" questioned Mr. Graham.

"That is my name for the principle that lies hidden in weak human nature—the principle of antagonism to happiness, which, with unholy impishness, tempts man to his own destruction. Don't you think it an apt name?"

"I don't believe I follow you."

"Then let me explain. Did you never, when standing upon some high point, become conscious of an influence irresistibly urging you to cast yourself down? As you listened—fascinated and horrified—to the voice, did you not feel an almost overwhelming curiosity to see what the sensations accompanying such a fall would be—to know the extremest terror of it? Your tempter was the *Imp of the Perverse*.

"Did you never feel a sense of glee to find that something you had said or done had shocked someone whose good opinion you should have desired? Did you never feel a desire to depart from a course you knew to be to your interest and follow one that would bring certain harm—possible disaster—upon you? Did you never feel like breaking loose from all the restraints which you knew to be for your good—throwing off every shackle of propriety, and right, and decency?—Mr. Graham, did you never feel like throwing yourself to the devil for no reason at all other than the desire to be perverse? Could any desire be more impish?—I will illustrate by my own case, I am in one respect not like other men. An exceptionally high-strung nervous temperament makes alcoholic stimulants poison to me. It works like madness in my brain and in my blood. The glass of wine that you can take with pleasure and perhaps with benefit drives me wild—makes me commit all manner of reckless deeds that in my sane moments fill me with sorrow!—and sometimes produces physical illness followed by depression of spirits, horrible in the extreme. More—an inherited desire for stimulation and the exhilaration produced by wine, makes it well nigh impossible for me, once I have yielded my will so far as to take the single glass, to resist the second, which is more than apt to be followed by a third, and so on. I am fully aware therefore, of the danger that lies for me in a thing harmless to many men, and that my only safety and happiness and the happiness of those far dearer to me than myself, lies in the strictest, most rigid abstinence. Knowing all this, one would suppose that I would fly from this temptation as it were the plague. I do generally. At present, several years have passed since I yielded an inch. But there have been times—and there may be times again—when the Imp of the Perverse will command me to drink and, fully aware of the risk, I *will* drink, and will go down into hell for a longer or shorter period afterward."

During this lecture upon one of his favorite hobbies, the low voice of The Dreamer was vibrant with earnestness. He spoke out of bitter experience and as he who bore the reputation of a reserved man, laid his soul bare, his vivid eyes held the eyes of his companion by the very intensity—the deep sincerity of their gaze.

Mr. Graham's last conversation with his new editor had dazed him; this one dazed him still more. What manner of man was this? (he asked himself) with whom he had formed a league? He could not say—beyond the fact that he was undoubtedly original—and interesting. Admirable qualities for an editor—both!

The readers of the new monthly thoroughly agreed with him. The history of Edgar Poe's career as editor of *The Southern Literary Messenger* promptly began to repeat itself with *Graham's Magazine*. The announcement that he had been engaged as editor immediately drew the attention of the reading world toward *Graham's*, and it soon became apparent that in the new position he was going to out-do himself. The rapidity with which his brilliant and caustic critiques and essays, and weird stories, followed upon

The Dreamer

the heels of one another was enough to take one's breath away. He alternately raised the hair of his readers with master-pieces of unearthly imaginings and diverted them with playful studies in autography and exhibitions of skill in reading secret writing.

About the time of his beginning his duties at *Graham's* he must needs have had a visit from some fairy godmother, the touch of whose enchanted wand left him with a new gift. This was a wonderfully developed power of analysis which he found pleasure in exercising in every possible way. To quote his own words, "As the strong man exults in his physical ability, delighting in such exercises as bring his muscles into action, so glories the analyst in that moral activity which disentangles. He derives pleasure from even the most trivial occupations bringing his talent into play."

He tried the newly discovered talent upon everything. In his papers on "Autography" he practised it in the reading of character from hand-writing, and in his deciphering of secret writing he carried it so far and awakened the interest and curiosity of the public to such extent that it bade fair to be the ruin of him; for it seemed his correspondents would have him drop literature and devote himself and the columns of *Graham's Magazine* for the rest of his life, to the solving of these puzzles. Finally, having proved that it was impossible for any of them to compose a cypher he could not read in less time than its author had spent in inventing it, he took advantage of his only safeguard, and positively declined to have anything more to do with them.

But he found a much more interesting way of exercising his power of analysis. In the April number of *Graham's* he tried it upon a story—"The Murders in the Rue Morgue"—which set all the world buzzing, and drew the interested attention of France upon him. In the next number, while the "Murders" were still the talk of the hour, he made an excursion into the world of *pseudo*-science the result of which was his thrilling "Descent into the Maelstrom;" but later in the same month he returned to his experiments in analysis—publishing in *The Saturday Evening Post* an *advance* review of Charles Dickens' story "Barnaby Rudge," which was just beginning to come out in serial form. In the review he predicted, correctly, the whole development and conclusion of the story. It brought him a letter from Dickens, expressing astonishment, owning that the plot was correct, and enquiring if Edgar Poe had "dealings with the devil."

Soon followed the "Colloquy of Monos and Una," in which in the exquisite prose poetry of which The Dreamer was a consummate master, his imagination sought to pierce the veil between this world and the next—to lay bare the secrets of the soul's passage into the "Valley of the Shadow."

Whatever else Edgar Poe wrote, he continued to pour out through the editorial columns of *Graham's Magazine* a steady stream of criticism of current books. While entertaining or amusing the public as far as power to do so in him lay, he did not for a moment permit anything to come between him and the duties of his post as Defender of Purity of Style in American Letters. He was unsparing in the use of his pruning hook upon the work of his contemporaries and the height of art to which by his fearless, candid and, at times, cruel criticism, he sought to bring others, he exacted of himself. In spite of the amount of work he produced, each sentence that dropped from his pen in this time of his maturity—his ripeness—was the perfection of clear and polished English.

But the evidences of this conscientiousness in his own work did not make the little authors one whit less sore under his lash. Privately they writhed and they squirmed— publicly they denounced. All save one—an ex-preacher, Dr. Rufus Griswold—himself a critic of ability, who would like to have been, like The Dreamer, a poet as well as a critic.

When Edgar Poe praised the prose writings of Dr. Griswold, but said he was "no poet," Dr. Griswold like the other little authors writhed and squirmed secretly—very secretly—

The Dreamer

but openly he smiled and in smooth, easy words professed friendship for Mr. Poe—and bided his time.

As for Poe himself, he had by close and devoted study of the rules which govern poetic and prose composition—rules which he evolved for himself by analysis of the work of the masters—so added to his own natural gifts of imagination and power of expression, so perfected his taste, that crude writing was disgusting to his literary palate. He had made Literature his intellectual mistress, and from the day he had declared his allegiance to her he had served her faithfully—passionately—and he could brook no flagging service in others.

Both his growing power of analysis and his highly developed artistic feeling were brought into full play in this review work. Under his guidance the writings of his contemporaries, whether they were the little authors or the giants such as, in England, Tennyson (who was a prime favorite with him), Macauley, Dickens, Elizabeth Barrett, or in America, Longfellow, Lowell, Hawthorne, Irving, Emerson, stood forth illumined—the weak spots laid bare, the strong points gleaming bright.

He unfalteringly declared his admiration of Hawthorne (then almost unknown) in which the future so fully justified him. The tales of Hawthorne, he declared, belonged to "the highest region of Art—an Art subservient to genius of a very lofty order."

Even the work of the little authors was indebted to him for many a good word, but the little authors hated him and returned the brilliant sallies his pungent pen directed toward their writings with vollies of mud aimed at his private character.

No matter what his subject, however, Edgar Poe always wrote with power—with intensity. He seemed by turns to dip his pen into fire, into gall, into vitriol—at times into his own heart's blood.

Of the last named type was the story "Eleonora," which appeared, not in *Graham's*, but in *The Gift* for the new year, and wherein was set forth in phrases like strung jewels the story of the "Valley of the Many-Colored Grass." The whole fabric of this loveliest of his conceptions is like a web wrought in some fairy loom of bright strands of silk of every hue, and studded with fairest gems. In it is no hint of the gruesome, or the sombre—even though the Angel of Death is there. It is all pure beauty—a perfect flower from the fruitful tree of his genius at the height of its power.

All of Edgar Poe's work gains much by being read aloud, for the eye alone cannot fully grasp the music that is in his prose as well as his verse. "Eleonora" was read aloud in every city and hamlet of the United States, and at firesides far from the beaten paths—the traveled roads—that led to the cities; for it was written when every word from the pen of Edgar Poe was looked for, waited for, with eager impatience, and when *Graham's Magazine* had been made in one little year, by his writing, and the writing of others whom he had induced to contribute to its pages, to lead the thought of the day in America.

And the success of The Dreamer made him a lion in the "City of Brotherly Love" as it had made him a lion in Richmond. The doors of the most exclusive—the most cultivated—homes of that fastidious city stood open to welcome him. The loveliest women, whether the grey ladies of the "Society of Friends" or the brightly plumaged birds of the gayer world, smiled their sweetest upon him. As he walked along the streets passers-by would whisper to one another,

"There goes Mr. Poe. Did you notice his eyes? They say he has the most expressive eyes in Philadelphia."

The Dreamer

Throughout this year of almost dazzling triumph the little cottage with its rose-hooded porch, in Spring Garden, had been a veritable snug harbor to The Dreamer. In winter when the deep, spotless snow lay round about it, in spring when the violets and hyacinths came back to the garden-spot and the singing birds to the trees that overhung it, in summer when the climbing green rose was heavy with bloom and in autumn when the wind whistled around it, but there was a bright blaze upon the hearth inside, his heart turned joyously many times a day, and his feet at eventide, when his work at the office in the city was over, toward this sacred haven.

And Edgar the Dreamer was happy. He should have been rich and would have been but for the meagre returns from literary work in his time. Men were then supposed to write for fame, and very little money was deemed sufficient reward for the best work. The poverty of authors was proverbial and to starve cheerfully was supposed to be part of being one.

Still, with his post as editor of *Graham's* and the frequency with which his signature was seen in other magazines, he was making a living. The howl of the wolf or his sickening scratching at the door were no more heard, and in the Valley of the Many-Colored Grass the three dreamers laughed together, and in the streets of the "City of Brotherly Love" Edgar Goodfellow whistled a gay air, or arm in arm with some boon companion of the "Press gang" threaded his way in and out among the human stream, with a smile on his lips and the light of gladness in living in his eyes.

And why should he not be happy? he asked himself. He had the snuggest little home in the world and, in it, the loveliest little wife in the world and the dearest mother in the world. He was upon the top of the wave of prosperity. His fame was growing—had already reached France, where "The Murders" were still being talked about. Why should he not be happy? His devils had ceased to plague him this long while. The blues—he was becoming a stranger to them. The Imp—he had not had a single glimpse of him during the year. He was temperate—ah, therein lay man's safety and happiness! By strict abstinence his capacity for enjoyment was exalted—purified. He would let the cup forever alone—upon that he was resolved!

This was not always easy. Sometimes it had been exceedingly hard and there had been a fierce battle between himself and the call that was in his blood—the thirst, not for the stuff itself, but for its effects, for the excitement, the exhilaration; but he had won every time and he felt stronger for the battle and for the victory—the victory of will. "Man doth not yield himself to the angels or to death utterly" (he quoted) "save only through the weakness of his feeble will." Upon continued resistence—continued victory—he was resolved, and in the resolution he was happy.

Best of all, Virginia was happy, and "Muddie"—dear, patient "Muddie!" The two women chatted like magpies over their sewing or house-work, or as they watered the flowers. They, like himself, had made friends. Neighbors dropped in to chat with them or to borrow a pattern, or to hear Virginia sing. And they had had a long visit from the violet-eyed Eliza White. What a pleasure it had been to have the sweet, fair creature with them! (He little guessed how tremulously happy the little Eliza had been to bask for a time in his presence—just to be near the great man—and meanwhile guard all the more diligently the secret that filled her white soul and kept her, for all her beauty and charm, and her many suitors, a spinster).

Eliza had brought them a great budget of Richmond news. It had been like a breath of spring to hear it. She talked and they listened and they all laughed together from pure joy. How Virginia's laugh had rippled out upon the air—it filled all the cottage with music!

It was mid-January, and he sat gazing into the rose-colored heart of the open coal fire going over it all—the whole brilliant, full year.

The Dreamer

"Sissy," he said suddenly, "Do you remember the birthday parties I used to tell you about—that I had given me when I was a boy living with the Allans?"

"Yes, indeed! and the cake with candles on it and all your best friends to wish you many happy returns."

"Well, you know the nineteenth will be my birthday, and I want to have a party and a cake with candles and all our best friends here to wish you and me many happy returns of the happiest birthday we have spent together. I only wish old Cy were here to play for us to dance! I'd give something pretty to have him and his fiddle here, just to see what these sober-sided Penn folk would think of them. My, wouldn't they make a sensation in the 'City of Brotherly Love!'" He began whistling as clearly and correctly as a piccolo the air of a recently published waltz. After a few bars he sprang to his feet and—still whistling—quickly shoved the table and chairs to the wall, clearing the middle of the floor. The tune stopped long enough for him to say,

"Come, Sweetheart, you must dance this with me. My feet refuse to be still tonight!"—then was taken up again.

The beautiful girl was in his arms in an instant and while "Muddie," in her seat by the window, lifted her deep eyes from the work in her ever-busy hands and let them rest with a smile of indulgent bliss upon her "children," they glided round and round the room to the time of the fascinating new dance.

At length they stopped, breathless and rosy, and the poet, with elaborate ceremony, handed his fair partner to a chair and began fanning her with "Muddie's" turkey-tail fan. He was in a glow of warmth and pleasure. His wonderful eyes shone like lamps. His pale cheeks were tinged with faint pink. While fanning Virginia with one hand he gently mopped the pleasant moisture from his brow with the other. Virginia's eyes shot sunshine. Her laughter bubbled up like a well-spring of pure joy.

"What would people say if they could see the great Mr. Poe—the grand, gloomy and peculiar Mr. Poe—the author of 'Tales of the Grotesque and Arabesque,' who's supposed to be continually 'dropping from his Condor wings invisible woe?'" said she, as soon as she could speak. The idea was so vastly amusing to her that she laughed until the shining eyes were filled with dew.

"If they could know half the pleasure I got out of that they wouldn't say anything," he replied. "They would be dumb with envy. I suppose it's my mother in me, but I just *must* dance sometimes. And this waltz! In spite of all the prudes say against it, it is the divinest thing in the way of motion that ever was invented. It's exercise fit for the gods!"

He drew her to him and kissed her eyes and her cheeks and her lips.

"It was heavenly—heavenly, Sis," said he, "And I don't suppose even the prudes could object to a man's waltzing with his own wife. I wonder will we ever dance to old Cy's fiddle again?"

CHAPTER XXVI.

It was a very modest party, but a merry one. The ground was covered with the unsullied whiteness of new-fallen snow and the coming of most of the guests was heralded by the tintinnabulation of the little silver bells so charming to the ear of the host.

The Grahams were among the first to be welcomed out of the frosty night into the glow of lamp and candle and firelight, by the cordial hand and voice of Edgar Goodfellow. Mr. Graham was in tune to most heartily take part in the commemoration of the birthday of the man who was making *Graham's Magazine* the success of the publishing world in

The Dreamer

America. His kindling blue eyes had never been kinder, his smile never more bland. Mr. Alexander, founder of *The Saturday Evening Post* which so gladly published and paid for everything that Edgar Poe would spare it from *Graham's* was the next, and close following him, Mr. Cottrell Clarke, first editor of the *Post*, and his charming wife. Captain and Mrs. Mayne Reid, who were among the most admiring and affectionate friends of the Poe trio were also there, and other congenial spirits.

They came in twos and threes, their laughter as light and clear as the tinkle of their sleigh-bells.

And Rufus Griswold was there. The Dreamer with his deep reverence for intellectual ability had a sincere admiration for Dr. Griswold—though he did say he was "no poet." He desired the approval—the friendship—of this brainy man and was proud and happy to have him of his party.

Coming in after the rest of the company had assembled, the brainy man's big frame, topped by his big head, with his prominent brow and piercing eyes, his straight, thick nose, his large full-lipped close-set mouth, his square jaw with the fringe of beard sharply outlining it, produced a decided effect. He seemed to fill up a surprisingly large portion of the room. Instinctively, the gentleman who had occupied the largest and heaviest chair vacated it and invited him to be seated in it—which he did, instinctively. He was a young man—under thirty—but looked much older. His face was a strange one. It could not have been called ugly. By some, indeed, it was considered handsome. It was strong, but it was strange. There was an indefinable something unpleasant, something to awaken distrust—fear—about it. Across the dome of the brow ran, horizontally, a series of wavy furrows that produced, in place of the benevolent air the lofty brow might have given, a sinister expression. The eyes beneath the wrinkled brow were piercing and spoke of the fire of active mentality, but they were always downcast and turned slightly askance, so that few people caught the full force of their gleam, and there was sternness and coldness, as well as will, in the prominent chin and jaw.

He came late, but he was a little more cordial in his expressions of pleasure in coming than any of those before him. His bows to Virginia and Mrs. Clemm were more profound—his estimation of Virginia's beauty he made at once apparent in the intense, admiring gaze he bestowed upon her. His words of congratulation and good will for his host were more extravagant than those of any of the others and were uttered in a voice as smooth—as fluent—as oil; while he rubbed his large, fleshy hands together in a manner betokening cordiality. When his host spoke, he turned his ear toward him (though his eyes glanced aside and downward) with an air of marked attention, and agreed emphatically with his views or laughed uproariously at his pleasantries.

Yet at Rufus Griswold's heart jealousy was gnawing. Heaven had endowed him with mind to recognize genius, yet had denied him its possession. He that would have worn the laurel himself, was born to be but the trumpeter of others' victories. He, like Edgar Poe, had an open eye and ear for beauty—for harmony. He could feel the divine fire of inspiration in the creations of master minds—yet he could not himself create. He was a brilliant critic, but (as has been said) his ambition was to be, like Poe, also a poet. His quick intuition had divined the genius of Poe at their first meeting. He knew in a flash, that the neat, slender, polished gentleman, with the cameo face, the large brow and the luminous eyes, and with the deep-toned, vibrant voice, was one of the few he had ever met of whom he could say with assurance, "There goes a genius—" and of those few the topmost. Poe's writing, especially his poetry, enthralled him. To have been able to come before the world as the author of such work he would have sold his soul.

And this man who had caught him in a net woven of mingled fascination, and envy, and hate, had, oh, bitter!—while generously applauding him as a critic and reviewer—as a compiler and preserver of other men's work—had added, "But—but—he is no poet."

The Dreamer

He had received the stab without an apparent flinch. He had even laughed and declared that Mr. Poe was right. That he himself knew he was no poet—he did not aspire to be a real one, but only dropped into verse now and then by way of pastime. The lie had slipped easily from his tongue, but his eyes drooped ever so little more than usual as it did so, their shifty gleam glanced ever so little more sidewise.

And though he came late to the birthday feast, his words of friendship were emphatic and the laugh that told of his pleasure in being there was loud and frequent. And he smiled and rubbed his hands together—and bided his time.

And Edgar Poe was pleased—immensely pleased—on his gala night, with the complimentary manner and the complimentary words of this welcome guest—of this big, brainy man whose good opinion he so much desired.

Alas, hapless Dreamer! Did the gleam of those eyes cast alway slightly downward, slightly askance—give you no discomfort? Did the fang-like teeth when the thick lips opened to pour forth birthday wishes or streams of uproarious laughter, and the square lines of the jaw, suggest to your ready imagination no hint of cruelty? If you could but have known that what time he laughed and talked with your guests and feasted at your board, with its tasty viands and its cake with lighted candles, and bent his furtive glance upon the beauty of your guileless Virginia—if you could but have known that in his black heart the canker jealousy was gnawing and that, behind the smile he wore as a mask, the brainy man was biding his time!

It was a goodly little company—a coming together of bright wits and (for the most part) of kind hearts, and the talk was crisp, and fresh, and charming.

Supper was served early.

"My wife and her mother have thought that you Penn folk might like to sit down to a Virginia supper," said the host, as he led Mrs. Graham to the table, and stood for a moment while Virginia designated the seats to be taken. Then still standing, said,

"Every man a priest to his own household, is our Virginia rule, but as we have with us tonight one who before he took up Letters wore the cloth, I'm going to abdicate in his favor. Dr. Griswold will you ask a blessing?"

All heads were bowed while the time-honored little ceremonial was performed, then seats were taken and the repast begun.

Virginia presided over the "tea-things," while Mrs. Clemm occupied the seat nearest the door opening on the kitchen, that she might slip as unobtrusively as possible out and back again when necessary; but most of the serving was done by the guests themselves, each of whom helped the dish nearest his or her plate, and passed the plates from hand to hand. All of the supper, save the dessert and fresh supplies of hot waffles was on the table. There were oysters and turkey salad and Virginia ham. And there were hot rolls and "batter-bread" (made of Virginia meal with plenty of butter, eggs and milk, and a spoonful of boiled rice stirred in) and there was a "Sally Lunn"—light, brown, and also hot, and plenty of waffles. In the little spaces between the more important dishes there were pickles and preserves—stuffed mangoes and preserved quinces and currant jelly. And in the centre of the table was the beautiful birthday cake frosted by Virginia's dainty fingers and brilliant with its thirty-three lighted candles.

There was just enough room left for the three slender cut-glass decanters that were relics of Mother Clemm's better days.

"The decanter before you, Mr. Graham, contains the Madeira; the Canary is before you, Captain Reid, and I have here a beverage with which I am very much in love at present—*apple wine*—" Edgar Poe said, tapping the stopper of a decanter of cider near his plate.

The Dreamer

All understood. He had served the cider that he might join with them in their pledges of friendship and good will without breaking through the rule of abstemiousness in which he was finding so much benefit.

The toasts were clever as well as complimentary, and the table-talk light and sparkling. Finally both Mrs. Clemm and Virginia arose to clear the table for the dessert.

"You see, my friends, we keep no maid or butler," said the host, "but I'm sure you will all agree with me in feeling that we would not exchange our two Hebes for any, and they take serving you as a privilege."

The cake was cut and served with calves-foot jelly—quivering and ruby red—and velvety *blanc mange*.

After supper Virginia's harp was brought out of its corner and she sang to them. With adorable sweetness and simplicity she gave each one's favorite song as it was asked for—filling all the cottage with her pure sweet tones accompanied by the bell-like, rippling notes of the harp. The company sat entranced—all eyes upon the lovely girl from whose throat poured the streams of melody.

She seemed but a child; for all she had been married six years she had but just passed out of her "teens" and might easily have been taken for a girl of fifteen. Her hair, it is true, was "tucked up," but the innocence in the upturned, velvet eyes, the soft, childish outlines of the face, the dimpled hands and arms against the harp's glided strings, the simple little frock of white dimity, all combined to give her a "babyfied" look which was most appealing, and which her title of "Mrs. Poe" seemed rather to accentuate than otherwise.

Rufus Griswold's furtive eye rested balefully upon her. And this exquisite being too, belonged to that man—as if the gods had not already given him enough!

From a far corner of the room her husband gazed upon her, and bathed his senses in contemplation of her beauty while his soul soared with her song. Mother Clemm noiselessly passing near him to snuff a candle on the table upon which his elbow, propping his head, rested, paused for a moment and laid a caressing hand upon his hair. He impulsively drew her down to a seat beside him.

"Oh, Muddie, Muddie, look at her—look at her!" he whispered. "There is no one anywhere so beautiful as my little wife! And no voice like hers outside of Heaven!... Ah—"

What was the matter? Was his Virginia ill? Even as he spoke her voice broke upon the middle of a note—then stopped. One hand clutched the harp, the other flew to her throat from which came only an inarticulate sound like a struggle for utterance. Terror was in the innocent eyes and the deathly white, baby face.

For a tense moment the little company of birthday guests sat rooted to their places with horror, then rushed in a mass toward the singer, but her husband was there first—his face like marble. His arms were around her but with a repetition of that inarticulate, gurgling sound she fell limp against his breast in a swoon. From the sweet lips where so lately only melody had been a tiny stream of blood oozed and trickled down and stained her pretty white dress.

"Back!—All of you!" commanded the low, clear voice of Edgar Poe, as with the dear burden still in his arms he sank gently to the floor and propping her head in his lap, disposed her limbs in comfortable, and her dress in orderly manner. "Back—don't crowd! A doctor!"

One of the guests from nearby, who knew the neighborhood, had already slipped from the door and gone to fetch the nearest doctor. The others sat and listened for his step in breathless stillness.

The Dreamer

Edgar Poe bent his marble face above the prostrate form of his wife, calling to her in endearing whispers while, with his handkerchief he wiped from her lips the oozing, crimson stream. His teeth chattered. Once before he had seen such a stream. It was long ago—long ago, but he remembered it well. He was back—a little boy, a mere baby—in the small, dark room behind Mrs. Fipps' millinery shop, in Richmond, and a stream like this came from the lips of his mother who lay so still, so white, upon the bed. And his mother had been dying. He had seen her thus—he would see her nevermore!... Would the doctor never come?—

Many days the Angel of Death spread his wings over the cottage in the Valley of the Many-Colored Grass. Their shadow cast a great stillness upon the cottage. Outside was a white, silent world. Snow had fallen—snow on snow—until it lay deep, deep upon the garden-spot and deep in the streets outside. There was no wind and the ice-sheathed trees that were as sentinels round about the cottage stood still. They seemed to listen and to wait.

Inside, in the bed-chamber upstairs, under the shelving walls of the low Dutch roof, The Dreamer's heartsease blossom lay broken and wan upon the white bed. It was a very white little blossom and the dark eyes seemed darker, larger than ever before as they looked out from the pale face. But they had never seemed so soft and a smile like an angel's played now and again about her lips.

Beside her, with his lips pressed upon the tiny white hand which he held in both his own was the bowed figure of a man—of a poet and a lover who like the ice-sheathed trees seemed to listen and to wait—of a man whose countenance from being pale was become ghastly, whose eyes from being luminous were wild with a "divine despair."

At the foot of the bed sat a silver-haired woman with saintlike face uplifted in resignation and aspiration. For once the busy hands were idle and were clasped in her lap. She too, listened and waited, as she had listened and waited for days. Oh Love! Oh Life! Are these the happy trio who lived for each other only in the Valley of the Many-Colored Grass?

The silence was only broken when the lips of the invalid moved to murmur some loving words or to babble of the flowers in the Valley. She was in no pain but she was very tired. She was not unhappy, for the two whom she loved and who loved her were with her and though she was tired she soon would rest—in Heaven. When she spoke of going the man's heart stood still with terror. He held the hand closer and pressed his lips more fiercely upon it.

He would not let her go, he vowed. There was no power in Heaven or hell to whom he would yield her.

But she sweetly plead that he would not try to detain her—that he would learn to bear the idea of her leaving him which now gave her no unhappiness but for one thought—the thought that after a season he might, in the love of some other maiden, forget the sweet life he had lived with her in the Valley, and that because of his forgetting, it would not be given to him to join her at last, in the land where she would be waiting for him—the land of Rest.

At her words, he flung himself upon his knees beside her bed and offered up a vow to herself and to Heaven that he would never bind himself in marriage to any other daughter of earth, or in any way prove himself forgetful of her memory and her love, and to make the vow the stronger, he invoked a curse upon his head if he should ever prove false to his promise.

And as she listened her soft eyes grew brighter and she, in turn, made a vow to him that even after her departure she would watch over him in spirit and if it were permitted her,

The Dreamer

would return to him visibly in the watches of the night, but if that were beyond her power, would at least give him frequent indications of her presence—sighing upon him in the evening winds or filling the air which he breathed with perfume from the censers of the angels.

And she sighed as if a deadly burden had been lifted from her breast, and trembled and wept and vowed that her bed of death had been made easy by his vow.

But it was not to be the bed of death. Little by little the shadow lifted from over the cottage—the shadow of the wings of the Angel of Death—and sunshine fell where the shadow had been, and a soft zephyr made music, that was like the music of the voice of "Ligeia," in the trees which dropped their sheath of ice. And the snow disappeared from the streets and from the garden-spot which was all green underneath, and by the time the crocuses were up health and happiness reigned once more in the cottage.

But it was a happiness with a difference. A happiness which for all it was so sweet, was tinctured with the bitter of remorse.

During the illness of his beloved wife, Edgar Poe had lived over and over again through the horror of her death and burial with all of the details with which the circumstances of his life had so early made him familiar—and had tasted the desolation for him which must follow. While his soul had been overwhelmed with this supreme sorrow his mind had been unusually clear and alert. He had been alive to the slightest change in her condition. Anticipating her every whim, he had nursed her with the tenderness the untiring devotion, of a mother with her babe. Through all his grief he was quiet, self-possessed, efficient.

But with the first glimmer of hope, his head reeled. His reason which had stood the shock of despair, or seemed to stand it, gave way before the return of happiness. A wild delirium possessed him. Joy drove him mad, and already drunk with joy—mad with it—he flung prudence, philosophy, resolutions to the wind and drank wine—and drank—and drank. When—where—how much—he did not know; but at last merciful illness overtook him and stopped him in his wild career.

With his convalescence his right mind returned to him; but he felt as he did when he awoke to consciousness in Mother Clemm's bed-chamber in Baltimore—that he had been down into the grave and back again. Only—then there was no remorse—no fiercely accusing conscience to make him wish from his soul that he might have remained in the abyss.

In dressing-gown and slippers he sat—weak and tremulous—in an arm-chair drawn close to the open fire in the cottage sitting-room. About him hovered his two angels, anticipating his every need, pausing at his side now and again to bestow a delicate caress. Virginia was more beautiful since her illness. Her face and figure had lost their plumpness and with it their childish curves—but a something exalted and ethereal had taken their place. Her eyes were softer, more wistful than ever. Through her fair, transparent skin glowed the faintest, most exquisite bloom. Her harp was mute. Her singing voice was gone. But the deep, low tones of her speaking voice, full of restrained feeling, could only be compared by her husband to the melodious voice of the dream-woman, "Ligeia." They recalled to him the impression that the voice of the priest as he read the funeral rite over his dead mother had made upon his infant mind—the impression of *spoken* music. His Virginia could no longer sing, but every word that fell from her lips was music.

As she and her tall, nun-like mother quietly stepped about the rooms ministering to his comfort, lifting the work of preparing the simple meals, mending the fire, and keeping the rooms bright into a sacred rite by the grace, the care, the dignity with which it was performed, no word, no look escaped either save of tenderness, patience, and boundless love. All the reproaches came from within his own breast—from that inner self that boldly tearing the veil from his deeds filled him with loathing of himself.

The years, his troubles, and his illness, had wrought a great change in him—outwardly. The dark ringlets that framed his face were still untouched with rime, and the dark grey eyes were as vivid, as ever-varying in expression as before, but the large brow wore a furrow and over it and the clear-cut features and the emaciated cheeks was a settled pallor. The face was still very beautiful, but in repose it was melancholy and about the mouth there was a touch of bitterness. The illumining smile still flashed out at times, and filled all his countenance with sweetness and light—but it was rarer than formerly.

He had many reasons for being happy—for being thankful. The genius with which he was conscious he was endowed in larger measure than others of his generation was being recognized. He had fame—growing fame—and money enough for his needs. He had what was as necessary to his soul as meat was to his body—the love of a woman who understood him in all his moods and who was beautiful enough in mind and in body and pure enough in spirit for him to worship as well as to love—to satisfy his soul as well as his senses. And this woman, at the very moment when he thought himself about to lose her forever, had been given back to him—given back clothed upon with a finer a more exquisite beauty than she had possessed before.

He had indeed found the end of the rainbow, but what did it amount to? He was dissatisfied—not with what life was giving him, but with what he was doing with his life. At the moment when his cup was fairly overflowing with happiness and he should have been strongest, he had suffered himself to be led away by the Imp of the Perverse, and had spoiled all. Nothing he had ever been made to taste he told himself, was so unbearably bitter as this dissatisfaction—this disgust with self.

Yet when again the tiny crimson stream stained the sweet lips of his Virginia, and again the Angel of Death spread a dread wing for a season over the Valley of the Many-Colored Grass, all his knowledge of the bitterness—the loathing—of remorse was not sufficient to make him strong for the struggle with grief and despair.

Again the reason of Edgar Poe gave way before the strain, and again he fell.

CHAPTER XXVII.

A day when the porch was rose-embowered once more and the garden-spot a riot of color and the birds singing in the trees round about, found Mr. Graham seated at Edgar Poe's desk in the office of *Graham's Magazine*. The door behind him opened, and he raised his head from his writing and quickly glanced over his shoulder. The look of inquiry in his blue eyes instantly kindled into one of welcome.

"Come in! Come in! Dr. Griswold," he exclaimed. "I am more than glad to see you! We are overwhelmed with work just now and perhaps we'll induce you to lend a hand."

The visitor came forward with outstretched hand, stooping and bowing his huge bulk as he came in a manner that to a less artless mind than Mr. Graham's might have suggested a touch of the obsequious. His furtive but watchful eye had already marked the fact that it was at Mr. Poe's desk—not his own—that Mr. Graham sat—which was as he had anticipated.

"Mr. Poe laid up again?" he queried.

The Dreamer

"Yes; he seems to be having quite an obstinate attack this time."

The visitor sadly shook his head. "Ah?—poor fellow, poor fellow!"

"Do you think his condition serious?" asked Mr. Graham, with anxiety.

Dr. Griswold cast a glance of the furtive eye over his shoulder and around the room; then stooped nearer Mr. Graham.

"Didn't you know?" he questioned, in a lowered tone.

"Only that the failure of his wife's health has been a sad blow to him and that after each of her attacks he has had a break-down. Is there anything more?"

Dr. Griswold stooped nearer still and brought his voice to a yet lower key.

"Whiskey"—he whispered.

Mr. Graham drew back and the candid brows went up.

"Ah—ah" he exclaimed. Then fell silent and serious.

"Did you never suspect it?" asked his companion.

"Never. I used to hear rumors when he was with Billy Burton, but I never saw any indications that they were true, and didn't believe them. How could I? Think of the work the man turns out—its quantity, its quality! He is at once the most brilliant and the most industrious man it has been my good fortune to meet—and withal the most perfect gentleman—exquisite in his manners and habits, and the soul of honor. Did you ever know a man addicted to drink to be so immaculately neat as he always is? Or so refined in manners and speech? Or so exact in his dealings? There is no one to whom I would more readily advance money, or with greater assurance that it will be faithfully repaid in his best, most painstaking work—to the last penny!"

Dr. Griswold's face took on a look of deep concern.

"The more's the pity—the more's the pity!" said he. "A good man gone wrong!" Then with a hesitating, somewhat diffident air.

"You say that you need help which I might, perhaps, give?"

Mr. Graham was the energetic business man once more. Dr. Griswold's visit was most opportune, he said, for while he had on hand a good deal of "copy" for the next number of the magazine—furnished by Mr. Poe before his illness—there were one or two important reviews that must be written and Dr. Griswold would be the very man to write them, if he would.

As Rufus Griswold seated himself at Edgar Poe's desk a look that was almost diabolic came into his face. The temporary substitution was but a step, he told himself, to permanent succession. As editor of the magazine which under Poe's management had come to dominate thought in America, he could speak to an audience such as he had not had before. *He* could make or mar literary reputations and he could bring the public to recognize him as a poet!

It so chanced that upon that very day the editor of *Graham's Magazine* found himself sufficiently recovered from his illness to go out for the first time. As he fared forth, gaunt and tremulous, the midsummer beauty of out-of-doors effected him curiously. It seemed strange to him that the rose on the porch should be so gay, that the sunshine should lie so golden upon the houses and in the streets of Spring Garden—that birds should be singing and the whole world going happily on when his heart held such black despair. As he went on, however, the fresh sweet air gave him a sense of physical well-being that buoyed his spirits in spite of the bitterness of his thoughts.

He was going to work again, and he was glad of it—but he made no resolutions for the future. In the past when he had fallen and had braced himself up again, he had sworn to himself that he would be strong thereafter—that he would never, never yield to the temptation to touch wine again. But he had not been strong. And now he looked the deplorable truth straight in the face. He hoped with all his soul that he would not fall again. He would give everything he possessed to ensure himself from yielding to the temptation to taste the wild exhilaration—the freedom—the forgetfulness—to say to the cup "Nevermore"—to ensure himself from having to pay the price of his yielding in the agony of remorse that was a descent into hell.

But he would deceive himself with no lying pledges. He hoped—he longed to be strong; but he could not swear that he would be—he did not know whether he would be or not. The temptation was not upon him now—he loathed the very thought of it now; but the temptation would most certainly return sooner or later. He hoped from the bottom of his soul that he would resist it, but he feared—nay, in his secret heart he believed—that he would yield. And because he believed it he loathed himself.

As he drew near the office he thought of Mr. Graham,—how kind he was—how trustful. He wondered if Mr. Graham knew the cause of his illnesses and if not how long it would before he would know it; and if the attacks were repeated how long he would be able to hold the place that had shown him the end of the rainbow? How bitter it would be to some day find, added to all the other disastrous results of his weakness of will—to find another in the editorial chair of *Graham's*.

Just at this point in his soliloquy he reached his destination. He mounted the steps leading to the office of *Graham's Magazine* and opened the door—quietly.

For a moment the two men in the office—each deep in his own work—were unaware of his presence, and he stood staring upon their backs as they sat at their desks. Mr. Graham was in his accustomed seat and in his—The Dreamer's—the giant frame of the man whose big brain he admired—though he was "no poet,"—the frame of Rufus Griswold!

Horror clutched his heart. Mr. Graham evidently knew, and knowing had supplied his place without deeming him worth the trouble of notifying, even. Had supplied it, moreover, with the one man who he himself believed would fill it with credit. The readers would be satisfied. He would not be missed. He turned and stumbled blindly down the stairs. Mr. Graham heard him, and hurrying to the door, recognized and followed him—trying to explain and to persuade him to return. But he was too much excited to listen. His reason prompted him to listen, but the Imp of the Perverse laughed reason to scorn. Seeing disaster ahead he rushed headlong to embrace it.

He understood—he understood, he reiterated. There was nothing to explain. Mr. Graham had secured Dr. Griswold's services. Mr. Graham had done well. No, not for any inducement would he consider returning.

He was gone! He was in the street—a wanderer! A beggar, he told himself!

He wandered aimlessly about for an hour, then foot-sore—exhausted in mind and body—he turned his face wearily in the direction of Spring Garden, with its rose-embowered cottage sheltering exquisite beauty—unalterable love—unfailing forgiveness—*heartsease*. He must go home and tell "Muddie" and "Sissy" that he was a ruined man! Oh, if they would only give him his desert for once! If they would only punish him as he felt he should be punished. But they would not! They could not—for they were angels. They were more—they were loving women filled with that to which his mind and his soul bowed down and worshipped as reverently as they worshipped God in Heaven—woman's love, with its tenderness, its purity, and its unwavering steadfastness. They would suffer—that horrible fear, the fear of the Wolf at the door which they had not known in their beloved Spring Garden and since he had been with *Graham's* would again rob them of peace. They would bear it with meek endurance, but they would not be able to hide it from him. He would see it in the wistful eyes of Virginia and in the patient eyes of "Muddie." But they would utter no reproach. They would soothe him with winning endearments and bid him be of good cheer and would make a gallant fight to show him that they were perfectly happy.

During the year and a half of Edgar Poe's connection with *Graham's Magazine* he had raised the number of subscribers from five thousand to thirty-seven thousand. His salary, like that he had received from *The Messenger*, had been a mere pittance for such service as he gave, but also, like what he received from *The Messenger* it had been a regular income—a dependence. With the addition of the little checks paid him for brilliant work in other periodicals, it had amply served, as has been said, to keep the Wolf from the door. In order to make as much without a regular salary it would be necessary for him to sell a great many articles and that they should be promptly paid for. And so he wrote, and wrote, and wrote, while "Muddie" took the little rolls of manuscript around and around seeking a market for them. Her stately figure and saintlike face became familiar at the doors of all the editors and publishers in Philadelphia.

It was a weary business but her strength and courage seemed never to flag. Sometimes she succeeded in selling a story or a poem promptly and receiving prompt pay. Then there was joy in the rose-embowered cottage. Sometimes after placing an article payment was put off time and time again until hope deferred made sick the hearts of all three dwellers in the cottage.

Oftentimes they were miserably poor—sometimes they were upon the verge of despair—yet through all there was an undercurrent of happiness that nothing could destroy—they had each other and even at the worst they still dreamed the dream of the Valley of the Many-Colored Grass, even though the heartsease blossom drooped and drooped.

Virginia's attacks continued to come at intervals, and each time the shadow hung more persistently and with deeper gloom over the cottage. It would be lifted at length, but not until the husband and mother had suffered again all the agonies of parting—not until what they believed to be the last goodbyes had been said and the imagination, running ahead of the actual, had gone through each separate detail of death and burial.

The Dreamer's thoughts dwelt constantly upon these scenes and details until finally the "dirges of his hope one melancholy burden bore—of Never—Nevermore."

Under the influence of the state of mind that was thus induced, a new poem began to take shape in his brain—a poem of the death of a young and beautiful woman and the despair and grief of the lover left to mourn her in loneliness. As it wrote itself in his mind the word that had thrilled and charmed and frightened him at the bedside of his mother and to whose time his feet had so often marched, as to a measure—the mournful, mellifluous word, Nevermore—became its refrain.

The composition of his new poem became an obsession with him. His brain busied itself with its perfection automatically. Not only as he sat at his desk, pen in hand; frequently it happened that at these times the divine fire refused to kindle—though he blew and blew. But at other times, without effort on his part, the spark was struck, the flames flashed forth and ran through his thoughts like wild-fire. When he was helping Virginia to water the flowers in the garden; when he walked the streets with dreaming eyes raised skyward, studying the clouds; when he sat with Virginia and the Mother under the evening lamp or with feet on the fender gazed into the heart of the red embers, or when he lay in his bed in the quiet and dark—wherever he was, whatever he did, the phrases and the rhythm of the new poem were filtering through his sub-consciousness, being polished and made perfect.

The Dreamer

Indeed the poem in the making cast a spell upon him and he passed his days and his nights as though in a trance. Virginia and Mother Clemm knew that he was in the throes of creation, and they respected his brown-study mood—stepping softly and talking little; but often by a silent pressure of his hand or a light kiss upon his brow, saying that they understood. They were happy, for they knew the state of mind that enveloped him to be one of profound happiness to him—though the brooding look that was often in his grey eyes told them that the visions he was seeing had to do with sorrow. They waited patiently, feeling certain that in due course would be laid before them a work in prose or verse, presenting in jewel-like word and phrase, scenes in some strange, fascinating country which it would charm them to explore.

At last it was done! He told them while they sat at the evening meal.

"I have something to read to you two critics after supper," he said. "A poem upon which I have been working. I don't know whether it is of any account or not."

The two gentle critics were all interest. Virginia was breathless with enthusiasm and could hardly wait to finish her supper.

"I knew you were doing something great," she exclaimed. "I *know* it is great! Nothing you have ever done has wrapped you up so completely. You've been in a beautiful trance for weeks and Muddie and I have been almost afraid to breathe for fear of waking you up too soon."

As soon as supper was over he brought out one of the familiar narrow rolls of manuscript and smilingly drew it out for them to see its length—giving Virginia one end to hold while he held the other.

She read aloud, in pondering tone, the two words that appeared at the top: "The Raven."—

Then, as she let go the end she held, the manuscript coiled up as if it had been a spring, and the poet rolled it closely in his hands and with his eyes upon the fire, began, not to read, but slowly to recite. His voice filled the room with deep, sonorous melody, saving which there was no sound.

When the last words,

"And my soul from out that shadow that lies floating on the floor,
Shall be lifted—nevermore!"

had been said, there was a moment of tense silence. Then Virginia cast herself into his arms in a passion of tears.

"Oh, Eddie," she sobbed, "it is beautiful—beautiful! But so sad! I feel as I were the 'lost Lenore' and you the poor lover; but when I leave you you must not break your heart like that. You and Muddie will have each other and soon you will come after me and we will all be happy together again—in Heaven!"

No word passed the lips of the mother. Her silvered head was bowed in grief and prayer. She too saw in "Lenore" her darling child, and she felt in anticipation the loneliness and sorrow of her own heart. She spoke no word, but from her saintly eyes two large bright tears rolled down her patient cheeks upon the folded hands in her lap.

And thus "The Raven" was heard for the first time.

Soon afterward it was recited again. Edgar Poe carried it himself to Mr. Graham and offered it for the magazine. Mr. Graham promised to examine it and give him an answer next day. That night he read it over several times, but for the life of him he could not make up his mind about it. Its weirdness, its music, its despair, affected him greatly. But Mr. Graham was a business man and he doubted whether, from a business point of view, the poem was of value. Would people like it? Would it *take*? He would consult Griswold about it—Griswold was a man of safe judgment regarding such matters.

The Dreamer

Dr. Griswold was indeed, a man of literary judgment and of taste. The beauty of the poem startled him. It would bring to the genius of Edgar Poe (he said to himself)—the poetic genius—acknowledgment such as it had never had before. It was *too good* a poem to be published. He had bided his time and the hour of his revenge was come. He would have given his right hand to have been able to publish such a poem over his own signature—but the world must not know that Poe could write such an one!

The candid eyes of Mr. Graham as he awaited his opinion were upon his face. His own eyes wore their most furtive look—cast down and sidelong. His tone was depressed and full of pity as he said,

"Poor Poe! It is too bad that when he must be in need he cannot, or does not, write something saleable. Of course you could not set such stuff as this before the readers of *Graham's*!"

For once Mr. Graham was disposed to question his opinion.

"I don't know about that," he said. "The poem has a certain power, it seems to me. It might repel—it might fascinate. I should like to buy it just to give the poor fellow a little lift. The lovely eyes of that fragile wife of his haunt me."

It was finally decided to let Mr. Poe read the poem to the office force, and take the vote upon it.

They were all drawn up in a semi-circle, even the small office boy, who sat with solemn eyes and mouth open and who felt the importance of being called upon to sit in judgment upon a "piece of poetry." Edgar Poe stood opposite them and for the second time recited his new poem—then withdrew while the vote was taken.

Dr. Griswold was the first to cast his vote and at once emphatically pronounced his "No!"

The rest agreed with him that the poem was "too queer," but as a solace for the poet's disappointment some one passed around a hat and the next day a hamper of delicacies was sent to Mrs. Poe, with the "compliments of the staff at *Grahams*."

Albeit "The Raven" was rejected by Graham's Magazine and others, enough of Edgar Poe's work was bought and published to keep his name and fame before the public—just enough (poorly paid as it was) to keep the souls of himself and his wife and his "more than mother," within their bodies.

And though Mr. Graham would none of "The Raven," he paid its author fifty-two dollars for a new story—"The Gold Bug." This sum seemed a small fortune to The Dreamer at the time, but he was to do better than that with his story. *The Dollar Magazine* of New York offered a prize of one hundred dollars for the best short story submitted to it. Poe had nothing by him but some critical essays, but remembering his early success in Baltimore with "The MS. Found in a Bottle," he was anxious to try. So he hastened with the critiques to *Graham's* and offered them in place of the story.

Mr. Graham agreed to the exchange and "The Gold Bug" was promptly dispatched to New York, where it was awarded the prize.

When it was published in *The Dollar Magazine* it made a great noise in the world and a red-letter day in the life of Edgar Poe.

The hundred dollars brought indeed, a season of comfort and cheer in the midst of the hardest times the cottage in Spring Garden had known. But the last penny was finally spent.

Winter came on—the winter of 1843. It was a severe winter to the cottage. The bow of promise that had spanned it seemed to have withdrawn to such a vast height above it that its outlines were indistinct—its colors well nigh faded out.

The Dreamer

The reading public still trumpeted the praise of Edgar the Dreamer—his friends still believed in him—from many quarters their letters and the letters of the great ones of the day fluttered to the cottage. And not only letters came, but the *literati* of the day in person—glad to sit at Edgar Poe's feet, their hearts glowing with the eloquence of his speech and aching as they recognized in the lovely eyes of the girl-wife "the light that beckons to the tomb."

But there were other visitors that winter, and less welcome ones. Though the master of the cottage wrote and wrote, filling the New York and Philadelphia papers and magazines with a stream of translations, sketches, stories and critiques, for which he was sometimes paid and sometimes not, the aggregate sum he received was pitifully small and the Wolf scratched at the door and the gaunt features of Cold and Want became familiar to the dwellers in the Valley of the Many-Colored Grass.

In desperation the driven poet turned this way and that in a wild effort to provide the necessities of life for himself and those who were dearer to him than self—occasionally appearing upon the lecture platform, and finally attempting, but without success, to secure government office in Washington.

And oftener and oftener, and for longer each time the Shadow rested upon the cottage—making the Valley dark and drear and dimming the colors of the grass and the flowers—the dread shadow of the wing of the Angel of Death.

Even at such times The Dreamer made a manful struggle to coin his brains into gold—to bring to the cottage the comforts, the conveniences, the delicacies that the precious invalid should have had. An exceedingly appealing little invalid, she lay upon her bed in the upper chamber whose shelving ceiling almost touched her head; and sometimes "Muddie" and "Eddie" fanned her and sometimes they chafed her hands and her feet and placed her pet, "Catalina," grown now to a large, comfortable cat, in her arms, that the warmth of the soft body and thick fur might comfort her shuddering frame. And oftentimes as she lay there "Eddie" sat at a table nearby and wrote upon the long strips of paper which he rolled into the neat little rolls which he or "Muddie" took around to the editors.

And sometimes the editors were glad to have them, and to pay little checks for them, and sometimes not.

The truth was, that though the fame of Edgar Poe was well established, there was an undercurrent of opposition to him, that kept the price of his work down. The little authors—venomous with spite and jealousy—the little authors, chief among whom was Rufus Griswold of the furtive eye and deprecating voice, were sending forth little whispers defaming his character, exaggerating his weakness and damning his work with faint praise, or emphatic abuse.

A day came when Edgar Poe realized that he must move on—that the "City of Brotherly Love" had had enough of him—that to remain must mean starvation. What removal would mean he did not know. That might mean starvation too, but, as least, he did not know it.

It was hard to leave the rose-embowered cottage. It was April and about Spring Garden and the cottage the old old miracle of the renewal of life was begun. The birds were nesting and the earliest flowers were in bloom. It was bitter to leave it—but, there was no money for the rent. His fame had been greatest in New York, of late. The New York papers had been the most hospitable to his work. It was bitter to leave Spring Garden, but perhaps somewhere about New York they would find another rose-embowered cottage. Virginia was unusually well for the present and the prospect of a change carried with it a possibility of prosperity. Who could tell what good fortune they might fall upon in New York?

The Dreamer

Edgar Goodfellow had suddenly made his appearance for the first time in many moons. *A change* was the thing they all needed, he told himself. In change there was hope!

He placed Mother Clemm and "Catalina" temporarily with some friends of the "City of Brotherly Love" who had invited them, and accompanied by his Virginia who was looking less wan than for long past, fared forth, in the highest spirits, to seek, for the second time a home in New York.

CHAPTER XXVIII.

New York once more! They went by rail to Amboy and the remaining forty miles by steamboat.

Certain cities, like certain persons, are witches; they have power to cast a spell. New York is one of them.

Edgar and Virginia Poe had known hard times in New York—the bitterness of hard times in a city large enough for each man to mind his own business and leave his neighbors to mind theirs. Yet as the boat slowed down and neared the wharf, and—past the shipping—they descried the houses and spires of town looming, ghostlike, through the enveloping mist of the soft, grey April day, it was with a thrill that these two standing hand in hand—like children—upon the deck, clasped each other's fingers with closer pressure and whispered,

"New York once more!"

It was their first little journey in the world just together, just they two, and much as they loved the dear mother—their kind earthly Providence, as they laughingly called her—there was something very sweet about it. It was almost like a wedding journey. The star of hope which never deserted them for long, no matter what their disappointments and griefs might be, shone bright above their horizon—their beautiful faces reflected its light. By it the lines of care and bitterness seemed suddenly to have been smoothed out of Edgar's face, and under its influence Virginia's merry laugh rippled out upon the moist air, causing the eyes of her fellow-travellers to turn admiringly her way many times.

Her husband hovered tenderly near her, drawing her shawl with solicitous hand closer about her shoulders and standing upon the windward side of her to protect her from the damp and keen breeze. He noted with delight the fresh color of her cheeks—the life and color in her eyes.

"Do you know, Sweetheart," he said, "You have not coughed once since we left Philadelphia! The change is doing you good already."

Both were blythe as birds. As the boat tied up at the wharf a gentle shower set in, but it did not effect their spirits. He left her on board with some ladies whose acquaintance she had made during the journey, while he fared forth in the rain in quest of a boarding-house. As he stepped ashore he met a man selling second-hand umbrellas. He bought quite a substantial one for sixty-two cents and went on his way rejoicing in the lucky meeting and the good bargain.

In Greenwich Street he found what he sought—a genteel-looking house with "Boarders wanted," upon a card in the window. Another good bargain was made, and hailing a passing "hack" he hastened back to the boat for Virginia and her trunk and soon they were rattling over the cobblestones.

"Why this is quite a mansion," exclaimed the little wife, as she peered out at the house before which the carriage stopped—for while the gentility of the establishment was of the

The Dreamer

proverbial "shabby" variety, the brown-stone porch and pillars gave it an air of unmistakable dignity.

Not long after their arrival the supper-bell rang, and they found themselves responding with alacrity. When they took the seats assigned them and their hungry eyes took in the feast spread before them, they squeezed each other's hands under the table—these romantic young lovers and dreamers. They had been happy in spite of frugality. Many a time while hunger gnawed they had kissed each other and vowed they wanted nothing (high Heaven pardoning the gallant lie!) Yet now, the traveller's appetite making their palates keen—the travellers weariness in their limbs—they were seized upon by an unblushing joy at finding themselves seated at an ample board with a kindly landlady at the head pouring tea—strong and hot—whose aroma was as the breath of roses in their nostrels, while her portly and beaming spouse, at the foot, with blustering hospitality pressed the bounty of the table upon them. A bounteous table indeed, this decidedly cheap and somewhat shabby boarding-house spread, and to their eager appetites everything seemed delicious.

There were wheat bread and rye bread, butter and cheese, cold country ham and cold spring veal—generous slices of both, piled up like little mountains—and tea-cakes in like abundance.

They feasted daintily—exquisitely, as they did everything, but they feasted heartily for the first time in months.

After supper they went to their room—a spacious and comfortably, though plainly, furnished one, with a bright fire burning in a jolly little stove. Their spirits knew no bounds.

"What would Catalina say to this solid comfort, Sis?" queried Eddie. "I think she would faint for joy."

For answer Virginia smiled upon him through a mist of tears.

"Why Virginia—my Heart—" he cried in amazement. "What is it?"

"Only that it is too beautiful!" she managed to say. "And to think that Muddie and Catalina are not here to share it with us!"

"Just as soon as I can scrape together enough money to pay for Muddie's board and travelling expenses we will have them with us," he assured her.

She dried her eyes and perched upon his knee while he went through his pockets and bringing out all the money he had, counted it into her palm.

"Four dollars and a half," he said. "Not much, but we are fortunate to have that. And with such fine living as we get here so cheap it will go quite a long way. Let me see—the price of board and lodging is only three and a half a week for both of us. Seven dollars would pay our way for a fortnight—and in a fortnight's time there's no telling what may turn up! Some editor might buy 'The Raven,' or money due me for work already sold might come in. If I could only contrive to raise this sum to seven dollars we could rest easy for at least a fortnight."

"I'll tell you how," said Virginia. "You have acquaintances here—hunt up some of them and borrow three dollars. Then you would have enough to pay two weeks board ahead and fifty cents over for pocket money."

"Wise little head!" exclaimed he, tapping her brow, "The very idea!"

And forthwith all care as to ways and means was thrown from both their minds, and they gave themselves up to an evening of enjoyment of the comforts of their brown-stone mansion.

While Virginia was resting her husband went out for a little shopping to be done with part of the fifty cents they had allowed themselves for spending money. First he

The Dreamer

exchanged a few cents for a tin pan to be filled with water and placed on top of the stove, for the comfort of Virginia who had been oppressed by the dry heat. Then a few cents more went for two buttons his coat lacked, a skein of thread to sew them on with, and a skein of silk with which Virginia would mend a rent in his trousers made by too close contact with a nail on deck of the steamboat.

Next day was a bright, beautiful, spring Sunday. The sky and budding trees had the newly-washed aspect often seen after a season of rain. The sound of church-bells was on the air; the streets were filled with people in their best clothes, and the new boarders in Greenwich Street, fortified with a breakfast of ham and eggs and coffee, jubilantly joined that stream of humanity which flowed toward the point above which Trinity Church spire pierced the clear sky.

On Monday, Edgar Poe was taken with what he called a "writing fit." For several days (during which Edgar Goodfellow remained in the ascendency) the fit remained on him, and he wrote incessantly—only pausing long enough, now and then, to read the result to Virginia.

"This will earn us the money to bring Muddie and Catalina to New York," he said with confidence.

At last the manuscript was finished and no sooner was the ink dry upon the paper than he took it to *The Sun*, which promptly bought and paid for it, and upon the next Sunday, April 13, printed it not as a story, but as news.

"Astounding News by Express, *via* Norfolk!" (The headlines said). "The Atlantic crossed in Three Days." Signal Triumph of Mr. Monck Mason's Flying Machines!!!

"Arrival at Sullivan's Island, near Charleston, S.C., of Mr. Mason, Mr. Robert Holland, Mr. Henson, Mr. Harrison Ainsworth, and four others, in the Steering Balloon, 'Victoria,' after a passage of seventy-five hours from Land to Land! Full Particulars of the Voyage!"

Strange as it may seem, the "astounding news" was received by the people of New York for fact. There was a rush for copies of the *Sun* which announced with truth that it was the only paper in possession of the "news," and not until denial came from Charleston, several days later, was it suspected that the "news" was all a hoax and that Edgar Goodfellow was simply having a little fun at the expense of the public.

The story did, indeed, earn money with which to bring "Muddie" and "Catalina" to New York. It did more—it brought the editors to Greenwich Street looking for manuscript. They begged for stories as clever and as sensational as "The Balloon Hoax," but in vain. Edgar Goodfellow had vanished and in his place was Edgar the Dreamer who only had to tell of,

"A wild, weird clime that lieth sublime Out of Space—out of Time,

Where the traveller meets aghast Sheeted Memories of the Past,—

Shrouded forms that start and sigh As they pass the wanderer by,— White-robed forms of friends long given In agony to the Earth and Heaven."

It was in vain that the editors besought him to try something else in the vein of "The Balloon Hoax," assuring him that that was what his readers were expecting of him, after his recent "hit"—that was what they would be willing to pay him for—pay him well. Was it the Imp of the Perverse that caused him to positively decline, and to persist that "Dreamland" was all he had to offer just then?

It was Mr. Graham who finally accepted this quaint and beautiful poem, and who published it—in the June number of *Graham's Magazine*.

The Dreamer

In October following the return of the Poes to New York—October of the year 1844—Mr. Nathaniel P. Willis who was then editor of *The Evening Mirror*, and had been editor of *The Dollar Magazine*, when it awarded the prize of a hundred dollars to "The Gold Bug," was seated at his desk in the "Mirror" office, when in response to his "Come in," a stranger appeared in his doorway—a woman—a lady in the best sense of a word almost become obsolete. A *gentlewoman* describes her best of all. She was a gentlewoman, then, past middle age, yet beautiful with the high type of beauty that only ripe years, beautifully lived, can bring—the beauty that compensates for the fading of the rose on cheek and lip, the dimming of the light in the eyes, for the frost on the brow—the beauty of patience, of tenderness, of faith unquenchable by fire or flood of adversity. A history was written on the face—a history in which there was plainly much of tragedy. Yet not one bitter line was there.

It was a face, withal, which could only have belonged to a mother, and might well have belonged to the mother, Niobe.

In figure she was tall and stately, with a gentle dignity. Her dress was simple to plainness, and might have been called shabby had it been less beautifully neat. It was of unrelieved black, and she wore a conventional widow's bonnet, with floating white strings.

The reader needs no introduction to this stranger to Mr. Willis, who in a gentle, well-bred voice, with a certain mournful cadence in it, announced herself as "Mrs. Clemm—the mother-in-law of Mr. Poe."

No connection with a famous author was needed to inspire Mr. Willis with respect for his visitor. She seemed to him to be an "angel upon earth," and it was with an air approaching reverence that he handed her to the most comfortable chair the office afforded.

Her errand was quickly made known. Edgar Poe was ill and not able to come out himself. His wife was an invalid, and so it devolved upon her to seek employment for him. In spite of his fame, she said, and of his industry, his manuscripts brought him so little money that he was in need of the necessities of life. Regular work with a regular income, however small, she felt to be his only hope of being able to rise above want.

Mr. Willis was distressed and promptly offered all he could. It was not much, but it was better than nothing—it was the place of assistant editor of his paper.

For months following, the figure of Edgar Poe was a familiar one in the office of the *Evening Mirror*. Neither in his character of Edgar the Dreamer nor that of Edgar Goodfellow was he especially known there, but simply as a modest, industrious sub-editor, doing the work of a mechanical paragraphist as quietly, as unobtrusively, as a machine. With rarely a smile and rarely a word, he stood from morning till night at his desk in a corner of the editorial room—pale, still and beautiful as a statue, punctual and efficient and the embodiment of courtesy always.

And quietly and unobtrusively his personality made itself felt. Mr. Willis came to love him for his innate charm and for his faithfulness to duty.

But the desk of a sub-editor could not long hold a genius like Edgar Poe. He bore its drudgery without complaint, but when an opening that seemed to invite his ambition, as well as to promise better pay came, he hailed it with enthusiasm. In March of the next year he formed a partnership with two New York journalists, as editors and managers of *The Broadway Journal*. A few months later saw him sole proprietor as well as editor, and for a short, bright period his old dream of a magazine of his own, in which he could write as he pleased, came true. Its realization seemed to inspire him with new energy. How many heads, how many right hands had the man—his readers asked each other—that he could turn out such a mass of work of such high order? His own and many other of the magazines of the day were filled with reviews and criticisms that made him the terror of other writers, and with stories and poems that made him the marvel of readers everywhere.

His works were translated into the tongues of France, Germany and Spain, and his fame grew in all of those countries.

Yet the most that he could afford in the way of a home was up two flights of stairs—two rooms in the third story of a dingy old house in East Broadway. Mother Clemm and Virginia kept them bright and spotless and "Catalina" dosing on the hearth gave a final touch of comfort, and they were far above the noise and dust of the streets, with windows opening upon a goodly view of the sky. They had a front and a back room, so that the beauties of the dawn and the noontide—of sunset and moonrise—were all theirs.

And the Wolf came not near the door, and the three whose natures were like to the natures of the oak, the vine and the heartsease, and who lived for each other only, dreamed again the dream of the wonderful valley—the Valley of the Many-Colored Grass.

CHAPTER XXIX.

Up, up the stairs, two steps at a time, sprang The Dreamer, one white January day, and burst in upon Mother Clemm who was preparing dinner, and Virginia who was mending his coat. He was in a great glee. He caught "Muddie" in his arms where she stood with her hands deep in a tray of dough, and kissed her, then stooped over Virginia and kissed *her*, and dropped into her lap a crisp ten dollar bank note. She gave a little scream of delight.

"Where did you get it?" she cried?

"From Willis. I've sold him 'The Raven.' He's vastly taken with it and not only paid me the ten, in advance, but will give the poem an editorial puff in the *Mirror* of the nineteenth. He showed me a rough draft. He will say that it is 'the most effective example of fugitive poetry ever published in this country,' and predict that it will 'stick in the memory of everybody who reads it!'"

"And it will! It will!" cried Virginia. "Especially that 'Nevermore.' I've done everything in time to it since the first night you read it to us."

"I've done everything in time to it since I was three years old," murmured her husband. He drew the miniature from the inside pocket of his coat where he had carried it, close against his heart, throughout his life, and gazed long upon it. In his grey eyes was the tender, brooding expression which the picture always called forth. "Ever since I heard that word for the first time from the lips of my old nurse when she took me in to see my mother robed for the grave, my feet and my thoughts have kept time to it; and generally when my steps and my face have been set toward hope and happiness it has risen before me like a wall, blocking my way."

Virginia arose from her chair letting her work and the bank note fall unheeded from her lap, and went to him. Gently taking the miniature from his hands she restored it to its place in his pocket and then with a hand on each of his shoulders lifted her eyes to his.

"Buddie," she said, calling him by the old pet name of their earliest days, "You frighten me sometimes. The miniature is beautiful but it makes you so sad. And when you talk that way about 'The Raven,' I feel as if I could hear your tears dropping on my coffin-lid!" Then, with a sudden change of mood, her laugh rang out, and she pressed her lips upon his.

"I'll have you know," she said, "I'm not dead yet, and you will not have to journey to any 'distant Aidenn' to 'clasp' me."

"No, thank God!" he breathed, crushing her to him.

It was upon January 29, 1845, that "The Raven" appeared, with Willis's introductory puff. In spite of Dr. Griswold and the staff of *Graham's Magazine*, it created an instant furor. It was published and republished upon both sides of the Atlantic. To quote a contemporary writer, everybody was "raven-mad" about it, except a few "waspish foes" who would do its author "more good than harm."

It brought to the two bright rooms up the two flights of stairs visitors by the score, eager to congratulate the poet, to make the acquaintance of his interesting wife and mother and to assure all three of their welcome to homes approached by brown-stone steps.

And it brought letters by the score—some from the other side of the Atlantic. Among these was one from Miss Elizabeth Barrett, soon to become the wife of Mr. Robert Browning.

"Your 'Raven' has produced a sensation here in England," she wrote. "Some of my friends are taken by the fear of it, and some by its music. I hear of persons haunted by the 'Nevermore,' and one of my friends who has the misfortune of possessing a bust of Pallas never can bear to look at it in the twilight. Mr. Browning is much struck by the rhythm of the poem.

"Then there is that tale of yours, 'The Case of M. Valdemar,' throwing us all into a 'most admired disorder,' and dreadful doubts as to whether 'it can be true,' as children say of ghost stories. The certain thing in the tale in question is the power of the writer and the faculty he has of making horrible improbabilities seem near and familiar."

Of all the letters from far and near, this was the one that gave The Dreamer most pleasure, and as for Virginia and the Mother, they read it until they knew it by heart.

When, some months later, his new book, "The Raven and Other Poems," came out, its dedication was, "To the noblest of her sex—Miss Elizabeth Barrett, of England."

And there was joy in the two rooms up two flights of stairs where Edgar Poe sat at his desk reeling off his narrow little strips of manuscript by the yard. His work filled *The Broadway Journal* and overflowed into many other periodicals.

While he created stories and poems, he gave more attention than ever to the duties of his cherished post as Defender of Purity of Style for American Letters, and the fame to which he had risen giving him new authority, he made or marred the reputation of many a literary aspirant.

Exposition of plagiarism became a hobby with him, and his attacks upon Longfellow upon this ground, brought on a controversy between him and the gentle poet which reached such a heat that it was dubbed "The Longfellow War." All attempts of friends and fellow journalists to make him more moderate in his criticisms were in vain; they seemed indeed, but to excite the Imp of the Perverse, under whose influence he became more merciless than ever. An admirer of this virtue carried to such an extreme that it became a serious fault, as it was assuredly a grievous mistake, humorously characterized him in a parody upon "The Raven," containing the following stanza:

The Dreamer

"Neither rank nor station heeding, with his foes around him bleeding, Sternly, singly and alone, his course he kept upon that floor; While the countless foes attacking, neither strength nor valor lacking, On his goodly armor hacking, wrought no change his visage o'er, As with high and honest aim he still his falchion proudly bore, Resisting error evermore."

Many of the "waspish foes" thus made turned their stings upon his private character, against which there was already a secret poison working—the poison that fell from the tongue, and the pen of Rufus Griswold. He had the ear of numbers of Edgar Poe's friends in the literary world, and what time The Dreamer dreamed his dreams in utter ignorance of the unfriendliness toward him of the big man whose big brain he admired, the big man watched for his chance to insert the poison. It was invariably hidden in a coating of sugar. Poe was a wonderful genius, he would declare, his imagination—his style—they were marvellous! Marvelous! His *head* was all right, but—. The "but" always came in a lowered tone, full of commiseration, "*but*—his *heart*!—Allowance should, of course, be made for his innate lack of principle—he should not be held *too* responsible. His habits—well known to everyone of course!"

No—they were not even suspected, many of his listeners replied. Might not Dr. Griswold be mistaken? they asked. Was it possible that an habitual drunkard could turn out such a mass of brilliant and artistic work? And consider the exquisite neatness of his manuscript!

Peradventure the listener persisted in believing his informant mistaken—peradventure he at once accepted the damaging statements; but in every case the poison had been administered, and was at work.

There was just one class among the writers of the day sacred from the attacks of Edgar Poe's pen. Before almost everything else The Dreamer was chivalrous. The "starry sisterhood of poetesses" and authoresses, therefore, escaped his criticisms. One of his contemporaries said of him that he sometimes mistook his vial of prussic acid for his ink-pot. In writing of authors of the gentle sex, his ink-pot became a pot of honey.

Several of these literary ladies living in New York had their salons, where they received, upon regular days, their brothers and sisters of the pen, and at which The Dreamer became a familiar figure.

"I meet Mr. Poe very often at the receptions," gossiped one of the fair poetesses in a letter to a friend in the country. "He is the observed of all observers. His stories are thought wonderful and to hear him repeat 'The Raven' is an event in one's life. People seem to think there is something uncanny about him, and the strangest stories are told and what is more, *believed*, about his mesmeric experiences—at the mention of which he always smiles. His smile is captivating! Everybody wants to know him, but only a few people seem to get well acquainted with him."

Chief among the salons of New York was that of Miss Anne Charlotte Lynch—who was afterward Mrs. Botta. An entré to her home was the most-to-be-desired social achievement New York could offer, for it meant not only to know the very charming lady herself, but to meet her friends; and she had drawn around her a circle made up of the persons and personages—men and women—best worth knowing. She became one of The Dreamer's most intimate friends, and always made him and his wife welcome at her "evenings." It was not long after "The Raven" had set the town marching to the word "nevermore," that he made his first visit there—a visit which long stood out clear in the memories of all present.

In the cavernous chimney a huge grate full of glowing coals threw a ruddy warmth into Miss Lynch's spacious drawing-room. Waxen tapers in silver and in crystal candelabra,

The Dreamer

and in sconces, filled the apartment with a blaze of soft light, lit up the sparkling eyes and bright, intellectual faces of the assembled company, and showed to advantage the jewels and laces of the ladies and the broadcloth of the gentlemen.

Miss Lynch stood at one end of the room between the richly curtained windows and immediately in front of a narrow, gold-framed mirror which reached from the frescoed ceiling to the floor and reflected her gracious figure to advantage. She was listening with interested attention to Mr. Gillespie, the noted mathematician, whose talk was worth hearing in spite of the fact that he stammered badly. His subject tonight happened to be the versatility of "Mr. P-P-Poe."

"He might have been an eminent m-m-mathematician if he had not elected to be an eminent p-p-poet," he was saying.

To her right Mr. Willis's daughter, Imogen, was flirting with a tall, lanky young man with sentimental eyes, a drooping moustache and thick, straight, longish hair, whose lately published ballad, "Oh, Don't You Remember Sweet Alice, Ben Bolt?" was all the rage.

To her left the Minerva-like Miss Margaret Fuller whose critical papers in the *New York Tribune* were being widely read and discussed, was amiably quarreling with Mr. Horace Greely, and upon a sofa not far away Mr. William Gilmore Simms, the novelist and poet, was gently disagreeing with Mrs. Elizabeth Oakes Smith in her contention for Woman's Rights.

At the opposite end of the room a lovely woman in a Chippendale chair was the central figure of a group of ladies and gentlemen each of whom hung upon her least word with an interest amounting to affection. She was a woman who looked like a girl, for thirty years had been kind to her. Glossy brown hair parted in the middle and brushed smoothly down in loops that nearly covered her ears framed an oval face, with delicate, clear-cut features, pale complexion and eyes as brown and melting as a gazelle's.

She was none other than Mrs. Frances Osgood, the author, or authoress, as she would have styled herself, of "The Poetry of Flowers"—so much admired by her contemporaries—whose husband, Mr. S.S. Osgood, the well known artist, had won her heart while painting her portrait.

Conspicuous in the group of literary lights surrounding her was Dr. Griswold in whose furtive glance, had she been less free from guile, she might have read an admiration fiercer than that of friendship or even of platonic love, and to whose fires she had unwittingly added fuel by expressing admiration for his poems—Mr. Poe's opinion to the contrary.

Mr. Locke, author of "The Moon Hoax," was of the group; and the Reverend Ralph Hoyt, who was a poet as well as a preacher; and Mr. Hart, the sculptor; and James Russell Lowell, who happened to be in town for a few days; and Mr. Willis and his new wife; and Mrs. Embury whose volume of verse, "Love's Token Flowers," was just out and being warmly praised; and George P. Morris, Willis's partner in the *Mirror*, whose "Woodman, Spare that Tree!" and "We were Boys Together," had (touching a human chord) made him popular.

The beloved physician, Dr. Francis, seemed to be everywhere at once, as he moved about from group to group with a kindly word for everybody—the candle-light falling softly upon his flowing silver locks and his beaming, ruddy countenance.

Suddenly, there was a slight stir in the room—a cessation of talk—a turning toward one point.

"There is Mr. P-P-Poe now," said Mr. Gillespie to Miss Lynch, and followed her as, with out-stretched hand and cordial smile, she hastened toward the door where stood the trim, erect, black-clad figure of Edgar Poe, with his prominent brow and his big dreamy

The Dreamer

eyes, and his wife, pale as a snow-drop after her many illnesses, and as lovely as one, and still looking like a child, upon his arm.

Instant pleasure and welcome were written upon every face present save one, and even that quickly assumed a smile as its owner came forward bowing and stooping in an excess of courtesy.

The pair became immediately the centre of attraction. Everybody wanted to have a word with them. It made Virginia thoroughly happy to see "Eddie" appreciated, and she chatted blythely and freshly with all—her spontaneous laugh bearing testimony to her enjoyment—while The Dreamer yielded himself with his wonted modesty and grace to the hour—answering questions as to whether he *really did* believe in ghosts and whether the experiments in mesmerism in his story, "The Case of M. Valdemar" had *any* foundation in fact, with his captivating but enigmatic smile, and a little Frenchified shrug of the shoulders.

It would have seemed at first that he had diverted attention from the fair author of "The Poetry of Flowers" to himself, but erelong—no one knew just how it came to pass—Edgar Poe was sitting upon an ottoman drawn close to the Chippendale chair, and the two lions were deep in earnest and intimate conversation upon which no one else dared intrude. The furtive eye of Rufus Griswold marked well the evident attraction between these two beautiful and gifted beings—*poets*—and something like murder awoke in his heart.

The tete-a-tete was interrupted by Miss Lynch, who declared that she voiced the wish of all present in requesting that Mr. Poe would recite "The Raven."

All the candles save enough to make (with the fire's glow) a dim twilight, were put out, and the poet took his stand at one end of the long room.

A hush fell upon the company and in a quiet, clear, musical voice, he began the familiar words.

There was scarcely a gesture—just the motionless figure, the pale, classic face, which was dim in the half-light, and the deep, rich voice.

Miss Lynch was the first to break the silence following the final "Nevermore." Moving toward him with her easy, distinguished step, she thanked him in a few low-spoken words. Mrs. Osgood, rising gracefully from her chair, followed her example, with Dr. Griswold at her heels, and in a few moments more the whole room was in an awed and subdued hum.

The girl-wife came in for her share of the lionizing. Her appearance was in marked contrast to that of the richly apparelled women about her. The simplest dress was the only kind within her reach—for which she may have consoled herself with the thought that it was the kind that most adorned her. She wore tonight a little frock made by her own fingers, of some crimson woolen stuff, without a vestige of ornament save a bit of lace, yellow with age, at the throat. Her hair was parted above the placid brow, looped over her ears and twisted in a loose knot at the back of her head, in the prevailing fashion for a young matron; which with her youthful face, gave her a most quaint and charming appearance.

Her husband's coat had seen long service, but it was neatly brushed and darned, and the ability to wear threadbare clothing with distinction was not the least of Edgar Poe's talents. Beside his worn, but cared-for apparel, costly dress often seemed tawdry.

Out from the warmth and the light and the perfume and the luxury and the praise of the beautiful drawing-room with its distinguished assemblage,—out into the streets of New York—into the bleakness and the darkness of the winter's night—stepped Edgar Poe and his wife. Virginia was wrapped against the cold in a Paisley shawl that had been one of Mother Clemm's bridal presents, while Edgar wore the military cape he had at West Point and which, except in times of unusual prosperity, had served him as a great-coat ever since.

Through the dimly-lit streets, slippery with ice, and wind-swept, they made their way to the two rooms up two flights of stairs, where the Widow Clemm mended the fire with a few coals at a time and sewed by a single candle, as she waited for them—the lion of the most distinguished circle in America and his beautiful wife!

Back from a world of dreams created by a company of dreamers to the reality of an empty larder and a low fuel pile and a dun from the landlord from whom they rented the two rooms.

"The Raven" had brought its author laurels in abundance, but only ten dollars in money. Editors were clamoring for his work and he was supplying it as fast as one brain and one right hand could; and some of them were sending their little checks promptly in return and some were promising little checks some day; but *The Broadway Journal* had failed for lack of capital. It was the old story. He had no regular income and the irregularly appearing little checks only provided a from-hand-to-mouth sort of living for the three.

Yet they had their dreams. Landlords might turn them out of house and home but they were powerless to deprive them of their dreams.

Mother Clemm's one candle was burning low—its light and that of the dying fire barely relieved the room from darkness and did not prevent the rays of the newly arisen full moon from coming through the lattice and pouring a heap of silver upon the bare floor.

"Look Muddie! Look Sissy!" cried the poet. "If we lived in a blaze of light, like your rich folk, we should have to go out of doors to see the moon. Who says there are not compensations in this life?"

CHAPTER XXX.

But it was not always possible to take a hopeful view. Continued poverty which oftentimes reached the degree of positive want, anxiety for Virginia's health and inability to provide for her the remedies and comforts he felt might preserve her life, were enough to arouse Edgar Poe's blue devils, and they did.

Why detail the harassments of the rest of that winter, during which The Dreamer led a strange double life—a life in the public eye of distinction, prosperity, popularity, but in private, a hunted life—a life of constant dread of the wrath of a too long indulgent landlord or grocer—a flitting from one cheap lodgement to another.

One gleam of genuine sunshine brightened the dreary days. The acquaintance with Frances Osgood begun at Miss Lynch's salon soon ripened into close friendship. She found her way up the two flights of stairs and Edgar and Virginia and the Mother received her with as ready courtesy and welcome as though the two rooms that looked on the sky had been a palace. Her intimacy became so complete—her understanding of, and sympathy with, the three who lived for each other only so perfect that it was almost as if she had been admitted to the Valley of the Many-Colored Grass.

Upon her The Dreamer bestowed in abundant measure that poetic love which the normal heart is no more capable of feeling than the normal mind is capable of producing his poetry. A love which was like his landscapes, not of this world or of the earth earthy—a love of the mind, the imagination, the poetic faculty. A love whose desire was not to possess, but to kneel to. In his rhapsodies over the phantasmal women his genius

The Dreamer

created or the real ones whose charm he felt, it was never of flesh and blood beauty—of blooming cheek or rounded form—that he sang, but of the expression of the eye, the tones of the voice, the graces and gifts of the spirit and the intellect.

In return for this love he asked only sympathy—sympathy such as he drew from the sky and the forest and the rock-bound lake and the winds of heaven—mood sympathy.

It was a love quite beyond the imagination of Rufus Griswold to conceive of, even. His furtive eye was on the watch, his jealous heart was filled with foul surmises and he added a new poison to the old, with which he was working, drop by drop, upon the good name of Edgar Poe.

Meantime the poet, harassed by troubles of divers kinds but innocent of the new poison as he had been of the old, welcomed the intimacy of this congenial woman friend as balm to his tried spirit; and delved away at his work.

Upon his desk one morning, were piled a number of the small rolls of narrow manuscript with which the reader is familiar. These were a series of critical sketches entitled "The Literati of New York," by which he hoped to keep the pot boiling some days. Virginia was listening for a step on the stair, for she had written Mrs. Osgood a note that morning, begging her to come to them, and she knew that she would respond. The door opened and the slight, graceful figure and delicate face with the gentle eyes, she looked for, appeared.

"What are all these?" asked the visitor, when she had embraced Virginia warmly and when the poet had, after bowing over her hand, which he lightly touched with his lips, led her to a chair.

Her eyes were fixed upon the pile of manuscripts.

"One of them is yourself, Madam," replied the poet.

"Myself?" she questioned, in amazement.

He bowed, gravely. "Yourself—as one of the Literati of New York. In each one of these one of you is rolled up and discussed. I will show you by the difference in their length the varying degrees of estimation in which I hold you literary folk. Come Virginia, and help me!"

The fair visitor smiled as they drew out to the full length roll after roll of the manuscript—letting them fly together again as if they had been spiral springs. The largest they saved for the last. The poet lifted it from its place and gave an end to his wife and like two merry, laughing children they ran to opposite corners, stretching the manuscript diagonally across the entire space between.

"And whose 'linked sweetness long drawn out' is that?" asked the visitor.

"Hear her!" cried Edgar Goodfellow who was in the ascendent for the first time in many a long day. "Hear her! Just as if her vain little heart didn't tell her it's herself!"

But the moment of playfulness was a rarity, and all the more enjoyed for that.

The papers came out in due course, serially, and created a new sensation and brought their little reward, but they also plunged their author into a succession of unsavory quarrels. As each one appeared, it was looked for with eagerness and read with intense interest by the public, but frequently with as intense anger by the subject.

Perhaps the most caustic of all the critiques was the one upon the work of Mr. Thomas Dunn English, whom Poe contemptuously dubbed, "Thomas Done Brown."

Mr. English bitterly retorted with an attack upon his critic's private character. A fierce controversy followed in which English became so abusive that Poe sued and recovered two hundred and twenty-five dollars damages—which goes to prove that even an ill wind can blow good.

The Dreamer

Long after the papers had been published the scene of playful idleness, with all its holiday charm, when Edgar Poe drew out the strips of manuscript in which were rolled up "The Literati of New York" remained in Mrs. Osgood's memory, and in his own. To him it was indeed a gleam of brightness amid a throng of "earnest woes," a season of calm in a "tumultous sea."

But, as been said, why dwell upon the details of that bleak, despairing winter? Spring brought a change which makes a more pleasant picture.

Ever since they had left Philadelphia the Poes had clung, in memory, to the rose-embowered cottage in Spring Garden. There, they told each other, they had a home to their minds. It was the dear "Muddie," their ever faithful earthly Providence to whom they were already so deeply indebted, who discovered in the suburb of Fordham, a tiny cottage which had much of the charm of which they dreamed—even to the infinitesimal price for which it could be rented.

It was only a story and a half high, but there was a commodious and cheerful room down stairs, with four windows, and from the narrow hallway a quaint little winding stair led to an attic which though its roof was low and sloping contained a room large enough to serve the double purpose of bed-chamber and study.

There was a pleasant porch across the front of the cottage which would make an ideal summer sitting-room and study, when the half-starved rose-bush upon it should have been nursed and trained to screen it from the sun.

The cottage stood upon a green hill, half-buried in cherry trees—just then in full bloom and filled with bird-song. Nearby was a grove of pines and a short walk away was the Harlem River, with its picturesque, high, stone bridge. It was an abode fit to be in Paradise, Edgar told Virginia and the Mother, and within a few days they and their few small possessions—including Catalina—were as well established there as if they had never known any other home.

The moving in recalled the earliest days of their life at Spring Garden. Again "Muddie" was busy, not with soap and water only, but with the whitewash brush. Again their hearts were blythe with the pleasing sense of change—of the opening up of a new vista of there was no knowing what happiness—just as children welcome any change for the change itself, always expecting to find pleasant surprises upon a new and untried road.

But there was a difference in themselves since the moving into the Spring Garden Cottage, which had been so gradual that they were scarcely conscious of it. The years since then lay heavily upon them. They showed plainly in the deepened lines in Mother Clemm's face, in the deepened anxiety in her Mater Dolorosa eyes, in the frost upon the locks that peeped from under her immaculate widow's cap. They showed in the fragile figure of Virginia—once so full of sweet curves;—in the ethereal look that had come into the once rounded cheeks and full pouting lips, in the transparency of her skin and in the sweet eyes that when not filled with the merry laughter that had through thick and thin filled her dwelling place with sunshine and music, had a faraway expression in them, as if they were looking into another world.

They showed most of all in The Dreamer himself. To him these years had been years of fierce battle; battle, not for wealth, but for bread; battle not so much for selfish ambition as for his country, and in a high sense—for he had fought valiantly to win a place for America in the world of letters; battle with himself—with the devils that sought mastery over his spirit—the devil of excitement and exhilaration that lay in the bottom of the cup, the devil of blessed forgetfulness, accompanied by magical dreams that dwelt in the heart of the poppy, the devil of melancholy and gloom to whom he felt a certain charm in yielding himself, the devil of restlessness and dissatisfaction with whatsoever lay within

The Dreamer

his grasp—a dog-and-shadow sort of desire to drop the prize in hand in a chase after that of his vision,—the impish devil of the perverse.

At times he had been victorious, at other times there had been defeat. But always the warfare had been fierce and the scars remained to tell the story. They remained in the emaciation and the deep lines of his still beautiful face; remained in the drooping curves of the mouth; remained above all in the ineffable sadness of the large, deep, luminous eyes.

Yet that sweet spring day when the three were moving into Fordham cottage, the years that had wrought upon them thus were as they had not been.

Their little possessions had dwindled pitifully. Virginia's golden harp that had been the glory of the sitting-room was gone to pay a debt. One by one others of their household gods had provided bread. But the spurt of prosperity the damages recovered in the "Thomas Done Brown" suit brought, made possible a new checked matting for the sitting-room floor and so bright and clean did it look that they felt it almost furnished the room of itself. It would mean much to them in saving the dear Mother the most laborious feature of her labor. It was a more difficult matter than formerly for her to get down upon her knees to scrub the floor and it had become impossible for the frail Virginia to help her in such work; yet as long as the floor was bare she had kept it as spotless and nearly as white as new fallen snow. When the matting had been laid, Eddie took her beautiful worn hands in his and kissed first one and then the other.

"No more scrubbing of the sitting-room floor, dear hands," he playfully said.

In addition to the matting there were in the way of furnishings only a few chairs, some book-shelves, a picture or two, vases for flowers, some sea-shells, and, of course, Edgar's desk. Above the desk hung the pencil-sketch of "Helen" from which somehow, he was always able to draw inspiration. Sometimes the wings of his imagination would droop, his pen would halt. In desperation he would look up at the picture.—Could it be (he would ask himself) that her spirit had come to dwell in this representation of her which he had made from memory? Her eyes seemed to look at him through the eyes in the picture—the past came back to him as it sometimes did when the mingled scent of magnolias and roses on the summer night air placed him back beneath her window.

From this portrait of the lovely dead upon the wall, from the miniature of the lovely dead that he carried always next his heart, and from the lovely being who walked, in life, by his side, but toward whose bosom death had this long time pointed a warning finger, came all his inspiration in the new, as in each of the old homes.

Upstairs, close under the sloping roof, was the bare bed-room, barer than the one below—for there was no checked matting upon the floor, and there were only such pieces of furniture as were an absolute necessity; but against a small window in the end of the room leaned a great cherry-tree. The windows were open and the faint fragrance of the blossoms floated in with the song and gossip of the nesting birds. Edgar and Virginia laughed together like happy children and told each other that they would "play" that their room under the roof was a nest in the tree—which was so much more poetical than living in an attic.

And roundabout the cottage on the green hill, with its screen of blossoming cherry trees and (hardby) its dusky grove of Heaven-kissing pines, and its views of the river and walk leading to the stone-arched bridge, the three who lived for each other only had erelong reconstructed the wonderful dream-valley—the Valley of the Many-Colored Grass.

And the cottage at Fordham became a Mecca to the "literati of New York," even as the cottage at Spring Garden had been a Mecca to the literati of Philadelphia. Among those who made pilgrimages thither were many of the "starry sisterhood of poetesses"—chief of whom was the fair Frances Osgood. Yet in his retirement The Dreamer enjoyed for the first time since he had left Spring Garden long intervals of relief from company, and in the pine-wood and on the bridge overlooking the river, he found what his soul had long hungered for—silence and solitude. Under their influence he conceived the idea of a new work—a more ambitious work than anything he had hitherto attempted—a work in the form of a prose poem upon no less subject than "The Universe," whose deep secrets it was designed to reveal, with the title "Eureka!"

Ah, Dreamer, could we but call the curtain here!—Could we but leave you in your cottage on the hill-top, overlooking the river, with the trees full of blossom and music about it, and the wood inviting your fancy, where as you pace back and forth with your hands clasped behind you your great deep eyes are filled with the mellow light that illumines them when they are turned inward exploring the treasures of your brain—leave you deep in the high joy of meditation upon God's Universe!

But "the play is the tragedy, 'Man,'" and it is only for the dread "Conqueror" to give the word, "Curtain down—lights out!"

CHAPTER XXXI.

All too soon the Wolf scratched at the door of the cottage on Fordham Hill. All too soon the shadow that had so often enveloped the rose-embowered cottage in Spring Garden—the shadow from the wing of the Angel of Death—fell upon the cottage among the cherry trees.

The Dreamer sat before his desk under the picture of "Helen," for hours and hours, or when Virginia was too ill to be up, at a little table beside her bed in the chamber which was like a nest in a tree. In fair weather and foul the stately figure and sorrowful eyes of Mother Clemm were to be seen upon the streets of New York as she went about offering the narrow rolls of manuscript for sale as fast as they were finished, or trying to collect the little, over-due checks from those already sold and published. Yet, with all they could do, had it not been for the generous gifts of friends the three must needs have succumbed to cold and hunger. And all the time the poison that fell from Rufus Griswold's tongue was at work. Even the visits of the angels of mercy who ministered to him and his invalid wife in this their darkest hour were made, by the working of this poison, to appear as things of evil. How was one of the furtive eye and the black heart of a Rufus Griswold to understand love of woman of which reverence was a chief ingredient?

These ministering angels—Mrs. Osgood, Mrs. Gove, Mrs. Marie Louise Shew, and others whose love for the racked and broken Dreamer and for herself Virginia so perfectly understood—Virginia the guileless, with her sense for spiritual things and her warm, responsive heart—brought to the cottage not only encouragement and sympathy, but medicines and delicacies which were offered in such manner that even one of Edgar Poe's sensitive pride could accept them without shame.

Summer passed, and autumn, and winter drew on—filling the dwellers in Fordham cottage with fear of they knew not what miseries. There had been ups and downs; there had been happiness and woe; there had been times of strength and times of weakness—of weakness when The Dreamer, unable to hold out in the desperate battle of life as he knew it; hungry, cold and heartbroken at the sight of his wife with that faraway look in her eyes, had fallen—had sought and found forgetfulness only to know a horrible awakening that was despair and that was oftentimes accompanied by illness. Now, there was added to every thing else the knowledge that she—his wife—his heartsease flower, and the Mother, in spite of all his striving for them, were objects of charity.

The Dreamer

When some of his friends, in the kindness of their hearts, published in one of the papers an appeal to the admirers of Edgar Poe's work for aid for him and his family in their distress, he came out in a proud denial of their need for aid. The need was great enough, God knows!—but the pitiful exposure was more painful than the pangs of cold and hunger.

At last the day drew near of whose approach all who had visited the cottage knew but of which they had schooled themselves not to think.

January 1847 was waning. For many days the ground had not been seen. The branches of the cherry trees gleamed—not with flowers, but with icicles—as they leaned against the windows of the bed-chamber under the roof. Sometimes as the winter blast stirred them, they knocked against the panes with a sound the knuckles of a skeleton might have made. There was not the slightest suggestion of the soft-voiced "Ligeia" in that harsh, horrible sound.

Upon the bed the girl-wife lay well nigh as still and as white as the snow outside. Now and again she coughed—a weak, ghostly sort of cough. Over her wasted body, in addition to the thin bed-clothing, lay her husband's old military cape. Against her breast nestled Catalina, purring contentedly while she kept the heart of her mistress warm a little longer. Near the foot of her bed the Mother sat—a more perfect picture than ever of the Mater Dolorosa—chafing the tiny cold feet; at the head her husband bent over her and chafed her hands. About the room, but not near enough to intrude upon the sacred grief of the stricken mother and husband, sat several of the good women whose friendship had been the mainstay of the three. Through the window, gaining brilliance from the ice-laden branches outside, fell the rays of the setting sun, glorifying the room and the bed. Scarce a word was spoken, but upon the request of the dying girl for music one of the visitors began to sing in low, tremulous tones, the beautiful old hymn, "Jerusalem the Golden." To the man, bowed beneath his woe as it had been a physical weight, the words came as a knell, and a blacker despair than ever settled upon his wild eyes and haggard face. To his dying wife they were a promise—the smile upon her lip and the look of wonder in her eyes showed that she was already beholding the glories of which the old hymn told.

And so wandered her spirit out of the cold and the want and the gloom that had darkened and chilled the Valley of the Many-Colored Grass, into the regions of "bliss beyond compare."

But her husband, left behind, was as the man in his own story, "Silence," who sat upon a rock—the gray and ghastly rock of "Desolation." "With his brow lofty with thought and his eyes wild with care and the fables of sorrow and weariness and disgust with mankind written in furrows upon his cheek," he sat upon the lonely grey rock and leaned his head upon his hand and looked out upon the desolation. She was no more—no more!—the maiden who lived with no other thought than to love and be loved by him;—his wife—in all the storm and stress of his troubled life his true heartsease!

Out of the desolation he perceived a thing that was formless, that was invisible—but that was appalling—*silence*. Silence that made him shrink and quake—he that had loved, had longed for silence! Silence would crush him now. And solitude!—how often he had craved it! He had solitude a plenty now.

Like a hunted animal, he looked about for a refuge from the Silence and the Solitude that gave him chase, but he knew that however fast he might flee they would be hard on his heels.

How white she was—and how still! Nevermore to hear the sounds of her low sweet voice, nevermore to hear her merry laughter, nevermore her light foot-step that—like her

The Dreamer

voice and her laugh—was music to his ears! Nevermore!—for she was wrapped in the Silence—the last great silence of all.

Nevermore would she sit beside him as he worked, or plant flowers about the door, or lay her hand in his and explore with him the wonderful dream-valley; nevermore lay her sweet lips upon his or raise the snow-white lids from her eyes and shine on him from under their long, jetty fringes. Henceforth a Solitude as vast as the Silence would be his portion.

Their sweet friend Marie Louise Shew robed her for the tomb and over the snow they bore her to rest in a vault in the village churchyard.

Then, for many weeks Edgar Poe lay in the bed-chamber under the roof, desperately ill—for the most part unconscious. The mother bereaved of her child had no time to give herself over to mourning, for as she had wrestled with death for the possession of a son when he was first given into her keeping, even more fiercely did she wrestle now that he must be son and daughter too. The kind friends who had made Virginia's last days comfortable aided her in the battle, and finally the victory was won,—pale, shaken, wraith-like, the personification of woe made beautiful—The Dreamer came forth into the air of heaven once more, and as spring opened was to be seen, as of old, walking among the pines or beside the river.

And ever and anon his clear-cut, chastened features and his great, solemn eyes were turned skyward—especially at night when the heavens were sown with stars; for from some one of those bright worlds, peradventure, would she whose absence made the Solitude and the Silence be looking down upon him. And as he gazed and dreamed, high thoughts took form in his brain—thoughts of the "Material and Spiritual Universe; its Essence, its Origin, its Creation, its Present Condition and its Destiny,"—thoughts to be made into a book dedicated to "Those who feel rather than to those who think—to the dreamers and those who put faith in dreams as in the only realities"—thoughts for his projected work, "Eureka!" Out of the Silence and the Solitude came the development and completion of this strange prose poem.

Like an uneasy spirit he wandered, night and day, up and down the river bank, in the wood or in the churchyard that held the tomb of his Virginia.

Meanwhile the Mother still kept the cottage bright. She asked no questions when he went forth, night or day, or when he came in, night or day; but her heart bled for him and sometimes when he would throw himself into a deep chair and sit by the hour, seemingly staring at nothing, but really (she knew by the harassed and brooding look in the great, deep eyes) "dreaming dreams no mortal ever dared to dream before," she would steal gently to his side and with her long, slim, expressive fingers stroke the large brow until natural sleep brought respite from painful memories. Her ministrations were grateful to him, yet he was barely conscious of her presence. Not even for her, and far less for any other human being, did he feel kinship at this time. His vision, when not turned within, looked far beyond human companionship to the wonders of the universe—the stars and the mountains and the forests and the rivers; but his only real companion was his own stricken heart. Many times he said to his heart in the prophetic words of his fantastic creation, "Morella,"

"Thy days henceforth shall be days of sorrow—that sorrow which is the most lasting of impressions as the cypress is the most enduring of trees. For the hours of thy happiness are over, and joy is not gathered twice in a lifetime as the roses of Paestum twice in a year."

Yet as the back is fitted to the burden and the wind tempered to the shorn lamb, so again, as in his early griefs, the sorrow of The Dreamer was not all pain, there was an

The Dreamer

element of beauty—of poetry—in it that made it possible to be endured. Out of the depths of the Solitude and the Silence he said to his soul,

"It is a happiness to wonder—it is a happiness to dream." And more than ever before in his life his whole existence had become a dream—the realities being mere shadows.

To dream, to wonder, to work; to work, to wonder, to dream—thus were the hours, the hours of sorrow, spent. The hours of which the poet lost all count, for between his dreams and his work so intensely full were the hours of vivid mental living that each day was as a lifetime in itself.

And as he wandered under the pines or along the river, wrapped in his dreams and wondering thoughts of heaven and earth, or leaned from the window of the chamber under the low sloping roof—the chamber that had been the chamber of death—and looked beyond the embowering cherry trees upon the sky; or at dead of night sat under his lamp pondering over his books—always, everywhere, he listened—listened for the voice and the foot-falls of Virginia as he had listened in his earlier days for the voice and the footfalls of the mythical "Ligeia." For had she not promised that she would watch over him in spirit and, if possible, give him frequent indications of her presence—sighing upon him in the evening winds or filling the air which he breathed with perfume from the censers of the angels?

And her promises were faithfully kept, for often as he listened he heard the sounds of the swinging of the censers of the angels, and streams of a holy perfume floated about him, and when his heart beat heavily the winds that bathed his brow came to him laden with soft sighs, and indistinct murmurs filled the night air.

And so the green spring and the flowery summer passed, and autumn drew on.

Then came a day of days—a soft October day when merely to exist was to be happy and to hope. And new life, like some sweet, rejuvenating cordial seemed to enter and course through the veins of The Dreamer and for the first time since the Silence and the Solitude had enveloped the cottage he laughed as he flung wide the windows of the chamber that had been the chamber of death, to let in the day. And as he looked forth he said, again quoting the words of his "Morella,"

"The winds lie still in heaven. There is a dim moisture over all the earth and a warm glow upon the waters, and upon the forest a rainbow—a bow of promise—from the firmament has surely fallen. It is not a day for sorrow but for joy, for it is a day out of Aidenn itself, and I feel that ere it has passed I shall hold sweeter, more real communion with her that is in Aidenn than ever before."

He went forth and wandered through the radiance of that perfect day hours on hours, and as he paced the solemn aisles of the pine wood, or strolled along the river walk which was veiled in a golden haze and carpeted thick with the yellow and crimson and brown leaves of October, he heard, clearly, the sound of the swinging of the censers of the angels, as his senses were bathed in the holy perfume, and the zephyrs that blew about his brow were laden with audible sweet murmurs.

As evening fell a pleasant languor possessed his limbs—a wholesome weariness from his long wanderings—and he lay down upon a bank littered with fallen leaves and slept. And as he slept in the fading light, the spirit of Virginia approached him more nearly—more tangibly—than ever before; and finally, when the red sun had sunk into the river, and when the afterglow in the sky and the rainbow that lay upon the forest were alike blotted out by the shadows of night, and the moon—a lustrous blur through the haze—wandered uncertainly up the sky, she drew nearer and nearer, and pressed a fluttering kiss—such a kiss as a butterfly might bestow upon a flower—upon his lips; then, sighing, drew away.

The Dreamer

The sleeper awoke with a start—a start of heavenly bliss followed by instant pain—for as he peered into the night he saw that he was alone—with the Silence and the Solitude. The winds lay still in heaven and bore him no whisper or sigh. The perfume from the censers of the angels still filled the air, but he was conscious of a great void—a pain unbearable. The kiss had awakened a thousand thronging memories; the kiss had robbed of their charm the elusive perfume, and the ghostly whisper of fluttering garments, and the shadowy foot-falls, and the faint, faraway sighs. Henceforth these would cease to satisfy. The kiss had made him know the want of his heart for love and companionship, such as the living Virginia had given him.

He listened and listened, but the winds lay still in heaven, and he was alone with the Silence—the dread Silence—and the heart-hunger, and the despair.

Then he arose from his bed of withered and sere leaves and as one distraught, wandered through the shadows of the misty, weird night. In the wood and by the waters he wandered, while the night wore on and the moon held its way—still a lustrous blur in the heavens.

On, on he wandered, seeking peace for his soul and finding none, till the moon was out and the stars fainted in the twilight of the approaching day, when lo, above the end of the path through the wood, the morning star—"Astarte's bediamonded crescent"—arose upon his vision!

And as he gazed with wonder and delight upon the beautiful star, hope was born anew in his heart, for he said,

"It is the Star of Love!"

He that had always looked for signs in the skies, had he not found one? What could it mean, this rising of the Star of Love upon the hour of his bitterest need but a sign of hope, of peace?

Vainly did his soul upbraid him and warn him not to trust the beacon—to fly from its alluring light and cast aside its spell. All deaf to the warning, he eagerly followed the star which promised renewal of hope and love and relief from the Solitude and the Silence—the desolation that the kiss had made so real and intolerable.

But alas, as he wandered on and on, his eyes upon the star, his feet following blindly, without marking the path into which they had turned, his progress was suddenly checked. Through the misty twilight of the approaching dawn there loomed an obstacle to his steps. It was with horror unspeakable that he recognized the vault in which lay, in her last sleep, his loved Virginia....

"Then his heart it grew ashen and sober As the leaves that were crispéd and sere,— As the leaves that were withering and sere!"

The Star of Love was fading in the eastern sky and through the ghostly dawn he turned and fled aghast to the cottage among the cherry trees.

Mother Clemm who had lain waiting and watching for him all night arose from her uneasy couch when she heard the latch of the gate lifted, and opened the door. He came in and walked past her like a wraith. His eyes were wild, his face was bloodless and haggard, his hair damp and disordered. The Mother's eyes were filled with dumb pain. He suffered her to take his hand in hers and to gaze into his eyes with pity and even raised the hand that held his own to his lips, as though to reassure her; but he spake no word—made no attempt at explanation—and she asked no questions.

For a moment he remained beside her, then straight to his desk he walked and began arranging writing materials before him, while she disappeared into the kitchen and started a blaze under a pot of coffee that stood upon the little stove.

He wrote rapidly—furiously—without pausing for thought or for the fastidious choice of words that was apt to make him halt frequently in the act of composition, and the words that he wrote were the wild words—wild, but beautiful and moving as an echo from Israfel's own lute—of the poem, "Ulalume:"

"The skies they were ashen and sober; The leaves they were crispéd and sere,— The leaves they were withering and sere,— It was night in the lonesome October Of my most immemorial year."

After that eventful night a change came over him that sat upon the Rock of Desolation. The Solitude and the Silence still enfolded him, but the Star of Love had arisen in his firmament, ushering in a new day and new hope to his soul. And he no longer trembled as he sat upon the rock, but with new energy he worked and with exceeding patience he waited. And as he worked interest in life returned to him, and ambition returned.

One day he copied "Ulalume" upon a long, narrow slip of paper and rolled it into one of the tight little rolls that all the editors knew and Mother Clemm made a pilgrimage to the city especially on account of it. First she tried it at *The Union Magazine*, which promptly rejected it. It was too "queer" the editor said. But *The American Review* agreed to take it and to print it without signature—for this poem must be published anonymously, if at all, the poet insisted. It soon afterward appeared and Mr. Willis copied it into the next number of *The Home Journal* with complimentary editorial comment.

The result was a new sensation—the reader everywhere declared himself to be brought under a magic spell by the words of this remarkable poem—though he frankly owned that he did not in the least understand them; which was as Edgar Poe intended.

Even the old dream of founding a magazine returned and possessed him as it had so often possessed him before. It was in the interest of the magazine, which he still proposed to name *The Stylus*, that he determined to give his new work, "Eureka!" as a lecture, in various places. He did give it once—in New York—coming out of his seclusion for the first time, upon a frosty February night. The rhapsody, delivered in his low but musical and dramatic tones, thrilled his audience, but it was a small audience, and when soon afterward, the work was published by the *Putnams* it was a small number of copies that was sold.

And again Edgar Poe was desperately poor. Yet he had seen the Star of Love— "Astarte's bediamonded crescent"—usher in a new morning; and he waited and worked in hope.

CHAPTER XXXII.

Autumn with its enchanted October night, and winter filled with work and spent in deep seclusion at Fordham, and spring with its revival of plans for *The Stylus*, and the appearance of "Eureka!" as a book, and its author's return to the world as a lecturer, slipped by.

About midsummer The Dreamer lay a night in the old town of Providence. It was a warm night and the window of his room was open—letting in a flood of light from the full moon. He leaned from the window which looked upon a plot of flowers whose many odors rising, enveloped him in incense sweet as the incense from the censers of the angels when the spirit of his Virginia was near. But it was not of Virginia that the fragrance told him tonight. Something about the blended odors, combined with the sensuous warmth of

The Dreamer

the night and the light of the moon, transported him suddenly, magically, back through the years to his boyhood and to the little room in the Allan cottage on Clay Street, hanging, like this room, over a space of flowers—the night following the day when he had first seen Rob Stanard's mother.

Back, back into the long dead past he wandered! The broken and jaded Edgar Poe was dreaming again the dream of the fresh, enthusiastic boy, Edgar Poe.

How every incident of that day and night stood out in his memory! He could feel again the wonder that he felt when he saw the beautiful "Helen" standing against the arbor-vitæ in the garden; could see her graceful approach to meet and greet him—the lonely orphan boy—could hear her gracious words in praise of his mother while she held his hand in both her own. As he lived it all over again, with the silver moonlight enfolding him and the breath of the flowers filling his nostrils, a clock somewhere in the house struck the night's noon hour. He started—even so it had been that other night in the long past. He half believed that if he should go forth into this night as he had gone into that he should see once more the lady of his dream, with the lamp in her hand, framed in the ivy-wreathed window, and seeing, worship as he had worshipped then.

Scarce knowing what he did, he arose and hurrying down the stair was in the street. The streets were strange to him but there was a pleasant sense of adventure in wandering through them—he knew not whither—and the sweet airs of the flowers were everywhere.

Suddenly he stopped. While all the town slept there was one beside himself, who kept vigil. Clad all in white, she half reclined upon a violet bank in an old garden where the moon fell on the upturned faces of a thousand roses and on her own, "upturned,—alas, in sorrow!"

Faint with the beauty and the poetry of the scene he leaned upon the gate of the

"enchanted garden Where no wind dared to stir unless on tiptoe."

He dared not speak or give any sign of his presence, but he gazed and gazed until to his entranced eyes it seemed that

"The pearly lustre of the moon went out: The mossy banks and the meandering paths— The happy flowers and the repining trees— Were seen no more."

All was lost to his vision—

"Save only the divine light in those eyes— Save but the soul in those uplifted eyes."

He continued to gaze until the moon disappeared behind a bank of cloud and he watched the white-robed figure glide away like "a ghost amid the entombing trees." Yet still (it seemed to him) the eyes remained. They lighted his lonely footsteps home that night and he told himself that they would light him henceforth, through the years.

Nearly a year had passed since that October night when the Star of Love ushering in a new morning had prophesied to him of new hope—nearly a year through which he had waited patiently, but not in vain. The time had evidently come for the prophecy to be fulfilled and Fate had led him to this town and the spot in this town where she that was to be (he was convinced) the hope, the guide, the savior, of his "lonesome latter years" awaited him.

Who was she?—

So spirit-like, so ethereal, she seemed, as robed in white and veiled in silvery moonbeams she sat among the slumbering roses, and as she was gathered into the shadows of the entombing trees, that she might almost have been the "Lady Ligeia." Yet he knew that she was not. The "Lady Ligeia" had been but the creation of his own brain. Very fair she had been to his dreaming vision, very sweet her companionship had been to his

The Dreamer

imagination—sufficient for all the needs of his being in his youthful days when sorrow was but a beautiful sentiment, when "terror was not fright, but a tremulous delight" but how was such an one as she to bind up the broken heart of a man? It was the *human* element in the eyes of her that sat among the roses that enchained him. Ethereal—spirit-like—as she was, the eyes upturned in sorrow were the eyes of no spirit, but of a woman; from them looked a human soul with the capacity and the experience to offer sympathy meet for human needs—the needs even, of a broken-hearted man.

How dark the woe!—how sublime the hope!—how intense the pride!—how daring the ambition!—how deep, how fathomless the capacity for love!—that looked (as from a window) from those eyes upturned in sorrow, in the moonlight while all the town slept!

Who was she?—this lady of sorrows. And by what sweet name was she known to the citizens of this old town?—Surely Fate that had brought her to the bank of violets beneath the moon—Fate that had led him to her garden gate, would in Fate's own time reveal!

As Helen Whitman flitted as noiselessly as the ghost she seemed to be up the dark stairway to her chamber, and without closing the casement that admitted the moonlight and the garden's odors, lay down upon her canopied bed, she trembled. What was it that she had been aware of in the garden?—that presence—that consciousness of communion between her spirit and his upon whom all her thoughts had dwelt of late? Herself a poet, from her earliest knowledge of the work of Edgar Poe she had seemed to feel a kinship between her mind and his such as she had known in regard to no other. She had followed his career step by step, and out of the many sorrows of her own life had been born deep sympathy for him. Since his last, greatest blow, she had more than ever mourned with him in spirit, for she too was widowed—she too had sat upon the Rock of Desolation and knew the Silence and the Solitude.

She and The Dreamer had at least one mental trait in common—a tendency toward spiritualism—a more than half belief in the communion of the spirits of the dead with those of the living and of those of the living with each other.

What had led her into the moonlit garden when all the world slept?

She knew not. She only knew that she had felt an impelling influence—a call to her spirit—to come out among the slumbering roses. She had not questioned nor sought to define it. She had heard it, and she had obeyed. And then the presence!—

She had never seen Edgar Poe, yet she felt that he had been there in the spirit, if not in the flesh—she had felt his eyes upon her eyes and she had half expected him to step from the shadows around her and to say,

"I, upon whom your thoughts have dwelt—I, who am the comrade and the complement of your inner life—I, whose spirit called to you ere you came into the garden—I am here."

It was almost immediately upon The Dreamer's return to Fordham, and when he was still under the spell of the night at Providence, that the identity of the lady of the garden was revealed to him, in a manner seemingly accidental, but which he felt to be but another manifestation of the divinity that shapes our ends. Some casual words concerning the appearance and character of Mrs. Whitman, spoken by a casual visitor, lifted the curtain.

So the lady of the garden was Helen Whitman! whose poetry had impressed him favorably and whose acquaintance he had desired. Helen Whitman—*Helen*! As he repeated the name his heart stood still,—even in her name he heard the voice of Fate.

The Dreamer

Helen—the name of the good angel of his boyhood! Were his dreams of "Morella" and of "Ligeia" to come true? Was he to know in reality the miracle he had imagined and written of in these two phantasies?—the reincarnation of personal identity? Was he in this second Helen, in this second garden, to find again the worshipped Helen of his boyhood?

He turned to the lines he had written so long ago, in Richmond, when he had gone forth into the midsummer moonlight, even as he had gone forth in Providence, and had worshipped under a window, even as he had worshipped at a garden gate. He read the first two stanzas through.

As he read he gave himself up to an overwhelming sense of fatality. Could anything be more fitting—more descriptive? The end of the days of miracles was not yet—this *was* his "Helen of a thousand dreams!"

His impulse was to seek an introduction at once, but this seemed too tamely conventional. Besides—he was in the hands of Fate—he dared not stir. Fate, having so clearly manifested itself, would find a way.

His correspondence was always heavy. Letters, clippings from papers and so forth, came to him by every post from friends and from enemies, with and without signatures. Yet from all the mass, he knew at once that the "Valentine," unsigned as it was, was from her.

By way of acknowledgment, he turned down a page of a copy of "The Raven and Other Poems" at the lines, "To Helen," and mailed it to her. He waited in anxious suspense for a reply, but the lady was coy. Days passed and still no answer. The desire for communication with her became irresistible and taking pen and paper he wrote at the top of the page, even as long ago he had written, the words, "To Helen," and underneath wrote a new poem especially for this new Helen in which he described the vision of her in the garden (but placing it in the far past) and his feelings as he gazed upon her:

"I saw thee once—once only—years ago; I must not say *how* many—but not many.

Clad all in white, upon a violet bank I saw thee half reclining; while the moon Fell on the upturned faces of the roses, And on thine own, upturned,—alas in sorrow! Was it not Fate, that, on this July midnight— Was it not Fate (whose name is also Sorrow) That bade me pause before that garden-gate To breathe the incense of those slumbering roses? No footstep stirred: the hated world all slept, Save only thee and me. (Oh, Heaven!—oh, God! How my heart beats in coupling those two words!) Save only thee and me!" ...

The paper trembled in the hands—tiny and spirit-like—of Helen Whitman. Her soul answered emphatically,

"It *is* Fate!"

So he had been there in the flesh—near her—in the shadows of that mystic night! The presence was no creation of an overwrought imagination. It was Fate.

Tremulously she penned her answer to his appeal, but was it Fate again, which caused the letter to miscarry? It reached him finally, in Richmond—*Richmond*, of all places!—whither he had gone to deliver to audiences of his old friends, his lecture upon "The Poetic Principle," in the interest of the establishment of his magazine, *The Stylus*. What could have been more fitting than that the gracious words of "Helen of a thousand dreams" should come to him in Richmond?

Not many days later and he was under her own roof in Providence.

The Dreamer

He waited in the dimness of her curtained drawing-room, ear strained for the first sound of her footstep. Noiselessly as a sunbeam or a shadow she entered the room, her gauzy white draperies floating about her slight figure as she came, while his great eyes drank in with reverent joy each detail of her ethereal loveliness—her face, the same he had seen in the garden, pale as a pearl and as softly radiant, and framed in clustering dark ringlets which escaped in profusion from the confinement of a lacy widow's cap—the tremulous mouth—the eyes, mysterious and unearthly, from which the soul looked out.

For one moment she paused in the doorway, her hand pressed upon her wildly beating heart—then, with hesitating step advanced to meet him. Her words of greeting were few, and so low and faltering as to be quite unintelligible, but the tones of her voice fell on his ear like strangely familiar music.

The man spoke no word. As her eyes rested for one brief moment upon his, then fell before the intensity of his gaze, he was conscious of spiritual influences beyond the reach of reason. In a tremulous ecstacy he bent and pressed his lips upon the hand that lay within his own and it was with difficulty that he restrained himself from falling upon his knees before her in actual worship.

Three evenings of "all heavenly delight" he spent in her companionship—sometimes in the seclusion and dusk of her quiet drawing-room, sometimes walking among the roses in her garden, or among the mossy tombs in the town cemetery—their sympathetic natures finding expression in such conversation as poets delight in. Under the intoxicating spell of her presence all other dreams passed, for the time, into nothingness and he passionately cried,

"Helen, I love now—*now*—for the first and only time!"

Yet he was poor, and the weaknesses which had caused him to fall in the past might cause him to fall in the future. How could he plead for a return of his love?

His very self-abasement made his plea more strong. Still, she did not yield too suddenly. True, she too, was under the spell, but she resisted it. As he found his voice, and his eloquence filled the room a restlessness possessed her. Now she sat quite still by his side, now rose and wandered about the apartment—now stood with her hand resting upon the back of his chair while his nearness thrilled her.

There were objections, she told him—she was older than he.

"Has the soul age, Helen?" he answered her. "Can immortality regard time? Can that which began never and shall never end consider a few wretched years of its incarnate life? Do you not perceive that it is my diviner nature—my spiritual being, that burns and pants to commingle with your own?"

She urged her frail health as an objection.

For that he would love—worship her—the more, he said. He plead for her pity upon his loneliness—his sorrows—and swore that he would comfort and soothe her in hers, through life, and when death should come, joyfully go down with her into the night of the grave.

Finally he appealed to her ambition.

"Was I right, Helen, in my first impression of you?—in the impression that you are ambitious? If so, and if you will have faith in me, I can and will satisfy your wildest desires. Would it not be glorious to establish in America, the sole unquestionable aristocracy—that of the intellect—to secure its supremacy—to lead and control it?"

Still the *yes* that so often seemed trembling upon her lips was not spoken. She received his almost daily letters and his frequent visits, listened to his rapturous love-making—trembling, blushing, letting him see that she was under the spell, that she loved him.

The Dreamer

Indeed she could not have helped his seeing it had she wished; but when he spoke of marriage she hesitated—tantalizing him to the point of madness, almost.

What was it that held her back?—She too, believed that it was the hand of Fate that had brought them together—that they were pre-ordained to cheer each other's latter years, to establish that intellectual aristocracy of which he dreamed. Yet she shrank from taking the step. When his great solemn eyes were upon her, his beautiful face pale and haggard with excess of feeling, turned toward her, his eloquent words of love in her ears, she sat as one entranced—bewitched; yet she would not give the word he longed for—the word of willingness to embark with him upon the sea of life. *Fear* checked her. Such an uncharted sea it seemed to her—she dared not say him yea!

The truth was the poison was working—the Griswold poison. The wildest rumors came to her ears of the worse than follies of her lover. She knew that they were at least, overdrawn—possibly altogether false—yet they frightened her.

"Do you know Helen Whitman?" wrote one of The Dreamer's enemies to Dr. Griswold. "Of course you have heard it rumored that she is to marry Poe. Well, she has seemed to me a good girl and—you know what Poe is. Has Mrs. Whitman no friend in your knowledge that can faithfully explain Poe to her?"

But Rufus Griswold had already "explained Poe" to those whom he knew would take pains to pass the explanation on to "Helen"—had dropped the poison where he reckoned it would work with the greatest speed and effect. The explanation, with the usual indirectness of a Griswold, was sugared with a compliment.

"Poe has great intellectual power," he said with emphasis, "*great* intellectual power, but," he added, with a sidelong glance of the furtive eye and a confidential drop in the voice, "but—he has no principle—no moral sense."

The poison reached the destination for which it was intended—the ears of Helen Whitman—in due course, and it terrified her as had none of the rumors she had heard before. Still her lover floundered in the dark—baffled—wondering—not able to make her out. Why did she tantalize him—torture him, thus?—keeping him dangling between Heaven and hell?—he asked himself, and he asked her, over and over again. He became more and more convinced that there was a reason,—what was it?

Finally she gave it to him in its baldness and its brutality, just as it had come to her—wrote it to him in a letter. It brought him a rude awakening from his dream of bliss. That such a charge should be brought against him at all was bitter enough, but that it could be repeated to him by "Helen" seemed unbelievable.

"You do not love me," he sadly wrote in reply, "or you would not have written these terrible words." Then he swore a great oath: "By the God who reigns in Heaven, I swear to you that my soul is incapable of dishonor—that with the exception of occasional follies and excesses which I bitterly lament, but to which I have been driven by intolerable sorrow, I can call to mind no act of my life which would bring a blush to my cheek—or to yours."

He followed the letter with a visit—again throwing himself at her feet and thrilling her with his eloquence and with the magic of his personality.

She gave him a half promise and said she would write to him in Lowell, where he had engaged to deliver a lecture.

In this town was a roof-tree which was a haven of rest to The Dreamer. Beneath it dwelt his friend and confidant, "Annie" Richmond—his soul's sweet "sister," as he loved to call her. And there he waited with a chastened joy, for he felt assured that the long wished for *yes* was about to be said, yet dared not give himself over prematurely, to the ecstacy that would soon be his. In the pleasant, friendly family circle of the Richmonds, he sat during those chill November evenings, seeing pictures in the glowing fire, as he

The Dreamer

held sweet "Annie's" sympathetic hand in his, while the only sound that broke the silence was the ticking of the grandfather's clock in a shadowy corner.

Thus quietly, patiently, he waited.

But in Providence the Griswold poison was at work. All the friends and relatives of "Helen" were possessed of full vials of it—which they industriously poured into her ears. Against it the recollection of the night in the garden and her belief that Fate had ordained her union with the poet, had no avail. The letter that she sent her lover was more non-committal—colder—than any he had received from her before, yet there was still enough of indecision in it to keep him tantalized. In a state of mind well nigh distraction, he bade "Annie" and her cheerful fireside farewell and set his face toward Providence; but he went in a dream—the demon Despair, possessing him.

Unstrung, unmanned, almost bereft of reason, his old dissatisfaction with himself and the world overtook him—a longing to be out of it all, for forgetfulness, for peace, yea, even the peace of the grave,—why not?

A passionate longing—a homesickness—for the sure, the steadfast, the unvariable love of his beautiful Virginia consumed him. Oh, if he could but lie down and sleep and forget until one sweet day he should wake in the land where she awaited him, and where they would construct anew, and for eternity, the Valley of the Many-Colored Grass!

He listened.... For the first time since the Star of Love had ushered in a new day in his life, he heard the swinging of the censers of the angels—he inhaled the incense—he heard the voice of Virginia in the sighing wind. She seemed to call to him.

"I am coming, Heartsease!" he whispered as he quaffed the potion that he reckoned would bear him to her.

But it was not to be. When he awaked, weak and ill, but sane, he found himself with friends. Calmness and strength returned and with them, horror at the deed he had so nearly committed, and deep contrition.

With all haste he again presented himself at the door of "Helen," beseeching her to marry him at once and save him, as he believed she only could, from himself. And the consequences of her indecision making her more alarmed for him than she had formerly been for herself, she agreed to an engagement, though not to immediate marriage.

He returned to Fordham and to faithful Mother Clemm a wreck of his former self, but engaged to be married!

Yet he was not happy—a new horror possessed him. As in the night when the Star of Love first rose upon his vigil it had stopped over the door of "a legended tomb," so now again was his pathway closed. Turn which way he would, the tomb of Virginia seemed to frown upon him. He remembered his promise to her that upon no other daughter of earth would he look with the eyes of love. Vainly did he seek to justify himself to his own heart for breaking the promise. No one could ever supplant her, or fill the void in his life her death had made, he told himself—this new love was something different, and in no way disturbed her memory.

But the tomb still stood in his way.

"I am calm and tranquil," he wrote "Helen," "and but for a strange shadow of coming evil which haunts me I should be happy. That I am not supremely happy, even when I feel your dear love at my heart, terrifies me."

Later he wrote,

The Dreamer

"You say that all depends on my own firmness. If this be so all is safe. Henceforward I am strong. But all does not depend, dear Helen, upon my firmness—all depends upon the sincerity of your love."

A month later the skies of Providence shone brightly upon him. He returned there, was received by Mrs. Whitman as her affianced lover, delivered his brilliant lecture upon "The Poetic Principle" to a great throng of enthusiastic hearers, and won a promise from his lady to marry him at once and return with him to Fordham. He scribbled a line to Mother Clemm notifying her to be ready to receive him and his bride and went so far as to engage the services of a clergyman, and to sign a marriage contract, in which Mrs. Whitman's property was made over to her mother.

But—just at this point a note was slipped into the hand of "Helen," informing her that her lover had been seen drinking wine in the hotel. When he called at her house soon afterward she received him surrounded by her family and though there were no signs of the wine, said "no" to him, emphatically—for the first time.

He plead, but she remained firm—receiving his passionate words of remonstrance with sorrowful silence, while her mother, impatient at his persistence, showed him the door. He prayed that she would at least speak one word to him in farewell.

"What can I say?" she questioned.

"Say that you love me, Helen."

"I love you!"

With these words in his ears he was gone. As he passed out of the gate and out of her life he saw, or fancied he saw, through the veiled window, a white figure beckoning to him, but his steps were sternly set toward the opposite direction—his whole being crying within him, "Nevermore—nevermore!" She had stretched out her spiritlike hands, but to draw them back again, in the fashion that fascinated and at the same time maddened him, once too often. The wave of romantic feeling which had borne him along since his vision of her in the garden suddenly subsided, leaving him disillusioned—cold. The reaction was so violent that instead of the magnetic attraction she had had for him he felt himself positively repelled by the thought of her unearthly beauty—her mysterious eyes.

He went straight to the depot and took the train just leaving, which would bear him back to the cottage among the cherry trees.

Mother Clemm, expecting him to bring home a bride, had spent the day putting an extra touch of brightness upon the simple but already spotless, home. A cheerful fire was in the grate; branches of holly, cedar and such other such bits of beauty as the woods afforded were everywhere about the house, and the Mother herself, in the snowiest of caps with the sheerest of floating strings and a gallant look of welcome upon her sorrowful face, stood at the window and watched for the coming of the son that Heaven had given her, and the woman who was to take the place of the daughter that Heaven had taken away from her. Her oak-like nature had quailed at the thought—but it had withstood many a blast, it could weather one more, and after all, if "Eddie" were happy—.

In the far distance a figure emerged out of the gathering dusk—a man. Could it be Eddie?—Alone?

Yes! It surely was he! The carriage of the head—the military cloak—the walk—were unmistakable.

But he was alone!—She grew weak in the knees.—The shock of joy more nearly unnerved her than had the pain. She had braced herself to bear the pain.

The Dreamer

She recovered her composure and hastened to the door just in time to be folded into the arms of the figure in the cloak.

"Helen?"—she queried.

"Is dead—to me," he answered, with his arms still about her. "We will have nothing more to say of her except this: Muddie, I have been in a dream from which, thank God, I am now awake. In the darkness of my loneliness—of my misery, of which you alone have the slightest conception, I saw a light which I fancied would lead me to the love for which my soul is starving—to the sympathy which is sweeter even than love to the broken heart of a man. I followed it. I was deceived. It was no real light, but a mere will o' the wisp bred in the dank tarn of despair."

He released her to hang up the cloak in the little entrance hall, then taking her hand, which he raised to his lips, drew her into the sitting room.

"Ah, but it is good to be at home again!" he exclaimed.

His whole manner changed; a mighty weight seemed to roll from his shoulders as he stretched his legs before the fire. His old merry laugh—the laugh of Edgar Goodfellow—rang out as he told "Muddie" of the success of his lecture, in Providence,—of the great audience and the applause.

"Muddie," he cried, "my dream of *The Stylus* will come true yet! A few more such audiences and the money will be in sight! And let me add, I am done with literary women—henceforth literature herself shall be my sole mistress. I am more than ever convinced that the profession of letters is the only one fit for a man of brain. There is little money in it, of course, but I'd rather be a poor-devil author earning a bare living than a king. Beyond a living, what does a man of brain want with money anyhow?—Muddie, did it ever strike you that all that is really valuable to a man of talent—especially to a poet—is absolutely unpurchasable?—Love, fame, the dominion of intellect, the consciousness of power, the thrilling sense of beauty, the free air of Heaven, exercise of body and mind with the physical and moral health that these bring;—these, and such as these are really all a poet cares about. Then why should he mind what the world calls poverty?"

"Why indeed?" echoed happy "Muddie." It was so delightful to have her son back at home, and in this hopeful, contented frame, she would have agreed with him in almost any statement he chose to make.

He gave her loving messages from "Annie" and told her in the bright, humorous way which was characteristic of Edgar Goodfellow, of many pleasant little incidents of his journey. One of the nights to look back upon and to gloat over in memory was this night by the fireside at Fordham cottage with the Mother—a night of calm and content under the home-roof after tempestuous wandering.

A quiet, sweet Christmas they spent together—he reading, writing or talking over plans for new work, while she sat by with her sewing and Catalina dozed on the hearth. Part of every day (wrapped in the old cape) he walked in the pine wood or beside the ice-bound river, and for the first time since the feverish dream of new love had come to him he was able to visit the tomb of Virginia and to dwell with happiness, and with a clear conscience, upon her memory. During these days of serenity a ballad suggested by thoughts of her and his life with her in the lovely Valley of the Many-Colored Grass took form in his mind. It was no dirge-like song of the "dank tarn of Auber," but a song of a fair "kingdom by the sea" and in contrast to the sombre "Ulalume" he gave to the maiden in the new poem the pleasant sounding name of "Annabel Lee." Out of these days too, came "the Bells" and the exquisite sonnet to his "more than Mother."

One flash of the false light that had lured him reached The Dreamer at Fordham. He held a letter addressed to him in the familiar handwriting of Helen Whitman long in his hand without opening it. This flame was burned out, he told himself—why rake its cold ashes? Yet he felt that nothing that she could say would have power to disturb his new peace. Still the Mother, though she kept her own counsel, trembled for herself and for him as she was aware (without looking up from her sewing) that he had broken the seal. Some minutes of tense stillness passed—then,

"Shall I read you her letter?" he asked.

"As you will."

"Then I will!—It is in verse and the place from which she dates it is,

"Our Island of Dreams," which she explains in a sub-heading is

"By the foam Of perilous seas, in faery lands forlorn"

—a line which she has borrowed from Keats. This is what she writes:

"Tell him I lingered alone on the shore, Where we parted, in sorrow, to meet nevermore; The night-wind blew cold on my desolate heart But colder those wild words of doom, 'Ye must part!'

"O'er the dark, heaving waters, I sent forth a cry; Save the wail of those waters there came no reply. I longed, like a bird, o'er the billows to flee, From our lone island home and the moan of the sea:

"Away,—far away—from the wild ocean shore, Where the waves ever murmur, 'No more, nevermore,' Where I wake, in the wild noon of midnight, to hear The lone song of the surges, so mournful and drear.

"Where the clouds that now veil from us heaven's fair light, Their soft, silver lining turn forth on the night; When time shall the vapors of falsehood dispel He shall know if I loved him; but never how well."

Silence followed the reading of the poem-letter. Finally the mother asked,

"Will you go back?"

He placed the letter upon the top of a pile in the same handwriting, tied them together with a bit of ribbon and laid them in a small drawer of his desk. Then, rising, he leaned over the back of "Muddie's" chair and lightly touching her seamed forehead with his lips replied,

"Quoth the raven, nevermore!"

Then took up a garland of evergreen which he had been making when the Mother came in with the mail, and set out in the direction of the churchyard with its "legended tomb."

CHAPTER XXXIII.

Back in Richmond!—The Richmond he loved best—Richmond full of sunshine and flowers and the sweet southern social life out of doors, in gardens and porches; Richmond in summertime!

In spite of the changes his observant eye marked as he rattled over the cobblestones toward the "Swan Tavern," on Broad and Ninth Streets, he almost felt that he was back in boyhood. It was just such a day, just this time of year, that—as a lad of eleven—he had seen Richmond first after his five years absence in England.

How good it was to be back upon the sacred soil! How sweet the air was, and how beautiful were the roses! When before, had he seen a magnolia tree in bloom?—with its dense shade, its dark green shining foliage, and its snow-white blossoms. Was there anything in the world so sweet as its odor, combined with that of the roses and the other

The Dreamer

flowers that filled the gardens? It was worth coming all the way from New York just to see and to smell them.

He caught glimpses of one or two familiar figures as he drove along. How impatient he was to see his old friends—everybody—white and colored, old and young, masculine and feminine. He could hardly wait to get to the tavern, remove the dust of travel and sally forth upon the round of visits he intended to make. His spirits went up—and up, and finally it was Edgar Goodfellow in the flesh who stepped jauntily from the door of "Swan Tavern," arrayed for hot-weather calling. In spite of the summer temperature, he looked the personification of coolness and comfort. The taste of prosperity his lectures had brought him was evident in his modest but spruce apparel. He had discarded the habitual black cloth for a coat and trousers of white linen (exquisitely laundered by Mother Clemm's capable and loving hands) which he wore with a black velvet vest for which he had also to thank the Mother and her skilled needle. A broad-brimmed Panama hat shaded his pale features and the grey eyes, which glowed with happiness. As with proudly carried head and quick, easy gait, he bore westward up Broad Street, no single person passed him that did not turn to look with admiration upon the handsome, distinguished stranger, and to mentally ask "Who is he?"

It so happened that Jack Mackenzie was the first acquaintance he met.

"Edgar," he said, as their hands joined in affectionate grasp, "Do you remember once, years ago, I met you in the street and you said you were going to look for the end of the rainbow? Well, you look as if you had found it!"

"I have," was the reply. "An hour ago. It was here in Richmond all the time and I didn't know it, and like a poor fool, have been wandering the world over in a vain search for it. The trouble is, I was looking for the wrong thing. I was looking for fame and fortune, thought of which blinded my eyes to something far better—scenes and friendships of *lang syne*. Jack—" he continued, as—arm in arm—the two friends made their way up the street. "Jack, life is a great schoolmaster, but why does it take so long to drub any sense into these blockheads of ours?"

"Damned if I know," replied his companion, who was more truthful always than either poetic or philosophic, "but if you mean that you've decided to come back to Richmond to live, I'm mighty glad to hear it."

"That's what I mean. I came only for a visit and to lecture, but made up my mind on the way from the depot to come for good as soon as I can arrange to do so. I think it was a magnolia tree in bloom—the first I had seen in many a year—that decided me."

"Well, all of your old friends will be glad to have you back; there's one in particular that I might mention. Do you remember Elmira Royster? She's a comely widow now, with a comfortable fortune, and she's always had a lingering fondness for you. I advise you to hunt her up."

The Dreamer's face clouded.

"Women are angels, Jack," he said. "They are the salt that will save this world, if it is to be saved, and for poor sinners like me there would be simply no hope in either this world or the next but for them; but they will have no more part in my life, save as friends. A true friend of mine, however, I believe Myra is. I saw her during my brief visit here last fall.—Ah, Rob! my boy! Howdy!"

The two friends had turned into Sixth Street and as they drew near the corner of Sixth and Grace, almost ran into Rob Stanard—now a prominent lawyer and one of the leading gentlemen of the town.

"Eddie Poe, as I'm alive!" he exclaimed, with a hearty hand-clasp. "My, my, what a pleasure! I'm on my way home to dinner, boys. Come in, both of you and take pot-luck with us. My wife will be delighted to see you!"

The Dreamer

The invitation was accepted as naturally as it was given, and the three mounted together the steps of the beautiful house and were received in the charmingly homelike drawing-room opening from the wide hall, by Rob's wife, a Kentucky belle who had stepped gracefully into her place as mistress of one of the notable homes in Virginia's capital. As she gave her jewelled hand to Edgar Poe her handsome black eyes sparkled with pleasure. She was not only sincerely glad to receive the friend of her husband's boyhood, but keen appreciation of intellectual gifts made her feel that to know him was a distinction. Some of the servants who had known "Marse Eddie" in the old days were still of the household—having come to Robert Stanard as part of his father's estate—and they were to their intense gratification, pleasantly greeted by the visitor.

That evening—and many subsequent evenings—The Dreamer spent at "Duncan Lodge" with the Mackenzies and their friends. A series of sunlit days followed—days of lingering in Rob Sully's studio or in the familiar office of *The Southern Literary Messenger* where the editor, Mr. John R. Thompson—himself a poet—gave him a warm welcome always, and gladly accepted and published in *The Messenger* anything the famous former editor would let him have; days of wandering in the woods or by the tumbling river he had loved as a lad; days of searching out old haunts and making new ones.

And everywhere he found welcome. Delightful little parties were given in his honor, when in return for the courtesies paid him he charmed the company by reciting "The Raven" as he alone could recite it. His lectures upon "The Poetic Principle" and "The Philosophy of Composition," and his readings in the assembly rooms of the Exchange Hotel, drew the elite of the city, who sat spellbound while he, erect and still and pale as a statue, filled their ears with the music of his voice, and their souls with wonder at the brilliancy of his thought and words. Subscriptions to *The Stylus* poured in. At last, this dream of his life seemed an assured fact.

One door—one only in all the town did not swing wide to receive him. The closed portal of the mansion of which he had been the proud young master, still said to him "Nevermore"—and he always had a creepy sensation when he passed it, which even the sight of the flower-garden he had loved, in fullest bloom, did not overcome.

The golden days ran into golden weeks and the weeks into months, and still Edgar Poe was making holiday in Richmond—the first holiday he had had since, as a youth of seventeen he had quarrelled with John Allan and gone forth to the battle of life. In the long, long battle since then there had been more of joy than they knew who looking on had seen the toil and the defeat and the despair, but from whose eyes the exaltation he had felt in the act of creation or in the contemplation of the works of nature, and the happiness he found in his frugal home, were hidden. But, as has been said, there had been no holiday, until now when he had come back to Richmond an older and a sadder and a more experienced Edgar Poe—an Edgar Poe upon whom the Silence and the Solitude had fallen and had left shaken—broken.

Yet that personal identity upon the mystery of which he liked to ponder—the unquenchable, immortal *ego* was there; and it was, for all the outward and inward changes, the same Edgar Poe, with his two natures—Dreamer and Goodfellow—alternately dominating him, who had come back to find the real end of the rainbow in revisiting old scenes, renewing old friendships, awakening old memories—and had paused to make holiday.

Even in these golden days there were occasional falls, for the cup of kindness was everywhere and in his blood was the same old strain which made madness for him in the single glass—the single drop, almost; and in spite of all the great schoolmaster, Life, had taught him, there was in his will the same old element of weakness. Had it been otherwise he had not been Edgar Poe. At times, too, the blue devils raised their heads. Had it been otherwise he had not been Edgar Poe.

But on the whole the holiday was a bright dream of Paradise regained at a time when more than ever before his feet had seemed to march only to the cadence of the old, sad word, Nevermore.

Two sacred pilgrimages he made early in this holiday—to the two shrines of his romantic boyhood—to Shockoe Cemetery, where he not only visited "Helen's" tomb, but laid a wreath upon the grave of Frances Allan—his little foster mother, and to the churchyard on the hill. The white steeple still slept serenely in the blue atmosphere above the church and, as of yore, the bell called in deep, sweet tones to prayer. But how the churchyard had filled since he saw it last! Graves, graves everywhere. It was appalling! He stepped between the graves, old and new, stooping to read the inscriptions upon the slabs. So many that he remembered as merry boys and girls and hale men and women still in their prime—could they really be dead?—gone forever from the scenes which had known them and of which they seemed an integral part? Oh, mystery of mysteries, how was it possible?—Yet here were their names plainly written upon the marbles! The church builded by men's hands, the trees planted by men's hands, the monuments fashioned by men's hands remained, but the living, breathing men, where were they? Could it be that God's highest creation was a more perishable thing than the lifeless work of its own hand? His spirit cried out within him against such a thought. No, it could not be! Gone from earth, or holden from mortal vision they assuredly were—departed—but dead? No!

Finally he came to the grave beside the wall. No marble tomb told the passer-by that there lay the body of Elizabeth Poe. Yet, what matter?—Was her sleep the less peaceful? Was her tired spirit the less free?—If in its flight it should visit this spot where it had laid the burden of the body down, surely it would find, for all there was no carven stone to mark it, a most sweet spot. The greenest of grass, and clover with blossoms white and red, waved over it—the summer breeze rippling through them with pleasant sound,—and the tall trees hung a green canopy between it and the midday sun.

As he laid his offering of roses among the clover blooms and turned to go away the bell in the steeple began to toll. How the past came back!—He stood with uncovered and bowed head and counted the strokes. Suddenly, there was a sound of horses tramping in the street below the wall. Then through the gate and down the walk it came—the solemn procession.

He waited until the last of the mourners had passed into the church, then followed, and as the bell stopped tolling and the organ began to play the familiar, moving chant, he passed in and took a seat near the door. Whose funeral service he was attending he knew not—but he was back in childhood, and it was beautiful to him to hear once more, in this very church, the words of spoken music and the old familiar hymns he had heard that day when his infant heart had been filled with a beautiful sorrow that was not pain.

More than one pair of eyes turned to see the owner of the fine tenor voice that joined in the singing of the hymns, and resting for a moment upon the dark, uplifted eyes of Edgar Poe, caught a glimpse of something not of this earth.

As he left the church and churchyard, he noted many changes in its immediate neighborhood but the only one upon which his eye lingered was a smug brick house of commodious proportions and genteel aspect. A pleasant green yard afforded space for a few trees and flowers. A dignified and prosperous, but not in the least romantic house it was. A house with no rambling wings giving opportunities for winding passageways and odd nooks and corners; no unexpected closets where skeletons might be in hiding, or dusky stairways to creak in the dead of night, or upon which, even by day, one was

The Dreamer

almost certain he caught a glimpse of a shadowy figure flying before him as he groped his way up or down them. A house with no mysteries—just the house in which one might have expected to find Elmira Royster who, as the Widow Shelton, the prudent housewife and good manager of a prosperous estate, was simply the frank, clear-eyed girl he had known, grown older.

He would call upon Elmira sometime, but not now little son, so that she could only use the income, was duly signed and sealed. The wedding ring was bought.

With visions of a new start in life, of which there were many happy years in store for him (why not?—He was only forty!) The Dreamer set out on his way back to Fordham to settle up his affairs and bring Mother Clemm to Richmond to witness his marriage and to take up her abode with him and his bride, in the brick house on the hill. He had been upon a holiday, but he carried with him a goodly sum of money realized from his lectures, and a long list of subscribers to *The Stylus*. Surely, Fortune had never shown him a more smiling face!

Baltimore!—

Why did his way lie through Baltimore? Baltimore, with its memories of Virginia—Baltimore where he had come up out of the grave to the heaven of her love, and where had been first constructed the most beautiful of all his dreams—the dream of the Valley of the Many-Colored Grass, in which he and she and the Mother had lived for each other only!

In Baltimore again he found his way stopped by the vision of "a legended tomb." It was paralyzing! He could go no further upon his journey, but lingered in Baltimore, wandering the streets like one bereft.

The words—the prophetic words—of his own poem "To One in Paradise," haunted him:

"A voice from out the future cries, 'On! on!' But o'er the Past (Dim gulf!) my spirit hovering lies Mute, motionless, aghast!"

And again, the words of his "Bridal Ballad"—more prophetic still:

"Would to God I could awaken! For I dream I know not how; And my soul is sorely shaken Lest an evil step be taken,— Lest the dead who is forsaken May not be happy now."

And that merciless other self, his accusing Conscience, arose, and with whisper louder and more terrible than ever before, upbraided him—reminding him of the vow he had made his wife upon her bed of death.

Alas, the vow!—that solemn, sacred vow! How could he have so utterly forgotten it? How plainly he could see her lying upon the snowy pillow—her face not much less white—her trustful eyes on his eyes as he knelt by her side and swore that he would never bind himself in marriage to another—invoking from Heaven a terrible curse upon his soul if he should ever prove traitorous to his oath.

Alas, where had been his will that he had so soon forgotten his vow? How he despised himself for his weakness—he that had boasted in the words of old Joseph Glanvil, until he had almost made them his own words:

"'Man doth not yield himself to the angels nor unto death utterly, save only through the weakness of his will.'"

Hours on hours he wandered the streets of the city whose every paving stone seemed to speak to him of his Virginia—the city where he had walked with her—where he had first

The Dreamer

spoken of love to her and heard her sweet confession—where, in the holy church, the beautiful words of the old, old rite had made them one.

All day he wandered, and all night—driven, cruelly driven—by the upbraiding whisper in his ear, while before him still he saw her white face with the soft eyes looking out—it seemed to him in reproach.

Finally the longing which had come upon him in Providence—the longing for the peace of the grave and reunion, in death, with Virginia, was strong upon him again—pressed him hard—mastered him.

It was sometime in the early morning that he swallowed the draught—the draught that would free his spirit, that would enable him to lay down the burden of his body and to fly from the steps that dogged *his* steps—from the voice that whispered upbraidings. He would lay his body down by the side of her body in the "legended tomb" while his spirit would fly to join her spirit in that far Aidenn where they would be happy together forever.

As he fell asleep he murmured (again quoting himself):

"And neither the angels in heaven above, Nor the demons down under the sea, Can ever dissever my soul from the soul Of the beautiful Annabel Lee."

When he opened his wondering eyes upon the white walls of the hospital he was feeble and weak in his limbs as an infant, but his brain was unclouded. Gentle hands ministered to him and a woman's voice read him spirit-soothing words from the Gospel of St. John. But the draught had done its work. He lingered some days and then, on Sunday morning, the seventh day of October of the year 1849, his spirit took its flight. His last words were a prayer:

"Lord, have mercy on my poor soul!"

Many were the friends who rose up to comfort the stricken mother and who hastened to bring rosemary to the poet's grave. But there was one whom he had believed to be his friend—a big man whose big brain he had admired—in whose furtive eye was an unholy glee, about whose thick lips played a smile which slightly revealed his fang-like teeth. To him was entrusted the part of literary executor—it had been The Dreamer's own request. In his power it would lie to give to the world his own account of this man who had said he was no poet and had distanced him in the race for a woman's favor.

The day was at hand when Rufus Griswold would have his full revenge upon the fair fame of Edgar the Dreamer.

"Out—out are the lights—out all! And, over each quivering form, The curtain, a funeral pall, Comes down with the rush of a storm; And the angels, all pallid and wan, Uprising, unveiling, affirm That the play is the tragedy, 'Man,' And its hero the Conqueror Worm."

Made in the USA
Columbia, SC
18 January 2024